second touch

BOOK TWO

 A.D. CHRONICLES®

second touch

Tyndale House Publishers, Inc.
Carol Stream, Illinois

BODIE & BROCK
THOENE

Visit Tyndale's exciting Web site at www.tyndale.com

TYNDALE and Tyndale's quill logo are registered trademarks of Tyndale House Publishers, Inc.

A. D. Chronicles and the fish design are registered trademarks of Bodie Thoene.

Second Touch

Authors' photo by Joe Dillon, Tuam, Co., Galway, Ireland. All rights reserved.

Cover designed by Rule29, www.rule29.com

Interior designed by Dean H. Renninger

Edited by Ramona Cramer Tucker

Scripture quotations for Parts I, II, and III section pages, as well as Joel 2:32, are taken from the *Holy Bible*, New International Version®. NIV® Copyright © 1973, 1978, 1984 by International Bible Society. Used by permission of Zondervan. All rights reserved.

Library of Congress Cataloging-in-Publication Data

Thoene, Bodie, date.
  Second touch / Bodie and Brock Thoene.
    p. cm. – (A.D. chronicles ; bk. 2)
Includes bibliographical references.
  ISBN-13: 978-0-8423-7509-2 (hc)
  ISBN-10: 0-8423-7509-0 (hc)
  ISBN-13: 978-0-8423-7510-8 (sc)
  ISBN-10: 0-8423-7510-4 (sc)
  1. Jesus Christ–Fiction. 2. Bible. N.T.–History of Biblical events–Fiction. I. Thoene, Brock, date. II. Title.
PS3570.H46S43 2004
813'.54–dc22
                                          2003021683

Printed in the United States of America

13   12   11   10   09   08   07
9   8   7   6   5   4   3

For Chance, Jessie, Ian, Titan, and Connor
—Psalm 91—
Love, Bubbe and Potsy

the middle east

FIRST CENTURY A.D.

SAMARIA

Jordan River

PEREA

Mediterranean Sea

Jericho .

Jerusalem . + Mount of Olives

← to Alexandria

Bethlehem . • Bethany

Ashkelon • • Herodium

JUDEA

IDUMEA

Dead Sea

EGYPT

N

Red Sea

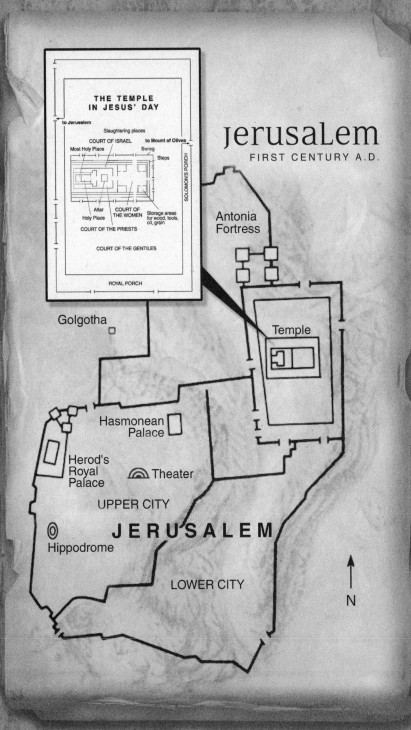

jerusalem
FIRST CENTURY A.D.

THE TEMPLE IN JESUS' DAY

to Jerusalem

Slaughtering places

COURT OF ISRAEL

Most Holy Place

to Mount of Olives

Soreg

Steps

Altar

Holy Place

COURT OF THE WOMEN

Storage areas for wood, tools, oil, grain

COURT OF THE PRIESTS

COURT OF THE GENTILES

SOLOMON'S PORCH

ROYAL PORCH

Antonia Fortress

Golgotha

Temple

Hasmonean Palace

Herod's Royal Palace

Theater

UPPER CITY

JERUSALEM

Hippodrome

LOWER CITY

N

Prologue

Adonai spoke to her softly as He formed her.

I AM sending you.

Adonai loved her, created her as a reflection of His great love. He swam beside her as she emerged from the warmth of the womb into the cold, far country called Life.

She hesitated. Tried to turn back.

He compelled her to go on. *Breathe! Don't be afraid! You are sent by Me beyond what you imagine are the boundaries of your world.*

At His urging she gasped, taking in her first breath of this new and foreign place. She wailed and longed for the steady beat of her mother's heart against her back.

But He stood by her cradle and touched her face in the night and comforted her. *Don't be afraid of anything! You are a tree. Let beauty and light and terror rage around you like a storm! It will not harm you!*

She longed for the safety of His presence. Her spirit begged to turn back.

He commanded her to go forward on the journey. *I AM your ship, your sail, your captain. I AM the wind, the water, the lighthouse guiding you to your destination!*

Together we will sail a great distance, face many sorrows, overcome great trials. Do not fear the journey. Trust Me! We travel together, you and I. Together! Together we carry priceless treasure to those who wait on the desolate shore.

Go on then! Live! Fearless!

Yes! That's my girl!

You will find the lost ones, like driftwood twisted and forsaken, strewn along the path of your own suffering. Find them. Embrace them. Feed them. Carry them. I AM at your side every step of the journey! And when we return home again together? Together those who were lost before you came will travel back with us!

And so her father named her Shoshana, which means "Lily." She was a beautiful child, almost perfect. Everyone said so. Flaxen hair, oval face, large blue eyes that gathered in the sky. Small nose. Mouth like a rosebud. Teeth straight and white. Ears petite and perfectly formed.

She was a cheerful baby. Met the eyes of every stranger who chanced by. Even the most irascible among the congregation would grin and coo and happily make fools of themselves when Lily was passed around the synagogue.

Papa used to say Lily was the most beautiful flower in his garden.

Lily was the eldest child. Three brothers followed in close succession. Lily was such a comfort, Mama would say, because a daughter stays a daughter all her life while sons grow up and get themselves wives. That was always the way of it, eh? Every mother needed at least one daughter. Mama had so many wonderful hopes and dreams tied up in Lily. Lily would grow up, get married, bring the grandbabies home to visit. Yes, it would be fine. Life ripening into something delicious and plentiful to be savored and enjoyed.

But it was not to be as Mama hoped.

Life ripened to become bitter, not sweet. So unfair. So full of suffering! Things never, ever turning out the way they ought!

Lily was twelve that terrible spring when the first sign of sickness touched her face with a strange beauty. Pale cheeks took on a rosy hue; blue eyes were brighter than usual. Papa mistook these changes as the indication of approaching womanhood. His bud was about to bloom, he declared.

But Mama had seen the progression of *tsara'at* before. Almost from the first she suspected all was not well with little Lily. She guarded her fears, kept silent, watched Lily when she was not looking. Prayed. Prayed a lot. To no avail.

Mama noticed when Lily's hands grew clumsy as she threaded a needle. She noted how awkward Lily seemed when she passed the jug of milk to her brothers or attempted to tie a string around a bunch of flowers. Still Mama could not bring herself to believe it could be true. Not Lily! Oh, Lord! Not Lily! The possibility was too horrifying to contemplate!

"Just growing." Papa waved away Mama's worry with his hand. "Children are always clumsy when they grow."

Then one morning Lily spilled scalding water on her left hand and did not seem to notice. She did not cry out, felt no pain.

Mama saw it happen, knew what it meant. All she had feared had come upon them! Mama dropped to her knees and began to wail, as if Lily had died right there before her very eyes.

Papa came running, picked up Lily's burned hand, stared at it in horror, searched Lily's serene face, then pushed her away.

With quaking voice Papa ordered Lily out of the house, into the empty lambing pen to wait. Wait until the elder would come and judge her case for himself.

She was to be isolated, separated. They would see. Yes. They would wait and see.

But no one really doubted the verdict. No one.

Lily slumped beneath the shelter in the corral and wept as they burned all her clothes, her things, even her bed.

Everything went up in smoke. Nothing of her life remained.

Nothing left but life.

Her brothers were commanded to stay away from her.

They peeked their sorrowful little faces out the door and cried for Lily. Lily reached out to them through the slats of the pen, mourned for her brothers as if they were condemned instead of her.

At night the house grew silent with anguish too deep for tears. Lily sobbed quietly alone. She was afraid. She wanted to go back inside, into her little room where she had always slept.

In the daylight Lily and her family peered at one another across the garden, which now seemed as wide as the gulf separating life and death.

Mama, weeping, brought food and water in a leather sack, hung it on the post, and hurried away. She cupped her hands and called to Lily over the berry vines, asking if there was anything else she needed.

Lily might have said she needed everything to be the way it used to be. Might have said she wanted to come inside and be home just like always. But she did not. What was the point?

"I'm sorry, Mama!" Lily cried. "I'm so sorry!"

But Mama, terrified of losing all her children, was too busy herding the boys to hear Lily. Her commands came sharply.

"Stay back! Boys!"

"Get back!"

"No! Aaron!"

"No! David! David! You can't!"

"Don't! Don't go near her!"

So they were certain even before the priest rendered final judgment. Even before the sentence was passed.

"Tsara'at!"

With that one word all the angels of heaven turned their backs on Lily. According to the laws of Moses, her family must drive her out as well.

No, Lily could not stay, no matter how she implored Mama. She could not live in the shed in the pasture with the sheep. She could not embrace her dear brothers or wrap her arms around Papa in one final farewell.

"Chadel! Baza! Tsara!" the elder declared. And so Lily was pronounced dead to her kin and to society, though she remained alive.

She sat in the dust before the house and pleaded for mercy. Begged not to be driven away!

Mama and Papa bolted the door and covered their ears against her cries.

Where was the One who formed her? Why had this happened? Where was His voice of comfort in all this?

After two days the people of the village came to the farm at the priest's demand. They remained at a safe distance. Before the whole congregation the elder adjured Lily to leave her home and the village . . . never to return!

The people who had loved her now picked up stones to stone her. They shrieked at her, flung dust into the air! They drove her away.

Some weeks after, she stumbled into the Valley of Sorrows, which is called in Hebrew *Mak'ob*. In that place the *tsara'im*, the Stricken Ones, lived out their half-lives until death eventually swallowed them up.

That had been six years and an eternity ago.

PART I

He was despised and rejected by men,
A man of sorrows, and familiar with suffering.
Like one from whom men hide their faces
He was despised, and we esteemed Him not.

Surely He took up our infirmities
And carried our sorrows.

ISAIAH 53:3-4

M idnight.
The sixth day of the month of Sivan.
Eighteenth year in the life of Lily.

Outcast. *Tsara*. Rejected. *Chadel*.

Lily, leper of the Valley of Mak'ob.

It was Shavuot. Pentecost. The feast was held each year on the anniversary of the giving of Torah on Mount Sinai. This was the night in which every generation of Jews since that day stayed awake to pray and await the descending to earth of Messiah, Israel's heavenly Bridegroom.

The moon had set behind the canyon wall hours ago, leaving the mist of the Milky Way as a bright streak across the sky.

Lily and Cantor sat shoulder to shoulder on the big boulder overlooking the Valley.

Far below them, in the center of the colony, a light burned in the hut of Rabbi Ahava.

"Look," Lily said. "It glows like a lantern, that house. Light beaming from every crack. Rabbi's awake."

"All scholars in Israel stay awake on Shavuot," Cantor replied. "Reading Torah. Studying. Praying for Messiah to come."

Lily hugged her knees and threw her head back to search the stars. "Wouldn't it be . . . something? Wouldn't it, Cantor?"

I'm praying again, heavenly Bridegroom. Are you on your angel horse? Galloping through the sky to gather your people? Scoop us up and fly away? Will you come tonight? Tonight? You know, of all your people . . . all . . . we here in Mak'ob have no hope but you. We're hoping you'll come! To save us. We're watching for you to come!

Her gaze shifted from constellation to constellation as she scanned the cold heavens for a sign of Messiah's approaching glory.

But stars were stars.

Cantor rattled off their names as if they were old friends. "Arcturus directly above us. Vega. Deneb. There's The Lion. There, The Bear. See them, Lily?"

"I wish I knew as much as you, Cantor."

"Learned the names when I was a boy. The old man who tended the goats taught us young ones. I'm the only one left alive of those boys. I was thinking, you know, maybe I should teach the little ones now. The star names. Like he taught me. Children in Mak'ob might forget stars have names when I die."

Lily frowned. "Don't talk like that, Cantor. Don't tempt the evil eye by speaking aloud such a thing. You're hardly sick."

Cantor laughed. "Impossible to avoid the subject in this Valley, I'm afraid."

"Yes. But no . . . but . . . don't. Not tonight, eh? You'll spoil it if you do. Keep watching."

There was a poignant pause.

Cantor spoke first. "What do you suppose it'll look like when Messiah comes?"

"Lightning. Maybe."

"Clear sky. No clouds. Crickets in the brush and then—"

"Lightning! Thunder! Maybe tonight." Lily dreamed. "Maybe tonight it'll really happen. He's supposed to come on Shavuot! Descend with mighty power. Like when the Lord descended to the mountain and gave Mosheh the laws! Wouldn't it be something if . . . if we were the first to see the flash!" A shiver of expectation passed through her.

Cantor hummed with pleasure. "Yes. It would be. Really something."

"Not impossible, eh? That the Son of David would stop in Mak'ob and gather us lost sheep up on his way to Yerushalayim? No place in all Eretz-Israel needs a visit from Messiah as bad as Mak'ob."

For a while the two sat imagining what it would be like. If *He* came.

Lily wondered what Scriptures the rabbi was reading.

She thought about her friend Deborah and the baby in Deborah's womb. Would the baby be instantly born if Messiah came tonight? Lily considered that this was a question worthy of discussing with Rabbi Ahava.

At last Cantor spoke. "There's Dubhe. Alkaid."

"You know so much. Everything. I just thought they were stars, that's all."

"The old man who taught us? He said King David learned the names of the stars when he was a shepherd boy. David found this Valley when he was searching for a lost lamb. Years after that he took refuge in one of our caves when Saul was trying to kill him."

"Imagine. One of our caves! Maybe where I live."

"When he became king, David returned to Mak'ob. His refuge. He set the Valley aside as a city of refuge for the lepers of his kingdom. His lost sheep, he called us."

"Imagine! Him . . . here."

"Ah, look, Lily. There's Antares. Spica."

"Which direction of the sky will Messiah come from, you think?"

"All the light from unseen stars will arrive with him when he comes to Yerushalayim! Blast the earth at once! Light! No north, south, east, or west anymore. Just light. Angel armies filling the sky everywhere we look! Singing! Singing."

Lily imagined it. Smiled. "And you'll sing with them."

"Yes. Yes. I'll sing." Cantor clasped her right hand in his. "You too."

"Yes. Wouldn't it be something if it was tonight?"

I'm praying again, Lord of the Angel Armies! Do the prayers of this Valley reach your home in heaven? If only . . . come tonight! Hear our prayers and gather us in! Don't forget your lost sheep! There are more of us than usual in the dying cave. My heart is shouting to you, Lord of all the Angel Armies. Here I am! Lily, leper of Mak'ob! Do you hear my prayers from where you sit? Don't forget your lost sheep in Mak'ob! We're here because everyone else wants to forget about us. But you! You! Son of David! Don't forget us, Lord. We're all waiting. Hoping! And we who live here and die here . . . we need you more than anyone!

What was the time?

The great city of Jerusalem was only just stirring. A merchant leading a donkey out to water passed by the gardenia bush where seventeen-year-old Peniel, the potter's son, and Yeshua of Nazareth sat together. Unnoticed. Unremarkable. Ordinary.

Yet Peniel knew the truth.

All who sought Yeshua tested Him. When they found Him they sized Him up, trimmed Him to fit their expectations, and tried to force His image into a puzzle of their own making.

But Yeshua did not fit.

Peniel knew Yeshua did not fit.

Peniel needed no miracles in order to believe He Was and He Is and He Will Be and He Can and He Wants To!

Nothing is impossible with God!

Peniel sensed the stars glistening on the night wind when the city was silent, and he *knew*.

Peniel heard the echo of creation in his heart and he *knew*.

The Great Timekeeper lived outside of time. Stepped into time. Just for a moment. Dwelt in *our* time! And Peniel *knew!*

Peniel needed no miracle in order to believe these things. And so, like an unbidden wind, the great miracle had caressed him, stirred him, root and branch, and *he knew!*

Now Peniel had seen The Face and *he knew* the certainty of what had been unknowable before!

The Great Potter!

He who made eyes had seen!

He who made ears had heard!

Wonder Worker. Origin of First Light. Knower of Secrets. He who sang galaxies and crickets into existence with equal delight!

Yeshua! He had stepped from eternity into time and stooped to make Peniel's eyes out of red clay! Paused to finish the creation of an unfinished life! To show one born blind . . . The Face!

And Peniel knew.

Yeshua clasped Peniel's hand in friendship. "This is the first light of a new day, and life will never be the same."

Never the same! Peniel grinned up at the colors of the morning sky.

Never the same! Peniel—no longer a beggar, but a man of Isra'el— stood and walked at Yeshua's side.

They passed slowly through the early-morning shadows of the city. Yeshua rested His hand on Peniel's shoulder as Gershon, Peniel's elder brother, had done long ago when they had walked together toward the Pool of Siloam.

Peniel took in the sights with wonder. He said without regret, "You've changed everything in my life, Lord. I'm cast out of the synagogue for giving true testimony of what you've done for me. Rejected by my parents. Now the religious rulers will kill you if they can. For giving me sight on the Sabbath, you know? I'm glad you did it. But they want you dead. Healing on the Sabbath and all."

Yeshua smiled, sharing His secret with Peniel. "They've missed finding the pearl because they stoop to grasp a copper, eh, Peniel?"

"Sure. I see what you mean. Yes. Point is, I was blind and now I see. No matter what day of the week it was, you healed me. It's the best day of my life so far."

"What's the best day to show mercy, Peniel?"

"Every day, I think, Rabbi."

"Well spoken."

"You know what I think. I'm glad you didn't turn away from my affliction because I'm poor and it was Shabbat."

"Not poor, Peniel. Just without . . . things."

"I live among the broken people, Lord. Castaways. Waiting without hope. They're left to pick through the rubbish heap beneath the viaduct."

"Who will care for them?"

"I asked myself that same thing. But . . . nobody. Nobody."

Yeshua gave Peniel an enigmatic smile, then abruptly changed the subject. "Today is Shavuot." Yeshua glanced up toward the light gleaming on the golden peaks of the Temple. "Today the heavenly Bridegroom comes to Yerushalayim. What do you think? Would you like to hear a story about a mighty king who prepared a wonderful banquet for his son's wedding?"

"You know me. I'm Peniel. I love a good story."

They walked.

"So. The king sent his servant to the prominent men in his kingdom to tell them that everything was ready. They should come to the wedding feast. But all those important fellows were too busy. One had bought a field and sent back the message that he had to go see it. The other had a new yoke of oxen to try out. Another had just got married and so sent his apologies. But apologies were not enough to the good king. He told his servant, 'Hurry up! Go out into the streets and alleys of the city! Bring in the poor, the crippled, the blind, the lame! Carry them on your back if you have to, but bring them!' When this was done there was still room in the palace so the good king sent his servant out again. 'Go out to the country roads and lanes. Make them come in so that my house will be full! I tell you, not one of those important men who were too busy to come will get a taste of my banquet.' "[1]

A few paces more.

Peniel digested the meaning. "Point taken. Well spoken."

"Who will go out? tell them? carry those who can't walk? bring them in? fill my Father's house?"

"But, Lord, the rulers. They'll try to kill you, Lord, and yes . . . maybe kill me too. Though I'm not so worried about myself as you. They'll try to put out the light. But why?"

"They prefer the darkness to light, Peniel."

They walked in silence for a time as Peniel wondered how anyone could choose blindness over sight.

"Morning has broken." Yeshua spoke at last.

"Yes. I feel it. I hear it! Listen! Listen to the cock crow!" Then Peniel followed Yeshua's gaze to a ragged beggar sleeping in a deserted door-way. A leper, judging by the stink. What was such an outcast doing here? Was he dead? "So . . . this is what the world looks like in the light."

"Darkness is a comfortable place. The candle of Adonai illuminates suffering which most would rather not see."

A chill of apprehension coursed through Peniel. "Beneath the via-duct where the paupers take shelter, I heard their moans. I smelled the lepers outside the camp. So hungry. So alone. I dreamed a dream that Mosheh, the lawgiver, spoke to me. He said I would be sent to tell them . . . tell them . . . something. It's not clear to me now. I always try to remember my dreams. But then I wake up and they fade away."

"The answer will come back to you. When you need to know."

"My ears saw their misery. Oh!" Peniel thumped his hand against his chest to indicate his pain. "I'm afraid, Lord. Afraid of what my heart'll feel now that I have eyes."

Yeshua paused and searched Peniel's face. Sad smile. Yeshua, like a father seeing himself in the expression of a son. "You have *my* eyes, Peniel."

"Who am I to do anything?"

"It's not who you are."

"So many, as you say. All around, I mean." Peniel shook his head.

"Yes. Seeing requires something, eh? That's all the Law and the Prophets. Summed up."

"So many men know the Scriptures. And still there's the viaduct. The rubbish heap. People who exist in the long, dreary waiting, like animals locked up and forgotten." How well Peniel knew this truth.

"Easy not to be bothered. Easy to follow the letter of the Law. Make a great show of keeping the Law. But men forget the true intention of the Law." Yeshua did not avert His eyes from the bundle of rags in the alcove, but neither did He slow His pace as they strode toward the Pool of Siloam. "And by turning away from those who suffer, they miss great blessings from heaven. Maybe the one they refused to help was an angel in disguise. Thus ends the lesson. Now, Peniel, practice what you've learned."

Why, Peniel wondered, did Yeshua not stop and heal the ragged man? He could have done so in an instant. Yet Yeshua walked on. The leper would never know how close he had been to his salvation.

Yeshua said, "There's much you won't understand until all things are complete, Peniel. The road ahead isn't easy."

They walked on, unspeaking, as Peniel attempted to reason out all that Yeshua had told him.

There were few other travelers abroad. Shops were mostly shuttered; the Lower City at the foot of the Temple Mount slumbered in the embrace of its shadow. Pentecost morning, the sixth day of the month of Sivan, in the seventeenth year of the Roman emperor Tiberius, was thus far serene.

Peniel shut his eyes and listened to the creak of hinges, the clatter of breakfast plates within still-barred doors. The trumpets of the morning sacrifice had not yet sounded, nor had he heard the Levite-led psalms ring down from the Temple Mount.

From first light until now? Such a tiny fraction of a life, and yet fuller in the company of Yeshua than any span in Peniel's memory. Had less than two hours passed? It was inconceivable.

Peniel opened his eyes again, reveling in his view of the translucent, pale blue sky and the glistening white marble of the Temple framed by it. It was as if the pillar of shimmering cloud by which the Almighty led His people in bygone times rested again atop the Holy City.

Peniel's gaze darted everywhere, eagerly sorting and cataloging. The dark green leaves of an orange tree hung over a garden wall. Its verdant foliage cooled the warm honey tones of the sandstone blocks.

A shaft of light lanced through a gap in the Temple structures overhead. The beam caromed off a bright brass candle sconce in a second-story window, ricocheting to dazzle Peniel's sight.

More people emerged from their homes; the city came to life as Peniel watched. Today was a holy day when no unnecessary work was to be done. A gaggle of yawning Torah schoolboys, having no doubt been up all night meditating on the five books of Mosheh, was herded along the street by their instructor.

The colors of the clothes, the objects the passersby carried, the myriad variety of gaits and postures—all these delighted Peniel.

But chiefly it was their faces that most fascinated him. Some were fresh, bursting with energy, like newly opened gardenia buds. Some were stiff and leathery, the passage of many sunrises and sunsets imprinted on their brows. Some were brittle as thin pottery, concealing inner turmoil, as if their lives were apt to shatter if examined too closely.

And this was merely the beginning, Peniel thought. After seventeen years of blindness, less than one day had passed since Yeshua of Nazareth had given him his sight. Peniel drank in the visions like one who came to a fresh spring after wandering the desert of Moab.

Peniel turned to study the Teacher. Slender of build, with brown curly hair and smile lines imprinted around his eyes, perhaps Yeshua was merely commonplace in His appearance. But not to Peniel. He stared openly at his benefactor, determining to memorize every single feature . . . and was caught in the act.

Peniel ducked his head, embarrassed, then raised it again at Yeshua's laugh.

They reached the entrance to the Pool of Siloam, where yesterday Peniel had been sent by Yeshua to wash away the clay that had covered his sightless eyes. Peniel had emerged from the portico able to see for the first time in his life.

The city gate, leading out into the countryside, was a few yards beyond them. Yeshua stopped there and looked back the way they had come.

"Yerushalayim! Yerushalayim!" Yeshua murmured as He took in the lofty towers. He let His gaze slide down the walls to linger on the multitudes moving up the street. "You kill the prophets and stone those sent to you." He winced as if some painful memory had struck Him. "How often I longed to gather your children together like a hen gathering chicks under her wings. But you weren't willing! So. Your house is left to you . . . desolate."[2]

Silence. It was as if the tumult in the city came to a halt in that instant. No one moving. Breathing. Speaking. Frozen. Then Peniel heard a distant rumble like thunder, only deeper, more penetrating, as Yeshua opened His eyes. The blue sky flashed bright white as if lightning had struck out of a cloudless sky.

And life resumed again.

Had anyone else seen or heard what Peniel saw and heard?

"You'll come back some day, Lord?"

"Yes. I promise. Soon. And what will you do with what you've been given?"

Peniel considered the gifts Yeshua had given him. Vision. Healing. Hope.

"I know Yerushalayim well," Peniel said at last, hoping this was the right answer. "Every corner. Every beggar. Every blind man."

"Yes. You're blessed."

"Can't say as I'd call it a blessing yet. We'll see. But I'll do what I can."

"I'll be in the north." Yeshua searched Peniel's face for some sign of fear. "Use your head. Be wise. They're wolves, these fellows."

"I know. But why would they bother with the likes of me? A blind man?"

"You're not blind anymore."

"Oh. Yes. Point taken. Well, you must stay clear of Yerushalayim. They hate you. I saw it in their faces at the meeting yesterday. They'll try to kill you."

No reply. Yeshua placed His hands on Peniel's shoulders and made a *b'rakhah* for parting. And then He melted into the crowds.

First light streamed through the high window of thirty-seven-year-old Simon ben Zeraim's bedchamber at his Bethany estate. He snuffed out the lamp that had burned on his study table through the night.

From twilight till dawn Simon had performed the Shavuot obligation of reading through the five books of Moses.

Legend held that during the long, dark hours of study, the heavens open for an instant. In that moment the Lord would hear and answer any prayer.

Any prayer?

How fervently Simon had prayed!

Every breath had contained a reminder to God of Simon's faithfulness, his righteousness! Where was the answer?

Simon held up his hands to the light. He clenched his fists and moaned.

So. Heaven had not heard his supplication.

With difficulty now he performed his final duty of piety.

Sunrise on the day of Shavuot marked the marriage between Messiah as the bridegroom and Israel as His beloved bride.

Simon rolled up the Torah scroll. Haltingly, he recited the *ketubah* of marriage between Messiah, the heavenly Groom, and His bride, the nation of Israel:

"On this day appointed by the Lord for the revelation of the Torah to his beloved people . . . the Invisible One came forth from Sinai. The Bridegroom, Ruler of all Rulers, Prince of Princes, said to his bride Israel, 'Many days will you be mine and I will be your redeemer. Behold, I have sent you golden precepts through the lawgiver Mosheh. Be my mate according to the law of Moshe and I will honor, support, and maintain you and be your shelter and refuge in everlasting mercy.'"

Simon paused. "Mercy." He muttered the word bitterly and shoved the *ketubah* to the side of his desk.

No bridegroom had descended with the golden dawn to redeem the nation of Israel. Today would be like every other day, Simon mused. A day when false messiahs, blasphemers, prophets, and rebels polluted the landscape, insulted the authorities, endangered the government, and duped the common people.

Simon's head throbbed. Shoulders ached. Eyes burned. He felt no enlightenment from his obligatory study of the Torah. The answers to his agonized questions remained elusive, even though he had been faithful in the performance of duty.

How long could he keep his secret? How long before he became an object of public humiliation and condemnation?

The stirring of servants seeped beneath the bolted door.

Simon's wife, Jerusha, had already been up for hours decorating the house with roses for the holiday.

Jerusha. Her gregarious youthfulness had blossomed and ripened over the years until now, at thirty, she was a beauty. The one thing in Simon's life that made sense. Their marriage had been arranged as an alliance between two prominent families, and yet Simon had loved her from the first night.

The political aspect of their union had gone sour after a fierce argument over the legitimacy of the high priest in Jerusalem. Jerusha had not seen her father in nearly fifteen years. Simon had forbade her any contact with her parents. Now her mother was dead. Only the old man remained. Young Jotham had never met his grandfather.

Through the fog of his despair Simon heard Jerusha's voice, her careful footsteps. He sensed her presence as she paused outside his threshold.

Had she spoken his name?

A whisper. *"Why, Simon? For sixteen years I shared your bed. Bore your son. Why, now, have you locked me out, Simon?"*

Had he heard her question? Or only imagined it?

The smell of baking bread brought him around. He raised his eyes. The quiver of new arrows, a gift from thirteen-year-old Jotham, hung unused on the rack beside the unstrung bow.

How proud Jotham had been of the dozen beautiful arrows he had presented to Simon three months ago. Jotham had collected and set the hawk feathers into the straight shafts of seasoned wood. Sharp iron tips imported from Alexandria guaranteed good deer hunting for father and son.

Yet days and weeks and months had passed since the gift had been presented. The bow remained untouched. The arrows untried.

A whisper. *"Why, Father? I'm a man now. At my bar mitzvah you promised we would go to Lebanon before Shavuot. Promised we would hunt together. Why, now, do you threaten to send me out of your presence when I mention your promise? Why do you say you're too busy when the fields are plowed and the seed is sown and lambing season is done?"*

Had he heard the accusation of Jotham yesterday in the barn? or merely seen it flash in his eyes? Resentment tempered by fear clouded the face of Jotham these days.

Simon studied the fingers that had once confidently grasped the bowstring and sent an arrow flying to the heart of its mark.

No more! No more!

A soft rap sounded on the door. "Simon? Shavuot tov! Will you eat with us?" Jerusha called him to breakfast. Even this brief message managed to pile guilt on him and rouse his resentment.

"I'm praying," Simon lied.

"We'll wait."

"Don't wait."

He knew he had hurt her. Knew she felt the sting of his rejection. Her passion for him was fierce. It was obvious in her glance—the way she moved across the room, looked over her shoulder, inviting him. In the way she leaned close to him to light the lamp at his table. He longed to take her in his arms. But at night he locked the door, keeping her out. And he could not tell her why. Why . . .

He rose slowly and fumbled for his clothes.

Removing the lid from the black onyx urn on his dressing table, Simon recited the prayers of purification. With the *antelaya*, the ladle, grasped in his right hand, he dipped pure water from the urn and poured it over his left hand until it was immersed. Lifting his hand heavenward, Simon allowed the drops to stream past his wrist before setting aside the *antelaya* and rubbing both hands together in the bowl.

How long had he kept himself spotless? Simon mused. How many years? The washings at rising, before meat, after meat, between courses. The first waters, the second waters . . . no one had been more scrupulous than he.

Dumping out the contents of the bowl, Simon ladled it full again and once more scrubbed. His final posture, like a supplicant, a beggar, ensured the fresh water completely carried away the polluted first washing, running down his arms even to the elbows.

Hoping . . . *hoping* . . . the Eternal took note of his piety.

Though he was not required to do so on a feast day, he tied phylacteries onto his forehead and then his forearm. The leather straps twined around his fingers like the jesses holding a captive falcon onto its master's fist. By obeying the commands of Torah, Simon kept his sanity from flying away. Each terrible new day he said the prayers and clung desperately to the outward image of what he was. Proud, arrogant, rich, an expert in the law and in the enactment of Pharisaic ritual, Simon ben Zeraim was among the most respected men of Israel.

No man imagined Simon's terror at what lay ahead.

None of his illustrious colleagues here in Jerusalem or in the region of the Galil suspected the truth.

Simon was sure that Jotham did not know.

If Jerusha guessed, she did not speak of it.

If his servants wondered at his reclusive behavior, they feared to mention it. After all, the downfall of their master could mean the end of the House of ben Zeraim.

Day by day, in performance of religious obligation, by outward display, Simon held his inevitable destruction at bay.

But for how long? Summoned to nearby Jerusalem by the keen-eyed high priest, or *cohen hagadol*, Caiaphas, Simon wondered if he could conceal his secret from him. Simon was anxious to pack up his family and return to the security of his Capernaum home.

He turned toward Jerusalem, toward the Temple of the Most High, and began absently to mutter the prayer: "Blessed are you, O Lord, King of the world, who forms the light and creates the darkness, and in your goodness day by day and every day renews the works of creation."

He spoke the words, though he no longer believed them. No longer believed in God's goodness.

Now only the formula remained.

Simon donned loose lambskin gloves. These provided an additional barrier between his flesh and the uncleanness of the earth. With this final step Simon ben Zeraim, would-be Pharisee of Pharisees, unbolted his door and emerged from the self-imposed exile of his room.

enturion Marcus Longinus sat on the broad stone ledge of the windowsill in the Antonia Fortress. His quarters, located on the corner of the fourth story, provided a clear view over the Jewish Temple Mount and Sheep Gate with vast stock pens brimming with sacrificial lambs.

"Stink of sheep is strong this morning," Marcus commented to his friend and superior officer, Tribune Dio Felix.

Felix downed a boiled egg. "I wrote Mother in Rome first day I saw this fortress. Told her it's one example of the way Jews insult Rome. Barracks of the legion is placed just so. When the prevailing wind is right, we Romans smell the stink of Jews on one side and their livestock on the other."

"Jews say the odor comes from us Romans." Marcus studied the throng of worshippers surging across the courtyard.

Below him Marcus spotted Zadok, Chief Shepherd of the flocks of Israel, as the old man waded into the herd like a common herdsman. A phalanx of Pharisees looked on as Yeshua of Nazareth and the old man conferred beside the gate to the fold.

"What're you looking at?"

Felix was clearly irritated, Marcus thought, by his unwillingness to have breakfast.

"Sheep."

"All right, Marcus, I'll rephrase that. What are you looking for? A beautiful woman? That might be worth skipping breakfast for."

"Wolves."

From the far side of the Temple platform a dozen of Herod Antipas' personal bodyguards entered. The crowds parted for them. At the head of the troop was Commander Eglon, a Samaritan well known for his enjoyment of cruelty. It had been Eglon who had hacked off the head of Yochanan the Baptizer and gleefully carried it into Herod's banquet.

"More wolves than sheep down there today, I'll wager." Felix seemed only slightly interested.

"Right. A pack of Herod's personal bodyguards is out hunting. And a committee of the high priest's jackals converging."

Felix yawned. "I hate these Jewish holy days. You know what the Emperor says about the Jews and their religion? Holy days give them an excuse to take the day off from work and rebel against Rome. Judea! Worst province in the Empire. And here I am!"

One day earlier Marcus had been expecting a death sentence for his part in the demise of the Praetorian Guard officer Vara. Though it had been Vara who attacked and Marcus who defended innocent lives, Marcus had anticipated being swiftly tried and summarily executed.

How the world had turned upside down between two sunrises!

Marcus had awoken this morning in the Antonia Fortress, but not in a prison cell. He had been fully restored to his former rank. He was again Primus Pilus, the lead centurion of all Roman forces in Judea. He was being honored by Pilate for the very deed he had presumed would mean his beheading.

Felix dabbed his mouth with a napkin. "Still, bad as things are in Jerusalem, I suppose there's less conspiracy here than in Rome, eh?"

"Rome is the gate to the world. And the hinges just turned," Marcus replied.

The tribune's youthful features relaxed in a smile. "When Praetorian Prefect Sejanus dreamed of exchanging his helmet for Caesar's crown, Tiberius rightly decided to remove helmet and head both."

Marcus did not express his belief that Sejanus was simply slightly more evil than Tiberius Caesar. "One more decapitation . . . I've lost count."

"Caesar sent a letter to the Senate, demanding Sejanus' arrest on a charge of *maiestas*—treason against the state and plotting against the emperor. The water of the Tiber will run red for months, they say. All of Sejanus' family, his friends, his appointees, even his slaves, were rounded up and—" Felix drew his thumb across his throat. "There's more: The Senate ordered their bodies left on the riverbanks to rot. Your enemy, the late unlamented Vara, as Sejanus' hatchet man in Judea, would have been arrested and executed too if you hadn't killed him yesterday and saved the Empire the bother. Which is why—"

"Governor Pilate is so eager to honor me," Marcus concluded as he followed the progress of Herod's guards across the platform. They were clearly searching for someone. Marcus was now almost certain it was Yeshua.

Oblivious to the drama unfolding on the Temple Mount, Felix continued with his speculation about the political upheaval in Rome and what it would mean in Jerusalem.

Pontius Pilate was also a Sejanus appointee. The governor was terrified that the fall of his patron would lead to his own summons back to Rome and death.

Felix leaned forward to relay the gossip about Sejanus' arrest and execution in Rome. "My uncle, the senator, heard the tale directly from the Imperial tribune commanding the troops who arrested Sejanus." Felix acted out the drama, putting on the shocked voice of Sejanus. " 'I'm Sejanus! It's a mistake! I'm Sejanus! You're arresting *me?*' The officer said the magic words, 'You are no friend of Caesar!' And Sejanus' knees buckled." Felix laughed.

Marcus pictured the scene: The arresting officer made the formal statement of *maiestas*. *No friend of Caesar* . . . not arguable. Not defensible. No doubt Sejanus continued protesting that it was impossible, right up until the moment the final twist of the silk cord went round his neck.

"So? Now?" Marcus murmured. "Is Pilate suspected by Caesar too?"

"Ah. For a man who says he wants to avoid politics, you come right to the heart of the matter." Felix cracked another boiled egg. "No evidence Pilate was part of any plot with Sejanus. After all, Pilate's been out here in the sticks of Judea for four years. On the other hand, our governor's made too many mistakes here to go unnoticed. Stirring up the Jews. Not that that's ever been difficult. Pilate will walk very carefully if he can. And hope nobody whispers the names Pilate and Sejanus in the same breath where Emperor Tiberius can hear it. Meanwhile Pilate knows my senator uncle was one of those who signed the *maiestas* warrant against Sejanus. Therefore Pilate's bound to respect my opinions, at least for a while."

Cautiously Marcus eyed the coming confrontation below him and inquired, "Yeshua of Nazareth? Is he out of danger?"

"Steady, there! Isn't it a bit soon after preserving your own hide to worry about another's? And him a Jew at that?"

"I tell you, Felix, Yeshua isn't guilty of any crime. You know it. Pilate knows it."

"Save it," Felix interrupted, raising a hand to halt the flow of Marcus' words. "I've heard this before. Rome's attitude remains that Jews can have their own religious practices . . . prophets, holy men, messiahs, or whatever they choose to call themselves . . . so long as they don't threaten rebellion or mar the security of the province."

"Yeshua hasn't done either!"

"Oh?" Felix said quizzically. "Then how do you explain the fact he's the one thing all the other Jewish warring factions—who usually hate each other's guts—agree on? How can such a one be anything other than a troublemaker? The high priest's party says he's a rebel. Herod Antipas thinks he's that other wild-eyed preacher come back to life. The fractious Galileans want him to be their king and are angry because he refuses . . . such a man has too many enemies to live out the year!"

"What if he leaves Jerusalem and remains quietly out of trouble?" Marcus asked anxiously as he observed Herod's troop making their way toward the sheep pens where Yeshua and old Zadok conversed. Were Antipas' men coming to take Yeshua into custody?

"You haven't heard? No, of course not," Felix answered his own question. "Your head's still spinning."

"Heard what? Yeshua's not to be arrested, is he?"

Tribune Felix tore off a chunk of bread. "Not by Rome. Today's a Jewish holy day. Plenty of time to jabber and gossip and pass stories around like bowls of wine. You'd think the town would be full of the news of the deaths of a Roman officer and Demos bar Talmai, ward of

Herod Antipas, but is that the gossip? Not at all! Today what everyone hears in the markets is how Yeshua of Nazareth made a blind man see."

"He healed Manaen bar Talmai?" Marcus asked.

"No," Felix returned. "Manaen's still sightless, poor creature. No use as a gambling partner now, is he? Susanna bat Maccabee's taking him back to the Galil. No, this was a beggar boy. Born blind, they say. I saw him myself once or twice. Of course, the tale grows with each re-telling."

Felix became uncharacteristically somber. "Think carefully, Marcus, before you plead with Pilate for the life of the Galilean . . . even if he is the holy man you seem to think he is. Remember, you and I were together when we saw him feed five thousand men on a handful of bread and dried fish that wouldn't keep a man alive for a week. Five thousand! There are only four thousand Roman legionaries in all Judea. Now it's all trickery, I'm sure, but it'll be just too bad for this Yeshua if too many come to believe it. Think, man! What will Rome do with someone who can feed an army out of thin air, heal their wounds, and even raise them from the dead? What? He'll have to be crushed before deluded masses start marching in his name, whether he gives them permission or not!"

Marcus nodded as he spotted Eglon question a group of priests who waved toward the sheepfold. "Trouble's brewing. Herod's buzzards. Circling." He rose and strapped on his sword.

"You know the only vultures who dare to circle the Temple of this Jewish God are the human type. You don't mind if I stay here and finish breakfast, do you?" Felix waved him away. "Besides, this is the best view of the circus."

Marcus scrambled down the spiral staircase to the barracks. Where was everybody? he wondered. He expected to lead at least a decuria of ten legionaries out to the sheep pens. Why were the Antonia's barracks deserted?

From the darkest corner of the bunkroom came a sonorous snore, like a camel bawling. On the bottom of a three-tiered rack of rope-lattice bunks was Guard Sergeant Quintus, sound asleep.

Marcus poked his old friend with his foot. "Get up, you drunk! Thirty-nine of the best for sleeping on duty!" he bellowed.

The old campaigner didn't fall for it. "*Off* duty," he retorted, opening one eye. "After being up all night, as the centurion would know if *he* hadn't slept so late."

"Where is everybody?"

"New order from Pilate. More pilgrims in town today than at Passover. Get everybody out on the street in full uniform. Stop any trouble before it starts. So I gave the orders . . . and turned in."

"Well, turn out again," Marcus demanded. "It's just you and me, then."

The urgency in Marcus' voice must have instantly alerted Quintus. It was an instinct that had kept him alive through wars against German tribesmen and Parthian archers alike. "What?"

"Trouble right outside our own door. Come on."

"Armor?"

"No time. Your sword."

Moments later the two soldiers were down the steps of the eastern exit from the fortress and only yards from the sheep pens. The smell of sheep and sheep dung made the still, ground-level air thick to breathe. Marcus worried he was already too late. Had Yeshua been arrested by Antipas' men . . . or worse?

But no: There was Yeshua, hemmed in by a gesticulating crowd. "For judgment," Yeshua said, "have I come into this world, so that the blind may see . . . and those who see may become blind."[3] The Teacher was flanked by Zadok the shepherd and two of the more reasonable Pharisees, Nakdimon ben Gurion and his uncle Gamaliel. On the other side of Yeshua was a handful of His talmidim, stout fishermen from Galilee.

Opposite these was a semicircle of others, neither reasonable nor calm. "Are we blind then too?" Marcus heard one red-faced, fist-waving Pharisee demand. Marcus recognized him: Simon ben Zeraim, from whose house Miryam had been barred by an overzealous servant until Marcus intervened.

And Eglon? Marcus spotted the ferretlike face of Antipas' bodyguard on the far side of the sheep pens. He had posted a ring of his men around the animal enclosures and was closing in.

"If you were blind, you would not be guilty of sin," Yeshua replied to Simon. "But now that you claim you can see, your guilt remains."[4]

A renewed uproar burst from the embarrassed and offended Pharisees. How dare this upstart preacher accuse them of sin and hypocrisy?

They shook their fists in Yeshua's face. His disciples looked anxious, Nakdimon angry, Gamaliel aloof and noncommittal.

Zadok brandished his staff as if ready to bash the whole lot of Yeshua's enemies. Able to do it too, Marcus judged.

"Found the new riot, have we?" Quintus asked dryly. "No armor?"

"This doesn't worry me," Marcus corrected. "But that does." The centurion pointed to Eglon and a half dozen of his men clambering over the first of several stone barricades. They waded through the flocks on a direct course toward the Teacher.

Yeshua apparently saw them too and offered a restrained smile. "I tell you the truth," He said wryly. "The man who doesn't enter the sheep pen by the gate, but climbs in some other way is a thief and a robber." Laying a restraining hand on Zadok's shoulder, He added, "The man who enters by the gate is the shepherd of his sheep. He calls his own sheep by name and leads them out. His sheep follow him because they know his voice." Then in louder, unyielding tones He continued, "But they will *never* follow a stranger; in fact, they will run away from him."[5]

Marcus fervently wished Yeshua was more alert to the danger He was in and ready to do a little running away Himself. Eglon was perfectly capable of slashing his way into a crowd to start a panic, then killing Yeshua in the commotion.

"Come on," Marcus ordered Quintus. "We'll head them off. You watch my back."

"Done," said the guard sergeant grimly, drawing his short sword. Quintus would not expend a drop of sweat, much less blood, defending a Jew, no matter how holy. But he would die protecting his centurion if the need arose.

Marcus crossed a stone wall himself, wanting to intercept Eglon before Antipas' hired assassin got any closer to Yeshua. Lambs scattered, crowding into corners. Shepherds remained attentively distant.

Yeshua continued speaking in unhurried fashion, as if teaching in the Temple courts surrounded entirely by admirers. "David, who was himself a shepherd before he was king of Israel, sang this song, *'The Lord is my shepherd, I shall not want.'*"[6]

Simon challenged Him. "You compare yourself to David?"

Yeshua replied, "I AM the good shepherd. The good shepherd lays down his life for the sheep."[7]

Not today! Not today! Marcus fervently hoped.

With Quintus guarding his left flank, Marcus strode unflinchingly toward the oncoming Eglon. Sheep bawled and scattered before them.

"Eglon! That's far enough." Marcus planted himself, arms folded across his chest. The noise of bleating lambs, the trapped heat, the oppressive stench formed one last barrier between the opponents . . . a blade's sweep apart.

"What right've you got here, Roman?" Eglon spat.

"Watch your tone!" Quintus barked, advancing menacingly. "This is Centurion Marcus Longinus."

Eglon looked left and right, licking his lips in indecision. Seconds earlier he'd been in control, eager for the kill. Now he was uncertain how he'd lost the initiative.

Behind him Yeshua continued, "I have other sheep who aren't of this sheepfold. I'll bring them with me also. I must bring them. They'll listen and hear my voice when I call them. There'll be one flock. One shepherd."[8]

"The centurion's out of uniform," Eglon growled. Sweat beaded on his forehead. "How was I to know? Besides," he resumed, motioning for his men to close in, "I'm here on official business for—"

"Doesn't matter who is your . . . master." Marcus' manner conveyed he was addressing Antipas' dog. "Be off with you. I'm in charge." Though the simple gray tunic he wore clung to his body, Marcus squared his shoulders as if for full dress inspection.

"You," Eglon said, screwing one eye shut. "You killed . . . you're the one . . . killed Vara."

Marcus dropped his hand to grasp his sword hilt. "True. And ready for anyone else who causes trouble. Tell that to your master, eh? And I know you, Eglon. The city is full of pilgrims again, but there won't be any corpses for you to pick over today."

Eglon cast a hard look toward Yeshua. Marcus saw murderous thoughts flash through his eyes. Eglon had been sent to murder Yeshua—that was plain enough.

Yeshua also seemed aware of the purpose of Eglon's visit. He turned His eyes full on Eglon, who suddenly grew pale.

Yeshua's next words were a challenge to the political and religious authorities who doubtless were watching the confrontation from their windows. He was calm, fearless, matter-of-fact. "The reason my Father loves me is that I lay down my life—only to take it up again. No one takes it from me. I lay it down of my own accord. I have authority to lay it down and authority to take it up again. This command I received from my Father."[9]

What could that possibly mean? Marcus wondered. There were so many things Yeshua said that required explanation, but this was not the time to be distracted.

"Leave," Marcus ordered Eglon, "before I arrest you for disturbing the peace."

"The tetrarch won't like this interference," Eglon rumbled. His men had already backed away from the fight. No one wanted to end his life spiked to a Roman cross for disturbing the peace or disobeying a Roman officer. "Governor Pilate'll hear about this."

"Yes. You can count on it." Marcus gave no sign of concern. "Take your curs with you. I give you two minutes. After that I'll flog any of them still within sight. And that includes you."

From the clench of Eglon's jaw Marcus knew the man was near exploding. This was the moment things could go either way. Without giving any other sign, Marcus clasped the sword hilt, making certain it would draw smoothly if needed.

Eglon stood rooted in place for a moment more then withdrew. Antipas' men and the Temple Guards followed him.

The jabber of Pharisees was even louder than before. "He's demon-possessed," Simon ben Zeraim asserted. "Raving mad. Why listen to him?"

Marcus heard Gamaliel respond, "These aren't the sayings of a man possessed by a demon."

To which Nakdimon added, "Can a demon open the eyes of the blind?"[10]

Taking a deep breath and releasing it slowly, Marcus glanced over his shoulder and got a reassuring nod from Quintus. Eglon's company was in retreat back through the herd.

Marcus turned round. Yeshua, Zadok, and Yeshua's talmidim were gone, leaving the Pharisees wrangling among themselves.

When High Priest Caiaphas reached his library in Nicanor Gate, he found Tetrarch Herod Antipas impatiently present. Visibly irritated.

Standing beside the chair of the bloated and sallow ruler of Galilee was the grizzled and unkempt chief officer of his guard and deputed assassin, Eglon.

Caiaphas looked expectantly from one to the other as his priestly assistant brought in the vestments: headgear, breastplate, and blue ceremonial robe of the high priest.

"You're late, Caiaphas." Antipas blew his nose on a silk kerchief.

"You're early, Antipas," Caiaphas countered.

"I haven't been to bed. Dreadful night. Herodias hardly slept. Everything in an uproar."

"Spirits haunting the palace? Only significant details, please. I have things to do." Caiaphas arched his brows. "Well, then? What news have you brought? Another prophet's head on a platter for breakfast?"

"Tell him." Antipas waved an impatient hand at his henchman. "Tell our high priest the latest news about our Messiah." The words dripped sarcasm.

Embarrassed, clearing his throat, Eglon obeyed. "I failed," he said. "I almost had him in Beth-Anyah, but some of his talmidim returned unexpectedly. This morning my men and I surrounded him near the Sheep Gate, but Centurion Marcus Longinus interfered."

Antipas grunted. Rome's involvement complicated things.

Caiaphas was religious head of the Jewish nation. His position had been bought and paid for. Herod Antipas was overseer of a fourth of Herod the Great's former kingdom. He was eager to reacquire the rest. These two rulers of Israel disagreed about most things.

On only one thing did Caiaphas and Antipas fully concur: Yeshua of Nazareth was a threat and must be silenced.

Herod Antipas had already decided that assassination was the simplest approach. Yochanan the Baptizer had been trouble enough. Now this Galilean preacher—a nobody, a carpenter's son—was being spoken of as if He were Yochanan come back to life! In Galilee there were rumblings that Yeshua would make Himself a king!

For his part Caiaphas spread the notion that Yeshua was a sorcerer and demon-possessed. He had tried to trap Yeshua with charges of breaking the Sabbath, of promoting immorality, of failing to properly recognize Rome's authority. When all those attempts at character assassination failed, he issued the formal edict, making any favorable comment on Yeshua cause for excommunication. This threat seemed to have a good effect on the people. To be cast out of the synagogue for speaking favorably about Yeshua meant an end to all commerce. Loss of business. Loss of home and family.

"I'm building a case against Yeshua," Caiaphas confided. "Testimony. I sent a summons to Capernaum, to Simon of the sect of the Pharisees. He entertained Yeshua and his talmidim some months ago. Yeshua claimed to have the power to forgive sins. Such details are important. Simon wrote me after the incident. He's coming to Yerushalayim to add his testimony to the others."

"Well and good." Antipas sucked his teeth. "Testimony means nothing in the face of what happened yesterday."

The whispers about Yeshua had certainly become more cautious. That is, until this matter about the blind beggar named Peniel.

Ultimately Caiaphas favored a permanent solution. A knife across the throat of Yeshua would end his arrogant babble!

"Yes. You're right. So where is Yeshua?" Caiaphas asked.

"By now I don't know," Eglon admitted. "There's a rumor he's going back to the Galil."

If true, this change was satisfactory to Caiaphas for the time being. Everyone living in Jerusalem regarded Galileans as hayseeds and brigands anyway. Let Yeshua get killed out in the countryside. By the time the news reached the capital it would scarcely raise an eyebrow, much less a riot. Besides, anything happening in the Galil was Antipas' problem.

"Well," Caiaphas said in a conciliatory tone to Herod Antipas, "the Galil. Your territory. You'll just have to pursue him there."

Caiaphas sat down, shifting the ritual turban so sunlight streaming in the window did not bounce into his vision off the brass plate forming the headband. *Holiness unto Yahweh* was lettered across it. Repressing an urge to smile, he gently nudged the headpiece so the shaft of light annoyed Antipas.

Squinting, Antipas interposed a fleshy palm. "Already ordered. But Yeshua is not the only problem, as I hear it. What are you going to do about Chief Shepherd Zadok in Beth-lehem? Trouble, that old man. Nothing but trouble. Brings up . . . certain unpleasant memories about my father, Herod the Great. That unfortunate incident with babies in Beth-lehem. Thirty years ago. Damning to the royal family. I hear Zadok spoke out openly in the council in favor of Yeshua. Urged the

Sanhedrin to recognize this imposter as Messiah. The Romans will cut all our throats if we don't nip this sort of thing in the bud."

Stiffly Caiaphas retorted, "Zadok is chief shepherd of the flocks of Israel. A hereditary position. But he's also a religious official under my authority. We discussed his case in council last night. You may leave him to me."

Antipas grunted and shifted his bulk ponderously in the chair. "And what about the latest supposed healing . . . the blind beggar? We can't have the common people—the *am ha aretz*—spouting nonsense about miracles and fulfilled prophecy, can we?"

"What do you suggest?" Caiaphas inquired sarcastically, knowing full well what was meant but willing to force the tetrarch to say it.

"Why not put out the beggar's eyes?" Eglon eagerly contributed. "If he's still blind, that'll prove Yeshua's a liar."

Both rulers stared at the officer and Eglon subsided. "Just an idea," he mumbled.

"And if Yeshua should heal him *again?*" Caiaphas drawled.

High priest and tetrarch stared into each other's face, knowing what the other was thinking: Both men believed Yeshua of Nazareth really did have the power to perform miracles. That said, His wonder-working was irrelevant beside the needs of the rulers to retain their authority.

"I think," Antipas conceded, "a permanent solution should be arranged for the boy as well. Peniel. Yes. Peniel. That's his name, isn't it? How hard can it be to locate a beggar if all Yerushalayim is talking about him?"

Wary of being spotted and arrested, due to Yeshua's warning, Peniel followed the most obscure route from the Lower City to the Sheep Gate quarter. His face concealed except for his eyes, Peniel wandered through corridors he had never seen. It took hours to reach the street of the potter's shop.

The alleyway between the fishmonger's stall and the cubicle occupied by the tripe seller was cramped, smelly, and heaped with things better left unexamined. It was also in exactly the right location for Peniel to approach his father's house unseen.

A man's voice spoke in gruff, no-nonsense tones of authority. Pauses were punctuated by Mama's shrill protests. Balanced precariously on cobbles slimy with fish guts, Peniel closed his eyes to listen.

"Why ask us?" Peniel's mother argued. "We don't know where he is."

"He's your son, isn't he? Don't try to deny it," the man's voice challenged. "You admitted it yesterday."

"Yesterday! Yesterday he was; today we have no son. Peniel's dead to us!"

Peniel winced. Best to turn and run! But Peniel needed to see who was after him. Sight was a powerful new tool, not to be ignored.

Bending low he peered around the corner from behind a heap of bones and scales.

There were two Temple Guards. Peniel recognized them from yesterday's interrogation. The third man, the one speaking, wore a different uniform. Brutish of face and body, he announced gruffly, "Now you listen to me. This isn't about who hasn't paid the Temple shekel or something. We're talking prison, see? I'm Eglon, chief officer of Tetrarch Antipas. My lords Antipas and Caiaphas put me in charge of finding your son, and find him I will. Once more! Do you know where he is? Listen: It'll go hard for you if you lie to me!"

Peniel's father stood with his arms folded across his chest. His chin tucked low. Face contorted with pain.

Mama's voice grew even more strident, matching Eglon's in intensity. "If we knew? If? We'd be first to tell you! Isn't that right, Yahtzar?"

Peniel's father mumbled something. Mama prodded him and he gave a jerk of his head.

Peniel's heart burst with the grief of it. Dead! *Papa! Papa! Oh, Mama!* He wanted to slink away but remained rooted to hear the rest.

"Good, loyal citizens we are!" Mama added. "We'll send word at once if there's any news of his whereabouts. We'll turn him in."

Eglon sneered. "Just the same, we're posting a guard here to keep a lookout for him. You—" he said to one of the Temple Guards—"you stay here. And you—" he ordered the other—"go door-to-door. Stop everyone close to the right age. Check their stories. Ask everyone about the boy. Mention the reward."

Before the instructions were finished, Peniel shrank back into the shadows. How could he ever go back home again? And yet if he had a chance . . . one more chance . . . to talk to Papa and Mama alone. Explain to them. He'd try again later.

It was midafternoon, still on the day of Shavuot. Cicadas hummed in the brambles beyond the well of Mak'ob. Cantor pulled up the bucket and poured the water into Lily's jar. She felt his eyes lock upon her.

Her worried gaze followed the progress of a lone woman descending the switchback into the Valley.

"So. Sarai's coming down," Cantor said sullenly. "After a night at the gatehouse with the Overseer. He's an animal, that fellow."

"Yes."

"You want to talk about it?"

"It's nothing."

"Tell me what's bothering you, then."

"I spoke to Sarai yesterday evening as she was on her way to the top. I asked her where she was going. Invited her to come eat supper with us. She spit on me."

"The Overseer's harlots. Five of them. All separating themselves from those of us who are already separate. Outcasts among the outcasts. It's almost laughable if it wasn't so pathetic. But you know how it is with that sort."

Lily sipped a cup of cool water. "I don't know what sort they are. They go up to the Overseer in the evening. Come down in the morning with extra things. Presents. I'm sorry for them. So much I don't understand."

Cantor was scornful. "What's to understand? They're young. Their bodies still mostly intact. They stay the night with him. He doesn't care what they are if he's drunk enough. All cows are black in the dark. He buys their bodies with food. Trinkets. They've sold their souls. Lowest of the low."

What did Cantor mean? How could a soul be bought? Lily did not pursue the discussion. Cantor clearly understood what happened in the stone cottage at the gate of Mak'ob, but Lily did not.

Lily felt sorry she had brought it up. "Sarai was such a frightened little girl when she first came to the Valley. And now? So hard. Suffering has made her so hard. She told me she hates God for making her a leper. And I'm sorry for her, Cantor. And now I'm angry that you judge her so harshly!"

He fell silent at her rebuke. Then, a minute later, he began, "Yes. You're right. You are. And I do pity her when I think about it. We're all lepers. Growing numb, then breaking off bit by bit. But this disease isn't just about what happens to the outside of a person. No, Lily. A leper is the visible picture of what the human soul looks like when sin takes over a life. When a person becomes numb to sin, he is eaten alive by it. That's why Outside people fear us so. Our bodies are the external image of corrupt souls. And yet I look at you and know it's possible for a beautiful soul to live in spite of physical suffering."

"But I'm not suffering, Cantor. Except, you know, my heart. When I think about Sarai and the others. And all the ones around me who are so lonely. So desperate that they'll do anything . . . anything for a little happiness."

"Their souls are like their bodies."

"Can a soul be *tsara*? Can a heart have leprosy? Can the inner man be so numb he no longer feels and so increases his injury day by day? God's mercy could heal such a heart. I believe it. Forgive and heal. Restore the feeling. Bring back what is eaten away in us."

Cantor placed the jug on his shoulder, and they walked together back toward the cave. "Ah, Lily. My Lily. I should listen to you more often. Yes. You're right. I was thinking about it last night. You know how we'll die here one day. Fade away inside this Valley with the other outcasts. How our headstones will crumble. Our laughter and tears and worries will all vanish in the air. No one on earth who comes after our time will even remember our names. Or care. Or know our stories. Believe we ever existed. But here we are, walking away from this well. Lily and Cantor. Lepers of Mak'ob. Our stories will never be told. But it doesn't matter. Because everyone . . . everyone . . . who lives out an ordinary life in the outside world will also die. Each person's physical body will become, in the grave, as we are now."

She said quietly, hoping, "Yet El Shaddai knows our names. Knows our stories. Lily. Cantor. He hears us when we cry to him."

Cantor agreed. "And one day we who have suffered in this Valley of Sorrow will stand alongside those who drove us away. Those who might have helped but turned from our suffering."

Lily imagined the moment. "They will see our souls, shining. Those who stoned us and hated us. Those who declared that we must deserve to suffer. Those who accused God of causing suffering! Accused God of causing the suffering of the children in the dying cave!"

Cantor shifted the weight of the water jar. "Those who were blessed with whole and healthy bodies. Then they will be judged by how they used their gifts on earth. Their health and wealth."

Lily frowned. "Oh, Cantor, there are so many here who hurt worse than me. I'm nothing in all this. All the little ones. Calling for their mothers in the night. I'm nothing."

"You are everything, Lily. Oh, that I could be more like you! Because when they cry out, you go to them and hold them as they die. Weep for them as if you were their mother."

"Because I hurt too."

"Yes. You feel. No leprosy in *your* heart, Lily. And think of this and be glad! You and I and all the little ones . . . our souls will stand as equals with everyone who ever lived. Yes! Stand before the Lord of heaven."

"I believe every knee will bow before him. Every voice will proclaim his name. It's all I have left to hold on to."[11]

"Soul to soul. Yes. Equal. We will stand without these corrupted bodies. Our accusers will stand without their possessions or wealth or success or any of the things by which an earthly life is valued. Then the lives of all mankind will be reviewed by the One, the Righteous Judge."

Lily smiled. It was good to talk of *olam haba*, the life of the world to come. "Rabbi Ahava says on that day the Knower of Secrets will reveal every secret thought. Every good deed will be rewarded and every neglected kindness will be clearly seen. Beneath the gaze of the Lord, darkness will become light."

With his gentle hand Cantor touched Lily's shoulder. "And we'll know the truth of who among mankind was merciful and whole. And also whose half-eaten hearts were beating inside trivial existence. We'll know who secretly blessed others. Helped the helpless. Touched the untouchables. No, more than that . . . who *embraced* the untouchables. Ah, Lily. My Lily. You will be the most beautiful soul of all . . . shining. I know I will see you on that day. And I am glad I came to this place and was allowed to love you."

Late-afternoon shadows deepened in the Valley of Mak'ob as Lily made her way slowly toward the cave she shared with Deborah and Deborah's seven-year-old son, Baruch. The shelter faced west, capturing the last rays of the sun. Cabbage soup simmered in a clay pot over the open fire.

Deborah sat nearby. Her eyes were nearly swollen shut, lips and face distorted by new sores. She squinted across the Valley toward the opposite slope of the cliff. A steep switchback snaked up a thousand feet to the Outside. She seemed not to notice Lily's approach. Lily guessed that Deborah was slowly going blind.

Deborah's clawlike left hand rested on her belly as she murmured endearments to the baby within her. "He'll come back. You'll see your papa's face first of all. He promised he'd come back to us before you are born."

The trail was empty. No one climbing up or coming down. Jekuthiel, absent almost four months, had not returned.

"Deborah," Lily hailed. "Where's Baruch?"

Deborah frowned, displaying some resentment that Lily had interrupted her reverie. "He stayed in the camp of the Torah Boys for the holiday. Last night and today. Midwife brought me soup."

"Did you rest? Midwife says you should rest. It'll be soon, she says."

Deborah shrugged and half turned away. She fumbled with a stick and poked at the fire. "I dreamed."

Lily did not ask. Did not need to ask.

Deborah continued, "I dreamed about Jekuthiel. He came back. He . . . he was . . . just like he used to be. Well. Whole. Handsome. I was sitting at the top." She gestured upward. "I was Outside at the head of the switchback. Above the Valley. He was leading a procession . . . others with him. Up and up the trail. An unbroken line of people . . . no one sick . . . they were following him. Climbing, climbing. Up to the Outside. To see our baby."

"A good dream, then! Mazel tov! A good dream for Shavuot."

"A dream." Deborah sighed. "What's the difference? I woke up and here I am. Awake and living in the nightmare."

"A good dream all the same. Was I there?" Lily sat beside her.

"I think so."

"And Cantor? Was he with me? Were we married?"

Deborah lifted her head in an attempt to make the vision clearer. "I don't know. I can't remember. Just a dream."

"Good though. Everyone coming up from the Valley. Outside. The old woman who dreamed dreams would have said such a dream means something good. If she was still alive she could tell us."

"Yes. Well. That's the point. She's dead. Everyone who lives here dies."

"Everyone who lives anywhere dies. Everywhere. It's just that the people Outside aren't smart enough to know they're going to end up the same as us. Rabbi says we're God's reminder, so they hate us."

"They have a life before they die."

"So do we. It's what you make of it, Cantor says."

Deborah snapped. "Stop! What do you know about it? You weren't even grown when you came here! What do you know about living? I had a real life Outside. Jekuthiel and I . . . we had a life together. Pleasant. Other people. People with hands. People with human faces." Deborah touched her deformed face with her claw. "What can you know about it?"

Lily fell silent. No use talking. Deborah had sunk into despair since her husband had left the Valley. As time grew nearer for the baby to be born, Deborah's mood grew darker every day. Her disease progressed further.

Lily dipped thin soup into a gourd and offered it to Deborah.

"No." She shook her head in adamant refusal.

"You must eat. Midwife says you must."

"No. When he comes back to me, then . . ."

This was Deborah's trick to make Lily speak openly what she really thought about Jekuthiel. Four months since he left. A long time in the life of a leper wandering on the Outside. One day was a long time for a leper to survive Outside. If exposure to the elements and starvation did not kill him, he may well have been stoned for attempting to draw water from a well. Who could say? He had been gone too long now for anyone but Deborah to continue to hope he would ever come back.

Still, for the sake of keeping Deborah going, Lily did not say what she and everyone in the Valley believed. Instead she said, "Suppose . . . just suppose . . . you die because you won't eat. And then the next day Jekuthiel comes back. What then?" Lily placed the full gourd beside Deborah and went inside the cave.

When she came back, the soup was gone.

Sundown.

With every deepening shadow Peniel grew more confident. More secure. Jerusalem—so hostile, so alien in the glare of day—bit by bit returned to a more familiar feel.

Even Temple Guards had to eat supper some time, Peniel reasoned. If the sentry was distracted, however briefly, Peniel would slip in.

East of the potter's shop was the warren of Sheep Gate streets, lanes, and alleys. Peniel's fingers lightly brushed the fence of the animal pens. He noted the well-known smell of the sheepfolds holding the Temple lambs. His eyes were open, but touch and scent carried him toward home. The chorus of evening sounds grew as Shavuot ended.

Peniel was two streets from where he grew up when he turned a corner and collided headlong with someone leaning against the wall.

"Here, you!" The hands that grabbed Peniel's arm were as coarse as the voice. "Watch where you're going!"

Eglon!

Peniel kept his head down, tried to pull away. He mumbled something unintelligible.

A grip like an iron band tightened around Peniel's wrist. "You live around here, do you?" Eglon demanded. "Haven't seen you here today. Who are you?"

Peniel's wits were frozen. He could neither speak nor move.

"Are you deaf or thick .... or something else, I wonder." Inexorably Eglon dragged Peniel from the alley into the greater remaining light of the adjacent lane. Jerking upward on Peniel's jaw he peered into Peniel's face, looked doubtfully into Peniel's eyes. "What's your business here, boy?"

"Going to the m-market," Peniel stuttered.

"Markets're all closed for Shavuot," Eglon returned, suspicion turning to triumph. "What do you say to that?"

"At sundown the baker opens briefly so we can buy bread," Peniel protested. "I forgot to get enough before the holiday," he explained. "Please, sir. My master'll beat me if I don't hurry."

"Your master, eh? Who do you work for? A potter?"

"No, sir," Peniel argued. "My master is . . ." Peniel's mind tumbled through all the facts. He was dressed as a beggar, so he could never pass as a household servant or a shop apprentice.

The bleat of an unhappy lamb struck his ear.

"My master is Zadok the shepherd," Peniel claimed. "You know him? Chief Shepherd?"

Eglon grunted. The boy was the right age and description to match Eglon's quarry, but he had come from the direction of the pens. Eglon sniffed, apparently judging the fact that Peniel smelled like a herdsman.

Taking a deep breath and steeling his resolve, Peniel raised his chin and stared back at the officer. Their eyes met, locked.

Eglon looked away first. "Your name?"

This time Peniel was prepared for the question. "Gershon," he replied, giving the name of his dead older brother.

"Exile, eh?" Eglon said. He shoved Peniel away. "Get on with your business then."

The instant the viselike grip was released, Peniel wanted to run. He forced himself to walk slowly and remembered to turn toward the bakery, even though that meant staying alongside Eglon for longer.

At the next corner Eglon turned one way and Peniel the other.

They were half a block apart when the wheelwright who lived near Peniel's parents emerged from his house. "Hey!" his voice boomed. "Is that you, Peniel? Did you know the Temple Guards are looking for you?"

Like an arrow leaving the bowstring, Peniel flew down the street.

"Stop! Here, stop you!" he heard Eglon yelling behind him. The clatter of Eglon's feet sprinting after him was joined by another and then another as more sentries took up the chase.

Beside the fruit seller's Peniel turned left; beside the tanner's, right. *Run!*

"Catch that boy! Grab him!"

Think, Peniel urged himself. *Think! Can't head toward Damascus Gate. Too many guards there. Which are the dead-end lanes? Mustn't turn up one of those. Double back? Run, dodge pedestrians!*

Eglon, puffing, no longer had voice to shout to passersby.

Peniel's legs started to ache, his chest to burn. Years as a blind beggar had not prepared him to race through Jerusalem.

Deepening blue sky gave way to purple.

Peniel closed his eyes and saw the route ahead clearer than before. The next fork led to a blind alley, but Peniel took it anyway. The wall across the end had a drainage ditch running underneath it. Peniel threw himself headlong into the channel, wriggled through, popped out the other side.

A yell of triumph turned to a yelp of dismay from the pursuers. Eglon shouted at his companions to boost him up, boost him up!

The officer cursed when he landed on Peniel's side of the wall. Eglon now ran with a limp.

Peniel pulled ahead.

Darkness closed in around the city, and into it, Peniel disappeared. The sounds of the chase faded in the distance.

Eglon returned to the Hasmonean Palace, which was the Jerusalem home of his master, Tetrarch Antipas. There he found Antipas at supper with the high priest.

"Well?" Antipas demanded. "Have you taken care of the problem?"

"The boy. Peniel," Eglon said, "is still at large."

Antipas grimaced, so Eglon added hurriedly, "But I've seen him now and can recognize him." Eglon had no intention of admitting that Peniel had been in his grasp. "He had help with his flight," the officer lied.

"Surprised you came back simply to admit another failure," Antipas remarked coldly, unhappy that Caiaphas was present to hear more of his retainer's ineptitude. "Go away, Eglon," Antipas said, waving a jeweled wine goblet. "If your news is all bad, there's no reason to bore our guest with it."

"Your pardon, lord," Eglon corrected, "but the rest of the news is of concern to the *cohen hagadol* and why I returned at once: Chief Shepherd Zadok is aiding the fugitive."

Caiaphas, whose eyes were bleary from too much drink, pushed himself up from the couch on which he reclined. "Zadok? How'd you know?"

"My sources," Eglon hedged. "Peniel ben Yahtzar is disguised as a shepherd. Put himself under Zadok's care."

"This morning you reminded me that Zadok was your problem," Antipas drawled to the high priest. "Well, Caiaphas? Are you going to do something about him, or only call another session of the council at which Zadok can spout more fables about Yeshua of Nazareth?"

Caiaphas was known for watching the direction of the winds of popular opinion before making any decision, but this time he was trapped. By his own decree, speaking well of Yeshua was grounds for excommunication. It was bad enough when the *am ha aretz* supported the carpenter, but a high religious official helping the fable grow larger by protecting the miraculously healed beggar? Enough!

Though both men were puppet rulers propped up by Rome, Caiaphas framed his next words as a formal request, one potentate to another: "By your leave, Lord Antipas," he requested portentously, "let Eglon go to Beth-lehem with a company of my Temple Guards. On my order Zadok is removed from his post. If the boy is there, Eglon will arrest him, and two problems will be solved at once."

Even by flickering torchlight, Pilate had visibly aged, Marcus thought. The governor's eyes appeared hollow, as if he was not sleeping well. His graying hair showed more silver. It was thinner too.

Marcus appeared before him in dress uniform, polished and shining. "Welcome, Centurion," Pilate said, inviting Marcus into his private chambers at Herod the Great's Jerusalem palace. "Wine for the centurion." He snapped his fingers.

An uneasy silence passed while goblets were filled and the servants dismissed. "I'm glad . . . ," Pilate began awkwardly. Then, more stiffly formal, "Congratulations, First Javelin of Judea."

"Thank you, my lord," Marcus acknowledged.

"A threat to the Empire has been removed," Pilate said, alluding to the removal of Sejanus and the Praetorian conspiracy. "A shadow over the sun, gone."

What else could a Sejanus appointee do but act shocked, appear grateful, and hope for the best?

"The emperor is well?" Marcus inquired.

"Well!" Pilate agreed. "Well and reasserting his control over the Imperial provinces."

Some of the conquered territories were administered by the Senate of Rome, but others, like Judea, were expressly reserved for the emperor himself. Till lately that distinction had meant the rule of Sejanus, but no longer.

Small wonder Pilate was anxious.

"Affairs of state call me," the governor said. "I must return to Caesarea."

After the season of Passover and certainly by Pentecost the weather was settled enough for safe sea voyaging. Official visitors from Rome could be expected at any time. Pilate needed to get the provincial capital in proper order to receive them. He would try to anticipate any challenges to his performance record he might face. And, of course, he would write glowing letters to the emperor, thanking the gods for Tiberius' deliverance from danger.

"Your job," Pilate said, "is to keep order, under Tribune Felix as your commander. First duty: King Aretas of Nabatea is acting uppity because of our . . . troubles here. Call on him within the week. Remind him not to interfere with the power of Rome. Make some examples: Round up rebels, put down insurrection, but keep the peace! No more riots!" Then, as if taking Marcus into his confidence, Pilate said, "These Jews! Cantankerous lot! Impossible to please them! Argue about anything and everything and then threaten to complain to Rome!"

On two previous occasions Pilate had made bad decisions that led to unrest in Judea. Unleashing Vara's malicious brutality had been the third mistake. He could not afford any more.

"I have some questions, my lord," Marcus said.

Pilate looked peevish. He waved a hand for Marcus to wait. "Don't think I don't know what's happening here," he said. "Herod Antipas would love to rule all Judea again, like his father. Happy to see unrest so he can tattle to Rome. Don't give him any excuses! He needs to go back to the Galil and keep his nose on his own affairs!"

This was also a tacit warning to Marcus. The governor knew Marcus and Felix had communicated with Caligula, who might one day be emperor. *Don't do it again*, Pilate's message insisted.

But perhaps here was the opening Marcus wanted. If Pilate was already suspicious of Antipas, maybe Marcus could use that distrust as a device to protect Yeshua.

Remembering Felix's warning about not pushing Pilate too hard, Marcus first tested the water by asking about Zadok. "There is a matter in which Herod Antipas is already meddling here in Judea," Marcus suggested. "He's urging the high priest to expel a good, upright man, Zadok of Bethlehem, the Chief—"

The warning palm lifted again. "I won't get in the middle of a Jewish religious squabble," Pilate instructed. "Had enough of that for life! You don't get into that mess either, Centurion! Keep the roads and cities safe, and taxes flowing. Anything else offends somebody, no matter how hard you try not to!"

Pilate was bitter, afraid, and eager to hole up in Caesarea, the least Jewish city in the Jewish province. He would leave Marcus to face the blame for anything else that went wrong.

"I'll do my best, sir," Marcus offered.

The governor scowled and dismissed Marcus.

There was no mandate from Pilate that Marcus could claim in order to protect Yeshua from the envy and hatred of the religious leaders. But for the moment he could extend the power he'd been given as best he could.

Marcus saluted and left.

CHAPTER 4

It was early morning. Before the heat of the sun awakened the flies and made the stench unbearable.

Lily, Cantor, Rabbi Ahava, and three other volunteers entered the large cavern that housed the dying of the community. There were thirty-six hopeless patients within, ranging in age from nine to seventy-one.

Leprosy in its last stages stole the senses incrementally. Taste, smell, sight, touch all vanished until finally only the sense of hearing remained. A dozen among the victims had reached this phase. They lay helpless, unmoving, listening to their own breathing and the voices around them.

Death would very soon press even breath from them.

Lily knew them all by name. Most were blind, yet they recognized her voice. She cleaned their sores and spoke to each as if she were mother, sister, daughter, or long-gone wife come to make these last days more bearable.

I'm praying again, Compassionate One. Oh, be here! Be here with them through my touch!

Few could taste the broth she spooned into their mouths. And yet they could hear Cantor singing softly to them, feeding their ravaged souls with Hope.

> *"I sought the Lord, and He answered me;*
> *He delivered me from all my fears."*[12]

The greatest battle for Lily was the fight against flies and maggots that hatched and swarmed in putrefied flesh from one day to the next. She covered her nose and mouth to keep from gagging. She picked them out of the sores one by one, then anointed the wounds with wine and oil. Lily reapplied the dressings day after day in a battle that could not be won.

I'm praying again, Creator of Me and Them and Us! Help me! Help me see them, not with my eyes, but as you see them. Faces featureless now. But you formed them body and spirit in your likeness. Do you suffer too? Is this your faceless face? your handless arm?

Cantor sang on and on, his voice a prayer for those who had no strength to pray.

> *"This poor man called, and the Lord heard him;*
> *He saved him out of all his troubles."*[13]

I'm praying again, Inventor of the Senses! How good of you to leave their hearing till the last. How good you are to bless Cantor with the sickness so he can sing to them in their darkness! How great is your wisdom to bless Rabbi Ahava with this suffering so he can be here with them!

Rabbi Ahava, always disregarding the levitical laws about who was unclean, embraced each patient. He spoke words of encouragement. "It will be over soon. Soon. Rest. It's all right to let go. But don't give up hoping. Yes! Messiah waits at the end of life to welcome us! Don't be afraid of darkness. There is light at the end of the dark journey!"

Lily scooped up the featherlight body of a small boy named Shalom. He could say only two words distinctly when he came: *Shalom* and *Mama.*

Shalom was only eight or nine. He had entered the Valley last summer. For years he had lived among the gravestones Outside. Then somehow he had come here. Dragging himself on stumps where feet should have been. Covered with disease. No face. He called Lily *Mama.*

Imagine.

She let him call her Mama. Didn't mind. Embraced him like his mama should have . . . if only . . .

"Shalom! Good morning, love," she whispered in the hole where his ear had been. "The sun is shining outside. Bright. I saw pink flowers blooming on the high slopes. We'll go hawking later. Catch a rabbit or a pigeon to feed you tomorrow. What do you think?"

The child replied with a moan of acknowledgment.

"When you get to heaven, you'll run through the fields. Would you like to fly with the hawks too?"

Another moan. Yes. Yes. He would very much like to fly.

"You will. You will. Angels fly. You have an angel, and soon he'll take you flying like a hawk. Put in a good word with the Almighty for me, love." She kissed his scab-covered head, then began to clean the filth from him.

"The angel of the Lord encamps around those who fear Him,
And He delivers them."[14]

Cantor sang. Rabbi Ahava spoke the psalms. Lily cleaned what remained of the calves of his legs.

Tears. Tears. Her tears. Little boy. Never had a chance to live. So near to flying away. Someday they would fly together in heaven. But for now the earth held her here, rooted like a tree.

I'm praying again, Soaring One. Do you remember what he looked like before? All of them? Me? Us? Will you restore us? Do the souls of children grow more beautiful in this refiner's cauldron? Am I seeing myself in these? And you? Are you here with him? in him? Am I tending your wounds?

The visit ended after two hours.

"No one dead today," Cantor said.

"I think little Shalom will leave us soon," Lily murmured.

Rabbi Ahava remarked, "There are always more to take the places of those who leave us. So many." Then, "How is Deborah? Is the baby due soon?"

"Any day," Lily told him. "I think she's somehow holding off until Jekuthiel comes back. She wants him with her when the baby's born."

"So long, he's been gone. So long." The rabbi shook his head slowly from side to side.

Avel stood on the pinnacle of the Tower of the Flock. The boy recognized the black horse pounding toward Migdal Eder. He likewise recognized its rider. Avel's heart drummed in his nine-year-old chest with violence equal to the thumping hoofbeats.

Good news never traveled this fast.

To Ha-or Tov, his friend in the pasture below, Avel shouted, "Centurion Marcus is coming!" Then he leapt for the ladder and disappeared into the upper story of the tower. Avel's feet did not touch the rungs. He controlled his descent solely by oak banisters polished smooth by generations of shepherds.

The lord of Migdal Eder, Chief Shepherd Zadok, was deep in conference with several of his deputies. "Master Zadok," Avel interrupted, panting, "Marcus Longinus is coming . . . and in a terrible hurry!"

Regarding the apprentice herdsman from under bushy brows topping one piercing eye and one menacing black patch, Zadok remarked, "Did y' think I didn't hear y' bellow, lad? Likely folks in Beth-lehem took note as well."

"Sorry," Avel said, only momentarily subdued before resuming the urgency of his report. "But he's in armor! Riding like the wind too! No mistaking that black horse. What should we do?"

Low growls from the others present greeted these words. Avel heard the men suggest staves, rocks for their slings. The boy's excitement grew. Battle could be coming to Migdal Eder!

"Aye," the shepherd named Lev agreed. "Shall I sound the alarm? Gather the men in from the far pastures?"

Zadok snorted. "Roman officer Marcus may be, but the man's a friend. Proved it more'n once. We'll wait for his news before yellin', 'All I feared has come upon me,' eh?" the Chief Shepherd scolded. "Go back up and keep watch, boy."

Avel stood his ground. "Let me send Ha-or Tov. His eyes are better than mine . . . and I want to hear what the centurion says."

Regarding his protégé shrewdly, Zadok acquiesced.

They had not long to wait for the news. Moments later the centurion's mount thundered into the yard, setting Red Dog barking violently.

Zadok stood in the doorway to greet him. Files of grim-faced shepherds flanked their chief on either side. Without dismounting Marcus announced, "Zadok, there's a company of Temple Guards on the way, forty of them. For supporting Yeshua of Nazareth you're to be turned out."

Avel noted the muttered concerns of the others. Forty was a sizable number when swords could only be opposed by wooden shepherd's crooks. The boy's anxiety mounted when he saw the tension in their faces. It was unsettling to witness consternation on the visages of sturdy, hardened men who slept rough most nights and encountered wild beasts alone.

On Zadok's face he saw resignation but no fear.

"It's the right of the high priest to put me out," Zadok said simply. "But I gather that's not all yer news. Come in. Lev, water the centurion's horse."

Avel saw tension ease in the broad shoulders and grim face of the centurion. The boy guessed the Roman expected bloodshed. Had he come to again fight alongside the Chief Shepherd of Israel?

While the other shepherds remained in a defensive ring outside Migdal Eder, Zadok and Marcus held a quiet discussion inside. Avel looked on from the corner by the fireplace, his presence uninvited but accepted.

Marcus explained: "I have a . . . source in Antipas' household. You already know your high priest has made it a crime to speak of Yeshua as the Jewish Messiah. Antipas and Caiaphas plot to kill Yeshua and others who oppose their plan."

Zadok grasped the twin corded braids of his coarse white beard and nodded. "I expected it. I saw it in that jackal Eglon's face at the sheep pens. Didn't have a chance to thank y'."

Slowly, measuring his words, Marcus continued, "Pilate restored my rank. But he refused to intervene for you. Said he had no authority to interfere in Judean religious squabbles."

Avel was surprised to see Zadok's chest swell up. "And right he is too! Do y' think I'd take something offered by the hand of Rome? Y' wrong me if y' think that, Marcus Longinus. More than thirty years have I been shepherd here with the Temple flocks—five and twenty of them as Chief. I never sought Rome's endorsement, and I would not take it now!"

"Then where'll you go?"

This was exactly the question Avel was aching to pose. Since being sent to Zadok by Yeshua, Avel had found in the grizzled shepherd a protector and grandfather, whom he vowed never to leave. Wherever Zadok went, Avel and his two friends would be going too.

"I shall go to him, of course," Zadok said quietly. "To Yeshua."

Avel watched the Roman officer indicate his acceptance. "I'm thinking of resigning my commission," Marcus said. "So I can do the same."

To Avel's disbelief Zadok contradicted Marcus. "Don't give up your office lightly," he argued. "Y' do more good where y' are."

Further discussion had to be postponed because of Ha-or Tov's treble cry, "In sight now: two columns of men marching. Round helmets, brown tunics. One man on horseback."

Temple Guards.

Avel had many times ducked away from the cuffs and slaps of such men while he was a Jerusalem Sparrow, one of the orphan boys who nightly carried torches to earn their daily bread.

Marcus stood up. "You won't accept the hand of Rome," he repeated, "but I trust you'll accept my hand, though it is a Roman who offers."

As Zadok stood, Avel saw the two men grasp each other by the forearm. Father and son they could have been, Avel thought. One looked the way prophets of old were described: visage like a mountain thunderstorm, implacable, able to speak to and for the Almighty with equal assurance. The other was short-haired, clean-shaven, and exuded physical confidence and courage. They were a formidable pair, corresponding in both integrity and force of will.

The sound of tramping feet approaching up the dusty lane echoed between the rock walls of the sheepfold.

"Troop halt!" Avel heard the shouted command. Then, "Zadok of Migdal Eder, show yourself!"

"They don't know I'm here," Marcus noted. "Let's see what they say before they know a Roman officer is a witness."

To Avel, Zadok said, "Hand me my staff, boy. And stay close to me." Avel retrieved Zadok's fire-hardened rod of almond wood. With it in hand the Chief Shepherd looked even more like the stories told of Elijah or Moses.

"Who calls for Zadok?" the man rumbled as he emerged from the tower.

Blinking in the sunlight, Avel stood behind him. The other shepherds still stood in postures of nervous defiance. The one called Lev had a sling dangling at his side. A rock the size of Avel's fist protruded from the leather pocket hanging by Lev's knee. Lev could knock a quail out of a tree or hit a badger in the eye; Avel had seen him do both. At this range at least one of the Temple Guards would fall as hard as Goliath before David.

There was a captain at the head of the marching columns of men, but he didn't speak. Instead the lone mounted man demanded again, "Chief Shepherd Zadok?"

"Eglon," Zadok identified in a voice dripping with disdain. "Y' have no business here. Go back and tell that old fox, your master Antipas, that the Chief Shepherd of Israel doesn't come when a butcher's son calls him."

"I'll have you dragged back in chains," Eglon blustered. "I'm here by special request of my lord Caiaphas. You're discharged."

"Where the body is, there will the vultures gather," Zadok said. "So Herod Antipas, the viper of the Galil, has taken refuge with the white-washed tombs of Yerushalayim."

Eglon nudged his horse forward a half-dozen paces, flicking the quirt in his hand as if he would lash Zadok in the face. Avel saw Zadok reach and restrain Lev's sling arm, though Eglon appeared not to notice. "Old man, you've insulted the tetrarch for the last time!"

Marcus stepped into the sunlight.

"C-centurion," Eglon stammered with surprise, "I didn't know—"

"Obviously not," Marcus intoned sternly. "I'm aware of your orders. The Chief Shepherd is correct. You're a messenger boy . . . nothing more." Then rejecting any further conversation with Eglon, Marcus addressed the captain of the Temple Guard. "Master Zadok will obey the command of the high priest. He'll leave here when he's ready . . . and in my company. You may go."

Avel saw Eglon's face tighten with rage. The man's hands clinched on the whip handle, and his body betrayed the temptation to spur his horse into Marcus.

Avel sensed the danger was not over yet. If Eglon led a charge, would the Temple soldiers follow? Then the herdsmen would certainly resist and blood would flow.

Marcus advanced quickly toward the side of Eglon's mount before

Antipas' hired killer made up his mind what to do next. The centurion beckoned for a private conference and said something too low for Avel to catch. Automatically Eglon bent forward from the waist to hear better.

In that instant Marcus reached upward with both hands, grasping Eglon by the lapels of his robe. The startled bay mare assisted by skittishly prancing sideways. With a twist of his shoulders and a jerk backward, Marcus lifted Eglon bodily out of the saddle. In the next instant Marcus slammed Eglon into the ground.

A puff of dust rose from the impact. This seemed to Avel to be the visible expression of the strangled explosion Eglon made when all his air abruptly left his lungs.

No one else moved a muscle.

Now Marcus spoke loudly enough for everyone to hear. "I said, 'You may go.' Or didn't you hear me the first time?"

Though Eglon was nearly as big as Marcus in height, the centurion easily swept the other man up from the ground and back onto his feet. "Be very clear about something," he said to Eglon, who wobbled visibly. "Zadok and any who choose to leave here with him are under my protection. And that means they are under the seal of Rome. Remember that and tell your keepers the same. Now go."

Though Eglon appeared manifestly furious, Avel knew Eglon was unwilling to openly tackle an Imperial officer. Remounting and wheeling his horse around, Eglon galloped off, leaving the captain of the Temple Guard to salute Marcus, then order his men to march away.

"Y' just made powerful enemies in Caiaphas and Herod Antipas," Zadok suggested to Marcus. "And I doubt Eglon will ever be your friend, either."

"One more thing you and I have in common," Avel heard Marcus reply. "But I've got to make use of Pilate's sense of obligation while it lasts. Doesn't your holy writ say not to trust in the goodwill of princes? Anyway," Marcus concluded thoughtfully, "Pilate wants me out of the way. I'm leading the diplomatic envoy to Nabatea the end of the week. No more use of you, I'm afraid."

"Then Shalom till we meet again," Zadok said, grasping Marcus' arm again. "We both serve as we're called."

Sweet breezes from the Great Sea of Middle Earth, urged eastward by the ginger and saffron rays of the setting sun, curled over the heights of Jerusalem. The prevailing wind kept the stench and squalor of the Lower City away from those who dwelt in the Upper City.

The palace of High Priest Caiaphas was well placed to take advantage of both the views and the cleansing drafts. Here, near the summit of the highest of the western hills, his three-story mansion was more imposing than any of its neighbors. The structure's grandeur was diminished only by its proximity to the sprawling palace built by Herod the Great.

Taken together, the high priest's mansion and Herod's citadel, now home to the Roman governors of Judea, stood in opposition to the Temple of El'Elyon, God Most High. *His* home lay on the Temple Mount promontory to the east.

Simon ben Zeraim turned his head to peer toward the marble of the sanctuary. His reception at the high priest's manor had been cordial. But the attentive slave's washing of his feet in perfumed waters had not completely alleviated the Pharisee's misgivings. Once more Simon looked longingly toward the Temple, where the *cohens*, or priests, were lighting the lamps and shutting the gates for the evening.

Pharisees had been pious keepers of the strict laws of Moses during the two centuries since Judah Maccabee cleansed and rededicated the Holy Mountain. They had little in common with the Temple authorities or others of their sect, the Sadducees.

Sadducee to the core, High Priest Caiaphas had married into a politically well-connected family. His name was derived from a Hebrew word meaning "low place," like the sink of a swamp or a valley where refuse was dumped. Caiaphas often joked about the reference, saying that it was proof how far above his origins a man of ability and ambition could rise.

Simon performed a quick mental calculation. Caiaphas had been raised to the high priesthood by Governor Pilate's predecessor, Gratus, about the third year of the reign of Tiberius. So Caiaphas had held the office for some eleven or twelve years now. Evidently his ability and ambition were satisfactory to the Roman overlords.

Simon wandered among rooftop gardens surrounding an expansive courtyard. Planter boxes encouraged fig, citron, and orange trees to flourish in the heart of the Holy City. Carefully tended miniature arbors produced grapes for the high priest's table.

The clatter of tramping feet from the quadrangle proved to be the sunset changing of the *cohen hagadol*'s personal squad of Temple Guards. For several months rumors had circulated throughout the province. They said Caiaphas allowed sacred korban funds from the Temple to be used unlawfully by Governor Pilate. Since then the high priest had received an increasing number of death threats. With Zealot rebels coming out of the hills to murder those they called collaborators, this was no time to be seen as working hand in glove with the Romans.

At the mental image Simon tugged at his own soft leather glove, then absentmindedly scratched his left ear . . . and jumped when Caiaphas spoke suddenly from behind him.

"Sorry to keep you waiting," the jovial voice of the high priest boomed broadly. "My secretary always pesters me for just one more letter . . . you know how it is." Caiaphas gestured with both hands. He included Simon in his portrayal of important men of affairs bearing up under the cares of their duty.

Everything about Caiaphas was done broadly. Whether he spoke to one man or a thousand, his speech had the quality of a lecture from a tutor to a class of simpleminded children. *Pay attention*, his manner implied. *I realize this is hard for you to grasp, but try, because everything I say is significant.*

"I'm sorry I can't invite you to stay to supper," Caiaphas added. "I'm entertaining the ambassador of the Nabatean king, Aretas. Diplomacy, you see, is one of the unexpected additional requirements of my office." Inclining his head to one side and tapping the side of his ample nose with an imperial forefinger, he added in a lower tone, "Tetrarch Herod Antipas needs my assistance in smoothing over some . . . but can't go into that, can I?"

Simon wasn't certain if he should nod or shake his head, so he merely responded with dignity, "I understand. You asked for my help?"

"Right to the point," Caiaphas rumbled. "I like that. Too many men want to know what's in it for them before they act as all good citizens should. All right, here it is: The troublemaker Yeshua of Nazareth has to be dealt with. Too many of the common people—" Caiaphas managed to make *common* sound synonymous with *defiled*—"flock to his speeches, neglecting their work. They give too much attention to his message, which, as we know, undermines proper submission to proper authority. You should know: Your father-in-law has been expelled from his post because of his support of Yeshua."

"The old man is nothing to me. Always was pigheaded. I've not allowed my wife to see him in years. Our son has never met him."

"It's a wise man who keeps a rebel from his door," Caiaphas counseled. "The old man talks too much."

Simon nodded his agreement with the high priest. For generations the Pharisees struggled to teach suitable piety to the masses, and in two short years Yeshua had convinced many of them that it wasn't all that important, that religion had more to do with the condition of the heart than a proper regard for the 613 dos and don'ts.

"Now many say this Yeshua is a rebel," Caiaphas continued, "and should be turned over to the Romans as a traitor. But I cannot in good conscience do this, for he is a Jew after all. We are a people of law and proper procedure, and he must be given a fair hearing. I never wish to act without giving an adversary a fair hearing." The weight of the warning hung in the air like an executioner's blade suspended overhead. "So I'm gathering all the information I can before proceeding further. I'm told you met this so-called rabbi in person . . . that you had him as a guest in your home?"

Simon recognized in this statement a demonstration of the high priest's network of informants. Since this event was exactly what he'd expected to be queried about, he felt no fear. "A year ago it was, and more," he admitted, "closer to two. Yeshua had been teaching in the synagogue in my hometown of Capernaum. At that time he had a decent enough reputation, performing healings and such."

Caiaphas narrowed his eyes and frowned.

"Done, of course, either through trickery or black magic," Simon added hurriedly.

Caiaphas nodded.

"At any rate, a story went round the Galil that Yeshua had brought a young man back to life . . . impossible, of course, but so ran the tale. Probably spread deliberately to make him sound like a prophet—Elijah or Elisha, I expect. I wanted to see for myself what the truth was, so I invited Yeshua and his followers to supper, and he agreed."

"Go on."

"Several of my brother Pharisees also attended, as well as other leading men of the Galil. Right from the first I wanted it to be clear that I was acting only as a concerned citizen, not out of some misguided personal interest."

"Unlike others of your faith, who have not been so cautious," Caiaphas muttered. "Nakdimon ben Gurion would do well to take a lesson from you."

Simon agreed. "So when I welcomed Yeshua I was cordial but reserved, proper but wary. You understand?"

"Perfectly."

"Supper passed pleasantly enough. Yeshua made several remarks about . . . oh, I don't know . . . inconsequential sayings about faith, not judging others, loving your enemies. The kind of philosophical twaddle that is of no practical value. Not straightforward, like a good set of rules and guidelines."

Simon noted that Caiaphas looked impatient so he hurried on. "Then quite unexpectedly, this woman appeared in the dining room. I don't know how she got in the house. I've since discharged my steward, because I think he lied about being ordered to admit her by some Roman officer. Anyway, there she was: a notorious sinner, a true harlot, a jezebel of scandalous reputation for her loose living. Why, even if I hadn't known her, it was clear from her manner and dress what she was! I was dumbfounded. And then before I could order her to be thrown out, the matter got even worse. She circled the tables to where Yeshua was reclining and stopped beside his feet. Great tears flowed down her cheeks. In her hands she carried an alabaster jar of perfume. I was stunned, stunned at her effrontery! This harlot let her tears fall on Yeshua's feet . . . on his feet, while he remained perfectly still, saying nothing."

Simon sensed the return of the same righteous indignation he had experienced when the event was in progress. "Unbinding her hair—masses of curly chestnut hair—she bent over Yeshua's feet and washed his feet with her tears and her hair!" Simon shuddered at the recollection. "She kissed his feet! Put her filthy, degraded lips on him. Laid her cheek against his feet! He gave no sign that anything was amiss; barely moved. Then she uncorked the bottle of ointment and poured the entire contents over his feet. Spikenard it was, hugely expensive."

Simon drew in a long breath, as if the air were again scented with the costly unguent. "Well, right then I thought to myself, *If this man is really a prophet, he'll know who is touching him and what kind of woman she is—that she is a sinner of the worst kind.*"

"He let her touch him like that?" Caiaphas inquired. "Did not rebuke her? Showed no revulsion?"

"None," Simon affirmed. "In fact he didn't even speak to her just then. Instead, turning to me he said, 'Simon, I have something to tell you.' With great difficulty I kept my composure, not wanting to make a dismal scene even worse, so I replied, 'Tell me, Teacher.' So he told me a story:[15] 'Two men owed money to a certain moneylender. One owed him five hundred denarii and the other fifty.' "

"Was he trying to bribe you to keep quiet about what you saw?" Caiaphas inquired. Simon saw the high priest's fingers twitch.

Simon lifted his gloved hands in denial. "No, no. Yeshua merely went on to say, 'Neither of them had the money to pay him back, so he canceled the debts of both.' "

"Anarchist," Caiaphas muttered. "Proceed."

Simon stared off toward the Temple, now rose hued from the twilight banners streaking the sky. "Looking right at me—he has a most direct gaze that cuts right through you—he asked me this question: 'Now which of them will love him more?' Naturally I said, 'I suppose the one who had the bigger debt canceled.' "

"Are you certain it wasn't the offer of a bribe?" Caiaphas said suspiciously. "It sounds like one."

"Listen," Simon urged a trifle brusquely. "Yeshua said to me, 'You have judged correctly.' Said that to me, like patting a Torah schoolchild on the head for answering how many days there were of creation!"

Simon's indignation came roaring in full force as recollection overwhelmed him. "Yeshua raised his palm toward the woman in a gesture of blessing . . . blessing that creature! But it was still to me he spoke when he said, 'Do you see this woman?' As if I had been able to take my eyes off her since she first arrived! Then Yeshua criticized me—*me*, not her! He said, 'I came into your house. You did not give me any water for my feet, but she wet my feet with her tears and wiped them with her hair. You did not give me a kiss of welcome, but this woman has not stopped kissing my feet. You did not put oil on my head, but she has poured perfume on my feet.' "

Simon interrupted himself. "Well, of course I hadn't offered to wash his feet. Part of his reputation is that he has no regard for proper washing. I wanted to see if he would *ask* for a basin, but he didn't do that. And of course I didn't put oil on his head. Why would I signal to my associates that I honored this charlatan, this demon?"

Caiaphas waived dismissively. By the high priest's expression Simon saw that self-justification was not of interest. "And then?" the high priest pressed. "Get to the point."

Simon, flushed with anger and smarting from the remembered rebuke, continued, "Yeshua said, 'I tell you, her many sins have been forgiven—for she loved much. But he who has been forgiven little loves little.' Then he took her hand. As if he hadn't endured enough of her foul touch, he deliberately took her hand and said, 'Your sins are forgiven.' "

"He said that?" Caiaphas' eyebrows slammed together like two rams butting heads.

Simon nodded emphatically. "While I and my esteemed friends challenged this aloud. After all, who is this country preacher to proclaim when someone's sins are forgiven? While we were still in shock, wondering if we hadn't heard correctly, Yeshua spoke again. as if to deliberately remove any doubt. To the woman he said, loudly enough for the servants in the kitchen to hear, 'Your faith has saved you; go in peace.' "

Simon's scalp prickled with his rage, and he tugged furiously at his ear. "Challenged the quality of my hospitality, challenged the sincerity of my religion. Then praised this harlot, this whore. Held her up to me and my guests as a shining example of faith!"

"You've not yet told me who she was," Caiaphas inquired.

"I'm sorry; I thought I mentioned it before," Simon apologized. "It was Miryam of Magdala."

"Just as my other sources suggested," Caiaphas noted. "But I thank you for this confirmation. Is it true that she's since sold property to support Yeshua?"

"Yes," Simon confirmed. "And turned her home in Magdala into a refuge for beggar children and unwed mothers with their fatherless whelps. It encourages wickedness of the worst kind."

"And she has been seen traveling with Yeshua since then," Caiaphas added. "Still we cannot arrest him for lechery. But claiming to forgive sin; that's something else again. Is that all?"

Simon agreed that it was. "You can imagine what a babbling uproar followed. In the confusion the woman disappeared. And through it all Yeshua remained uncannily serene, as if he'd said or done nothing wrong—nothing at all! This from the same devil who called my brother Pharisees 'whitewashed tombs full of dead men's bones'!"[16]

Calling for a servant, who approached with a lighted torch, Caiaphas abruptly ended the interview. He was apparently not interested in insults leveled against Pharisees. "Thank you for your time," he commended Simon. "We wish for you to return to the Galil immediately. Follow Yeshua. Challenge his teaching whenever opportunity presents itself."

"At your service," Simon acknowledged in a shaky voice, puffing as if he'd just completed a footrace. "For the high priest of Israel."

With a curt nod, Caiaphas acknowledged the deference. As he stalked away he called over his shoulder, "Help yourself to some of the early figs. The ones near the southern wall are quite nice."

Smoothing his beard with both hands, Simon sought to calm down. His pulse was racing and his head throbbed. Ignoring the empty basket extended by the servant, Simon stared over the wall, past Jerusalem's city barricades, and down into the Valley of Hinnom beyond. It was there that ancient idol worshippers had burned infants alive in the fires of Molech. Now it was merely a garbage heap, a shallow depression where refuse was dumped and burned.

Accepting the wicker container half full of ripe figs, Simon surveyed the high priest's palace once more before departing. Caiaphas was right about his ability and ambition: He had risen very far above his origins indeed.

On the way out of the high priest's compound Simon passed another man arriving. They bowed curtly to each other.

It was a few paces into the lane before Simon remembered the new arrival's identity: Eglon, reportedly the hired assassin of Herod Antipas.

Despite the tokens of friendship presented by Caiaphas, the skin on the back of Simon's neck prickled.

"hen your mama has her baby, who do you think will die?"

It was a question in the minds of many more than these small boys who trailed after Lily and Cantor.

Little Baruch was troubled by the thought that the birth of a new baby in his family could cause the death of someone living in the Valley. He frowned. "Who says anybody's going to die?"

A childish treble piped, "It's the way it always is with us lepers. When a new prisoner comes Inside from Outside, one of us Inside dies to make room. That's all. So who will die, do you think?"

"My baby brother won't be a prisoner like us when he's born. Not a leper. Not sick. He comes from heaven, not from Outside. So. Not an outcast. Not a prisoner. Nobody has to die to make room for him."

Something to hope for, Lily thought. She glanced at Cantor. Did he hear the grim discussion?

Deborah's baby would not be a prisoner in the Valley of Mak'ob. Not outcast from the world. He would be new. Perfect.

"There's more than usual in there. Lying in the dying cave," chirped the second boy. "Charities bring food to us. Dump it at the top of the Valley every new moon. Like feeding caged animals. But there's only one road out of here for us. We're prisoners until we die. And when a new one arrives? Somebody always dies."

This seemed to be more than coincidence. The population of Mak'ob's captives never varied. It was a stark fact. Even so, those lepers who existed inside Mak'ob were better off than those who attempted to remain free.

Outside there were many stricken ones who chose not to endure imprisonment and exile in the Valley. No matter that they might have food and some shelter here; the terror of the place kept many from entering freely.

In hopes of perhaps catching a glimpse of loved ones, these Outside lepers haunted graveyards. They roamed the countryside after dark in search of food. They were the stuff of a child's nightmares: wormy, rotting flesh that could not speak except to wail for mercy.

But there was no mercy for a leper on the Outside, Lily knew.

Lily no longer thought of herself as a prisoner, an outcast.

Yes, her left hand had been robbed of fingers. Her ears had bloomed like cauliflower. The latter deformity was concealed beneath hair and head scarf. In the world Outside, perhaps few would notice unless they came in close contact with her for a time.

Her face was still her face. Though suntanned and six years older, Lily often thought if Mama had ever come to visit her . . . if . . . ever . . . Mama would have found that Lily was still mostly herself. After years of exile Lily was not eaten away by the disease that devoured some quickly and others, bite by bite, over many years.

She had come to love those who lived on and on, half eaten.

Surrounded by the thousand-foot-high cliffs that rose from the Valley of Mak'ob, she was at home among the *chadel*, the "Rejected Ones."

Outside they were known as *chedel*, the "living dead." Strange how fear, loathing, and a vowel or two could make such a difference in the definition of a person's worth, Lily thought.

Inside they were Lily's People. Beloved. Men. Women. Lots of children here. The God of them was the God of Abraham, Isaac, and Jacob. Inside there was a rabbi, and a Torah school held every other morning in the grove of date palms.

Lily had a family of her own now. Inside. Jekuthiel, who had gone away but would come back. His wife, Deborah, was pregnant. Their son, Baruch, seven years old, did not remember Outside.

And best of all, though no one Outside would think it possible, Lily was in love and loved in return by Cantor.

Cantor had spent the fifty days between Passover and Pentecost building a hut for the two of them. It was a modest shelter, with only room enough for sleeping out of the weather. Lily looked at it across the gulch and felt as if God was watching over her after all.

Shavuot was over. The season of weddings had begun. Lily and Cantor would be married by the rabbi as soon as Deborah's baby arrived.

Like Lily, the evidence of Cantor's condition was not far advanced. His right foot was crippled. No matter. With the help of a stick he hopped and skipped over the rough Valley floor as quickly as any man with two good feet. Cantor had a tiny lesion on the lobe of his right ear, and the beginnings of invasion on his forehead. But this went unnoticed beneath locks of red hair that tumbled down over his brow.

Cantor was twenty-three. He had first come to the Valley when he was nine. He had lived in Mak'ob as long as anyone ever lived in Mak'ob. This was his home. He knew every one of his fellow sufferers by name. He sang kaddish over each new grave.

Cantor often told Lily that if he was ever given a chance to leave, to go Outside again, he would not go. Everything he needed or wanted was here, he told her. Especially now that she had consented to marry him.

Today, followed by a flock of children, Lily and Cantor set out to train the Hawk.

I'm praying again, Awesome One. I know you hear me as I thank you for him. The sun on his copper hair. The Hawk riding proudly on his shoulder. Baruch and the others skipping all around him! Thank you for the suffering that brought me here to Mak'ob! To him.

Cantor's hawk never had a name after he came to be an accepted resident of the Valley. Though this seemed like an oversight, it was, within Mak'ob, an honor. He was simply the Hawk, as if there was no other hawk in all the wide world.

Names were important Inside Mak'ob, but not in the same way they were important Outside. Many residents kept their Outside identity. Deborah was still Deborah. But to be known by your skill or particular talent or some aspect of your personality? Perhaps even some long portion of Scripture learned by heart? Inside Mak'ob, virtues and talents became identity.

The carpenter of Mak'ob was the Carpenter. He did not have much wood to practice his craft, but he had brought his tools Inside with him, and on occasion he assisted in construction of a shelter or a well-made crutch.

The shoemaker was the Shoemaker. He had no feet, but for those with goatskin leather and a few toes remaining, he could craft a miracle of style and comfort. There was no glove maker in residence, but the Shoemaker also filled that role as needed.

The Cheesemaker and the Goatherd were closest of friends. They discussed at length the virtues of grazing in the upper pasture or lower pasture in relation to the taste of cheese. The result of their long conferences was goat cheese.

Two afflicted sisters, who had made a living in the Outside world dyeing clothes, were now known as the Cabbage Sisters. They were extraordinarily skillful in the gardens. Cabbages flourished when they waded among them, watering, plucking, fussing, discussing this and that.

There were five vintners Inside. Old. New. No Nose. Drunk. Crusher. They worked together in vines and vat to create about one hundred gallons of wine each season. Not much when spread around over six hundred inmates, but greatly appreciated and of high alcohol content for medicinal purposes.

The midwife was the Midwife.

Rabbi Ahava, whose name meant "love" in Hebrew and whose real identity was long forgotten, declared this was proper.

What was best about a person should be what he was known by.

Lily was perfectly named.

Little Baruch, as his name conveyed, was full of praise.

Cantor, because he had a strong, pleasant tenor and led the psalms from the heart, was the Cantor.

And so on.

And so the hawk was the Hawk.

Cantor's eyes were hawklike in their intensity. He studied things, reasoned out the ways of cloud and wind till he could give warning to those living near the creek bed that a flash flood was coming. He studied the bark of the apple trees, letting Pruner and Grafter know if there was a need to lime wash the trunks.

Most of all, Cantor loved to study the ways of the animals in the

Valley. He knew where conies lived among the rocks and could tell from an empty circle of crushed grass where a deer had hidden with her fawn. Cantor spied on the places where birds nested in the craggy gorge, a good source of eggs and meat for the hard times.

Cantor had prepared a home for the Hawk long before he had ascended the narrow ledge. In the nest he placed a net of woven palm fronds, then waited two days and nights. Cantor wanted a hawk, but he wanted one parent-reared to the point of independence. He also timed the capture so as to snare only one, lest a brace of hawks injure each other struggling to escape.

Afterward Cantor tamed the Hawk with love, patience, and dead mice. It was a partnership, he said. The Hawk hunted for Cantor and returned when called because Cantor fed him regularly. The Hawk found the teamwork more than satisfactory. He was never tame, Cantor said, nor obedient like a slave, only agreeable.

Lily loved the Hawk. Brown and black lines. Mottled underneath. Little spots on feathers. Patterns of light and dark shimmering on his wings when he soared. A sharp orange beak that cracked open the skulls of mice like nuts when the children of Mak'ob caught them for his training sessions.

And when he sat on Cantor's glove? Golden eyes, piercing, staring over Cantor's shoulder, as if he was studying something important. The Isaiah scroll maybe? To Lily the Hawk's eyes and Cantor's eyes shared a quickness of perception she found nowhere else.

Oh! The Hawk was an intelligent, faithful bird!

Lily loved the Hawk because Cantor did and she loved Cantor. Man and raptor were inseparable, it seemed, and when the Hawk soared, circling on rising currents of air, Lily sensed Cantor's soul soaring upward as well.

Cantor exercised him every day. With Baruch and many other children as onlookers, Cantor put the Hawk through his paces, and Lily helped with the training.

Sometimes Lily looked at Cantor's broad shoulders and the unhurried movements of his skillful hands. She thought how it would be to be a family of three: Cantor, the Hawk, and herself.

Keeping the jesses wound loosely from thumb to between third and fourth fingers, Cantor nodded to Baruch, who was posted across the clearing about twenty-five yards away. Proud that Lily had shared this responsibility with him, Baruch urged the others to get back, make room, then set the swing lure in motion. A leather pouch the size of a pigeon and stuffed with feathers was overlaid with pigeon wings. In place of the decoy's head was the eyelet through which a stout cord was knotted. When Baruch paid out the line and swung the lure around his head, it fluttered and rustled like a bird in flight.

The Hawk, knowing what was coming, plucked the talons of his left foot against Cantor's glove. He never actually tried to pull free from the restraints when Cantor held him; he merely signaled his readiness to participate.

When Cantor judged the lure to be rotating properly, not too slowly and not too fast, he cast the Hawk. As he did so he shouted, "Ho!" even though this time the Hawk needed no help identifying his goal.

Pinions beating powerfully, the Hawk gained altitude, then abruptly folded his wings and dove at the lure. At the last second he flared, so as not to overshoot his target, and seized the lure in midair.

The surrounding circle of children applauded.

Immediately Baruch let the slack of the line slide through his fingers, and the Hawk and his catch landed softly on the ground. As Cantor approached, he put a chunk of meat on his glove. The Hawk, though he knew the game well, mantled his wings in possessiveness of the prize. Cantor bent toward the ground and presented recompense. Gravely, with great dignity, the Hawk relinquished his grip on the lure and stepped across to the glove and his reward.

On other days Cantor and Lily led a parade through the settlement. Flanking Baruch were two friends near his age, Scrounger and Catcher. Together the three boys were allowed the duty of taking turns feeding the Hawk as he trained.

Once away from the distractions of the chickens in their coops, Cantor cast the Hawk and he darted onto the highest branch of an apple tree. Cantor and Lily walked on, while a dozen children strung along after her on both sides.

Strolling, not too quickly because Scrounger and several others used crutches, Cantor led the Hawk through his schooling. The bird moved ahead when he was ready, needing no cue. Sometimes he was in full view of the audience, posted like a sentinel on the dead snag of a lightning-blasted oak. Sometimes his whereabouts could only be guessed at from the tinkling of the bell on his ankle. When the procession plunged into the willows along the dry creek bed, the Hawk was completely out of sight for some time.

After a few minutes Cantor stopped and called Baruch to his side. From a pouch the boy carried, Cantor retrieved a dead mouse and placed it on top of the glove. Then, raising his gloved fist in the direction where he had last heard the bell, Cantor whistled sharply.

Darting and turning, weaving through gaps in the foliage that scarcely admitted sunlight, the Hawk swooped toward him. The dive seemed swift enough that it would knock Cantor down or carry the bird right past. But with scarcely one extra beat of his wings, the Hawk settled lightly on Cantor's fist.

Lily loved Cantor and she loved the Hawk. These outings muted the ever-present gloom over Mak'ob, at least for a time. They stopped children from talking about death.

Despite the narrow confines of her world, Lily was content, having a family, a future, and a hope.

It was late. Lily lay awake and listened to Deborah's ragged breathing. At any moment Lily expected to hear the rattle in Deborah's throat, followed by the long sigh of death. But hours passed and it did not come.

Lily was exhausted. Why could she not sleep?

She tried to pray. Only broken phrases and solitary words escaped her lips.

Lord? You. Can you? Scared, Lord. Deborah. Baruch. Alone. And Jekuthiel. Cantor! Oh! Lord! Without him, what? Home. Papa milking the cow. Mama kneading bread. Clearly. So clear the memory! I remember home! Oh! Mama? Do you think of me?

Her prayers were nonsense. Jumbled-up thoughts. Overwhelming longing. She felt lonely and yet could not define the reason.

The waning moon, framed in the entrance to the cave, illuminated the mat where Deborah slept so restlessly. Lily could clearly see the rounded mound of her stomach. Pregnancy. A beautiful thing, anywhere but Mak'ob. Would Deborah survive to give the child life? And after the baby was born? How long could Deborah keep it?

Lord! Sorrows! Place of separation! Lord! Do you? Can you? Oh! Remember?

Suddenly Lily was aware of a halting step on the gravel path that led to their dwelling.

The figure of a man stood silhouetted by the moon.

Instinctively Lily pulled the thin blanket up to her chin.

And then a whisper. "Lily?"

"Cantor." She sat up. "What are you doing?"

"Couldn't sleep."

"Me neither."

"Want to come talk a bit?"

"A minute. Maybe."

Deborah stirred but did not awaken as Lily wrapped the blanket around her shoulders and slipped out into the cold night air.

Cantor smiled and waved his stick toward the big boulder where they often sat together and discussed everything.

Without speaking he led the way up the slope and spread his cloak on the stone for them to sit on. She sat beside him and hugged her knees. They watched as the moon sank lower on the horizon.

At last she broke the silence. "Soon we'll be in our own shelter."

"And when I can't sleep I'll reach out and there you'll be." He finished her thought. He did that often.

"You suppose we'll still come up here? Sit on this old rock?"

"Sure. We've solved all the problems of the world up here." He took her hand and kissed it.

"Now, look. The moon is leaving. I'm always sorry when it sets." She was determined to be morose.

"But the stars are shining."

"Good old Cantor," she replied. "You won't let me be sad even when I want to."

"No. No. Not if I can help it."

"Well then. It'll be good when we're married."

"Yes. After the baby's born. The rabbi says that's only right. Deborah needs you now. But once the child is born . . ."

"I think . . . Jekuthiel's not coming back," Lily confessed.

"I've thought that for a long time. But you can't let her know you think it."

"I won't. I wouldn't." They both knew that such a thought expressed would be Deborah's death warrant. "She's barely hanging on. Hoping he'll come."

"I'm sorry," Cantor said at last. "It's despair that'll carry her to the dying cave, not the sickness."

They sat in silence, contemplating this for a long time. The moon vanished. Stars carpeted the heavens.

Cantor cleared his throat. "I wonder sometimes—" he squeezed her hand—"what's behind all the stars. I mean, just behind the curtain, you know?"

"I thought you knew everything," she teased.

He covered her eyes. "I think about it. Yes. Nights like this. When the dying cavern is so full. I think about how the worries of this world blindfold our souls. Little things keep us from really seeing. You know?" He removed his hand. "But look up. See? That's how it is when worry doesn't block our vision. And when we die, the blindfold will be altogether gone. That's what we have to look forward to."

"But, Cantor, not too soon. Not for you and me. Now that we have one another."

"I'll bet it's beautiful, behind the curtain, Lily. I mean, really beautiful."

"I prayed the other day," she ventured. "I really prayed, you know? That when it comes for us . . . that you and I could both see it at the same time."

"Yes. A good prayer." Cantor embraced her. "I'll tell you something that happened when I first met you."

"You were my first friend here in the Valley."

"After you came I stopped caring so much that I was dying. And once I knew I would have you to love for the rest of my life? It made everything right, somehow."

"Me too." She swallowed hard, hoping they would have time together. A long time.

I'm praying again, Inventor of Love. I'm asking. No, I'm begging. Please give me and Cantor years and years together. Even with everyone dying around us. Years . . . sitting up here on our old stone, looking at stars and wondering. And when it finally comes, let us take off the blindfold together.

With Pentecost past, the spring season of religious holidays was completed. The next big festival, Yom Kippur, the Day of Atonement, was still several months away.

Ceremonial duties completed, High Priest Caiaphas turned his full attention to administrative affairs. The latter category included dealing with Yeshua of Nazareth.

Even with the country preacher reportedly out of Judea and heading back to the Galil, Caiaphas demanded that he be kept informed. He wanted no slipups this time, no chance that another riot could break out and he be blamed.

Eglon reported the dismissal of Zadok and another instance of interference by the Roman centurion. "Peniel is not there. But I've learned Marcus Longinus is leading a delegation to Nabatea. Shall I go back and drag Zadok here in chains?"

Caiaphas angrily refused the suggestion. "More important matters need our attention. Since Yeshua's left Yerushalayim, what're your plans?" he demanded. "You missed arresting him; you missed killing him. Now what?"

"There are thousands around him when he teaches. He travels surrounded by his talmidim," Eglon explained. "A hundred or more. Plus an inner circle who're never far from his side."

"No excuses!" Caiaphas warned. "What's your plan?"

"It's his closest group that interests me," Eglon said, scratching his beard and staring down at the passersby below the wall.

"One of them will turn traitor?"

Eglon shook his head. "Working on that angle," he admitted. "But no luck yet. No, I'm thinking of adding a new member, as it were."

"Slip a spy into his camp? But who can we trust who won't instantly be suspected?"

"Been giving that some thought," Eglon said. "Doubt if that boy, that Peniel, would have any trouble getting close." Eglon raised his hand to stifle a protest. "Not that I think the boy'd turn traitor. Heard how he spoke up in the council. No, but if we plant someone next to Peniel . . . the boy's so trusting. The plan is simple. Instead of killing Peniel, we follow him to Yeshua. If he vouches for our man, we're in."

"Do you have an agent in mind?"

Eglon nodded slowly, deliberately. "Yeshua likes to surround himself with the *am ha aretz*, the common folk. Likes to heal beggars, does he? Let's send another beggar along and see what happens."

From the second-story terrace of Simon ben Zeraim's Capernaum home it was possible to look down the full length of the Sea of Galilee from north to south. To guests who remarked on the marvelous view Simon replied that on a clear day he could see himself making money. When new acquaintances fell for this ploy, he pointed out the triangular sails of fishing boats. Simon then reminded them that fully a quarter of the tilapia caught in the lake ended as dried fish sold by the House of Zeraim.

Clouds hung heavy over the western hills. Whitecapped waves scudded across the lake. The fishing scows stayed home. Even so, Simon could still note the increase of his coffers. Yellow morning light on the plain around Magdala revealed the dark emerald inscription of grapevines written on the parchment of the paler green slopes. The juicy clusters of fruit would soon find their way into Zeraim winepresses.

But today, as for all the five days since returning from Jerusalem,

Simon paid no attention to either ships or waves. He ignored the visions of both heavenly colors and earthly profits.

His attention was focused solely on the mortar and pestle that stood by his elbow and the unfolded wooden frame of the wax tablet propped up before him. Consulting the scribbled notes again, Simon added a pot of olive oil to the mortar and then a handful of bay leaves. When these had soaked up their fill of the oil, Simon crushed them against the sides of the stone bowl with short, rapid strokes of the alabaster pestle. Three drops of sweet gum were added next, then a shekel's weight of costly frankincense. The perfumed resin was sticky and difficult to force into the solution. It clumped and refused to add its virtue to the mix.

Simon transferred the concoction to a fire-hardened clay jug, then secured the container on a stand over a charcoal brazier. Satisfied that the brew was heating gently, the Pharisee turned his attention to a leather scroll. The rolled-up parchment lay partially covered by his prayer shawl and his gloves on a nearby table. Where had his attention been that he had allowed such a thing?

Nervously he twitched the shawl aside from the document. When he next covered his head for prayer, perhaps some defilement would transfer itself from the scroll to his shawl to him. Simon could not think of any specific regulation covering such a transaction, but he always erred on the side of caution where the Law was concerned. He decided to substitute his second-best head covering for the suspect one until he could investigate the matter.

The wind rose even further, gliding down the funnel of the upper Jordan from the heights of Mount Hermon. The breeze that sighed around the eaves of Simon's house raised prickles on the back of his neck. He heard accusation on the currents of air, condemnation in the rustle of the leaves of the sycamore fig towering over his house.

Simon rebelled emotionally against the charges. The scroll was not Torah or interpretation, true enough, but its contents were not evil. It was even reputedly of Jewish origin, although written in Alexandria, in Egypt. The bookseller, Ma'im of Gadara, swore it dated from the time the son of the murdered high priest Onias had fled there. Practical advice, that's what it was, no more immoral than a recipe for rosemary and garlic chicken or a commentary on the proper production of perfume.

Simon's mixture was warming nicely, the frankincense giving off its sweet-spicy aroma, mingled with the sharper tang of the bay leaves.

Jerusha liked perfume, Simon thought. She especially favored sandalwood. Dabbing it behind each ear, she would then place a single drop in the hollow of her throat. She never put perfume there unless he was watching. She would always wait until he glanced her way before anointing herself there.

Other images tumbled over Simon like a great fall of stones from the heights of the limestone quarry outside Hazor: Jerusha on their bed in the moonlight. Jerusha inviting him, welcoming him, smiling at him. Silvery rays dancing over her tawny skin. The arch of her neck when he kissed the perfumed secret. Simon felt again her nails on his shoulders. All his passion, all his desire, concentrated, seemed condensed into that one dab of perfume, signaling she was his alone.

"Father?" Jotham queried from the landing of the outside staircase. "Are you cooking something?"

Simon whirled around. In his haste to conceal the wax tablet and the scroll with a sweep of the prayer shawl, he bumped the bubbling flask with his elbow. The support scooted sideways. Simon grabbed for the tilting jug and seized it. There was an instant before the temperature of the heated clay registered; then Simon yelped and flung it from his burned fingers. It shattered against the wall.

"Get out!" he bellowed at his son. "Get out!"

Jotham retreated from his father's wrath. "But I only came to say—"

The contents of the pot splashed across the scroll and prayer shawl. A trail of droplets leading back to the oil lamp caught fire, igniting the fringes of the shawl, the ragged border of the parchment.

"Get out of my sight!" Simon bellowed, snatching up a three-legged stool as if to brain his son with it. "You idiot!"

Jotham fled back down the staircase. Simon threw the prayer garment and document to the floor, then stomped out the flames with sandaled feet, but not before shawl and scroll were both ruined.

The cleanup would have to wait. The servants, having seen an enraged Simon on other occasions, would maintain a respectful distance until summoned. But Jerusha might well come up to investigate the commotion. Besides, even though Jotham had fled back down the exterior stairs, he might still have reported to his mother what he had seen.

Some explanation would have to be offered.

Gripping his burned hand by the wrist, Simon scanned the room. The sticky sweetness of charred frankincense cloyed the air much the same as the bubbles of oil smeared his worktable and oozed onto the floor. And Simon's deliberations moved just as ponderously, as gummed together as the now useless scroll and defiled shawl.

What if the mixture had worked? Would Simon ever be able to reproduce the proportions again?

A noise reminded him of the need to intercept his wife, and Simon hurried down the staircase. It was well he did so, for Jerusha's foot was even then on the bottom step.

"What's happened?" she asked. "Jotham flew by me! All I could get from him was that you're going to kill him! And what have you done to yourself?"

Simon grimaced as she took his injured hand in her delicate fingers. "It's nothing," he said, closing a concealing fist.

"Nothing!" she exclaimed. "Your skin's blistered. Here. Let me put it in a bowl of cool water."

There was such tenderness in her voice, such compassion for his injury. Her love for him flowed from her words, her eyes. He felt her willingness to take his pain and ease it by the sharing. Her profound concern touched Simon's deepest longing. For an instant . . .

"Don't bother," Simon snapped, jerking his hand away. "I left strict instructions that I wasn't to be interrupted. Jotham startled me, that's all." Simon led the way into the kitchen at the rear of the house.

"What were you up to anyway?" Jerusha inquired.

"I wasn't *up to* anything," Simon retorted crossly.

How quickly Simon's thoughts of Jerusha's perfumed throat vanished; the closeness they had always shared was as shattered as the clay pot. Then, realizing he had to supply a plausible account, Simon said, "I was working on a mixture of perfume."

Jerusha regarded her husband with disbelief. "But you're a landlord and a merchant in wine and fish! Where does perfume fit?"

"Are you criticizing me, or calling me a liar?" Simon demanded savagely.

The harshness of the assault stopped Jerusha from asking anything else. Her voice cracked a bit when she shook her head and said, "Neither."

"Anyway," Simon continued, "it's spoiled now, thanks to Jotham! He'll have to be punished so he won't do it again."

Jerusha's hand flew to her mouth. "Oh no, Simon!" she exclaimed.

"It's my fault. A messenger came and it sounded important. I gave Jotham permission to go up and tell you about it. He was eager to be useful to you; he's felt so cut off from you lately."

Simon ignored the twinge of guilt. "Couldn't it wait?" he insisted. "What's so urgent?"

Jerusha was on firmer ground now, and the evenness of her tone showed it. "Ma'im of Gadara. He sent word he'll be at the oil press of Hazor tomorrow night. He says he has something you'll be interested in. You said to me just last week that if any word came from him you were to be told at once."

"Yes," Simon agreed, all other thoughts instantly banished from his mind. "Ma'im of Gadara. Tomorrow night, you say?" Then recollecting his anger, Simon asserted, "But Jotham still shouldn't have interrupted me. It was very wrong." Casting a glance out the window, Simon noted the decreased length of the shadow of the sycamore fig. "I'll be late for synagogue," he concluded brusquely. "Get me some linen for this burn. Once inside my glove again it'll be fine."

Jerusha nodded and retrieved a roll of scrap cloth kept as a bandage. "Would you like me to dress it for you?" she asked.

"I'll do it myself," Simon replied, taking the linen from her outstretched palm without touching her fingers.

"Simon?" Jerusha stopped Simon's departure with his name. "Ma'im of Gadara? He scares me."

Simon snorted. "Woman's imagination. He's a bookseller, a fellow merchant, that's all."

"And the oil press of Hazor?" she queried. "Why not here or in Capernaum?"

There had been a time—much of their life together in fact—when Simon opened his heart to Jerusha about everything. He valued her quick wit, her ability to help him view a problem from a different angle. He shared every confidence with her: his ambition to be recognized as a leading Pharisee, his worries over money, his fears that she might die in childbirth, even the times he found himself attracted to another woman.

Jerusha was always understanding, always helpful.

But no longer. It wasn't possible.

Simon thought of connecting his story about the perfume with a greater tale involving a new venture in olive oil. He settled for a gruffly dismissive, "Women shouldn't trouble their heads about business."

With that, he left her alone and reascended the stairs.

Perhaps he had been too harsh with the boy, Simon mused a while later. He'd make it up in some way.

He and Jotham had always been close, ever since Jotham's birth thirteen years ago. Simon regarded his son as both the present and future blessing of the House of Zeraim, and his only offspring returned the esteem. Since first being able to walk, Jotham toddled after Simon through the cool artificial canyons of the wine-storage caves and among the fish-drying racks.

Once, on a lakeshore near Magdala, Simon had laughed out loud at the closeness of the connection. Four-year-old Jotham, one hand on his hip, shook an admonitory index finger in the face of a laborer wielding the salt at the fish-drying tables. The mimicry was perfect; Simon often instructed his workers using such a pose.

In those better days Jerusha had teased Simon, cautioning him that Jotham's regard for his father was akin to idolatry.

Simon glanced down at the straps of his phylacteries. There was nothing to be done about the matter at the moment. Simon's thoughts were concentrated on his one overwhelming secret concern. He could scarcely remember the proper order of the obligatory benedictions, much less deal with hurt feelings. The boy would just have to get over it. Later—not much later, Simon hoped—all would be put right and things would return to normal.

It was time for prayers as Simon arrived at the Capernaum synagogue. Today was a market day, not a Sabbath. With no teacher of repute on hand, few worshippers joined the morning readings. Simon reflected grouchily that when Yeshua of Nazareth was present the crowd overflowed the hall and the porch and swarmed around the windows.

Such was the foolishness of the *am ha aretz*. They confused popular acclaim with true piety, clever demonstrations with the weightier matters of the Law.

Simon paused to look up at the lintel over the doorway. A pot of manna was carved there, reminding worshippers of Elohim's provision of bread in the wilderness. Entwined around the sharply incised image of an overflowing amphora was a flourishing grapevine with lush clusters of fruit: Elohim delivering far greater blessings than mere sustenance when His wandering children finally reached Eretz-Israel.

The carving was also a metaphor for the Law and the Prophets; the study of Torah was the bread of life given by Moses. The promise of a coming Messiah-King as recorded by the ancient prophets was the wine that gladdened the hearts of the chosen people.

Simon grunted with disapproval as he always did when he saw the symbols. The restoration of the Capernaum synagogue had involved the charity of a Roman centurion. As much as Simon enjoyed praying in the recently refurbished building, it wasn't right for pious believers to be beholden to a pagan, and a Roman soldier at that! Even worse, this particular pagan was once the lover of the notorious Miryam of Magdala. More odious still, if such a hierarchy of wickedness could be imagined, was the widely repeated rumor that this centurion, Marcus Longinus, was sympathetic to Yeshua of Nazareth.

Simon started to sputter and make the sign against the evil eye. He stopped himself only at the last second from actually spitting on the synagogue steps.

Once inside Simon made his way to his accustomed place among the chief places at the front. He inclined his head to the other men of note, seated himself facing the audience, and composed himself for worship.

Or rather appeared to compose himself for worship.

Standing for the two blessings that preceded the Shema, Simon's lips moved. The appropriate sounds came from his mouth, but he heard nothing of them.

Nor of the "Hear, O Israel."

Nor of the morning benediction that followed.

His thoughts were both far away and painfully near at hand at the same time.

Today it was easy to go into the innermost room of his mind and bar the door. The principal lector was an elderly scholar who mumbled his way through his Torah portion. Rabbi Shamel sat to deliver a confused analysis of the levitical proscription of the forbidden degrees of marriage. He seemingly concluded that a man might not marry his own great-grandmother unless she was also his uncle, but this astounding revelation had no impact on Simon.

The service ended, Simon's mind continued on the subject of Jotham's message. Might this summons from Ma'im be the answer to his worries? Perhaps by tomorrow night all would be restored, with no one the wiser and nothing lost. What business in Hazor could Simon say called him there? What appointments for tomorrow would have to be put off?

Outside again and headed home at an eager clip, Simon's fellow Pharisee Melchior bar Snoqed caught up with him. "Simon!" Melchior called in an aggrieved tone. "In too big a hurry for an old friend?"

Simon paused midstride and fixed a welcoming smile on his face before turning round. "Never too busy for an old friend," he exclaimed.

"You know," Melchior pontificated, "the scribes say that one should hasten *to* synagogue in your zeal to learn, but *go slowly* away after. You seem to have reversed the order today."

Simon flushed, caught by his own distracted mind.

"You look well, Melchior," he said, diverting the subject. "And your voice when reading the passage from D'varim . . . such power and clarity."

"It was from B'Midbar," Melchior corrected.

"Of course," Simon returned with forced cheerfulness, glowing deeper crimson in spite of willing himself to remain self-possessed. How much guilt was evident on a man's face?

"You look well yourself," Melchior observed. "Such a ruddy glow to your skin. But you are obviously busy, so here's why I stopped you: Can you come to dinner at my house tomorrow? I have a chance to buy a supply of new wine from Ramoth-Gilead, but I'd like your opinion before investing."

"Tomorrow night," Simon repeated. "No, no. Can't make it. Sorry. Called away on business."

Melchior's face displayed frustration. "The day after perhaps?"

Simon tumbled calculations and visions of himself laboring over another boiling flask in his upstairs chamber. Best not to agree and then have to break the engagement. He shook his head. "Not then either, sorry. This is a cluttered week for me, I'm afraid."

"Is everything all right with you?" Melchior inquired in an understanding tone. "But I see it's not. Is it business or family? You can count on me, you know."

Simon's mind raced, weighing which lie was the better to offer since he could not supply the truth. If he said his investments were in trouble, it might lead to gossip that Elohim was disciplining Simon for wrongdoing. Among Pharisees, business reversals were widely regarded as the sign of God's disapproval. Simon was too near to advancing upward another degree within the fraternity to have such a tale circulate.

A dreadful rumor to start!

"It's my son," Simon said. "He's been disobedient and willful. It disturbs me."

Melchior nodded sympathetically. "Children," he said, raising his eyes heavenward. "Blessing and curse at the same time, eh? But with such a good man as yourself as instructor, he'll soon get straightened out. If you need my help, you know you have only to ask. Ever since you sponsored me for my first degree as a Pharisee, you know you have no greater ally than me."

"I know and I appreciate it," Simon returned. "Now please excuse me. A revelation came to me in today's sermon which I'm anxious to share with Jotham. It may be just what he needs to hear."

Simon did not witness Melchior's curious stare following him out of sight.

"Use your head," Yeshua had warned Peniel. *"They're wolves!"*

For days Peniel laid low, hiding in back alleyways of Jerusalem or mingling among the hordes of pilgrims in the city. He did not return to the camp of the beggars beneath the viaduct. The place was being watched.

He longed to speak to Mama and Papa. To tell them he loved them. To ask them to come away with him to meet Yeshua face-to-face. But so far there had been no opportunity to show himself to his family.

Peniel kept his head covered, his face concealed behind the hem of his keffiyeh. Only his eyes were visible. No one who knew Peniel would recognize his eyes!

At his parents' house the danger was much worse than Peniel had imagined. Temple Guards asked questions everywhere about him!

Peniel listened. Listened to the whispers among the common folk as they retold the story on the corners and in the marketplace. He saw the watchers standing guard outside his father's pottery business. If Peniel dared to come home, they would arrest him!

One sentry remained on duty during the daylight hours. Another came at sunset for the nightlong vigil.

This evening, as the shops of his old neighborhood were shuttered in preparation of Shabbat, Peniel walked the length of the block behind a group of gossiping women.

Some had been neighbors. He recognized their voices. He took great care that they not get a good look at his face. Any one of them might turn him in for the reward.

Half a year's wages for each eye of Peniel ben Yahtzar!

"Mama. Papa." Peniel whispered a prayer as he lowered his head. An ache, a longing pierced his heart. If only they could meet Yeshua! Hear Him speak even once! If only they could see His compassion at work among the needy. Could their lives also be changed forever?

As twilight fell Peniel set out for home.

The city's twisting lanes teemed with people. Broad-faced, swarthy, suspicious Galileans mingled uneasily with manicured and perfumed pilgrims from Antioch. Travelers from the Jewish settlement of Corinth kept themselves aloof from hot-tempered Syracusans. All were under the watchful gaze of Roman mercenaries hired from Samaria, Syria, and Idumea.

Keeping the Temple Mount on his right side, Peniel struggled against the tide. Somewhere beyond the elevated viaduct connecting the Upper City with the Temple enclosure, Peniel realized he was lost. There were so many people, so many turnings. He who could walk its streets without light, who knew Jerusalem better than he knew his own face, was suddenly baffled.

Peniel's senses swirled. Putting out his hand, he leaned against a plaster frieze of vines and grape clusters decorating the front of a wine merchant's shop and closed his eyes.

It came to him that he was still blind in a way. It was more comfortable walking in the familiarity of darkness.

He heard the call of the Roman sentries atop the Antonia Fortress, smelled the fresh challah baking in the Street of the Bakers. Through the soles of his sandals Peniel discerned the rumble of carts entering the city by the Gennath Gate, and his whereabouts clicked back into place. Peniel proceeded confidently once more, pausing occasionally to verify his location with his other senses whenever the newfound oracle of sight overloaded with visions.

Peniel recognized his home street two turnings before he reached it. The aroma of sun-ripened early figs swirled toward him from the fruit seller's on the corner. This sensation was overwhelmed seconds later when a shift in the wind brought an avalanche of musk from the sheep pens.

Almost home.

Keeping to the shadows, he opened his eyes.

The watcher had gone at last.

A sense of delicious freedom filled Peniel. He could go home. Speak to his family!

Closing his eyes again, he listened for any unfamiliar sound or voice as the lane emptied out. He sniffed the air. No. Everything was as it should be. As it had always been.

Darkness fell. Absolute. The flicker of lamps appeared in windows.

Peniel swallowed hard and walked the few paces across the street. He raised his fist at the front door, then thought better of knocking. He would go around the side of the house. Like always. Call in to Mama from the side entrance of the workshop.

As he rounded the corner Peniel came face-to-face with the squat figure of Mama. Beads of perspiration stood out on her leathery brow. Grizzled hair framed her blotchy face in wild curls. She stood athwart the shop doorway, like an angel with a flaming sword. "Peniel!" A shriek, as if she were seeing the walking dead. "Get back," she hissed. "Back! You can't come in here. Can't! Hear me? You're a curse! Anathema! Go away!"

"Mama," Peniel implored. "I can see you, Mama. I see your eyes, Mama. You're afraid." He put out his hand. "Don't be afraid."

She slapped it away.

"Don't be afraid," Peniel began again. "Yeshua sent me—"

"Don't!" Peniel's mother commanded, flinging up her palm and spitting three times to ward off the evil eye. "You'll not speak that vile name here. They've forbidden it! He's a son of the devil, that one!"

Peniel reeled as though she had struck him, felt more physically sickened than all the times when she had actually delivered a blow.

"Mama," he tried again, "I know you're afraid of the Temple rulers and the Pharisees, but don't be. Now everything can be all right, better than before. Come with me. Come on. Just listen to him once and—"

"You've brought disgrace! On us! Defying the rulers! Where do you think you're going that I would want to come? Prison! That's where they'll put you if they catch you here!"

"To meet Messiah."

"Messiah!" she scoffed. "Go against the command of the rulers? You think we want to be cast out of the synagogue too? Ruin our business? Lose our friends?"

"But, Mama! Then . . . let me stay awhile. I can help you and Papa. Help you work."

Peniel searched her face for some sign of compassion, a glimmer of kinship, some spark of love. She spat at his feet. "Go on! Before I fetch the Temple Guard back to arrest you myself! They've been here all week lurking! Lurking! Driving away good customers. You're no son of mine!"

Peniel's father appeared. His cheeks were streaked with clay. He mumbled something.

"Papa! What?" Peniel implored. "Papa, what?"

At an instructive glare from his wife Papa announced, "You can't come back here. Not as long as you support the Galilean. You know the decree."

"But my eyes!" How could they deny what had happened? deny the power of the miracle?

"Enough!" Mama concluded as someone gave a shout from across the road.

"You all right there? Trouble? Has the lad come back?"

"Now you've done it!" Mama accused. Lifting her voice still louder so that it carried down the length of the street, she shouted, "Neighbors! Friends! Bear witness for us! See his arrogance? Do you hear him? The spirit of dishonor to parents? Disrespect for the Law? Who but a devil would think he knew more than the teachers of the Law and the Levites? Would our rulers cut off any who speak well of the Nazarene if he weren't evil and dangerous?"

Then to her husband she commanded, "Do it!" For the benefit of the unseen audience she cried, "Neighbors! You all be our witnesses! We've not broken the decree of the judges! You see how we turn him away! They won't find fault in us! Witness this!"

With hands made powerful from a lifetime of working stiff clay, Papa grasped his tunic collar and ripped it open to mid-chest. "Peniel! Boy? You're . . . dead . . . to us. And there's an end to it," he said in a monotone. "I have no . . . son!" Then, urgently, under his breath, he warned, "Get out of here, boy! Run, Peniel! There's a price on your head! Go now! And don't come back!"

The child known as Shalom died in the night.

In the morning when Lily came to feed him, his soul had flown. Angels cared for his soul now.

Tenderly she washed him. Combed his hair.

Lily cried for the boy who had called her Mama. And as she prepared him for the grave, how she longed for the comfort of her own mother!

I'm praying again, Father of the Fatherless. Mama has forgotten me by now! And this boy's mother. Will she think of him today? Will she sense that he is gone? Oh! Lord! We are forgotten! Make Shalom especially welcome in your home. Hold him tonight. Sing him a lullaby.

There were no perfumes or costly spices in Mak'ob. Not even the homely spices of bay leaves and sage, hyssop and mint were available in Mak'ob to sprinkle over the dead. The boy was wrapped in palm fronds. Into Shalom's folded arms was placed a bundle of *keneh bosem*, the sweet-smelling reed that grew beside the willows.

Then this tiny fragment of humanity was placed in an oblong wicker basket. The bier served most of the funerals in Mak'ob. But it never looked so melancholy as when the occupant took up such little space.

Today Lily was the only woman walking before the body. The spot would have been reserved for the boy's mother if she had been there.

Mama! He called me Mama!

I'm praying again, O Comforter of the Brokenhearted. What am I feeling today? Is this grief? The senseless loss of one so small? Relief his suffering's over? Fear that though we lepers live together in this place, everyone dies alone? Help me find some meaning in this.

Stout poles protruding from the sides of the bier provided hand-holds for six pallbearers, though today the strength of one would have been more than enough. Lily could have carried the body in her arms.

The procession wound through the settlement. As it passed, those who were strong enough to rise stood in silence to honor the child.

He had been one of *them: chadel.* Rejected by the world Outside.

But Inside, loved by all his fellow sufferers.

Cantor joined Lily, grasping her hand and lending her his strength.

I'm praying again, Approachable One. Grateful for Cantor. Glad I'm here. Glad I'm sick because he's here. And we're together.

Rabbi Ahava waited beside the shallow grave as the body was lowered into the ground.

"The prophet Isaias says of Adonai, *'You will keep in perfect shalom him whose mind is steadfast, because he trusts in You.'"*[17]

The rabbi paused to collect his thoughts before continuing, then again referred to Isaiah. "But Zion says—and perhaps we say at times—*'The Lord has forsaken me! The Lord has forgotten me!'"*[18]

The old man searched Lily's face as if he knew her question. Then he spoke again. "This is what the Lord says to your aching heart: *'Can a mother forget the baby at her breast and have no compassion on the child she has borne? Though she may forget, I will not forget you! See! I have engraved you on the palms of my hands!'"*

Rabbi Ahava raised his arms, spread them wide, showing all present his bloody hands, stumps of fingers, open sores. "We are, each of us, like this child. Forgotten. And yet Adonai, the Lord, has engraved our names. No, he's done much more than that. The word used in this passage says he *hacked* out our names, as with hammer and chisel, into the flesh of his palms! Love for his children has made the wounds we will see one day when we look at the outstretched hands of our Redeemer! The prophet Isaias tells us . . . the Lord hasn't forgotten this boy. No, and he won't forget you either."

Around the grave in an arc of suffering, rejection, and hope, Lily, Cantor, and the other lepers raised their half hands toward heaven.

"By his wounds we will be healed!"[19]

I'm praying again, Wounded One. Look at your palms and remember me! Remember this little one. We are your children.

The brief ceremony concluded. The grave was filled in.

Lily stood to one side, waiting for Cantor. He set down the spade, wiped sweat from his brow. His sharp eyes stared off into the haze around the trail leading toward Outside. "Someone's coming."

Lily followed his gaze, adding, "Shalom is gone. And another comes to us."

"Yes, well, this one needs help," Cantor noted. "He's small. Scared. He moves two steps forward and one back. I need to go to him."

"I'll go with you," Lily said.

"I'm sure it was near here I saw him," Lily asserted. Pointing toward a wind-sculpted terebinth shaped like the Hebrew letter *resh*, she added, "I saw him duck under—"

"Shh," Cantor cautioned.

It was so unlike him to reprimand her in any way that Lily stopped midsentence.

Cantor crouched beside the trail as if studying the spore of a wild animal. Lily stooped also. What was he looking at? There was no sign of the newcomer, nor was there any mark in the dirt or on the tree trunk that she could see.

She spread her hands in a questioning gesture. Cantor pointed to a single green leaf lying under the dogleg bend in the tree, then up to a broken stem directly above it.

Use your eyes, his motion said. Someone must have climbed over the low crook in the terebinth and knocked that leaf loose.

Lily understood. But where, then, had he gone from there? The rest of the path and the hillside had been in plain view all during their approach. Had this stranger vanished into thin air? Why was he being so secretive?

Cantor studied the surrounding slope.

Earlier in its existence the terebinth had been a spreading growth of magnificent proportions. Three limbs of nearly equal size had sprouted near its base. But of these, two died. Winter storms or summer Khamseen winds sent them crashing to the ground. Their tangled heap lay partly propped against the surviving trunk of the tree. Though most of the space beneath was filled with dirt cascaded down from above, there was one opening as big as the mouth of a large wine jug.

If the hollow space below the debris was itself as big as an amphora, it might make a den for foxes or badgers . . . or a hiding place for a small boy.

"Don't be afraid," Cantor coaxed. "We won't hurt you. Are you thirsty? hungry? Take your time."

There was a momentary reflection of light within the gap, like the reflection of a wild animal's eye.

Lily had seen Cantor approach timid creatures before. She had seen him persuade a roe deer to accept grain from his hand, been with him when wild sparrows flew down to alight on his outstretched palm.

"My name's Cantor," he called soothingly. "Are you hurt?"

Lily heard a faint whimper, a muffled sob that seemed to come from the pierced heart of the crippled tree.

"Are you hurt?" Cantor repeated.

"Nuh . . . no," the cavity sniffed. "Scared."

"What're you scared of?" Cantor asked. "It's a bright day. The sun is shining. Do you like birds? There are birds here. Listen."

It was true. In the hard-packed earth beside the trail a family of lapwings had their nest. When everything was very still Lily heard their rhythmic two-note calls.

"There's food and water waiting for you below," Cantor offered. "But take your time. I have a hawk. Actually, he's not mine, but he lives with me."

A tousled mop of curly dark hair jutted out of the hole.

A face showed the lost eyebrows and thickened forehead ridges of early *tsara*. Black marks on each cheekbone demonstrated the progress of the scourge. In size and apparent age the newcomer was around eleven or twelve.

"I'm Cantor. And this is Lily. Do you have a name?"

"Tobias. But they told me I couldn't use it no more. Said creatures don't have regular names. That's when they threw rocks at me. Told me I better go live with the other creatures."

Comprehension dawned on Lily. "So you were afraid of the creatures here?" she asked.

"I was scared to come here," Tobias admitted, "and scared to stay . . . out there."

"Do you want to come out now?" Cantor inquired. "Come home with me? You'll have a meal, and you can ask me anything you want about us and how it is here in the Valley."

There was a lengthy hesitation. Then slowly, unbending one joint at a time, one shoulder, then an elbow, then another arm emerged from the burrow. "I am hungry," Tobias said.

Tobias greedily devoured a meal of goat cheese and dried figs as he shared his story with Lily and Cantor.

"I was studying for my bar mitzvah. I'm twelve this year. The rabbi saw the spot on my hand. And that's how it started. It was all done according to the Law. I was isolated. When I was examined, there was a spot on my right earlobe. My family didn't want to believe it at first," he said. "Didn't believe it," he corrected himself. "Mother didn't want to send me away. Later . . . I don't know. They got scared or something. Scared of the priest? Scared of the other people in our village? Scared of *me?*" His inflection rose on the last syllable.

This was the most wrenching question of all.

Lily's heart constricted as she experienced the echo of her own lost family in the boy's words. Betrayed and abandoned. Willing to take the blame for being *tsara* if only . . . if only . . . there was a way to escape the terrible rejection. *Me! Mama! I'm still me! Blame me! Punish me! But don't send me away! Could I have done something to prevent it?*

"Mother fought them. Tried to keep me. Held on to me. They beat her and pulled me away from her. They locked her up when they sent me out. I saw my father among them . . . when the first rock was thrown . . . just standing there! He just stood there! Ashamed. His head bowed. He let them!" Tobias' thin shoulders jerked up and down with his strangled words.

Lily saw again the implacable resolve of her own parents.

"Like a dog!" Tobias cried. "Once I got beaten for throwing a stone at a stray dog! What did I do? What did I do wrong?"

"Shhh," Lily comforted, sliding her good arm around the boy's back and pressing him to her side. "No more being driven away. Never again."

I'm praying again, Rejected One. I was his age when I was driven away from my village. Let him find some joy among the outcasts as I have.

Overhead, dead palm fronds rattled in the breeze with the sound of dead bones. Tobias huddled closer.

"Hid outside the village. Watching. Watching my house! No good." He shook his head. "Heard Mother crying inside. Like I had died. Grandmother left bread out for me. Wrapped it so nothing would get it till I came at night. Then Father shouting. Raging. They'd be unclean too, he said. They'd be driven out if they kept me around. I was dead, Father said. Dead to them. Someone told, I guess. Next time they threw rocks again, I ran away. Ran till I dropped. Stole apples from the orchard. The farmer caught me and told me he'd kill me. I left there."

Tobias sniffed, experiencing again the final good-bye from all he'd known as a child.

Cantor nodded at Lily then slipped away.

"Where did you go then?" Lily asked, encouraging the boy to get it all out. Every leper in Mak'ob arrived with a story of grief to tell. She knew he needed to tell it before he could accept his new home in Mak'ob.

"Lived in a graveyard." Tobias shuddered at the recollection. "I met another . . . another like me. Like us. Only . . . you know . . . his face." The boy still could not call himself a leper. It was always hard because it was so horrible and so final, so inescapable.

"He told me about a Prophet. A Teacher who could do miracles. Said he wanted to find him. Maybe he could heal us. If we could only get close enough to touch him."

Could it be Jekuthiel? Eagerly Lily inquired, "What happened to this man, this *tsara*? Where was he?"

"Died," Tobias explained. "One night he just . . . gave up."

Lily's heart plummeted. "What did he look like? What color eyes?"

"Eyes?" Tobias repeated doubtfully. "Almost blind he was . . . but they had been hazel, I think."

Lily gave a small sigh of relief. "And his hair?"

Tobias replied with greater assurance, "No hair. No eyebrows neither."

"Then you left?"

Tobias nodded. "Didn't know what else to do. Afraid to come here, you know? This place. So I tried to find this Prophet on my own. Lived in graveyards, ate—"

From the unfinished sentence Lily conjured up whole worlds of horror: existing on the garbage dumps; picking through rotten fruit, moldy bread; finding a chicken bone with a scrap of gristle.

"Came to a place where he—the Prophet, I mean—where he'd been. Heard people say how he healed a cripple. A deaf man too!" The boy's excitement faded as quickly as it rose. "Too late. He'd moved on. Another time, by the river, they say he'd been teaching there for a week. But I missed him again. Always too late."

Tobias was almost done, his tale of steeling himself to seek shelter in Mak'ob nearly complete. "Got caught pulling up a bucket from a well. Been walking all day, you know? Couldn't wait for dark. Thought it was safe. No one to see." He shook his thatch of black hair sadly. "They threw stones and set dogs on me! I ran! So thirsty . . . hungry. Couldn't find the Prophet. No place else to go. I decided to come here after all," Tobias concluded.

Lily held him close for a while. It was, she thought, as though she were someone else . . . holding the child she had been. How she wished she could tell him everything would be all right. That he would find a new life, a family of outcasts who had also lost everything.

"I miss my mother," he cried. "Oh, Mother! Do you think she remembers me too?"

"Of course. Yes. And she's praying for you. Praying you'll be safe. And so you are. This is the answer to her prayer. You're safe now, Tobias. Here, no one will throw stones at you. No one will drive you away."

Lily and the boy sat together for a long time and wept for what was lost forever.

Cantor returned with Rabbi Ahava. The old man stooped to sit beside the boy. He waited in silence until Tobias looked up and wiped his eyes with the back of his hand.

"Shalom," said Tobias.

"Shalom." The rabbi nodded. "I am Rabbi Ahava. Also *chedel*. Also *tsara'at*." He held up his desiccated right hand. "Cantor says you've been searching for Messiah?"

"A Prophet. I heard rumors. I searched for him but never found him."

"His name? Did they tell you his name?"

"No. No. I heard stories."

"Ah," the rabbi said solemnly. "Yes. Always. There are rumors. But never mind. You're here now. Safe with us. We have a Torah school. We meet just there, beneath those trees. There are three who are completing studies for their bar mitzvah. You look the age."

Peniel huddled in the doorway of the shoemaker's shop. Even though darkness concealed him, closed around him, sleep would not come. He felt shattered, like one of Papa's clay lamps thrown against a stone wall.

Despite Peniel's new eyes, Mama and Papa could not accept him. Nor would they hear the good news he had returned to share. Fear of being separated from all that was familiar prevented them from embracing him.

Messiah had come at last . . . and there was no one he could tell!

All his life Peniel believed blindness had separated him from his family. He imagined that if he had vision everything would be different. Mama and Papa would love him. Accept him. They would be a family, whole and happy.

And now that he could see? Now that he could prove his worth? Ah, well. What difference did it make? Nothing changed. Mama was still Mama, hating him. Papa was too afraid of her to argue. So. Having sight made no difference to the one thing in the world that mattered to Peniel.

He was useless. No one listened to him when he was blind; no one would listen to him now that he had eyes. Why not lie down here and wait for Eglon to arrest him? wait to die? He could never, ever go home again.

In all the years Peniel had been blind he'd felt grief, yes. Sorrow, in plenty. Aching loneliness, often.

But never despair. Not like this.

The miracle had been wasted.

He must rejoin Yeshua. The Rabbi was Peniel's only hope to escape from the despondency that threatened to drown him.

Maybe in the morning. Maybe I'll go find him. If Eglon hasn't caught me by then . . . maybe?

At last Peniel slept.

It was halfway between the call of the sentries for the midnight watch and the tramp of feet for the changing of the guard at cockcrow when Peniel heard the voice, smelled the stench of a leper. A rustle. A stirring. The stink of rotting flesh was intense.

"Who's there?"

Shalom, a voice whispered gently to Peniel. *May I share your doorway with you?*

"Depends. Are you a leper then?"

A deep sigh of resignation replied. *It's cold. Herod's guards are searching everywhere.*

"Not for you."

No. For you, I think. If you're Peniel ben Yahtzar, the potter's son.

"I'm no one," Peniel replied bitterly. "The Sanhedrin says I'm dead."

Well then, said the visitor, *we have something in common.*

Yes, the smell was something like death. "You're a dream," Peniel whispered, covering his face and peering out at the apparition.

Of course.

A dream. A very bad dream. The thing was dressed in rags. Where the face should have been was a veil. Peniel could hear the labored breathing, characteristic of the late stages of leprosy. And yet he was polite enough. Pleasant.

May I sit with you? share your shelter?

Somehow Peniel had not expected a visit tonight. How kind of Adonai to send a Ushpizin. *"Te-vu Ush-pi-zin."* Peniel murmured, remembering his manners. "Welcome, exalted wanderer."

Exalted? returned the other. *It's been a long time since anyone called me that.*

"What's your name?"

You've dreamed my dream before. Don't you remember?

Peniel searched his memory, hoping to recollect the voice. "I've never dreamed a leper before."

You were never before in need of a leper's help.

"Keep talking. It'll come to me."

What should I say, Peniel?

"Do you have a story for me?" Peniel asked.

Is that the fee for joining you?

A brace of nightingales offered a chorus to the rising moon. The two beggars crouching in the doorway listened to the warble of rising and falling chords.

A story, eh? Peniel's visitor reflected. *How's this? Do these words jar your memory? "Who am I that anyone wants to listen to me?"*[20]

Peniel studied the shapeless form beside him. "Mosheh the lawgiver said such a thing to the Lord when he was sent. But Mosheh didn't stink like a leper or wear the rags of a beggar when he went to deliver the children of Israel from bondage."

Rags. Ah, well. The term is all relative. I was a prince of Egypt before I was driven out to become a shepherd. After wearing the robes of a king, putting on the clothes of a shepherd is . . . humbling. But I did it. No other way, really. And as for being a leper? Well, think now. Think what you've heard in Torah about me.

"You're the lawgiver. They still talk about you. About how they follow you."

Talk is cheap. They've missed entirely what is written in Torah. Not myself. Not others. No. Everything . . . everything is about the One who gave you sight, Peniel: the Great Leper.

"What's gone wrong in Israel? First, the Sanhedrin throws me out because I was blind and Yeshua gave me eyes. Next they'll kill him. And me too. Nothing I say makes a difference. What's wrong with everybody? Are they blind too?"

Yes. Yes. Blind souls. But you know that.

"People listened to you when you spoke. Why don't they listen to Yeshua?"

But they didn't listen to me! It was the same in my time as now. Humans seldom listen. Not really. The truth is inconvenient. The rulers have their own agenda. The common folk don't want to be bothered.

"How will they ever learn the truth? If even this sign with my eyes doesn't convince them, what will it take?"

There was a long pause. In the distance Peniel heard the tramp of boots. Harsh voices called his name, demanding he give himself up. The visitor seemed unperturbed.

Nothing is too hard for God.

"I believe that. I do. Now that I have eyes."

If you believe it, then why doubt? Nothing . . . nothing . . . is too hard for God.

"No one else seems to believe it."

You find this discouraging.

"Yes. Honestly. Well? Who wouldn't?"

You should have tried wandering forty years in the wilderness with a million Jews who had a five-minute memory about Adonai's miracles! Now that's discouraging. Why should it matter what others believe? You've met Him. You know the truth. Is creation wiser than the Creator? Why does it matter what they think?

"Point taken. Well spoken."

Thank you. And yet I was once like you. It mattered to me what people thought. Remember when Adonai Elohim picked me to return to Egypt? to tell the Hebrews I had been sent?

"Ah," Peniel said, pleased with the way the dream was unfolding.

I was afraid to go. I believed Adonai must have chosen the wrong messenger: "Who am I, that I should go? What if they don't believe me or listen to me, and they say Adonai did not appear to you?"[21]

Then Adonai said to me, "What is that in your hand?"

"A staff."

"Throw it on the ground."

I threw it on the ground and it became a snake. Not just any snake. Deadly. Same sort as the cobra that adorns the golden crown of Pharaoh. Symbol of Egyptian power and divine protection. A cobra . . . yes. Scared me witless, I can tell you! I ran from it as any man in his right mind would do. Just as I had run from Pharaoh years before. Then Adonai said to me, "Reach out your hand and take it by the tail."

By the tail, Adonai said! Ever try taking a cobra by the tail? One blink and it'll hook its fangs in you. You're dead within minutes! But I did as Adonai commanded. Now that took courage. By the tail . . . I picked it up! And the thing I most feared—Pharaoh's might—turned into an ordinary shepherd's crook. And later my staff swallowed up the cobras Pharaoh's magicians produced.

The lesson was hard to miss. True might is found only in Adonai. But still I wasn't convinced.

Then Adonai said, "Put your hand inside your cloak."

I obeyed Him.

"Now remove it again."

And when I took it out again my hand was white as snow, encrusted with leprosy! Worse than a cobra, I can tell you! No way I could run from my own rotting flesh! All of my hand! Consumed! Neh-geh! This means "One Touched" by the judgment of Adonai! I was afflicted! Smitten! Tsara! In that moment I became one of the living dead! Chedel! Cut off from all others. Chadel! From my family. Forsaken! Likewise, anyone who touched me became unclean. Adonai showed me the truth of what I really was! Unclean! Corrupt! Powerless! I cried out in anguish at the sight of my own mortality.

And then Adonai said to me, "Put your hand back into your cloak and take it out again."

Weeping, I did as He told me. And when I took it out again my hand was completely healed.

"I had forgotten about that," Peniel mused. "Leprosy on the hand of Mosheh the lawgiver. Curious. But that sign was never used to convince anyone that Adonai spoke to you."

Until now.

"Now?" Peniel was puzzled.

All these things are written not simply as stories about Mosheh the lawgiver. These are prophecies, recorded in Torah, which speak of the One yet to come. Written so this generation and those yet to be born will read and know the true identity of Messiah. Like Mosheh, Messiah is the Son of a King. The King of Heaven! The Prince of Light has laid aside His royal robes and clothed Himself in the poverty of our human flesh, taking on the appearance of an ordinary man. And yet He is the Good Shepherd that David sang about in one of his psalms! He will confront and defeat the Prince of Darkness and liberate His flock, not by the rod of fear and oppression, but by raising the simple staff of righteousness and love. And by the staff of our Shepherd-King, all power that the Prince of this world has over mankind will be swallowed up just as the staff of Mosheh swallowed the serpents of Pharaoh's magicians!

"But your hand. The leprosy. You were stricken by the Almighty! Tell me what it means!"

And Adonai said, "It's not who you are . . . it's who I AM! Fear not, Peniel!"

"Fear not? There's nothing more horrifying than being eaten alive by leprosy! Tell me! What meaning can such an awful sign have?"

Everything in Torah foretells something about Messiah. Remember, Peniel, nothing is too hard for God.

The whisper receded as Peniel cried out, "But what's it mean? Mosheh? Mosheh?"

The lawgiver did not reply.

The twittering night birds stopped abruptly. From around a nearby street corner came the noise of tramping feet, low commands, harsh words. "Check everywhere! Look under those steps. Down in that culvert. He's here somewhere."

Dancing torchlight appeared less than a block away. Peniel's eyes snapped open. Searchers! Coming this way. He knew, felt with a certainty, that he was the object of their quest. He cowered back in the doorway.

With a gasp he saw that the leprous Ushpizin was still with him! "Mosheh?"

The thing whirled and hissed him to silence.

The indistinct form of a cloaked and hooded man crouched between Peniel and the street. His outline was blurred by the orange glow of the firebrands. The figure stretched out his arms. No hands emerged from the empty sleeves. A twisted shape writhed up from the ground like a snake uncoiling. Eyes reflected the light. But his face . . . where was his face? A smear of less-than-human features, a misshapen, distorted countenance, almost like a child's charcoal rendering of a face!

Peniel drew back. Yes. Yes. Leprosy was more horrifying than a deadly snake! He was more frightened of this apparition than of impending capture. A ghost? A demon?

The nodding torches drew closer. "There's someone there. Move up! Here's someone."

Then, from the depths of the thing, a horrible wail rose up. "Unclean!" the apparition intoned loudly. "Unclean!" He glided forward into the center of the alleyway.

He faced the soldiers and screamed, "Unclean!"

The troops shouted in alarm to one another, "Leper! It's . . . a . . . leper! Get back! Back!"

They stumbled over each other in their haste to get away. Searching for a defenseless beggar was one thing; discovering a ghoul, one of the living dead, by flickering flames, was something else again.

The hunters fled, pelting back around the corner.

Peniel hunched in the corner, wondering if he should run away as well.

Then the leper turned slowly toward him. The stench was like an open grave.

"Come on." The specter breathed with difficulty. "I don't . . . don't . . . think we . . . should be . . . here when . . . they get . . . their courage . . . back."

An owl hooted in the branches of an ageless olive tree. The last dregs of a wine-colored sunset had drained into the basin of night. Simon ben Zeraim, out of breath from climbing a steep hill, paused for a beat, allowing the sheen of a newly risen moon to aid his steps.

The lights of Hazor, less than ten miles north of the Sea of Galilee, twinkled nearby. The city, still a stop on the trade route connecting the Galil with Damascus, was only a shadow of its former magnificence. At the height of its glory King Solomon had favored this northern outpost of his empire. He endowed it with massive city walls and enlarged its role to encompass royal storehouses of grain, wine, and oil. That was long before Hazor was sadly reduced by a millennium of conquest and neglect.

As he rounded a sharp curve, a lantern hanging from an acacia limb attracted Simon's attention. At first he saw no one near the camp. As he drew closer a lean, dark shape stood up and detached itself from the shadow of an olive press. It was as if the handle employed in rolling the crushing stone had suddenly come to life, advancing to meet him.

"Greetings to Simon of the House of Zeraim," the tall figure intoned.

"And to you, Ma'im of Gadara."

Ma'im wore a blue turban around his head with the tail of the cloth across his throat and over one shoulder. His skin was dark brown and his eyes so deep set it was difficult for Simon to distinguish them except when they glinted in the lantern light.

"Since the master of Zeraim doesn't wish to meet in the comfort of Hazor's caravansary, shall we conduct our business here?" Ma'im suggested. He indicated the recumbent stone wheel of the olive press.

Simon looked nervously around. The highway was deserted at the moment, but it was only a hundred yards away. A passing squad of soldiers might decide to investigate if they spotted the lantern light. "Isn't there somewhere else?" he asked.

Ma'im chuckled in his throat, then turned it into a feigned cough. "Certainly," he agreed. "The wishes of the customer must always be considered. It's why I suggested this location. Follow me." Retrieving the lamp, Ma'im led the way toward the base of the acacia and seemingly disappeared, as if the earth had swallowed him up. "It's quite safe," came his voice, echoing hollowly. "Go slowly down the steps."

Beside the olive press was the entrance to an underground water cistern. It was dug in times so long past that even the memory of the tale of its builders had long since vanished. Ninety-three worn stone slabs led downward, the incline so precipitous that the top of the shaft was lost to Simon's view long before the bottom came into sight.

When he was no more than a dozen paces down, Simon wanted to change his mind and get back up into the Galilean night. The air inside the tunnel felt close and muffled, as though something holding its breath was listening to the sound of his footsteps. The walls of the passage, three man-widths apart, towered overhead. The quarrymen must have been giants to need twelve feet of headroom.

There was nothing wrong with this meeting, Simon reminded himself. What had he to fear of passing soldiers or the tales that would circulate after? What?

Simon kept moving downward.

Nearing the bottom, the light gleamed off a pool of water. The stone steps continued into its opaque surface, vanishing into its depths.

Around the tip of the cistern there was a ledge, barely wide enough for one man to pass. On the far side of the circular chamber the shelf widened, and rough benches had been hewn out of the rock face. It was to one of these spaces that Ma'im conducted Simon.

"Well?" Simon inquired brusquely. "You'll have to do better than last time. That scroll didn't tell—" Simon stopped to compose and correct himself—"that source doesn't meet my needs." Then, unable to keep the eagerness from his voice, he added, "Where is it?"

Ma'im of Gadara took a seat on the stone protrusion and gestured for Simon to do the same. Reaching into a dark recess under the bench, he withdrew a linen-shrouded object about the size of a man's sandal. This he handed to Simon.

"What's this?" Simon challenged, hefting the inconsequential weight in his hand. "This can't be the scroll. I won't pay except for the original article, as agreed."

"But of course," Ma'im said soothingly. "If the good Pharisee would but open the parcel, all will be made clear."

Still suspicious, Simon undid the drawstrings of the pouch, withdrawing from it a wooden cylinder.

"Open it," Ma'im encouraged.

Simon's gloved fingers trembled slightly as he unscrewed the jointed tube. Could this be the answer? Could he at last have the solution to his dilemma in his grasp?

A single scrap of papyrus, loosely rolled, emerged from its protective case. The exterior of the flattened reed paper shone a soft yellow against the dark red wood. As Simon unrolled it, exposing the inner surface, the lantern light glanced off a gilded border and flung back glints of lapis and turquoise illumination.

Facing Simon was the illustration of a man with the head of a falcon: Horus, one of the gods of Egypt.

Simon was hit by a wave of revulsion. Idol worshippers! Pagan graven image! Violation of the Second Commandment!

Fighting the bile in his throat, Simon demanded, "Where's the rest of it?"

Ma'im spread his hands in a gesture of conciliation and remorse. "Surely the learned scholar Simon understands my position. The value of the original is far too great to carry about this unsettled and dangerous land merely to satisfy a whim of curiosity. But this much I offer as proof that the entire scroll is in my possession . . . in my shop in Gadara. Look there."

Ma'im's bony finger protruded from the drooping sleeve of his robe to stab at the drawing of the bird-man. Horus' right hand held an ankh, gripping the Egyptian symbol of life by the ring on top of the cross.

But it was the row of symbols depicted beneath his outstretched left hand that caught Simon's attention. He drew his breath in sharply as he scanned the hieroglyphs.

"So," Ma'im said thoughtfully, "it does not disappoint? Does the learned Simon wish a translation?"

"No," Simon retorted. "I can make it out easily. I told you, I'm a student of ancient writing, accounts going back to the days when my ancestors were slaves in Egypt. I'm seeking to write a history of that period using Egyptian sources."

"Of course," Ma'im agreed obsequiously.

Simon shot a glance at the trader to see if the eyes held scorn or sarcasm, but Ma'im's face was turned away from the light and could not be read.

"It would be good for my business if other of your Pharisee colleagues took similar interests in antiquities," Ma'im suggested.

"You are not to mention it!" Simon responded curtly. Then, in a softer tone, he added, "This is original research. It's important to me that I continue it without interruption or competition. Once complete, I'll be happy to introduce you to everyone."

Ma'im raised a placating hand. "As Master Simon wishes. You'll come to my shop then? You know its location?"

"Yes!" Simon agreed, fumbling in his mind to determine how soon he could get away and what excuse he could use for the journey.

Ma'im coughed delicately. "It is customary to advance a small sum . . . a mere token really . . . for which I will gladly reserve the article, even if another offer is presented before our transaction is concluded."

Simon unlooped the strings of a money pouch from the sash of his robe and passed it over.

Ma'im peered in, judged the amount to be sufficient, and nodded his thanks. "In exchange you may keep that title page until you have the rest."

Simon replaced the papyrus in the tube and cloth and secured it beneath his sash.

"Our next meeting," Ma'im noted, "will be in somewhat more comfortable surroundings. Allow me to conduct you back up."

When Ma'im stood and raised the lamp over his head, a previously unseen niche located in the wall behind the stone bench was revealed. In the alcove were a pair of stone statues.

Simon recoiled from the black basalt figures. One statue was a male, seated and wearing a bowl-shaped hat. The other, simpler and yet more sinister, was a pillar whose surface bore the stylized carving of a pair of upraised hands. But instead of a face, the idol possessed a single eye surrounded by the rays of the sun.

"The scholar Simon recognizes these images also? No? Perhaps his studies do not extend to the Canaanites and Phoenicians. Before your King Solomon possessed this land, it once belonged to King Og of Bashan and later to the kings of Tyre."

"But why are they here?" Simon demanded, keeping a close watch on the two figures, as if expecting them to move. "Do you deal in antique figurines as well as books?"

Ma'im shrugged. "As it happens, these are not mine. In this place sometimes followers of the old ways still make appeals to their gods. You know that some link the worship of Melkarth of the Phoenicians with Horus of Egypt? But of course that is of no concern to a follower of Yahweh of the Jews."

Outside, the air atop the cistern by the olive press of Hazor was cool, even chilly. Yet drops of sweat clung to Simon's hair and beard and burned his eyes as he hurriedly returned to the highway.

It was late when the meeting was called at Rabbi Ahava's hut.

Clean, fed, and reassured by the fact that he was in the company of dozens of children, the new boy, Tobias, slept in the children's camp.

Lily and Cantor walked toward the gleaming light in the old man's shelter.

There were eighteen members of Mak'ob's council. Twelve men were chosen in honor of the twelve tribes of Israel. Six women were also seated as advisors. Lily, though young herself, was chosen by the rabbi to represent the children.

Cantor and Lily were late. The council was already in session.

Rabbi Ahava poked the fire with a stick. "This boy is the twenty-second witness to come Inside with news of some prophet. Some have said Messiah. This time we have some detail. 'Son of a carpenter,' the child says."

Midwife, the shadows and firelight making her grotesque features even more exaggerated, frowned. "Rumors. That's what they are."

Carpenter rubbed his forehead where eyebrows once had been. "I agree. As long as I've been here—and even Outside, before I was stricken—there were rumors among those in my guild. Rumors about a lad, that he was . . . extraordinary."

"In what way?" Ahava leaned forward with interest.

Carpenter raised a shoulder in indecisiveness. "Nothing, really."

"Tell us what you heard," the rabbi urged.

"I knew the lad's father. What was his name? Escapes me now. But we all talked, you know. Everyone talked. Gossip, really. About the mother. Pregnant before he married her. So there were circumstances about the child's birth. Well, no one believed what the fellow said. Angels appearing to him and such like. 'Marry her,' these angels said to him. Well, I can tell you plainly, no one believed it. That's all."

Rabbi Ahava sighed. "Gossip. Rumor. Whispers from Outside. It's not enough."

I'm praying again, God of Promises. Are the prophecies empty promises? Or is there reason for those of us who are the least of all mankind to hope?

Carpenter cleared his throat. "I met the lad. Passover it was. Some of us in the Carpenter's Guild traveled to Yerushalayim together. The lad was twelve years old or so."

"The age of bar mitzvah." Rabbi nodded.

"Yes. That's it. Well, the lad spent all his time in the Temple Courts, at Solomon's Portico. He sat all day and listened to the learned men. Not just listening but *discussing* Torah, as if he were a rabbi himself. They were amazed, these rabbis, when they heard him. He had no education to speak of. Common Galilean stock. Came time to leave and the lad didn't leave with us. Somewhere along the road his mother missed him. The family turned back to Yerushalayim. Three days later the lad was found in the Temple, setting the learned doctors straight on points of the Law. Nothing like it ever came out of the mouth of a child. They all said so. When I heard the end of it, the lad had told his parents he was just going about his father's business. Now I ask you, since his father was a carpenter, what's all that got to do with his father's business?"

"How long ago was this?" Ahava stared at Carpenter intently.

Carpenter calculated. "Nineteen. Maybe twenty years."

"That would make the boy . . . in his early thirties? About the age . . ."

"Rumors." Midwife sniffed. "We've sent poor Jekuthiel Outside to find this Prophet, this Messiah. Four months he's been gone. Poor Deborah's due to have the baby any day. And Jekuthiel isn't back. No one's prayed more than I have for deliverance from this scourge, but we've got to face facts. Do we risk the safety of any one of us by sending someone out again? Chasing a shadow? a hope?"

"Aye! We must! Hope's all we've got left," Shoemaker declared. "We're condemned anyway. If this fellow can heal us and we miss him because we're all snug and content to live and die in this open tomb, think what we might miss."

"A chance to live," said Cantor. "I mean, if he's the prophet Elisha, as some are saying, it was Elisha who cured the leper. Just think . . . what if . . . and if we stay here . . . wait here to die."

I'm praying again, God of Hope . . . what if? What if he is among us? Would he come even to us? to me? to Cantor and all the rest of us? Six hundred and twelve.

Rabbi contemplated Cantor's words. "We've sent one Outside alone. He didn't return." Everyone knew that implicit in his words was the belief that Jekuthiel would not come back.

Cantor spoke again. "Suppose we send out ten men. A minyan from our synagogue."

A favorable murmur circled the campfire. "Well spoke, Cantor," Rabbi agreed.

Encouraged, Cantor continued, "We choose ten faithful men from among us."

Patting the stumps of his legs, Shoemaker interjected, "They must have legs to walk on. Feet that will survive the journey. There's scarcely ten men in all the Valley who aren't missing toes or legs. We chose Jekuthiel to go Outside because he could walk. He was a strong man. Yet he never returned."

"And you know he would have returned if he'd been able," Midwife insisted. "For the sake of his wife and unborn child. For the sake of his young son, Baruch. We all know Jekuthiel would've returned if he was able."

Cantor agreed. "Then we'll send women out too. And children of bar mitzvah age if we must. But we must send a minyan to Messiah. Ten of us. Then, if one dies, there'll still be nine. If five die, there will still be five. Surely at least one will get through. Find out the truth once and for all if we in the Valley of the Shadow of Death have reason to hope! If there is a Messiah. If even one got through . . . think of it! Even if one could make it back Inside to report. And then we'll know. Won't we? Should we stop looking? stop hoping? wait here till death takes us all? Or is there a chance?"

Carpenter said, "You know if ten of us go Outside there will be ten more to come Inside. It's always that way. The same number. And if the minyan comes back to report, ten will die Inside to make room for them."

"We'll have to take the chance," Cantor replied. "What if the ten come back healed?"

I'm praying! Oh, yes! I'm praying again . . . what if . . . do I dare hope?

Shoemaker wagged the stump of his left leg. "Now there's a dream to dream of."

Rabbi cradled his chin in his hand. "Who will we send?"

Cantor had it all thought out. "I'll go! My stick is no hindrance. I can skip along as well as any man on two legs."

Lily's heart sank. She thought about Jekuthiel. Gone four months. No one who left the Valley for Outside ever came back. She raised her hand. "Then I'll go as well."

Yes! I'm praying again! I'll go Outside with Cantor! Die with him if we're stoned! At least we'll die together!

"But what about Deborah?" Midwife asked. "She'll need you when the baby comes."

Lily pressed her lips together in consternation. "I . . . yes . . . then . . ."

Rabbi thumped his stick on the ground. "So. Cantor is going. And the others?"

Cantor's expression was bright with excitement. "We'll draw lots for the others. Choose nine others to go with me. Nine of the most healthy from among us. That's it. We'll draw lots from among those of us who still have strength for the journey."

"Well spoken, Cantor," Ahava agreed. "What do you say? Aye for the plan. Nay against it."

The vote in favor was unanimous.

The leper led the way along hidden alleys, through passages, and into sewers Peniel did not know existed.

They approached the northern city wall near Gennath Gate. Peniel whispered, "We've wasted our time. Still trapped inside Yerushalayim."

Silently, apparently undaunted, the shrouded figure plunged into a culvert, beckoning the younger man to follow. Amid stinking filth, the two disappeared into a labyrinth of tunnels . . . and reemerged outside the city wall.

Moonlight showed Peniel the outline of a whitewashed stone fence gleaming starkly against the dark earth. Within the gaping mouth of the enclosure were the jutting teeth of gravestones. The faceless face of Peniel's guide was clearly illuminated. His eyes, unblinking, stared at him. Eyebrows were gone. An open, running wound was where his nose should have been. Ears were eaten away like dead leaves clinging to a tree. Surely this was not Mosheh, the great lawgiver, but a true leper! *Tsara!* One of the living dead who lived in the cemeteries around Jerusalem by night and came out to beg during the day.

Peniel fought the terror of his imagination. Would other ghouls come shrieking to surround him? pull him down to rob him and murder him?

He recoiled from the last step, shuddered on the brink of the cemetery.

The apparition in front sensed his hesitation. "We'll be . . . safe . . . here."

Peniel shook his head. "City of the dead."

"I'm a man . . . like . . . you . . . though . . . I'm . . . leper," the guide replied. "Are you . . . afraid . . . of me? Why not? All the guards . . . were."

Peniel was unwilling to admit that he was secretly terrified. "You saved my life."

The thing gave a wheeze that might have been a laugh. The reply was labored. Words formed through collapsing palate and wormy lungs. "Then don't . . . be afraid . . . now. This . . . safest place . . . for us. No one . . . comes . . . not Temple Guards . . . not Eglon. Did I lead you . . . wrong . . . in getting outside . . . the walls?"

Peniel shook his head.

"Trust . . . me. I'm right . . . about . . . this too. The dead . . . in their . . . graves . . . aren't offended . . . because we . . . lepers . . . take . . . refuge with them."

Peniel gulped and followed the leper into the land of death.

Peniel and the leper sat down silently within an enclosure of monuments on three sides, sheltered from the wind.

Listening. Listening. Were they followed?

Peniel thought about this creature, one of the living dead, consorting with the really dead.

Were there evil spirits about?

What did he fear more? Eglon? Caiaphas? Death by torture in a prison? Or the haunts of demons?

After long hours, Peniel forced himself to speak. "You have a name?"

"Long time . . . since anyone . . . asked. No one . . . Outside . . . seems to care . . . names."

"My name's Peniel," Peniel offered, but he did not extend his hand to the creature. "You?"

"Je-ku-thiel," was the reply.

"The lawgiver? Just like Mosheh?" Peniel mused. Amid moon-cast shadows of family tombs and the rustling of palm branches, it was hard to separate vision from reality. "I've seen you somewhere." Peniel's mind conjured up a picture of walking the streets with Yeshua. "I know! You were lying in a doorway beside the Herodian Way! But lepers aren't allowed inside the city! I mean, you could be stoned! What're you doing there? It must be terribly important to you."

"Life and . . . death." Jekuthiel's throat rattled as he spoke. Peniel was glad the darkness covered his shudder. "I came . . . Outside . . . to find a prophet . . . Yochanan. Baptizer. I thought perhaps . . . you know . . . maybe he . . . Messiah."

"But he's dead . . . murdered by Herod Antipas. Head cut off by Eglon."

"I know," Jekuthiel replied sadly. "I . . . almost . . . gave up. Didn't know . . . what . . . to do. Where . . . to turn. Heard stories . . . of another . . . Prophet, but . . ."

"Yeshua of Nazareth!" Peniel exclaimed.

"Him. Yes. You . . . know?"

"Messiah! Here in Yerushalayim! He healed me, my eyes! I was blind since birth, and now I can see." Peniel recounted the entire tale of his miracle then added, "I was with him. That's who I was with when I saw you."

Jekuthiel gave a cry of anguish. He rocked back and forth, as if he was mourning for the dead. "So . . . so close . . . that . . . close? Ah, Adonai! Mocks . . . me. But where . . . now?"

Peniel pressed his back harder against the cold tombstone. "North. North, he told me. I wanted to go home to my parents. Talk to them. Bring them. But they don't want to come." Peniel tried to cover his nose from the stench without Jekuthiel noticing. He coughed. "I'm going to find him. . . ."

"Find? You'll take . . . take . . . me . . . too?"

Peniel coughed again, resisted the impulse to gag. Sitting beside the leper was something akin to stumbling over a dead cat in an alleyway.

"Take you?" The thought was like scooping up the dead cat and carrying it in to supper.

"So long . . . I've been . . . looking. Praying . . ."

Guilt. Poor creature. Peniel considered the leper's words. Did lepers pray? And could the Lord hear the prayers of those who were so stricken by the judgment of the Almighty?

If Peniel was seen in the company of a leper, he would be unclean also. Prevented from going to the Teacher. And yet . . .

"Where have you come from?"

"Mak'ob."

"No one ever leaves the Valley of Mak'ob," Peniel argued.

"I have . . . no other hope . . . to find . . . the one . . . we heard about. Rabbi . . . sent me . . . four months . . . no luck. Will die soon. . . . Will you . . . help?" He leaned closer. Too close. Rancid breath turned Peniel's stomach.

Peniel covered his eyes with his hands as the setting moon slid from behind a cloud, revealing again the horrific visage of the one who had saved him. So this was seeing! As if smelling them was not bad enough!

Take him? What choice did Peniel have? He was obligated. And yet, what if he caught the sickness?

"I owe you my life," Peniel agreed. And then, "But, please, don't come too near me. I beg you. No closer. I fear your disease more than any other thing. I've heard the lepers moaning outside the camps and . . . not so close. I'm sorry."

"But . . . you'll take . . . me?"

"Yes."

The leper nodded once and moved away, settling at the base of a monument ten or so paces from Peniel. The creature curled into a lump of rags. Soon the rattle of unnatural snoring filled the air.

Peniel did not sleep as the constellations spun away above his head.

At dawn the Gennath Gate opened with a shrieking complaint of hinges. Bawling camels and cursing drovers pushed past vigilant, unsympathetic guards. Pilgrims, beginning homeward journeys and anxious to put miles of dusty travel behind them before the heat of the day, chafed at the delay.

Leaning across a headstone marking the resting place of the Motola family, Peniel studied the scene.

A few yards inside the gate, Peniel saw the beleaguered sentries still searching for him among departing travelers. New arrivals into the Holy City were waved through with barely a glance.

It was possible. Just possible, Peniel thought. He could reenter the city openly, return to his beggar friends beneath the viaduct, and come out after nightfall by way of the hidden culvert.

Peniel smelled Jekuthiel before he heard him, knew the leper stood only feet behind him. "I have to go back." Peniel turned round.

The leper's face was swathed up to the eyes. Shrouded, like a corpse. "You . . . promised . . . take . . . me to Messiah."

"I will. I promise," Peniel pledged. "But in the night it came to me. There are others inside the city. I'm sent, see? Have to go back for them.

Take the cobra by the tail, if you take my meaning. I thought it all out in the night. My dream. I don't want to go back, but I have to, see?"

The eyes of the leper remained locked on Peniel's for a time, judging what he saw there. "Back? Crazy."

"Yes. Point taken. All the same. I've got very good friends living under the viaduct. And now that I can see . . . see? Well, maybe I was thinking of everything all wrong. I thought it was Mama and Papa. But maybe he meant the others. Understand?"

The leper shook his head from side to side. "You . . . just . . . going . . . to leave me, eh?"

"I'll come back. Unless I'm nabbed by Eglon and nailed to a tree. But look there. The guards are searching everyone coming out. Nobody going in. They'd never suspect that once I got away I'd want to go back in again."

"They'll . . . wring your . . . neck . . . like a chicken."

"Point taken. But see, they've given up looking for me at Papa's workshop. That means they won't be looking for me anymore among the beggars beneath the viaduct. I can go back. Fetch as many as can walk. And I won't be going back to the Teacher empty-handed."

"They'll . . . cut . . . off your . . . hands . . . to make you . . . squawk."

"It's possible. But what else have I got to lose?"

"Lose? . . . Everything. You'll look . . . worse than . . . me . . . if the Temple Guards get . . . hold of you. A rooster . . . changed into . . . a hen."

"Descriptive. Yes. Well spoken. But it all came to me last night. I'm sitting on this gravestone, and I told the Almighty if he would let me live till morning I'd go back for them."

"You go . . . back . . . in there . . . you'll never come out. And who . . . will help me?"

"Stay here. Pray. That's all. Maybe I'll come back. If not, it means we're both going to die and that's the end of our story."

"Then . . . here." Jekuthiel produced a canvas sack from beneath his robe and from it withdrew a dark green cloak. "Take this," he offered. "Disguise."

A leper's cloak? How could Peniel even touch it, much less wear it? He drew back as if it were a snake. "No. Thank you very much but . . . no, thanks. But I will come back."

"Scared, eh? Take the . . . cobra . . . by the tail. It's clean . . . never worn."

"Well, then." Peniel winced and put it on. He itched, but just maybe a different cloak would save him. "Thanks, friend."

The leper nodded once and did not speak again. He slumped down in the shade of a sepulchre to wait.

At the back of the cemetery Peniel slipped over the wall. He emerged from beneath a pair of hills alongside the Caesarea road. No one saw him leave the graveyard.

Several wagonloads of barley were en route to Jerusalem, and behind these came a herd of goats being driven to market. Peniel joined the procession between the two groups, able to slip forward or back as circumstances required. Just one more traveler on the highway. Just another Jewish pilgrim arriving at the Center of the World.

And then a commotion at the gate: Two sentries pounced on a young man close to Peniel's age. He resisted. They clubbed him to the ground, trussed him up, and hauled him away.

"Halt!" soldiers ordered a merchant. "You there! Unload your stock! All of it!"

They opened every container. The searchers rummaged through the contents, as if Peniel might be hiding inside.

Madness! Peniel pulled out of the flow and looked over his shoulder. Why did the cemetery seem so much farther away in daylight?

A guard atop the parapet stared down at him.

Peniel, near panic, forced himself not to run.

No choice now. Had to go forward.

Goatherds. Peniel faded back to walk alongside them. "What's all this, then?" one of them complained loudly. "Figure on catching rebels in broad daylight, do they?"

"Here, you," a guard sergeant bellowed.

Peniel's heart sank. Trembling, he pivoted toward the command.

"Yes, you!" The sentry pointed to a teenage boy hefting one of the poles of a rich woman's litter.

The matron shrieked, asking by what right he held up the progress of the household of Demetrius of Tyre. "I don't care if you're mighty Caesar's grandmother herself," was the shouted reply. "This one goes nowhere till I say, got it?"

The gate jammed. No one advancing. None turning back. Wagons and carts, foot traffic and horseback, all piled up.

A pair of goats seized the opportunity to jump atop the barley wagon.

A fight broke out between the carters and the drovers.

"Enough!" the guard sergeant barked. "Nobody leaves Yerushalayim till I say. Clear a path there! Clear a path. Now, all of you going into the city, get on with you! Speed it up! Go!"

The sentries at Jerusalem's northern portal did not spare a second glance at Peniel in his new green cloak. Harried, cursing, and sweating as they searched for a youth trying to escape Jerusalem, they missed their quarry altogether.

Peniel nodded and waved as he walked past a trio of guards and back into the den of vipers that was Jerusalem.

The minyan of ten lepers was chosen by lot right after morning prayers.

The list was varied. The only requirement was strength and willingness to go. Cantor was the chief delegate. Carpenter was second in command. The two Cabbage Sisters, each of whom had lost ears and joints of fingers. Fisherman, who had no nose and had lost his eyebrows and right ear. Crusher of the vinegrowers was in the early stages, as were the four young Torah scholars from the camp of the boys.

And so it was settled. Citizens of the Valley donated various foods and a coin or two where they could be found. In a day or two at the most, the minyan of lepers would be ready to travel.

I'm praying again, God Who Knows I'm Afraid. Afraid. Of what? Of being left alone forever? Of never seeing Cantor again? Of losing the dreams I have dared to dream about being his wife? Yes! All those things I fear more than if he never finds the Messiah! I am more afraid of this than I am of finding out we have no hope of deliverance! Do you hear me, God Who Knows I'm Afraid? Do you? What if Cantor never comes back to me?

Lily did not share her trepidation as she watched Cantor pack his meager supplies in his rucksack. If he sensed her fears he did not mention it or seek to console her.

"I'll leave Hawk with you."

"I don't know how to handle him. Not without you."

"Hawk fancies you."

"I can't hunt with him . . . not unless you're here."

"You can. You will. It'll all be fine. He'll come when you whistle."

"What if he doesn't?"

"He will. We trained him together. He'll come to you as quickly as to me."

"But . . . the wedding . . ."

"I'll be back before you know it!"

"But, Cantor . . . what if . . ."

"There's no what if . . . only when. And when I get back we'll be married just like we've planned. By then the baby will be big enough. Deborah back on her feet. We'll be married." He smiled and touched her cheek. His red hair glistened in the sunlight. Eyes seemed feverish.

"Are you feeling well?"

"Well enough!"

"You're glad to be going."

"Think of it, Lily! What if we find him? What if he really is the one? Think! Lily! You and I can leave this Valley and never look back!"

"You'll come back for me. I mean . . . if . . . you won't forget . . . us." Her chin trembled.

He wrapped his arms around her. "Never. Never. Forget you? I'll be back. One way or the other. I promise I won't forget."

Just as Jekuthiel had left Deborah, Cantor was leaving Lily for the Outside in search of a dream. Perhaps, like Jekuthiel, Cantor would never come back.

For the second time in her life, Lily was terrified.

Peniel was hungry. He made his way to the foot of the causeway leading onto the Temple Mount. Silver trumpets inside the Temple signaled the procession of Levites, choir, and high priest. The roar of worshippers swelled up and rolled over the walls that enclosed the platform.

Resisting the urge to ascend the bridge and enter the Temple grounds, Peniel drew aside into a shadow and considered his next move. Beneath the viaduct was the colony of the outcasts.

Would he be recognized? Coming through a crowded gate ignored by harried guards who'd never met him was one thing, but how to approach those who knew him? What if they reacted like Mama had? threatened to turn him in?

Peniel examined the open palms of his hands. Long slender fingers. He wondered what his face looked like. Other people might recognize him easily enough, though he could not recognize himself. He kept the tail of the keffiyeh wrapped around his head.

He gazed longingly at the Temple Mount. How often had he sat outside Nicanor Gate and held up his begging bowl as men entered the Court of the Israelites? "I would have liked to see the Beautiful Gate just once more before I leave." He shrugged. "But I don't fancy dying for it."

Sun glinted on the gold-capped pinnacles of the structure. Peniel shielded his eyes from the glare. It was so much bigger, so much grander than he had imagined. But the glory of Herod's construction had not healed Peniel. Nor had priestly benedictions. Not the sacrifices. Nor the trumpets. Not processions, nor priests, nor alms.

Yeshua wielded a power more glorious than could be contained in the white stone and gilded cornices of Jerusalem. Such might was never meant to be hoarded, but must be shared. "Lord, I gave my word. How can I follow you unless I bring someone else? But who?"

Behind him, from the causeway, came the familiar bump and scrape of Gideon, the lame. "Peniel!" An old friend. "Peniel! Brother beggar!" Even from the back and dressed in the green cloak Peniel could be recognized? A new wave of fear swept over him.

Gideon had been good company, though they had fallen out because Peniel called Yeshua Et Ha-or, "the Light," after it had been forbidden by the Sanhedrin's edict. What did Gideon think now?

Peniel turned to face him. Gideon was young. Perhaps a year or two older than Peniel. Not much. The perfect mendicant. Skinny. Underfed. Ridiculous tangle of dirty blond hair. Beard wild and wiry. Teeth yellowed with a gap in front. Wide forehead, large ears. Ragged, dirty clothes. Smooth, twisted walking stick. The right leg spindly and useless. Foot turned inward.

Peniel put the face with the familiar voice of Gideon. Everything matched perfectly.

Peniel held his breath to see what would follow. Would Gideon call for the guards?

Gideon gawked then stammered, "B-bless me, I thought you was somebody else! You look enough like him to be himself. I see now you're not blind. I see you're not him at all. I mean no disrespect."

"Gideon!" Peniel cried out, rushed to him, and embraced him. "Sure! Gideon! Brother! I am myself! I am Peniel! Like you thought I was!"

Gideon took some convincing. "If you're Peniel, then how did we last part company?"

"Badly. A religious disagreement."

Gideon's cheek muscle twitched. "How . . . how . . . do you know that?"

"How else?"

"But . . . a fine pair of brown eyes. How?"

They sat together on the parapet of the bridge as Peniel explained from start to finish what had happened between last Shabbat and today.

"The Temple Guards came snooping about. Looking for someone named Peniel. And I heard about a miracle and someone named Peniel, but, bless me," Gideon said, "I never thought it was you! I mean, miracles don't come to the likes of us now, do they?" Gideon examined his face and whispered conspiratorially, "You're a fool for staying in Yerushalayim after they've passed judgment on you! They can gouge out those new eyes of yours, you know. Easier to make you blind again than to have to explain away what Yeshua did for you! Not safe for you here!"

"I'm leaving Yerushalayim. I am! Come with me!"

"Where?"

"The Galil. He's there."

Gideon glanced cautiously up at the Temple edifice. "They won't take kindly to it. You know what they say around here."

"They'll never miss you."

"That's true enough."

"I'll take you to him! Gideon! He'll fix your foot."

"Even after I tossed you out?"

"Sure."

"After what I said about you being a fool for speaking out in his defense and all?"

"Forgotten."

"They'd like to keep us poor folk in line. Hush up the ones like you."

"He'll straighten your leg right out!"

"Make us march to their drum. A Roman drumbeat it is."

"If he can give me eyes to see, then he'll give you straight legs to walk on!"

"The people of Yerushalayim are afraid to openly declare he's a prophet. These religious sorts don't like prophets from the Lord much!

Look what Antipas did to the Baptizer." Gideon drew his finger slowly across his throat.

"Come on, Gideon!"

"I've never been outside Judea. Never been outside Yerushalayim, if you must know."

"Don't be scared!"

"Galil. It's a long way to walk. Uphill." Gideon rubbed his bad leg like it was an old dog who might not be able to walk so far.

"I'll help you!"

"Galilean pilgrims always have sore feet after the walk from the Galil. I hear them grumble. Makes for good opening conversation. They show me their blisters. I show them my crippled leg. There's usually a coin or two in it for me. A long walk."

"I'll carry you on my back if I have to. And after you see him you'll be able to run and skip back to Yerushalayim if you want to come back."

"They'll pinch you on the way out the gate. Searching everyone I hear."

"I know another way out. After dark."

"Well then. Another way out? We can rest beneath the viaduct till nightfall."

"Is it safe?"

"They haven't been back in a couple of days. They don't like to poke around our hovels. Safe enough. Here! That's a fine cloak you're wearing. Where'd it come from? Have you turned thief?"

"A gift." Peniel thought about Jekuthiel, decided not to mention they'd be traveling with a leper—not yet. Nor did it seem wise to go in and out again, increasing the risk. This seemed like a sensible idea.

"You're dressed too fine for Peniel. I'll make up a story about you. You're not you at all."

"Sure. Then we can set out tonight."

"You'll have to keep quiet about where we're headed. The others—the beggars beneath the viaduct—are scared of the authorities. Turn you in for speaking up for Yeshua. You'll be arrested. Then we'll never be able to leave."

"Tonight. Then, like a couple of stones from a sling . . ."

Gideon jangled pennies in his pocket. "Hungry?"

Peniel put a hand to his belly. It seemed a very long time since he had eaten. "Hungry. Yes."

"Good day for alms today. Enough to spare." Gideon threw an arm over Peniel's shoulder. The two set out. "Cheese and dates for supper. Apples. Bread. Food enough to take with us on our journey. Come morning I'll let you guide me to this miracle worker. Then we'll see if he's as clever with a dead foot as he's been with those brown eyes of yours. Solemn and sincere as a faithful dog's, your eyes! He fashioned them very fine. As fine a pair of matching brown eyes as ever I saw plugged into a face. Are you pleased with the way they've turned out?"

Peniel touched his index finger to his eyelid and blinked rapidly in demonstration. "They work very well."

Gideon leaned in close to study them. "He's added a bit of gold there. Near the center. I saw a horse with eyes that color once."

Peniel supposed this was a compliment. He thanked Gideon as the two set off.

They left the souk with cheese and dates.

Peniel sensed the danger, heard it, before he saw the Temple Guard approach. Men on horseback. Men who meant business.

Behind Gideon came the tramp of hobnailed boots and iron-shod hooves on the street. A dozen. Two dozen. Marching as if to war. Peniel heard them well before they were in sight. The back of his neck prickled with fear.

Gideon hissed. "Peniel? You've gone white as a shroud."

Peniel took Gideon's arm and turned away from the approaching soldiers. "Nothing. They're just . . . I can't be seen, that's all."

Gideon's eyebrows arched, and his mouth formed a small *O* of understanding. "Here! Here, then. Lean on my stick. That's it. Limp. I'll lean on your arm."

The two hobbled away as the soldiers rumbled past at a clip.

The cloud of dust stung Peniel's eyes. He watched as the troops retreated down the road toward the Sheep Gate.

"Yes." Gideon sucked his teeth. "Doesn't take a blind man to see what they're after. If we wait long enough in Yerushalayim, they'll come back with Yeshua in chains."

"A ray of sunlight, your brain."

Gideon pantomimed the stabbing, the garroting, the slitting of a throat. "After they do whatever they've a mind to do to him, they'll make you blind as a post again." He finished his play by acting out a knife gouging out eyes.

Peniel chewed his lip. "Ah, Gideon. You always were an optimist."

"Well then. Much good it'll do me to have your Rabbi heal my leg if they break both my legs afterwards on a Roman cross."

"You're right," Peniel apologized. This had all been a stupid idea, putting more people at risk than just himself. "I should be alone. Anyone seen with me is in danger." He saluted Gideon and jogged away quickly in the opposite direction of the soldiers.

Gideon called him back. "Wait! Wait! Fool! Come back!"

Peniel wheeled around. "What?"

Gideon hobbled after him, lowered his voice. "It came to me. See? While you were running off like that. You know. *Running* off to your Rabbi."

"Just running off."

"Yes. Well, if I go with you . . . after I got my leg fit and strong? I could run. I could *run* away, see. They'd have a time catching me. I've dreamed of running. Maybe it's worth the risk. Maybe."

"Yes. Maybe."

"So? Will you still take me with you then?"

Peniel would be grateful for the company. "Sure. Yes. Sure."

It was washday in the Valley of Mak'ob. Water drawn from the well, boiled in enormous cauldrons. Women and children who were able to do the work gathered at the trough with bundles of dirty clothes and bandages and gossiped as they scrubbed.

Lily was grateful for a chore to keep her mind off Cantor's impending departure.

She knelt beside the wash stone and pounded Deborah's shift. Two women, Widow and Old Thing, discussed the minyan's quest.

Widow cast a furtive glance toward Lily. "Tomorrow morning they're leaving. Imagine! Going Outside!"

Old Thing concurred. "Outside, Samaritan mercenaries patrol the top of the cliffs. Looking for the likes of us, they are. Looking for any who might try to leave. Kill the likes of us, they do, if we try to leave."

"Aye. Dangerous for our kind out there. They'll stone you first and ask questions later. What do you think, Lily? Scared for Cantor, are you?"

Though Lily did not want Cantor to leave her, she was cautious in her reply. Old Thing and Widow were the yentas of the Valley, spreading and enlarging on every word until it became unrecognizable. "Those who're chosen to go were given a choice. Don't have to go."

"Cantor's got them all stirred up," Old Thing argued. "Excited by the thought of the journey. Four of the ten are just boys. Bar mitzvah age. Practically children. Barely old enough to know how to think. He's got them all stirred up."

Lily added solemnly, "I'd go if I was picked. If I didn't need to stay here with Deborah."

"Not me," Old Thing countered. "All nonsense. Nothing Outside for the likes of us. Our only hope is to live here best we can and die when death comes knocking. You get used to it after a few years. I wouldn't want to leave. Nothing for me Outside."

Lily argued, "But what if . . ."

Old Thing slapped a wet shift hard against the rubbing stone. "There's no what if . . . only them that lives Outside Mak'ob and those of us that live Inside. It's the Law. We don't mix with them, and they don't hurt us. We stay put, don't cause trouble, and by the charity they send each new moon there's food enough to live until we die."

Widow worked on her clothes. "And we're better off for it. Being left alone. Yes. A poor widow's got better sympathy Inside than Outside. Them as is Outside have no mercy."

From across the trough came a halting question from a young woman whose face had dissolved away. "But . . . what about . . . this Messiah . . . they're going . . . to hunt for?"

Old Thing, who had lived in Mak'ob longer than anyone, cried, "Messiah? Nonsense! What about him? Even if he exists! So what if he heals a blind man? or a cripple? What's that compared to the likes of us? Living dead, that's what they call us Outside. If this Prophet's a righteous man, he'll never come near the likes of us. It's the Law! If he comes near or so much as touches one of us, he's declared unclean by the rabbis. Then who'd listen to him?"

Widow, whose husband had been a scholar, agreed. "True. True. The Law makes it clear. The prophet Elisha, when he healed Naaman the Syrian? Elisha didn't even come out of the house. Sent his servant to give the instructions. We contaminate everything we come near. When you've lived Inside long enough, you forget what it's like Outside. How the Outside people treat lepers. This Valley's the only place on earth where we aren't required to shout our shame at the top of our lungs."

Old Thing probed Lily's thoughts. "So? Lily? What do you think about all this? Your dear Cantor leading the minyan to the Outside and all? And Jekuthiel never bothering to come back? Deborah, alone up there. Waiting. Waiting."

Lily beat the cloth harder on the stone, attempting to scrub the smell of leprosy from the fibers. Impossible task. The stink would return the instant it touched the leprous sores again. Lily said, "Safety in numbers."

"Why! Them as is Outside would just as soon kill ten lepers as kill one trying to come out," Widow said. "They'll think it's a rebellion!" She cackled.

Lily suppressed her anger. "I'd go. If I could. Yes. I'd go back Outside. In a minute I'd go if it wasn't for needing to care for Deborah and Baruch. Go with Cantor and never mind what happened."

Widow was snide. "Deborah told us you still talk about your mother and father when you sleep."

Lily frowned. "Maybe I do."

Widow shoved the knife deeper. "Not thinking about trying to go back home, are you, girl? You can't ever go home again once you're declared *tsara*."

Lily wrung out the water from the shift as if it were Widow's neck and shrugged. "Dreaming and planning are two different things."

Widow's comeback stung Lily. "You know that as well as anyone, dearie. Dreaming and planning, eh? How long you and Cantor been dreaming of being wed?"

Emboldened by her friend's cruel remark, Old Thing said, "Aye. That Cantor of yours is a dreamer who doesn't know the difference. Ought to stay here and wed you. Have a few weeks or months of happiness before one of you dies anyway. What's he trying to prove? Isn't it enough that Jekuthiel's lost? Never coming back? Shouldn't have gone Outside. Not with a wife and a baby on the way. Isn't it enough? Sanity comes by accepting our fate. Accepting the fact that God has no sense of what's fair. What did I ever do to deserve such punishment? But here I am. Messiah indeed! They're chasing after shadows."

Lily would not argue further. "We're all in the hands of El Olam, the Eternal God." She loaded her wet clothes into a basket and hiked back toward the cave.

Saying nothing, watching everything, Avel and the two other boys followed Zadok on his final rounds.

Today they were leaving the flocks and herds of Migdal Eder forever.

Zadok, Avel, Emet, and Ha-or Tov spoke little of their loss. The old man was leaving behind a lifetime of memories. His three adopted boys were saying farewell to the only place that had ever been home.

The morning had begun like always. Avel was not surprised that Zadok was up before dawn, since that was his habit. But the very ordinariness of the day was surprising. The sun rose over hills and pastures of sheep and shepherds. Where once heavenly choirs had sung to herald Messiah's birth, now cicadas clicked in the sage. Birds flew overhead in the same sky where archangels had soared and the great star had shone so brightly.

How could life go on when it felt as though life was coming to an end?

Avel, long-faced, poked at breakfast. He ate without tasting. The bunches of lavender still hung from the rafters where Zadok's wife had placed them to dry the night before she died. Emet nudged Avel as the old shepherd reached up to break off a sprig and held it to his nose.

For an instant, an image threatened to overwhelm Zadok. He gazed solemnly around the room where they had lived together. Where their little sons had died at the hands of Herod's soldiers. Where Zadok and Rachel, after they had wept together, had somehow rebuilt a life.

How to capture a lifetime in one last, long look?

Suddenly conscious of the miserable stares of the young threesome,

Zadok cleared his throat, blustered about something being ill packed, and strode from the house.

From all that had been his life.

And so the Chief Shepherd spent most of the morning in the limestone lambing caverns on the ridge above the Tower of the Flock. Zadok went from stall to stall, with Lev following close behind. "This one'll do right well," Zadok noted, indicating a pregnant ewe who bulged sideways as wide as she stood tall.

At the next pen he suggested, "This one'll bear watchin'. Triplets last time, y' remember. Apt to do it again, I fancy."

Out of the corner of his eye, Zadok saw a puzzled look on Avel's face. Evidently, Zadok's attention to detail and obvious concern for the routine matters of the flock were confusing Avel. The Chief Shepherd was issuing orders and handing out advice as if he were not going anywhere.

Ordinary. So ordinary. As if his great heart were not breaking. As if the injustice of this expulsion did not eat at his soul and rage within him. When they reached the end of the row of stalls Avel asked him, "Like every other day?"

"Tomorrow," Zadok said, "it'll be on someone else's shoulders. It won't be my lookout anymore. But while I remain in charge here, if it's only hours, I won't shirk nor give less than my best."

At the entry to the cave a deputation of shepherds waited for Zadok to emerge. They had come to honor the old man. To say farewell.

"Master Zadok," offered a shepherd named Joel, "we all come here to say to you . . . well, we want you to know, sir . . . it's not right what they're doing to you—putting you out and all. And sending down someone from Yerushalayim to take your place! It'll never work out. We'll see to that. We'll send him packing in a fortnight."

"Aye," agreed another gruffly. "He'll leave double-quick, or likely find an adder in his bed."

An undercurrent of approving laughter was smothered when Zadok lashed out. "Never!" he bellowed. "I won't hear of it! Y' will serve your new master better than y' ever served me or I'll come back and whip you myself!"

The shepherds shuffled uneasily. Stared at their feet. Muttered that they meant no harm. No harm.

Zadok clapped a broad calloused hand on each man's shoulder in silent gratitude for their support and then said quietly, "Whose flocks do we care for here? Whose? Not the high priest's nor the Sanhedrin's nor any high-and-mighty Pharisee's, but the lambs of the Lord Almighty himself. It is he alone I have served these two and fifty years. Avel, why do y' cull the herd before y' drive them to Temple?"

Nervous at being called on in front of all the older herdsmen, Avel took a deep breath and replied, "Because only spotless lambs can be brought to Yahweh. Only perfect lambs will do for the sacrifices."

"Just so," Zadok agreed. "And tending them is no less important duty than any *cohen* who burns the sacred incense, any Levite singer, or the high priest himself! If any of y' think otherwise, clear off now, today! Come with us if y' cannot do your duty for the Lord."

"But, Master Zadok," Lev protested, "it's still not right."

Avel saw a rare thing: A new crease appeared on Zadok's face, at right angles to the ancient scar from forehead to jaw.

It was a smile.

"I thank y' for your concern on my behalf, Lev," Zadok admitted. "But I am following my Lord no less now in what I am about to do than in all I have done these three decades past. Remember our King David was a shepherd before ever he was king. Hear what he wrote. *'Commit your way to the Lord,'*" Zadok quoted. "*'Trust in him and he will do this: He will make your righteousness shine like the dawn, the justice of your cause like the noonday sun.'* [22] He himself will do this," Zadok rumbled. "It is not for me to show the justice of my cause or complain how I am abused. The sheep are his, my life is his, and what he chooses to do with either is for him to say. My only concern is to commit my way and trust. All else is up to him.

"And so, lads, y' have been like sons to me. I shall not forget y'. No. Nor this place. Nor shall I deny all that I have lived to see here! For this reason alone I am put out. Because I have spoken the truth about the Lord and all the wonders of a single night thirty and two years ago! And I will not say it never happened. I dare to speak his name to those who would deny him! My own babies were martyrs for this cause. Would I change my story?"

Zadok touched the scar on his face. "But now I am called to serve the Good Shepherd. Yeshua. He is the son of David. And so shall I serve him as I served the flocks of his Father. Yes. Even if it is by laying down my life for him. And so, Shalom. Farewell. All of y'. Brothers. Sons. Farewell."

"Gideon! Shalom!" From all quarters of the squalid encampment beggars greeted the lame youth.

Peniel recognized the voices of old friends. Amos the dwarf. Jeremiah the idiot. Shana the ancient woman pickpocket. Hosea the young spastic, whose cousins carried him to the Pool of Bethesda six days a week. But among those dozens who had shared the misery of a beggar's existence with Peniel for years, no one seemed to recognize him. Furtive glances examined him as he passed by. Faces turned quickly away from him.

And as he viewed them all, Peniel's new eyes confirmed truths his ears had only hinted at.

Before, when he was blind, his senses had warned him that all was not well. Now vision verified the worst.

The world beneath the viaduct was indeed a harsh and pitiless place.

Tears, unbidden, misunderstood, began to flow silently down Peniel's cheeks as he took it all in for the first time.

"What's wrong with you, then?" Gideon mocked. "Never mind. Just remember what I said. Keep your mouth shut."

Beneath the viaduct, where the dregs of Jerusalem drained away, lived the ragged people. Shelters constructed of cast-off lumber and brush gathered from the hillsides were packed into the culvert mostly out of sight of the respectable citizens of the city.

Through the center of the colony ran a polluted brook. Children of the homeless darted through swarms of flies as they played along the bank of this open sewer. Three small boys under the age of five, brothers by the look of them, stared listlessly at Peniel and Gideon as they passed. Hair spiked with filth, they were nearly naked, clothed only in torn fabric tied around hunger-swollen bellies.

If Yeshua saw this place, Peniel thought, *surely he would embrace them all. Heal them all. Feed them all.*

Here and there among the hovels were smoldering campfires. Near the shelter of Gideon three cripples, stretched out in various stages of disability, roasted pigeons skewered on long sticks.

Pigeons? Or something else? Peniel wondered. *The little carcasses seem to have four legs.*

Gideon, noting Peniel's questioning stare, explained the grisly menu. "That's the last of Red's kittens. But the cat of the old man without legs just had another litter. Nine kittens. There'd be a feast in a few weeks if he didn't always kill them so early. Every time. He says he can't bear to eat them after they open their eyes because they're so . . . so human then, he says. Kittens romping round his shelter are comfort to him when he's lonely, he says. If only he'd let them get some meat on their bones, I say. Wait awhile. But he's a sentimental fool. He won't let them open their eyes before he's picking his teeth with their bones."

Peniel choked back a sob and covered his face.

"What's wrong with you, then?" Gideon demanded irritably.

Peniel attempted to reply. The more he saw of life, the more his heart ached and the more tears streamed from his new eyes. He could not stop them.

Gideon nudged him hard in the ribs. "Never mind. Shut up, will you! Keep it to yourself. You're supposed to be deaf. You're mute, remember? Remember what we agreed. I'll be up to the neck in trouble for taking you in if they get wise to who you really are. There's a reward for turning in followers of Yeshua."

When Gideon paused, Peniel instantly recognized the glint of temptation that brightened Gideon's expression. Then, giving his head a little shake, Gideon patted his lame leg, as if to remind himself of why he must shield Peniel. Peniel would take him to Yeshua. Yeshua would heal Gideon's leg. Yes. It was important that Peniel survive.

With a shrug and a wave of his hand, Gideon indicated that they had arrived at his home. It was a lean-to of dried olive branches propped against a stone pillar.

Exhausted, Peniel sank down on the straw mat, leaned his back against the pillar, and adjusted his keffiyeh. Concealing his identity behind the green cloak, hiding himself, he closed his eyes and clasped his knees. He slept.

Hours passed. It was twilight when Gideon broke bread without making the blessing and jabbered in a lowered voice, "No doubt what they're all afraid of . . . Pilate, I mean . . . Caiaphas . . . the rest . . ." He passed a chunk of bread to Peniel, who regretted that he could not pray the prayer out loud.

Stuffing his mouth, Gideon continued his monologue. "Think what Yeshua could do with an army of beggars. Now wouldn't that be a sight? The lame. The deaf and the blind all sitting in the Chamber of Hewn Stone. Well, I suppose in a way the lame, the deaf, and the blind are *already* sitting in the chamber. But I mean, what if it was us, not them?"

Peniel wished he could tell Gideon to shut up, but he couldn't even open his mouth to do that. He had promised to play the part of a deaf mute. Exchanging one infirmity for another so he would not be found out.

He heard the stumping of Amos the dwarf, as the little man approached the shelter. His large head tilted on sloping shoulders as he peered in at Peniel and smiled.

"Who's your friend, Gideon? Introduce me?" Amos scratched grumpy jowls with stubby fingers.

"A friend." Gideon had not thought far enough ahead to have a good story at hand.

"To every answer you can find a new question, eh?" Amos bowed curtly to Peniel. "Shalom."

Peniel did not respond, though it was difficult. He had always liked Amos. The dwarf's soul was straight and tall, though it was trapped inside this bent and stunted skeleton. He was a fountain spouting proverbs for all occasions.

"He's deaf," Gideon blurted, as if to remind Peniel that he must not reply.

Amos scrunched his face and raised his hand in silent greeting. "Better dignified silence than a lie, eh? Deaf, eh? He looks like Peniel, don't you think? A lot. Almost identical. Except for the eyes."

Peniel would have liked to invite Amos to come along to Galilee. Couldn't Yeshua make a small man large? Was such a thing any more difficult than giving a blind man eyes?

Gideon, as if reading Peniel's mind, cast a stern look of warning in his direction.

"I say," Amos croaked in his pinched voice, "he does look a lot like Peniel. Only Peniel didn't have brown eyes, did he? Is he crying? Are those tears? When the eyes don't see, the heart doesn't ache, eh? But to see what's here. Oy! The suffering! Now that'll make you weep."

The lie grew. "This is Peniel's cousin. A relative from Hebron."

"His cousin? Well, then. That explains it. They look an awful lot alike. The whole family must be accursed."

Peniel pretended not to hear the insult. Now that he had seen Amos in the light of day, it was clear the dwarf had no right to criticize Peniel. Or Peniel's cousin either.

"So what's Peniel's cousin doing here?" Amos leaned close to examine Peniel's eyes. "And why is he crying?"

Gideon feigned unconcern, though beads of sweat popped out on his brow. "Looking for Peniel, I suppose. Yes. That's it. He's looking for Peniel. Weeping because he can't find him."

The huge head bobbed up and down in comprehension as the dwarf whispered conspiratorially. He pronounced each word very carefully, as though attempting to help Peniel read his lips: "Well . . . tell . . . Peniel's . . . deaf cousin . . . he's . . . not . . . the . . . only . . . one . . . looking . . . for . . . Peniel . . . will you?" A grin. A rapid batting of eyelashes. "This morning, Gideon, after you left, four men of the Temple Guard returned. Still looking for Peniel. Peniel the blind beggar, they said, somehow got his sight. Some sort of pretend miracle, they said. Some charlatan from Galilee pretended to heal Peniel on the Sabbath. Broke the Sabbath. Made Peniel a new set of brown eyes out of spit and clay. And now the Temple rulers would like to take out the brown eyes and examine them close up." Amos raised his brows and tucked his chin in a way that let Peniel know that Amos knew the truth.

Gideon grew very pale. "They came back?"

"Looking for Peniel," Amos confirmed.

"Anyone else know?"

Amos glanced over his shoulder. "No," he said hesitantly. "But I think Zacharias suspects."

"The scum."

"He just left. Good thing he stutters. It'll take him an hour to spit out the fact that Peniel is . . . well . . . you know . . . so! If this cousin of Peniel wants to save Peniel's life, it'd be wise if he left. Better a live dog than a dead lion, eh? I'm betting Zacharias will be back, and he won't be alone."

Gideon's expression was stunned. "Will you tell them you've seen us?"

Amos smirked. "No."

"Good."

"Not if you take me with you, eh?" Amos patted Peniel's head as if he were a child. "Whoever can make a blind man see can make a small man grow, eh? Take me with you. I'm weary of spending my life staring at the knees of Pharisees. The only time I'm equal is when they kneel to pray. Then I'm a bit taller. Can he make me like other men, you think?"

Peniel opened his mouth to speak. "You must come."

"Shut up!" Gideon slammed his fist on Peniel's shoulder.

Amos laughed. "Keen sight does not make for brains, eh? So. Now. Another miracle for the family of Peniel. The deaf cousin hears and speaks. I must meet the miracle worker who's done this!"

"All right." Gideon, disgusted, scrambled up and grabbed his crutch. "You can come. And we're leaving now."

The shrill cry of the Hawk sounded as he circled above Lily. His shadow brushed her. Lily glanced up the slope.

Cantor was waiting on their boulder. Grinning, he waved broadly to her and cupped his hands around his mouth to shout, "Lily! Hey! Come up!"

She hiked slowly up the hill. She did not want him to see the ache that filled her at the thought of his leaving.

"You're finished packing?" she asked, sitting next to Cantor.

He scoffed. "Packing? I've got enough dried venison for a week and a note to the Messiah written by Rabbi Ahava."

"Messiah. You believe the stories then? The legend of King David's prophecy? About God's Son coming here some day to lead the lepers out of the Valley of the Shadow of Death?"

Cantor frowned. "I've dreamed of green pastures. Looked for the coming of the Good Shepherd every time some half-dead exile stumbles down the path to us. I have to go see for myself. For the sake of everyone here in Mak'ob."

"Sure."

"But . . . what, Lily?"

"When will you come back?"

"Soon as I know for certain."

Lily wrapped her arms around her knees and gazed out over the Valley. "Jekuthiel said the same thing to Deborah. Can you tell me when? When I can look for you? What month I should stop looking and say, 'Well, then, I guess he's never coming'?"

"The end of summer. I'll come to you when the vine leaves turn."

"Well, then. When the leaves turn." She was resigned. "It'll feel like forever."

"But the day will come! The people of this Valley have been waiting since the time of David for their deliverer to come."

"What's another thousand years to wait until we marry?" She gave a bitter laugh.

"Time passes. And maybe we won't come back alone. Maybe we'll bring Messiah here!"

"The women at the wash trough this morning said that any prophet who entered our Valley—or touched a leper—couldn't be righteous or the Anointed One. To touch a leper is to become a leper."

"You know the stories. Isaiah says that Messiah will be like us. *Chadel!* Rejected! *Tsara!* Stricken! *'And by his wounds we will be healed.'*"[23]

"If only I could believe it. No one knows what that can mean. Messiah? A leper like us?"

"It is written that he will be made like us, yes. I don't understand how it will happen, but if he's out there—Outside—I want to see for myself."

"But I won't know what to believe when you're gone, Cantor. Who will teach me? Who will make me laugh?"

"The children."

"Will you come back for me? Even if you don't find your Messiah? Or will you stay Outside? Perish looking for him?"

He took her shrunken hand and kissed the place her fingers once had been. "Listen! I was talking to the rabbi a while ago. He says he has nothing to do tonight that would keep him from performing a wedding. Would you? Would you marry me tonight, Lily? We don't have to wait. We'll have tonight, Lily. And when we say good-bye tomorrow, you'll know I'll come back for my wife."

Peniel, Amos, and Gideon had not gone far in the twilight before proof of Zacharias the hunchback's crooked soul became evident. Just as Amos suspected, Zacharias had indeed hopped off to fetch the Temple Guard. Now, just beyond the junction of the roads, Peniel heard the traitor's stammering voice, accompanied by the plodding noise of well-shod feet.

"P-Peniel! The beggar's name. We all knew him. He's a sly one, that one is. I always suspected he might not truly be b-blind. His p-parents will be losing a good bit of income from his alms now that the truth is out."

Peniel, terrified, froze in place.

"Hide!" Amos snapped.

Peniel covered his face with his hands. Darkness! It was the only shelter he knew.

"No, no, you fool!" The dwarf jumped up, grabbed Peniel's arm, and dragged him to the ground. "Get down!"

Gideon clutched Peniel's sleeve and grasped Amos by the hair. He pulled them into an alleyway and thrust them behind a rubbish heap just in time.

The troop rounded the corner. Gideon peeked out and then displayed ten fingers to indicate the number of guards following the hunchback.

Amos nodded. Peniel peered between his fingers.

Zacharias' voice rang out clearly. "Never knew exactly where P-Peniel stood on issues about priests and such. Careful about what he said, he was. But he's made it clear enough now, your honor. Tried to recruit us all, with talk about Messiah and the like," he lied.

A gruff reply. Eglon. "You'll testify to what you heard?"

"For a p-price."

"The high priest has announced the condition for collecting the reward."

"Well then, I'll say whatever his honor likes."

Peniel swallowed hard. Amos kneaded Peniel's forearm. The dwarf trembled.

Another guard with a higher-pitched, singsong quality to his voice: "You say this Peniel's in the beggar's camp? The beggar's camp?"

"Sure. Sure. Under the viaduct. Came a while ago. In the company of G-Gideon the lame."

The bolts of shop doors slammed home; window shutters thudded into place.

"And was Yeshua with him?" Eglon persisted.

"No. No," Zacharias answered.

"But did Peniel say anything about this Galilean?"

"Oh, yes. Yes. Said he's the Messiah," Zacharias insisted.

"Well, then. Out of his own mouth, eh?" Eglon laughed harshly. "The imposter must still be around the city somewhere. Or P-Peniel wouldn't be here."

"So. Takes guts to stay in Yerushalayim what with the chief priests being in such a dark mood. I'll give him that. Guts." Eglon shook his head.

The hunchback scuttled like a crab on the sand before the boots of the police. "Caiaphas will have his guts," Zacharias quipped. "And I'll have the reward, eh?"

They passed the alleyway where the trio hid.

"Yes. Well done, you, if he's caught. A year's wages. All the better if Peniel's trail takes us to Yeshua."

"Well done, well done," the other guard cackled. "To Yeshua!"

Peniel's heart raced. *What am I doing? Will I lead this pack of wolves straight to the Teacher?*

The voices faded, blended in with the tumult of the street. The last carts leaving the city for the evening rattled by, drowning out the last of their conversation.

It was a long time before any of the three fugitives ventured to speak.

"Better a good enemy than a bad friend. And that's the proof of it."

Gideon exhaled a long sigh of relief. "Nothing else to do. I'm going back there. Under the viaduct. I'll spy out the lay of the land."

Amos screwed up his face in consternation. "The lay of the land? What's that?"

Gideon yanked the dwarf's beard impatiently. "Idiot! I'll find out what they're up to, that's what! Tell them Peniel left on his own. Say he headed south, I'll say. Toward Ashkelon, I'll say. Not north. I'll throw them off the scent, see? Then I'll wait awhile after they leave, sneak out, and come back here."

"What about Zacharias the hunchback?" Amos challenged. "He's a jackal. He has teeth."

"I'd kill him if I had a knife," Gideon snarled. "But I don't have a knife. I've always wanted a knife."

Amos chewed his lip knowingly. "Someone else will kill him later, no doubt."

Gideon erupted in fury. "He's a dung heap! No! Ha! He's the fly that sits on the dung heap! No! No! Listen to this! He's the fly speck of the fly that sits on the dung heap!"

Amos' tiny feet pawed the ground in disgust. "Yes! Yes! I wipe Zacharias the hunchback off the sole of my shoe!"

Gideon proclaimed, "And I avoid stepping on him altogether! Thus my shoe is not spoiled!"

These were brave words for a coward like Gideon, Peniel thought. He shook his head solemnly. "Dangerous. Dangerous. Suppose they throw you in jail?"

Amos slapped Gideon's back in congratulations. "I like this idea. Spy. Lay of the land. It's a good plan," the dwarf argued. "Oh-ho! Send them all to Ashkelon!" He guffawed.

For the dwarf to tell a man to go to Ashkelon was akin to telling him to go to perdition, Peniel mused. What fierce and courageous companions he had found in Amos and Gideon!

Tears of gratitude stung Peniel's eyes. "Gideon! Friend! You'd do this for me? And for Yeshua? But what if you don't come back?" Peniel fought down the panic that welled up in his chest. Had he placed the lives of his brothers in danger?

Gideon tried this thought on. "If I don't come back? Then, you know, if I'm not back . . . if I don't come back in an hour . . ." He pursed his lips and stared off, as though he was trying to form an answer.

"Yes? If you're not back in an hour?" Amos threw in.

Gideon snapped. "What do you think? Fool! Then I'm not back. That's all. I'll be back when I get back. Wait here!" He rose unceremoniously and set off to spy.

The village of Gadara was inland from the east shore of the Sea of Galilee. It existed roughly on the border between Tetrarch Philip's province of Trachonitis and the Greek federation called the Decapolis. The bookshop of Ma'im of Gadara was not actually inside the city walls, but not because he was unwelcome there. Gadara was a freethinking city, where age-old pagan deities mixed with Greek philosophy and Syrian cults.

Had this business been located within Jewish territory, Ma'im might have been stoned by religious zealots for sorcery or for encouraging Jews to violate the ban on graven images. He still had Jewish clientele, however.

A cluster of shops and small houses was tucked up against the west-facing wall below the brow of Gadara's hill. The air itself spoke to Simon the Pharisee of foreigners: Curried spices announced dishes prepared for non-Jewish palates. Heavy, musky perfumes offered visions of exotic, forbidden women.

For this nighttime excursion, Simon dressed in his plainest traveling clothes. He laid aside both anything that spoke of wealth or connected him with the Pharisee sect.

When he arrived at the bookshop after twilight, the street was dark and so was the shop. However, the door opened at his first knock, and Ma'im greeted him with the words, "Welcome. I've been expecting you."

Simon was relieved that Ma'im had not announced his name yet disturbed and wary that his arrival was apparently anticipated.

From the recess of an inner room the light of a single flame wavered, casting dancing shadows on the walls. As Simon's eyes grew accustomed to the dim interior, he saw that the room was cluttered with scrolls. Some were bound and lay stacked, ends outward, like orderly piles of cordwood. Others, partially unrolled, rested one atop another, spreading across tables like heaps of fallen leaves.

"Most of my trade is prosaic," Ma'im informed Simon. "Shipping news from Alexandria and Corinth, political reports from Ephesus and

Pergamum, the latest plays from the theaters of Athens . . . broad as to subject matter but no more than knucklebone deep. My shop and the reading room adjoining are a crossroads of the Empire. People from many lands come to find their native scripts, to satisfy their longing for news of home. What will satisfy the longings of Simon the Pharisee? I wonder . . ."

"You know what I'm here for," Simon growled. "Do you have it?"

In reply Ma'im turned to a curtained recess in the wall behind the counter. From its dark interior he produced a locked mahogany strong-box and a bronze key, both of which he presented to Simon. "More significant than provincial news or theatricals," he explained. "You may take it and examine it at your leisure. The learned Pharisee will no doubt wish for privacy to make his assessment, and my accommodations—" he gestured around the cramped and cluttered shop—"are less than comfortable. I have a condition that affects my eyes," he added. "I never go abroad in daylight and prefer dim to bright light."

"What about your payment?" Simon asked, though already hugging the coffer greedily to his chest.

Ma'im shrugged. "Master Simon and I are now partners, are we not? Both of us have secrets best kept strictly between us. It is a bond of sorts, true?"

Simon blustered, "Are you suggesting that I'm dabbling in something I shouldn't? Practicing magic or the like? Was that a threat?"

"Not at all," Ma'im soothed. "Merely an observation. Interesting, isn't it, that your family name means 'seeds,' and in my native tongue, *Ma'im* means 'water'? We need each other, I think."

Time was passing. Simon perceived the risk of exposure yet would not—could not—draw back now. Too much was at stake. Perhaps the answer to his dire predicament was within his grasp, within an unremarkable mahogany box. "If it suits my needs," he said stiffly, "I'll send the payment I offered before."

"It is well," Ma'im returned, bowing. "And may the gods assist you . . . whoever they are."

Gideon the cripple hurried past the dark archways supporting the viaduct. His left arm swung furiously, and the tip of his crutch scraped white marks on the paving stones. Beside the southwestern end of the Temple Mount platform he hesitated. The beggar looked first down Herodian Way, then at the steep steps rising toward the Royal Stoa.

Tucking the prop more firmly under his armpit and clenching his teeth, Gideon began the ascent.

Beside the exit of a tunnel leading beneath the Royal Stoa and from there giving access to the Temple precincts, Gideon paused to rest.

A burly arm collared him around the neck. Gideon was dragged into the shadowy overhang.

"Took you long enough," Eglon growled. "Where is he?"

"Waiting for me to come back and report my spying on you," the beggar added. "He trusts me."

"Yeshua with him?"

"No."

"Did he say where they was to meet?"

"No," Gideon repeated. "If he knows, he's keeping it secret."

Eglon shoved the cripple against a stone wall. The hired assassin grasped Gideon's left hand and bent the fingers back. "Sure?" Eglon persisted. "You aren't holding back anything, eh?"

"Let me, Captain," a lean, red-haired guard offered with a chortle. "I'll find out! Find out good!"

"Not now, Alek," Eglon refused.

The guard's head pecked at the air like his namesake rooster, and his sandals scratched the cobbles with eagerness to cause pain.

Gideon shook his head violently. "I swear it, your honor. That's all I know."

Eglon maintained the pressure until beads of sweat popped out on Gideon's face. When Eglon released his grip, the beggar slipped to his knees and knelt there, cradling his injured fingers.

"We don't much care about the blind one," Eglon said. "Pick him up any time. But if he's got an in with Yeshua and we follow him, then maybe we can slip you in close enough to take care of the trouble-maker."

"Not me," Gideon protested. "I couldn't!"

"I know that, you miserable coward," Eglon confirmed. "But you can open doors, can't you? Lead him off somewheres alone?" Eglon's hands shot out again, this time encircling Gideon's throat. "Not trying to back out, are you?" he threatened. "It'd go bad for you."

"Bad for you!" Alek chorused.

The guard captain released his grip just enough to allow Gideon a rasping breath.

Once Gideon could speak again, he protested that no such thought had crossed his mind. "I want the reward," he said flatly. "I won't fail."

"See you don't," Eglon warned, pushing the beggar away from him. "You just tell me which direction you're headed, and I'll tell you where our next meeting will be. Got it?"

The ridge above the Valley of Mak'ob had reddened with sunset. The starry sky reflected a portent that tomorrow everything familiar would end for Lily and Cantor. Still, Lily would not let herself think such thoughts as she and Cantor stood beneath the canopy of Cantor's tallith and spoke their vows.

Only a few were invited to the wedding.

Deborah, great with the burden of new life within her, lumbered down the slope from the cave for the first time in weeks to take her place at Lily's side. Little Baruch peered shyly from behind his mother.

Carpenter proudly stood as Cantor's witness. He read aloud the written *ketubah:* the promise of bride and groom to love and cherish one another for a lifetime.

The boys of Cantor's hawking class leaned upon one another as they observed the ceremony with crooked smiles on their ravaged faces. Lily knew the members of the wedding company each concealed rampant thoughts.

How long will they have together?

A lifetime? How long is that?

Leaving her tomorrow.

Perhaps I'll grow up and someday marry . . .

Will he return?

Can it be? Might I also find love in such a place as this?

Oh I remember! I remember! My love, I remember our day like it was yesterday!

Yet all were silent as the questions of the rabbi were answered by murmured pledges.

"I will . . ."

"I do . . ."

"Till death . . ."

". . . parts us."

I'm praying again, Inventor of Love. I thank you, thank you, thank you for him!

Look upon these stricken ones, as I am stricken . . . my family, they are. We have no beauty to offer you. No wealth. Nothing that the world esteems. We are the least of mankind. Judged unworthy to live. There is nothing left of what we once were, except souls held captive in our flesh.

And so, praise to you, O Adonai. You have given us this one last hour of happiness before we breathe ourselves out into eternity. Steam rising from a kettle.

Like dew in the morning we pass away. You are the sun that sparkles and warms us on the leaf. You are the light drawing our vapor up and up. You are the cloud we rise to meet.

Gather us in, oh cloud, when that hour comes!

"There you have it." Rabbi Ahava smiled. "And so, Lily and Cantor are man and wife. Will the groom speak a word? A word to us before he takes his bride away?"

Cantor cleared his throat. His eyes brimmed. He attempted to speak but could not. Had he heard her thoughts? plumbed her prayers?

"Lily . . . Lily . . . Lily . . . oh!" His voice cracked, and he could not continue.

Applause, laughter, and cheering from the witnesses.

Rabbi Ahava raised his hand. "For the first time in his life Cantor is speechless! A good sign! Marriage has a welcome effect on you, Cantor! We will all enjoy your company more now, I am certain." More laughter.

"Now, Lily! The bride must say a word."

Lily nodded, clutching Cantor's hand tightly. She scanned the faces of her dear friends. "My family! For this moment we are alive!

And for Cantor, to our friends, to the Lord who has let us live this long, for this time I am truly thankful!"

She reflected that her speech was shallow compared to the great well of emotion in her heart. But there were no words. No words. No words. Only this moment. Only Cantor. No tomorrow.

Night birds sang in the evening. Crickets chirped. A frog or two croaked. One moment whispered into another as they slipped away into the shadows.

From nearby homes overheard discussions filtered into Peniel's hiding place. Unhappy conversations swirled around his head like a whirlwind, swooping up the dust and debris of daily anxiety.

Ordinary family matters were thrashed out: A child's misbehavior. An argument between man and wife about . . . nothing of consequence. The price of shoes? The too-plump, irascible aunt. The too-stern grandfather who corrected the children! The lack of enough lavatories around the Temple Mount.

"No word about you, Lord," Peniel murmured. "No mention of Messiah."

It seemed the Sanhedrin's edict forbidding talk about Yeshua had been effective. Or was this just the natural state of man: ignore the miracles and concentrate on the trivial?

"Listen to them all," Amos mumbled. "The wife wails and the dog whimpers and the child whines and poverty howls! Yet on their worst days they're better off than me on my best!"

Peniel's senses were assaulted by the misery. First under the viaduct and now from those who had homes, who had families. Desperate! Anxious! They all seemed to be drowning! Drowning!

Peniel looked down. His unfocused eyes fixed on the wiry-haired top of Amos' head. He whispered, "Sorrow. Sorrow. Everywhere in Yerushalayim. Sheep. Hungry. Thirsty. Crying out. No shepherd to lead them. Is this what you see in the faces of the people, Lord?"

Amos tugged on Peniel's tunic. "You say something, Peniel?"

"No. Nothing." Peniel wiped his face.

Amos complained, "Yerushalayim stinks. Smell it? Enough to make my eyes water."

Rousing himself from his gloom, Peniel encouraged, "It's cleaner in the north. And I hear in Galilee you can pick leftover fruit right off the tree and eat without paying."

"If you're tall enough," Amos added dubiously.

Peniel heard the scrape of Gideon's crutch and presently the cripple reappeared.

"I hid in the bushes," he reported proudly. "Good spying, if I do say so myself. Heard every word. That Zacharias! Bragging how he saw you, knew you were still in the city. How he could pick you out of a crowd. Heard them hatch a plan: Double the guards, then stop everyone under twenty-five from leaving Jerusalem until Zacharias passes them. Guards talking all polite to him, like he's somebody. All puffed up, he is!"

"Scum," Amos put in. "Sell his own father to the Romans if he had one."

"Sell somebody else's father to 'em!"

"Sell their mother *and* their father!"

Before the renewed competition over Zacharias' depravity could wind up still further, Peniel interrupted. "And so? Did you put them on the wrong scent? Send them to Ashkelon?"

"Yes. Yes, I did," Gideon replied, scuffing the toe of his right sandal against the pavement.

"You talked face-to-face with Temple Guards . . . with Zacharias knowing your name and all?" Amos prodded.

"Not exactly," Gideon admitted. "But I know a miller whose wife's sister is married to a guard. I told him to tell her to tell him to look for Peniel in Ashkelon. Straight-out I said it: 'Ashkelon is where he's bound, I said.' " Gideon, who was by nature a coward, looked back through the cramped canyon of the lane toward the viaduct. "I've never been outside the gates of Yerushalayim. I made a fine living here." Then, as if recollecting the present danger, he added, "Peniel, your neck's in a noose and no mistake. Best get out now, if it isn't already too late."

So back they went, along the wandering path leading to the hidden culvert.

They squeezed through the drain with Amos hanging on to Peniel's ankle. Gideon lay on his back and propelled himself with his crutch, like a fisherman poling his boat through a shallow passage.

Presently they emerged from the confining darkness of the sewer into the expansive darkness of the Judean countryside. Behind them loomed the city whose walls channeled orange light skyward, as if from an immense glowing cauldron.

"Told you we'd make it," Gideon announced. "Knew they weren't as smart as the likes of us. But it's too late to travel farther. So where do we spend the night?" A warm wind from out of the desert collided overhead with the cool, moist breeze off the sea. A bolt of lightning flashed. Thunder growled in the east.

Peniel could see that Gideon was afraid of what lay ahead.

"Don't worry about that," Peniel said encouragingly. "I know just the place."

The choice of the graveyard as a refuge was not instantly approved. "There's good shelter from the storm that's coming. Nobody will ever think of looking for us there," Peniel urged.

"Of course not!" Gideon retorted.

"Are you crazy?" Amos demanded. "Evil spirits? Demons? The demon-possessed? Maybe even . . . lepers? So far we're alive. But luck without sense is a sack with holes." There was a barely controlled edge of panic in the dwarf's voice.

Rain began to fall: big, fat, methodical beads, hinting at a deluge lurking inside the racing black clouds. Lightning arced behind the veiled sky, leaving a sharp aroma on the breeze. Thunderclaps butted heads, spilling warm rain like pattering drops of blood.

"Under those trees along the ditch!" Gideon suggested.

"Better than a graveyard!" Amos announced.

Peniel conceded the point. Perhaps a late-night rendezvous in a cemetery was not the time to introduce their remaining traveling companion. "Then hide yourselves," he said, "in that ditch over there. We'll go on at first light."

"What about you?" Gideon queried warily. "Where're you going?"

"I've got some . . . something I have to do," Peniel replied.

It was their house. Small. One room. Cantor's. Lily's.

Until he left in the morning this would be their universe. As if it had always been. As if it would always be. This one night. This one room. Lily. Cantor. An eternity of love reflected in the microcosm of this night. This place. Lily. Cantor.

I'm praying again, Knower of Our Souls. Tomorrow he will leave me. Can you make tomorrow never come for us? Make time stand still? Give us this moment forever?

Torrents of rain bucketed on the Valley, but inside the hut was dry. Cantor had made it ready for her. The floor was carpeted in newly cut palm fronds. Fresh. Clean. A blanket of sheep fleece was spread out. Soft. Warm.

The two sat opposite one another, holding hands in the darkness.

"The smell of rain. A gift to us, Cantor. Sweet. This rain on our wedding night. Listen."

"What do you know about . . . love, Lily?"

Lily, suddenly shy, whispered, "Cantor? I . . . don't know anything."

"You didn't ask Deborah?"

"I was . . . too . . ."

"Well, then—" Cantor's voice trembled—"I asked Rabbi Ahava what should be done. He told me some. A little. He says that the Lord made man and woman to fit together. And that it's a very fine thing. The Lord made a man and wife to take pleasure in one another."

"I have always found pleasure in your company, Cantor."

"There's even more to it than that. I mean, you've seen the rams with the ewes. Yes?"

"Oh."

"That's what I mean. Carpenter was married when he lived Outside. To a very nice woman from the sound of her. She liked Carpenter very much. He sired five children before he came here, you know? He explained . . . things . . . to me. Details, you know?"

"Well, then." Lily reached for him. "You'll teach me?"

"I will . . . show you . . . if you like."

"All right then."

"Yes." Cantor touched her face. "All right." He pulled her close. Her heartbeat raced as he fumbled with her clothes. He held her in his arms. Stroked her. "Yes?"

"Nice."

"And this." His lips brushed her cheek, her throat, her mouth. Fire uncoiled deep within her.

Through his quickened breath he asked, "Yes? Lily? This? All right, Lily?"

"Yes! Teach me, Cantor! Teach . . . me! I want to learn . . . everything!"

"We'll learn . . . together."

Lily slept in the arms of her husband. Warm. Did he have a fever? She laid her ear against his chest. The heartbeat was deep and regular. How she wished he would wake up again.

The rain had stopped. At the far end of the Valley a dog barked. It was after midnight. Moonlight briefly appeared from behind a passing cloud and then vanished again.

Lily heard the sound of footsteps on the muddy path.

The piping voice of Baruch called, "Lily? Lily? You in there?"

Cantor stirred and sat up. He coughed. "Lily?"

"Baruch's outside." She pulled on her shift.

"Lily?" The boy sounded desperate. "You in there?"

Cantor snapped, "Yes. Yes. She is. What do you want at this hour, boy?"

"It's Mama," Baruch explained. "She said I should get Lily. Bring her back. And get Midwife, too. Mama says she's sorry to disturb, but it's time. Baby's coming."

In the tiny rented room in Gadara, Simon ben Zeraim pored over the Egyptian manuscript. Unrolled on the table before him was a document composed on papyrus with a mixture of powdered charcoal mixed with oil. The markings, though faded from the passage of time, were still legible enough if Simon tilted the page of flattened reeds toward the sputtering lamp.

The Pharisee scrutinized another sequence, then rubbed his tired eyes. What time was it? The midnight watch was long past. Simon heard the exchange of challenge and password as the captain of the city guard made his rounds.

Even with the door bolted and a curtain firmly pinched in place across the lone window, Simon looked up from his study at every passing footfall in the street below.

Another turn of the scroll revealed a cryptic diagram, together with some notations. The illustration appeared to be a tree with drooping, narrow, pointed leaves. One side of the tree was shown with star-shaped greenish white flowers.

Simon's excitement grew.

The next turn of the spiral exposed several drawings of a dark brown fruit. One rendering depicted a section through the egg-shaped growth, exposing twelve or fifteen black seeds.

This was the answer! Simon knew it, and none too soon either.

His right hand, the one he had burned, was considerably crabbed, stiffly disobedient. Simon struggled to hold the page of the scroll in place.

Bordering the diagram on both sides was a double file of hiero-glyphics: falcon, bread, water, sky, life, then another symbol whose meaning Simon did not recognize. He consulted his memory. He thought it might mean oil or perhaps pitch.

Moistening the tip of the sharpened reed in the dish of water by his elbow, Simon touched it to the round cake of dry ink in his wooden writing case. With definite strokes he recorded his conclusions in He-brew on a smooth sheet of leather. Halfway through his effort Simon studied his fingertips thoughtfully, then completed his copying chore.

Laying aside his pen, Simon laced his hands together and stretched his arms over his head, arching his stiff neck and back. The oil in the lamp was almost exhausted. Simon refilled the lamp's reservoir from the jug, though his sight was blurring. The subject was too important to allow fatigue to make him careless.

He'd rest awhile then resume his perusal.

Simon was both eager to return to his home in Capernaum and dis-turbed about the prospect. Discovery haunted his every outing. How much longer could he live in such uneasiness of mind?

As long as necessary to find the way out of his dilemma, he re-minded himself.

Rerolling the scroll, Simon put it in a linen sleeve and tucked both it and his notes into a leather pouch, which he tied carefully shut. This parcel went into the bottom of his traveling case, to be covered by spare robe and tunics, all shoved beneath his bed.

Only then did Simon blow out the lamp. Lying down on the bed made of cords, he composed himself for sleep . . . or tried to.

The face of Horus, the falcon-headed god of the Egyptians, haunted his dreams.

Inside the cemetery Peniel called softly, "Jekuthiel." Thunder rumbled in the distance. "Jekuthiel?" Silvery lightning grasped the rim of the eastern sky with crooked fingers. Rain pelted him and ran in rivulets from headstones.

Peniel's heart pounded with fear. Breath came in short gasps. He recognized the unreasonableness of his dread, tried to talk himself out of it. Why should he be scared? A graveyard. What was it? An early summer thunderstorm was not uncommon. The leper was just a man in a decaying body, not a demon.

A mouse skittered away underfoot. Startled him. The lonely hoot of an owl sounded. The rush of blood in his ears threatened to deafen him. The downpour soaked his clothes.

He closed his eyes, preferring darkness to sight. "Jekuthiel?"

He opened his eyes again just as a shapeless mass detached itself from the shadows under an acacia tree and limped to meet him. "Thought . . . you'd left without . . . me," Jekuthiel panted.

"I have two friends with me. I left them outside. They won't come in here. Never mind the rain. They'd rather get wet than come in. But me? I've been cast out of the synagogue. My mother says I'm dead to her. Can't get much more unclean than that. So, I bought you bread. A few dates." Peniel offered a cloth-wrapped bundle.

Jekuthiel didn't immediately reach for the sack.

"Go on. Take it. You must be starving."

"Come . . . a place . . . to shelter."

He led Peniel down a slick path toward a newly hewn tomb in the rock face. The leper ducked and entered. Peniel hesitated, frightened of what he would find inside.

The leper called to him, "It's . . . never . . . been used. New. See? Just finished. Look . . . there . . . beside you. Still a heap . . . of broken rocks. Not hauled away yet. Come . . . on . . . before you drown."

Lightning forked, striking a tree beside the city wall. The thunder-clap nearly knocked him down.

Peniel held the cloak tighter and entered the tomb. Plenty of headroom. A clay lamp burned feebly on a narrow stone ledge. By this light the leper looked like a dead man, half rotted. As if a corpse had awakened long enough to devour a cake of figs. This eerie sight gave more credence to the myth that lepers were really human bodies inhabited by demons.

"There's a lamp?" Peniel hung back at the entrance, ready to run if his fears proved true.

"The workmen . . . left this lamp . . . burning . . . today. They're almost . . . finished. New tomb . . . carved . . . rich man's tomb. Heard them say . . . rich merchant."

"Well, then. No worse than the rock quarry, I suppose. If it's never had a dead man in it."

Behind him another jagged flash lit the sky. Rain drummed.

"We're . . . safe . . . here. Your two . . . friends?"

"Ah, them. They'd never set foot in a cemetery after dark. Dark's nothing to me. But . . . them? Darkness. A tomb? And they'd rather be washed away in a deluge than . . ."

"Than come near . . . a leper?"

Peniel wiped water from his face. "Well . . . yes." Peniel sank down on the dry stone floor. It was as far away from the leper as he could manage without remaining outside.

Seated in the recess where a body would one day be placed, Jekuthiel devoured the provisions. "Good." He chewed the dates with difficulty.

Perhaps the disease had begun to eat away the roof of the leper's mouth, Peniel thought.

"Good," Jekuthiel said. Then, unexpectedly, he began to sob softly. "I was . . . afraid you . . . weren't coming . . . back. Didn't know how . . . I'd go . . . on."

Odd, Peniel thought. He could not imagine confronting anything more frightening than a leper in a tomb in a cemetery at night during a thunderstorm! And yet it was Jekuthiel who spoke of fear. "My wife . . . my child. But . . . sent to find . . . Messiah. If I fail . . . no hope left . . ."

"We'll go together." Peniel squared his shoulders.

"Your friends . . . they'll . . . travel . . . with me?"

"It's a long road. They'll keep us in sight."

Peniel composed himself to sleep, wondering what the day would bring.

12 CHAPTER

P eniel lay stretched across the threshold of the tomb like a sentry. The night air was cold but fresh compared to the putrid odor of the leper who shared his strange lodging.

The flame of the oil lamp guttered and died. Peniel's last waking thoughts were troubled. After all, here he was in an open grave with one of the walking dead, in search of the Messiah, while a band of cutthroats sought his life. Not exactly the stuff sweet dreams were made of. Maybe Mama was right: Peniel was as good as dead now. A failure. Even if he was able, he couldn't enter the Temple again. Could never sit at Nicanor Gate. How could Peniel be more defiled than this? More exiled from all the laws of Torah? More outside the camp of his people than this? In the company of a leper, who in all of Israel would listen to what Peniel had to say about the wondrous sign Yeshua had given to him?

At last Peniel slept. Rain pelted down.

He was vaguely aware of someone stepping over him to enter the tomb. Then, rumble like thunder. A flash of light. Followed by a whisper, *Peniel! . . . Peniel!* The scent of lavender filled the space. So. A visitor had entered his uneasy dreams.

"*Ulu Ush-pi-zin.*"

A firm touch on his shoulder urged him to sit up and make room. He opened his eyes, surprised to see the leper fast asleep on the ledge. Towering over him was a dark-eyed, coarse-bearded fellow with a shepherd's staff in his right hand. Outside, tethered to a large stone on the rubble heap, was a donkey.

"Shalom." Peniel sat up and braced his back against the wall.

Shalom, Peniel. It's raining. May I share your lodging?

Peniel recognized the voice. Mosheh, the lawgiver. By now such dreams did not surprise Peniel. He welcomed the chance to discuss Torah with someone who knew something about it. Had Mosheh come to chastise him for violating every precept about staying away from that which was unclean?

"Enter then, exalted wanderer. Be seated, faithful guest . . . if you like. It's dry here. But I'm duty bound to warn you this is a tomb. No dead man's ever yet been in it. It's newly carved, as you can see by the rubble heap where your donkey's tied. But there's a leper sleeping where the dead man will lay one day, so it's defiled all the same. And I'm defiled as well because I've touched him. I admit it. I may as well have eaten a whole hog. A big fat one at that. There's the truth of it."

You talk a lot, Peniel.

"Point taken. Just thought I should warn you. Not that you don't have eyes to see and a nose to smell him just the same as me. Mama's right. I'm a failure. Look at me. If my brother, Gershon, were here, he'd know what to do."

Is it my turn to speak? We haven't much time, and I have a lot to tell you tonight.

Peniel settled in, pleased that Mosheh did not mind the tomb or the leper. "Will you tell me about parting the sea with that staff of yours? leading our people out of bondage in Egypt? drowning the horses and charioteers of Pharaoh?

No. No. Not tonight. Nothing so well known as that. But just as important all the same. About the love of our Messiah, the heavenly Bridegroom, and His redemption of His bride. Listen. I'll tell you a story about Gershon.

"My brother? Have you met him, then, where you come from? Is he there with you?"

Of course. But I haven't come to tell you about Gershon, your brother . . . but about my firstborn son, Gershon.

"You named him Exile. Because you were in exile from your family. You were in Midian."

That's it. Forty years. Married to the daughter of Jethro, a priest of Midian. Zipporah was her name. It means "Little Bird," like a sparrow. And so she was. Plain. Small. Lively. A good wife. A good mother.

"Sounds pleasant enough."

That she was. I loved Zipporah, my little sparrow. Loved her even though the blood in her veins was not the blood of Yitz'chak, Ya'acov, or any of the tribe of Israel. Zipporah was my wife, yet she was outside the covenant of circumcision that Adonai had made with Avraham.

"Point taken. Yes. I never thought about it. The great lawgiver marrying outside the Law. Must have presented a problem since you were sent to lead the twelve tribes of Israel."

Yes. Indeed. And eventually a difficulty even in my own family. For now, this is a story about my failure. Yes. My failure to understand the enormity of Yahweh's love for all mankind. My failure to understand the importance of Yahweh's provision for our salvation. This is a story that tells what the covenant of circumcision says about Messiah and His love for us. My wife understood, though I did not.

When Adonai first appeared to me, I gave Him several reasons I could not return to Egypt and lead anybody anywhere. Who would believe me? What proof could I offer? I was not a good speaker. And besides, there were men in Egypt who wanted me dead.

At last Adonai answered even my final objection. Yahweh said to me in Midian, "Go! Return to Egypt, for all the men who wanted to kill you are dead!"[24]

At last I had no excuses to stay away from everything I had run from in my life. I took my wife and sons, put them on a donkey, and started back to Egypt. I took the staff Adonai put in my hand. And Adonai said to me, "When you return to Egypt, see that you perform before Pharaoh all the wonders I have given you power to do. But I will harden his heart so that he will not let the people go. Then say to Pharaoh, 'This is what Adonai says: "Israel is my firstborn son, and I told you, let my son go so he may worship me!" But you refused to let him go! See! I will kill your firstborn son!"'

I was also sent to bring the Hebrew slaves the good news that the blood of a sacrificial lamb daubed on the doorpost of every Hebrew home would be a sign of Adonai's protection over that family. When the Angel of Death saw the blood on the doorpost, he would pass over that house and spare the firstborn children of Israel. Redemption was near for Israel! For all who placed themselves under the protection of the blood of the lamb!

The word I was sent to deliver to Pharaoh troubled me greatly. Who was I to say such a thing to anyone? Who was I to demand that the Hebrew slaves be allowed to go out and worship Adonai? How could I lead when I had so neglected to follow the commands of the Almighty? I found a new reason to doubt myself. I looked at my own family. My wife, the mother of my children, was an outsider. A Cushite.

Zipporah had a good heart. She respected me and was in awe of the One who had appeared to me. But Zipporah was no Jew! I had never explained to her about the blood covenant of circumcision between Avraham and Adonai, nor had I circumcised our own sons.

In the culture of Midian, circumcision was merely a legal and civil transaction: a rite performed by the father-in-law upon the bridegroom before the daughter was given in marriage. The blood of the bridegroom's foreskin sealed the ketubah, *the marriage contract. Henceforth forever the world knew that the bridegroom had made a covenant with the father of the bride to keep her and care for her as his wife. By shedding his blood, the bridegroom took her under his protection. By this sacrifice the bridegroom pledged that even to death and the spilling of his own blood he would care for her. After such pledge any objections to the union were forever silenced.*

This was the custom in Midian. But it had no connection with the covenant Adonai made with Avraham. So Zipporah and my children were outsiders. They were not Jews. They were unclean. I was certain Pharaoh would use this fact against me with my own people when my failure came to light. After all, I had neglected to perform the first commandment Adonai gave to Avraham and his descendants. After Adonai had showered eternal blessings upon Avraham, Adonai declared that "any uncircumcised male shall be cut off from his people; he has broken My covenant."[25] I admit this decree was on my mind as I set out for Egypt with my family.

On the way, we stopped at a caravansary for the night. We were sleeping there in the straw. The four of us: me and Zipporah, our boys between us. Little Gershon tucked under my arm as always. He was my firstborn. My beloved son. I went to sleep, troubled by all I had neglected in the raising of my own children, in the teaching of my dear wife.

Suddenly I was aware of the presence of Adonai standing over us. And this time it was not only me, but Zipporah, who knew that He was with us. She gasped, sat up, then bowed her face to Him.

He did not speak to us, and yet in my mind I heard again what I was sent by Adonai to proclaim: "I told you, let my son go that he may worship me! But you refused to let him go. See! I will kill your firstborn son!"

Suddenly I knew Adonai was speaking not only to Pharaoh but to me, because I had also disobeyed Adonai's command! Pharaoh's sin against Adonai was a deliberate hardness of heart. My sin against the Lord was ignoring the precepts plainly stated by the Almighty! Because of my neglect, my sons could not go out with Israel to worship Adonai! By my neglect to obey Yahweh's word my children were cut off from their kin! The Lord was speaking to me when He said, "I will kill your firstborn!"

I do not know what Zipporah heard in that whisper, but suddenly she cried out! She stared in horror at little Gershon, who had gone white as lamb's wool. His breathing became shallow. His lips tinged with blue.

"No!" She snatched up our little boy and held him to her. "Not Gershon! No! No! Don't take him from me!"

In that moment I understood the grief that would come upon all of Egypt. In a flash I saw all the firstborn children . . . all . . . laid out for burial! I heard the lament of every mother and father outside the covenant, who would, by neglect and unbelief, fail to place their children under the protection and provision of the blood of the Passover lamb! And that grief, that unbearable loss, would begin with my own beloved firstborn son!

I did not know what to do. What to say. How could I plead for the life of my own son when I was about to pronounce doom on all the households of Egypt?

But Zipporah! Ah! My little sparrow! There's a mountain of strength and sharp wit in her name! She dug through her pack and took out a flint knife. She held it up before Adonai and cried, "He is my firstborn! My dearest boy!" With one quick stroke of the blade she circumcised the child. Gershon was too far gone to even cry out. His breath had ceased. He was slipping from us.

Then Zipporah took the blood of the circumcision and daubed it on him.[26]

Listen now and understand! The words used in Torah for applying the blood are the same used to describe the way the Hebrew slaves in Egypt placed the blood of the sacrificial lamb upon the doorposts of their houses! This was the same sign given to the Angel of Death that they were under Yahweh's protection. Zipporah's actions, therefore, were a clear prophecy about the future of Egypt.

I, like Pharaoh, had defied the command of El Olam, the Eternal One. My little sparrow was like the Hebrew slaves, faithful to obey the word of Adonai.

After Zipporah had placed the blood upon our dying son, my wife whispered to Adonai, "Surely you are to me the bridegroom of blood!"

Adonai replied to her pledge with a nod.

My last objection to returning to Egypt had been vanquished. Zipporah was not an outsider. She had done what I failed to do. I was ashamed of my sin of neglect.

Gershon gasped. Breathed. Whimpered as life and awareness flowed back into him. The presence of Adonai receded from us and once again we were alone in the little room. Zipporah took our son in her arms. Kissed his tears away. Laughed and cried. The life of her firstborn was redeemed.

I asked Zipporah later what she had heard when Adonai had come. And why she had thought to do such a thing. She said, "There is no covenant stronger than circumcision, whereby the bridegroom's blood is shed for the sake of the bride . . . his pledge of everlasting faithfulness. This is what circumcision means. I have made Adonai, your God, my bridegroom! I have sealed the contract with the blood of a covenant. This silences any objection to my belonging to your people. I have pledged my life and the lives of my children to your Yahweh by the blood of my firstborn son. By this I am no longer outside. Our sons are no longer outside. We belong to Him just as you do. And I heard Him say that one day He would give His firstborn Son to save all who believe in Him."

There is a saying. You know it. "If a man's wife be short, he should bend low so she can whisper advice in his ear." Yes. I should have bent low to listen to her sooner.

Everything in Torah means something. Every detail. This story about Zipporah is often read and misinterpreted. But she taught me something I would not have fully realized without her: that Messiah makes provision for those who believe they are outside the boundaries of His love. For all the nations and peoples of the world.

Father Avraham, a man, circumcised his firstborn son and thus, by faith, the covenant between his descendants and Adonai was sealed.

Zipporah. Gentile. Woman. Wife of Mosheh the lawgiver. She circumcised her firstborn son and thus, by faith, opened the door for many nations to enter into Yahweh's covenant of blessing and redemption.

This was the promise Adonai gave Abraham through the picture of circumcision: that in a future time not only Avraham and his descendants, but all the nations of the earth will be blessed through this covenant. Zipporah was the first convert to fully understand its significance. When she saw Adonai face-to-face, her obedience and faith in Adonai's mercy were far greater than mine.

I was the lawgiver, yet the commandment of Adonai, which I transgressed by neglect, brought death to my son. The Law brings death because no one, not even the lawgiver, ever kept every law. In the end all we can do is ask God for His mercy. Act on that mercy. Hold to it. Claim it as my little sparrow did! Then His grace pours out life to us freely, abundantly.

Very soon now, in the city of Yerushalayim, the blood of Messiah, our heavenly Bridegroom, will be shed to redeem His people, His bride. This is the price He is willing to pay. Messiah's blood daubed upon our souls will be our seal that we are His beloved—forever. It is the seal to the ketubah, *the marriage contract of our salvation. And He will be our Yahweh, and we will be His people for all eternity. All objection to our union with Him will be silenced forever. He will guide us, protect us, love us, free us from sin, and redeem us from the curse of death and sorrow.*

Yet Messiah is not only the Bridegroom-Redeemer of Israel but the Redeemer of people from all nations who will call upon His name for salvation! Many who are outside Yahweh's covenant will be saved by The Light. By faith they will claim the blood of Messiah's sacrifice for themselves.

Adonai promises to take in all who ask Him for refuge. Believe it!

Peniel considered this new twist on an old tale. The rabbis had never thought much of Mosheh's wife. She was, after all, an outsider in their eyes. Peniel had never understood before. He asked, "You mean the covenant is not only for sons of Avraham, Yitz'chak, and Ya'acov?"

Mosheh replied, *By the One, The Light, the Messiah, all the nations of the world will be blessed.*

"Does that mean lepers? untouchables? sinners? people whose lives are so far outside they think they can't ever be saved?"

For Yahweh so loved the world He gave His only Son that all who call upon His name will be saved. All, yes! And all who call upon His name will be saved.[27]

"All?"

Yes. That's it. Mosheh's words echoed and faded as he vanished.

"But when? When will this be? We're looking for him now! So much suffering to set right! My friends! This leper! We all need his touch! Will Messiah die and leave us here, still seeking him? Still needing his touch?"

There was no reply.

Peniel felt the wind brush past him. He opened his eyes and looked around. The leper slept soundly, snoring, on the ledge. Peniel glanced outside as the rain slowed to a stop. On the heap of rubble lay a lead rope where the donkey had been tethered.

The Khamseen wind howled from the east.

Deborah labored to give birth inside the cave.

Would Deborah die tonight?

The feeble light of the oil lamp flickered, casting enormous shadows against the rough walls. Midwife laid her ear against Deborah's stomach.

The old woman, her countenance all sores and distortion, urged life to come forth. "Yes. Yes. Come on then, little one. Light is waiting. Life is . . . waiting!"

"So . . . tired . . ." Deborah's eyes rolled back in her head. Once she was pretty. But at twenty-nine, she was wasted by *tsara'at* and now further by the struggle to bring this baby into the world.

"I know, love. You're tired. But hold on. Baby's moved low. He's trying to come into the light. Yes. Yes. Hold on, love! You can do it!"

"Another one . . . here comes . . ." Deborah's breath caught with a grunt as the muscles closed around her abdomen like strong fingers.

Lily grimaced as pain washed over her friend. She held her breath, counted to forty, and prayed.

Oh! I'm praying again, Breath of Life! Oh! Help! Help her! Oh! Have mercy! See how she suffers!

The vise released its hold on Deborah.

Lily exhaled and cradled Baruch in her arms. Midwife hovered over his mother.

What more could Lily do to help? Pray feebly. Comfort Baruch. But what if Deborah died?

The old woman issued a command, not allowing Deborah to quit the fight. "You can do this, Deborah. You *will* do it! We're near the end now!"

Deborah, bathed in sweat, shook her head from side to side as she rubbed her stomach. "So tired."

"Don't give up!" Midwife commanded.

"Where . . . is . . . Jekuthiel?" Deborah's voice was tinged with panic as yet another strong contraction gripped her.

The Midwife exchanged a look with Lily. "Breathe!" Midwife soothed. "Come on, now! Let it . . ."

Deborah gritted her teeth, tried to ride it out. She gasped and blurted, "Jekuthiel!"

Baruch buried his face against Lily and cried, "My mama! Mama! Is Mama going to die?"

"No. No." Lily attempted to comfort him. "Just . . . just . . ." Midwife threw Lily a stern look. *Yes. Maybe Deborah will die.*

"Come on. Don't give up, Deborah!"

Lily needed to escape! *She is my family!*

Except for Cantor, Lily had no one left but Deborah! Deborah had taken her in, consoled her! What would Lily do if Deborah died now? "Should I take Baruch outside? Should I? Yes. Yes. I'll take him outside. We'll wait outside."

A single nod from the old woman dismissed Lily and Baruch. Yes. It would be better, if Deborah were to fly away, that Baruch not witness it.

The moon was setting in the west. Windswept pillars of thunderclouds built up over the distant mountains, where lightning forked and split.

Lily and the boy sheltered in the lee of the great boulder, and she held her palms over Baruch's ears to shield him from the sound of his mother's agony.

Lily listened for the soft heavenly whisper she had often heard when she was very small. It had been such a long time since she had heard the Voice. How she had hoped that tonight she would hear it once more!

I am praying again, Indifferent One! Some answer, please! Some explanation!

But tonight the Voice was not in the wind.

The little boy heard his mother cry out in spite of the gale, in spite of Lily's efforts to protect him.

"Is Mama dying?" The child huddled closer to Lily.

Lily did not reply at first. Baruch had seen so much. Known too many partings in his life.

Then Baruch demanded, quietly, patiently, *"Will* Mama die, Lily?"

"No. Not tonight. Mama won't die . . . tonight. She's working hard. Bringing a new life into the world tonight. It's a good thing. Good, Baruch," Lily replied, though she was not certain of the outcome.

"Mama hurts," the boy said.

"A baby. A brother or sister for you. Would you like that?"

"But where is Papa?"

"Gone Outside to fetch help." Lily held Baruch close, stroked his hair.

Little Baruch showed signs of the sickness that had claimed the older brother. The same sickness that would soon carry away his mother and that had perhaps killed his father. Baruch would have been a beautiful child if he was not *tsara*. Dark hair like his papa, liquid brown eyes like his mother. His presence in the camp was a gift to those who had lost everything.

Baruch was among the youngest Inside. He was cherished by all. Spoiled. A surrogate child for those who had left sons and daughters Outside.

Now Baruch's tiny fingers were disintegrating, the bones consumed. His ears, face, and nose were covered in ulcers. He felt no pain, but *tsara'at* had attacked his lungs. It was only a matter of time. He would not survive another winter. Everyone knew it.

"I want Papa." Baruch was frightened. "Where is he, Lily? Why did he leave?"

"He'll be back."

"*Jekuthiel!*" Deborah's cry rang out loudly.

"Mama is calling for Papa. See? Just there! I heard her," Baruch insisted.

"Rabbi Ahava sent your papa Outside . . . to pray in Yerushalayim. Maybe to find Messiah. Remember? To bring him back. To fetch us back a miracle."

"Why doesn't Adonai hear our prayers here? Why did Papa have to go all the way to Yerushalayim?"

Lily smelled the stench that wafted through the night air. The odor was in her clothes. In her hair. No one could escape it. When she had first come to Mak'ob, the smell of others was so overpowering she had vomited for days until she became inured to it.

She did not tell Baruch what she was thinking: that the Valley of Mak'ob was the one place on earth where the stink of rotting flesh was so terrible the Lord would never come. Lily had not heard the whisper of Adonai in her heart since she had come to this place.

"Yerushalayim is . . . where Adonai lives. So your papa went to speak to him there. To ask him what to do about Mama and you and the new baby."

"And you, Lily?"

"Oh. I reckon the Lord stopped thinking about me a long time ago."

I am praying again, Comforting One. When I was cast adrift in the sea, you promised you would carry me over. Now I'm fighting the current that pulls me under! I will drown soon. We will all drown soon. Even this little one!

Baruch's eyes widened as his mother's cry was carried on the wind. "I want Papa now."

"Yes. Yes. He'll be back. And when he comes, you'll be here with a new baby brother or sister. Right here with Mama."

Lily looked up into the star-sprinkled sky. Almost morning. She had imagined somehow that Jekuthiel would be back before the baby was born, that he would bring a miracle with him.

Where was he? He promised he would come back before the baby was born! What if Deborah died before he returned?

Baruch at last fell asleep in Lily's arms. The stars faded as predawn light colored the eastern sky. At last the wind died down. A bird sang from the nodding spikes of a broom tree.

Lily's head sank lower, chin against her chest. So tired. Had there ever been such a long night? So much. Too much to think about. Where was Jekuthiel? Why was he not back? Where was the miracle they had all been hoping for?

P eniel's companions stirred just as he emerged from the grave-yard in the gray hush of predawn. Raindrops still dripped from the tree branches.

Gideon sat up, blinking, his hair sticking up in all directions as he felt about for his crutch. Peniel guessed the cripple relied so much on his wooden prop even when not standing or walking that he needed its reassuring comfort.

Amos awoke with greater difficulty. A second touch of Peniel's hand on the dwarf's shoulder was required. "Get away," Amos snapped, flailing at the air with arms like short, thick clubs. "I . . . oh, it's you, Peniel. Shanna was picking my pocket. Too clever, she is. She can show you all ten fingers and still have two around a coin!"

Gideon rose, stretched, and hoisted himself on crutch and toes to gaze back longingly at the looming walls of Jerusalem. "How far'd you say it was to the Galil?"

"We can make it," Peniel said reassuringly. "It'll be worth it. You'll be able to run all the way back if you've a mind to."

"Yes, well," Gideon intoned uncertainly, then brusquely, "we should get on the way, then. I always like to get an early start."

"Away from Yerushalayim," Amos announced. "About time. Everybody looking down on me all the time. 'Wonder what sin this one's parents committed to be so cursed,' people say! I hope Messiah makes me ten feet tall! I'll come back and thump them all good, I will."

"Yeshua says true healing comes from mercy."

Gideon noted, "First things first. The brotherhood of beggars, an *army* of beggars to kick out the rest! Teach them a lesson and then show them more mercy than they ever showed us! The world turned upside down! Ha!"

"We can be merciful," Amos agreed. "We can be kind. We can . . . what's that smell?" the dwarf queried, wrinkling his nose with disgust.

"Listen," Peniel said hurriedly, "someone's coming with us. I promised. He's coming along too."

"Where is he? Who is he? Are you sure you can trust—"

From a clump of acacia trees growing just inside the cemetery gates Jekuthiel appeared. Though his back was to the leper, Peniel recognized his arrival by the wide-eyed, horrified stares on the faces of Gideon and Amos.

Peniel turned. Jekuthiel looked like one of the bundles of sticks swaddled in ragged canvas toted on the backs of the poorest firewood sellers.

Amos' cry of "unclean" was stifled at the first syllable by Peniel's hand over his mouth. "Stop!" Peniel ordered. "This is the man I told you about. The one who's joining us."

Though only Jekuthiel's nose, eyes, and forehead were visible, the features were misshapen, grotesque. The pallid hand extended in supplication from beneath the rags was clawlike and monstrous.

"Are you crazy?" Gideon yelped. The cripple hastily backed away, tripping over a stone and falling awkwardly sideways. "It's a ghoul! A demon! The only people who associate with lepers are other lepers! If we're seen with him, we'll all be stoned!"

"Come on! Peniel!" Amos hopped on one foot and then the other. He waved his little arms like a bird wanting to take flight. "Peniel! Get back from it! It's . . . unclean! It's . . . get away from it!" For once the dwarf had no proverbs to define the occasion.

Gideon gawked in horror. His lip curled like he might be sick. "Never been so close to one before. Get back from it, Peniel! It's . . . accursed!"

The leper stretched out his hands toward Gideon.

Gideon brandished his stick like a club in defense. "Stay back! Ghoul! Death! Corpse with breath! Come no nearer or I'll knock your arm off with my stick!"

"No! No, no, no, no!" Amos warned. "Peniel, you'd do this? No! We won't go with you if you do this."

"I gave my word," Peniel said forcefully. "Aren't we all a brotherhood of beggars?"

"Beggars, yes! But not living dead! Are you crazy? Messiah won't come within miles of us if we're with . . . *it!* You think the Anointed One of Israel is going to make himself unclean by touching this . . . this . . . thing? If your Rabbi from Galilee would do that, then he can't really be Messiah, can he?"

"His name's Jekuthiel. Jekuthiel of Mak'ob."

"Mak'ob! Valley of Sorrow? Nobody ever comes outside that place alive!"

"He's got a wife. A child," Peniel pronounced very carefully. "Inside. He was sent out by a rabbi to find Messiah. And so we're going. I promised."

Excitement at nearing the end of his quest drove Simon ben Zeraim out at daybreak. He had deciphered enough of the scroll to at last identify the key ingredient in the potion and how to use it. But he did not know its name or where it might be found.

Simon wanted that information and he wanted it immediately. The desire—the need—for absolute secrecy in what he was pursuing forced Simon to avoid the more suitable, appropriate informants for one of his station and reputation. So he went instead in daylight to the reading room of Ma'im of Gadara.

He found the lean, dark-skinned proprietor engaged in conversation with a Greek-speaking trader. "Back so soon?" Ma'im greeted Simon in Aramaic. "Does the purchase not suit you?" he asked, pointing to the pouch under Simon's arm.

"No, that is, yes, it's exactly what I hoped." Simon faltered. "But I find I need clarification and thought you could help."

Ma'im bowed. "My poor abilities are entirely at your service, for whatever good they may do you." To the other merchant Ma'im said,

"Please excuse me," and he led Simon to the dim recesses of a storage room.

Simon wasted no time in preliminaries. Unrolling the scroll to the depiction of the tree with its leaves and fruit, he inquired, "Do you know the name of this and where it's found? I want a supply of the seeds, but I don't know where to turn."

No further attempt to maintain the fictional historical research. Simon no longer cared if Ma'im knew the real reason for the question. "This?" Ma'im confirmed, using a two-inch-long fingernail to trace the outline of the fruit. "Yes. I know this."

Eagerly Simon leaned forward. "Where does it grow? How can I obtain it?"

"Chaulmoogra, it's called," Ma'im offered, "in the lands far to the east, beyond Parthia, where it grows. In your language, *khalav mooglah* . . . 'pus milk.' "

Simon's nose wrinkled at the name, but he pressed ahead. "So far away? Do you—" he was suddenly afraid he'd come to a blank wall— "do you know anyone who sells this?"

The query hung in the air for a long time. As seconds ticked away, Simon's anxiety grew.

Finally Ma'im also leaned forward until his pointed nose approached Simon's; the trader stared into the Pharisee's eyes. "What you propose to do cannot be achieved without the proper spells," he said. "A word in the wrong ear could get us both stoned to death. Do I trust you that much, Simon the Pharisee?"

Grasping Ma'im's arms in his gloved hands, Simon demanded, "Tell me! You are in less danger than I am. Help me!"

"It will be expensive," Ma'im suggested, indicating the sole remaining hurdle.

"No matter," Simon retorted, throwing his hands wide. "Name it."

Ma'im's eyes glittered. He quoted a figure that shocked Simon, despite his fervor. Swallowing once, Simon said hoarsely, "How soon?"

"When can you have the money?"

Ten fingers and ten toes. Perfect. Pink little fists wagging in the air. Mouth open like a little bird's searching for supper. Eyes dark, unfocused, but seeing! Ears like flowers, buds unfolded, just as they were meant to be. Spindly arms and legs. Kicking, pedaling legs; knees drawn up to the round tummy where the stub of the umbilical cord hung limp and useless.

"See how much he looks like Jekuthiel." Deborah studied the baby with pleasure as he lay nestled in the crook of her arm and frantically squirmed to latch onto her breast. "Don't you think he looks like his papa, Lily?"

Of course Deborah was speaking from a memory of what Jekuthiel had looked like. Lily could not see any resemblance since most of Jekuthiel's face had melted like the wax of a candle.

"Yes. A handsome little boy," Lily agreed, smiling.

So this is what Jekuthiel must have looked like. Little Baruch before he got sick. Oh what beautiful, beautiful people they must have been!

"See how much hair he has!" Deborah was so proud.

"Dark. Yes. Lots of hair just like Jekuthiel." In this Lily saw the similarity.

Baruch crowded in to see his new brother. "Look, Mama! No hurts on him! Except there . . . that one there on his belly. Is he *tsara* too?"

"No. He's not sick, Baruch. No. No. Don't touch. Please . . . don't touch. . . . This is how he ate his supper when he was growing inside Mama. It came through there into his body. Now he eats through his mouth. This will dry up and fall off."

"Like my fingers?" Baruch frowned.

"No." Deborah struggled to keep her voice even.

Baruch reached toward the baby with the stub of his little hand and touched his arm. This time Deborah did not reprimand him. "He's so nice. Smooth. Just like when the goats have babies and they're all so nice. He's all nice just like that. I like him, Mama. I never saw anybody so pretty as this."

Deborah's eyes glistened as she reached up to stroke Baruch's thinning hair. "You looked very much like him when you were born."

Baruch chewed his lower lip and narrowed his eyes, as though he were trying to remember the time so long ago when he was a beautiful baby too. "I'm not handsome now, Mama. Yochan says we lepers are monsters, *chedel*, he says. Like dead people—only not dead. The Outside people are afraid of us. So we stay Inside and wait."

Lily sat back on her heels as if the child's words had struck a blow.

She covered her face with her hands. Poor Baruch! Poor little one! He could tell the difference. *Ten fingers. Ten toes. Perfect, smooth complexion.* Yes, he could see plainly that he was different from this baby brother.

"Oh, Baruch!" Deborah reached for him, pulled him down to her, embraced him. "You are still my handsome boy! What a fine, strong soul you have! Just like Papa."

Baruch seemed comforted by his mother's words. He smiled through swollen lips. "Sure. Like Papa."

"A beautiful soul stays beautiful forever!"

"Sure. But . . . will this brother get sick too, Mama?"

Deborah faltered. Her mouth worked as she made some attempt to reply. "I . . . I . . . hope not, Baruch."

Lily knew the truth as well as Deborah. If the baby stayed Inside, he would become *tsara*. There was no avoiding it.

Lily changed the subject abruptly. "So what will you call him? Have you thought of a name?"

Deborah's expression of joy turned to anguish. "Name?"

"Yes. Yes," Lily urged. "What's his name? What will we call him?"

Deborah gazed sadly at the baby as he nursed contentedly. "I . . . I . . . can't think of that until Jekuthiel comes back."

A shadow blocked the entrance to the cave. The old Midwife had come round to check on Deborah. She hobbled forward, peered down at the baby on his mother's breast. "Getting along fine there. Fine, healthy appetite. Your milk will come in strong on the third day and then!" The old woman patted Baruch's head affectionately. "What do you think of this, boy? What? What do you think of this fine little brother? He's a blessing, eh?"

"He hasn't got a name yet. But he's got all his fingers and toes. See here!" Baruch touched the tiny foot.

The old woman interjected, "He'll have to be named when he's circumcised. A fine healthy son of Abraham. Yes. His papa would be proud. He'll have to have a name on the eighth day."

Deborah did not smile. She said in a subdued voice, "Jekuthiel will be back by then." She cast a look at Lily. "He will be back. And then we'll decide what we must do."

Midwife fixed her gaze on Lily. One eye was marbled, white and blind. "Take Baruch out for a while. Tend to the chickens. We must have a talk, Deborah and I."

Lily gratefully snatched up Baruch's hand. She knew what the old woman's topic of conversation would be.

I'm praying again, Considerate One. What will become of this baby if he stays Inside among us? Ten fingers. Ten toes. Altogether in one place on one perfect little person. It won't remain that way if the baby stays Inside with his mama. No. It won't take long for the tsara *to take hold of him either.*

Lily mastered her sorrow at this certainty and forced herself to act as though nothing at all was wrong. Cheerfully she led Baruch outside.

Morning clouds, whipped by the wind, stampeded across the sky. Lily watched them move, wondered what distant places they would pass over in the course of the day. Cities? Farms? The sea? People. Outside people living their ordinary lives would see the same clouds Lily looked at.

Would Mama, living in the west, glance up and whisper a prayer for Lily? Or had Mama forgotten her by now? put it all behind her? moved on with her life? Did Mama smile again? Maybe she had another little girl. It had been long enough. Anything could have happened.

Lily wondered if she should write a letter to Mama. Tell her about Cantor. Tell Mama that in spite of everything Lily had fallen in love. Tell her what a beautiful voice Cantor had. How he sang and sang and filled the Valley with praise every morning! Let Mama know that even here, in this Valley, were happiness and life.

Shadow and light played on the steep face of the gorge. Lily and Baruch ate boiled eggs and flatbread on a boulder. They spotted the old rabbi hobbling up the trail with the new boy, Tobias.

"Rabbi Ahava! Tobias! Shalom!" Lily called, relieved when he raised his hand in greeting.

The old scholar huffed. He was clearly not cheerful. "So. The baby?"

"Strong and healthy."

"New life. Replacing the old. I've come to make the blessing."

"Deborah will like that."

The old man tugged his gray beard thoughtfully. There was something else he wasn't telling her. Something he did not want to say. "Cantor is calling for you, Lily. He's . . . not well."

Lily felt the blood drain from her face. "Cantor? Not well. He was warm last night, but . . ."

"After you went to help Deborah with the baby, he didn't join the minyan for prayers. Carpenter went to see about him. I came later. Cantor became suddenly weak. He's asking for you. His lungs. His lungs . . . they filled in the night. You know how it can happen."

Lily nodded. Yes. She knew. And now the rabbi had told her without saying it. Why didn't he just say it plainly?

"He's only twenty-three," she argued. "Cantor's hardly sick at all. Only his foot. Just his foot. The tip of his ear. Hardly sick. We just got married . . . last night."

"Yes. Yes." But the old man shook his head. "He wants to see you. Hurry." Rabbi Ahava took Baruch's hand. "Baruch can stay with me. I'll tell Deborah where you've gone. She'll understand. Stay with Cantor as long as you can. Send for me when . . ."

Lily brushed the dust from her cloak and hurried toward the hut.

Smoke from dozens of campfires snaked upward to be dissipated in the wind. Like her prayers, Lily thought. Torn apart before they reached heaven.

I'm praying again, Merciless One! Not Cantor! Oh! Don't take him from me now! Not when we have had only one night of happiness! Not when I can live with him and love him and pretend to be alive for a while! Make room in this corner of the world some other way! Don't take him from me now! Not yet!

But when she reached their hut, Cantor's campfire was nearly out. The Carpenter hunched before the dying embers. He glanced up and then away as Lily came near.

"Cantor's been asking for you, Lily." Carpenter poked the embers. "The baby was born and . . . and you know how it is."

Not believing, she rushed past Carpenter into the hut.

Cantor, whose songs had carried over all the congregation, now spoke in a barely audible whisper. Each word required a breath. "Lily. Been . . . waiting . . . the . . . baby?"

Lily sank down beside the sheep fleece. Red hair was plastered to his head. Skin was the color of white ash. Green eyes were bright with fever.

"Cantor," she moaned.

Nothing ever turned out the way it ought to.

"Sorry . . . Lil . . ." He groped for her right hand. Caressed her fingers, pressed her hand against his fluttering heart.

Dying.

"Don't!"

"Sorry . . ."

I'm praying again, Cruel One! How can you do this? Choose someone else to die today! Not Cantor! Oh, not him! I can't say good-bye! I saw Cantor with me every time I dreamed about tomorrow!

She pleaded, "I'll take care of you! You'll get better! You can't leave me here alone! Not now! I had hope!"

"Can't . . . stay. The baby . . . born . . . you . . . know . . . how . . . it . . . is."

"No! Stay with me! . . . Someone else can fly away today! Not you, Cantor! Cantor!"

"Sorry . . . Lily."

"Who will sing for me? Cantor! No! Who will . . ."

"Ah . . . look . . ."

Some unseen beauty above her head surprised him.

Cantor smiled softly. Looked beyond her. Exhaled long and slow. Death rattled in his throat. Light faded from his eyes.

And he was gone.

The Carpenter laid aside his hammer and the Potter left his wheel. Every few yards the file of mourners paused, and new bearers took up the burden. This was not so much because of weakness as to give everyone opportunity to share in caring.

Cantor had been a joy, cheerfulness, and hope in their lives. He would be sorely missed.

Today they all dropped their tools, stopped their planting, banked their cook fires, set aside their lives to join in the funeral procession. Hobbling on crutches, supported by friends, or even carried on litters behind the bier, the whole community of Mak'ob turned out. In all the Valley no one stayed away from the Cantor's funeral except in the cave of the dying, where those too ill to come were tended only by two others.

Women trudged ahead, wailing their grief. Reed pipes played shrill, mournful airs in minor keys.

Among lepers, whose clothes were already in tatters, there was no rending of garments. But something vital had been ripped away from all of them.

Lily walked beside Cantor's body; one hand clutched the woven frame of the basket.

Where are you today, Unfeeling One? Wasn't this Valley dark enough without blotting out the sun? Couldn't you have just taken me instead? It would have been less cruel by far.

There was no color in the Valley. Lily heard words of comfort murmured in her ears but understood none of them. She felt hands grasp hers, pressing love and concern upon her, but none of it registered.

Or couldn't you take me too?

Rabbi Ahava met them at the grave. Already there were bundles of bright red anemones strewn alongside the mounded earth, painstakingly gathered from the rocky slopes. Sprays of mulberry branches, whose name *baka* means "weeping," were bound with clumps of dark blue lupines.

A semicircle of mourners gathered on the dusty tableland. Another *tsara* to be planted in the hope of raising a crop of whole, clean, unwounded souls when Messiah came.

Soldiers were coming from Jerusalem at a brisk march. The rhythmic click of hobnailed boots and the jingle of harness fittings against mail shirts gave away their profession.

At Peniel's urging Jekuthiel increased his pace from an agonizingly slow hobble to a marginally faster shuffle. At the nearest dry wash Peniel led the way off the highway. Dragging Jekuthiel behind him, Peniel sought the meager shelter of a lone broom shrub's brushy trunk. The spindly branched tree spread out some twelve feet overhead. Nearer the ground it was no wider than Peniel's arm span.

The leper sat down and leaned his back against the trunk of the tree. Peniel burrowed into the dirt alongside as best he could. "Elijah . . . sheltered under a . . . broom tree," Jekuthiel haltingly observed. "Like this . . . but . . . near Beersheba."

"Shhh!" Peniel urged.

From a quarter mile away Peniel saw a quartet of Temple Guards overtaking Gideon and Amos. Peniel was stunned at how far this sense called vision supplied information. The leader was heavyset and half a head shorter than his troopers. He was apparently out of shape, since his tunic was dark with sweat. The other guards were the same size and age. All were youthful, with practiced scowls and darting eyes.

Peniel gulped, certain the fugitive they sought was him. And he had only this pitiful, scrubby broom tree for cover.

After a few more paces closed the gap, Peniel saw their eyes!

It was impossible that they did not see him. Surely they could not miss seeing him!

The four soldiers reached Amos and Gideon. Peniel heard the demand for his friends to halt. He was grateful the other two beggars turned round and went back toward the troopers. Several feet of distance might be the difference between discovery and escape.

Fear rose in acrid waves from Peniel's trembling frame. For the first time since leaving Jerusalem, Peniel no longer noticed the foul stench coming from Jekuthiel.

The leper seemed too exhausted by his exertion to care. Perhaps a man already under an irreversible sentence of death had no reason to care what else could be done to him.

The officer of the squad gestured as he spoke.

Gideon waved his crutch.

The fickle wind had died; Peniel could no longer hear well enough to decipher the conversation. What was happening?

He had to know!

The expanse on which the road was built was elevated, Roman fashion, above the surrounding landscape. There was a narrow berm along the rim. Peniel thought he could wriggle near enough to overhear the conversation.

"Stay here, keep still, and keep quiet," he instructed Jekuthiel.

With that Peniel belly-crawled back to the road.

God grant that no one strolled close enough to the edge to look over; he'd be right under their nose!

Creeping in the dirt took forever, but eventually Peniel could make out the conversation. Neither the captain's words nor the scraps of commentary offered by the others matched any voices Peniel had heard in Jerusalem.

How many soldiers were out looking for him anyway? How many

more searchers had the price on his head motivated? Had all the Temple Guards turned out in quest of one person?

Maybe even the Galil wasn't far enough away!

"You two seem remarkably dense," the leader of the patrol observed. "Even for beggars."

"Your worship is no doubt right," Gideon agreed jovially.

"We heard he left Yerushalayim with a dwarf and a cripple."

"A dwarf and a cripple, you say," Gideon repeated, as if pondering the words.

"Don't try to lie to me," the officer warned. "How many dwarfs and cripples do you think there are on the Jericho Road?"

"I know this one," Amos croaked. "Let's see if I can remember how to work it out. It's something to do with being on the road and not—"

"Shut up!" the captain bellowed. A lash whistled through the air, but there was no corresponding yelp. He must have aimed too high and swung over Amos' head.

"Now listen very carefully," the officer tried again. "Have you seen a blind boy—that is, one who used to be blind but now can see?"

There was a painfully protracted silence. Then Amos observed in his unreasonably deep, gravelly voice, "I don't understand. Is the one you seek blind or not? Or is he blind only in one eye?"

"Let me bounce him on his head," offered one of the soldiers. "I don't think either of them is as dumb as they pretend."

"Oh, yes we are," Gideon argued. "You can ask anyone."

"There's a hundred denarii offered as a reward," the captain wheedled, as if coaxing a reluctant child to eat his porridge. "Four months' wages for a working man. The prize of a lifetime for a beggar. How about if we offer to split it with you? Think. His name is Peniel."

Peniel's heart beat in his throat. Would Gideon betray him now? A hundred denarii? A beggar might not earn such a sum in years of huddling in blistering sun, driving rain, withering dust storms.

Gideon whined, "I saw a blind boy named Peniel in Yerushalayim. Begged at Nicanor Gate, he did."

"That's the one."

This was getting too near the truth! Was Gideon wavering? Should Peniel take off running right now?

What would happen to Jekuthiel? What about Peniel's promise to take the leper to Yeshua?

The youth commanded his breathing to slow down and his trembling body to remain static.

"Peniel," Amos contributed. "The face of God? Stupid name for a blind boy."

"Well," the captain demanded again, "have you seen him?"

Another silence. Were Amos and Gideon conferring with a look? Deciding to exchange Peniel for a hundred silver coins?

Amos mumbled, "Haven't seen him."

"We're wasting our time," the captain concluded abruptly. "If these two are lying, they'll change their minds soon enough. Hear me: The high priest wants this beggar boy, dead or alive. Dead or alive," he reiterated. "If we find out you lied, it'll be just too bad for you, won't it?"

"Of course, your worship," Gideon concurred. "Most everything is too bad for us, except when folks say something is too good for us."

This time the lash did not miss, and Peniel winced at Gideon's cry of pain.

But the soldiers marched away, on toward Jericho.

Peniel was drained. Even after the immediate danger was past, he was spent physically and emotionally. All he could think to do was get away from the view of any other travelers and rest for a while.

When Peniel returned from the highway with Amos and Gideon following some distance behind, Jekuthiel still reclined against the broom tree's trunk. The leper showed no concern over Peniel's near escape; in fact, he did not speak or move at all. Had he died? Had Peniel's urging him to greater speed brought on the man's end?

While the other two beggars waited some distance off, Peniel bent close to check the leper's breathing.

"Is he dead?" Gideon called. "It'd be a mercy if he is."

"Can't be much more dead than he was already," Amos pointed out. "Save us all a lot of bother."

"Look there. The embroidery on his cloak. He must have been rich once."

"The best horse is still a carcass when it dies."

But Jekuthiel was not dead, just asleep.

Peniel approached his friends to relay this information.

"You're as contaminated as he is," Gideon warned. "Breathing the same breath!"

"More than that," Amos added. "Don't come near us or any decent folk until you've burned your clothes, bathed, and put on something else."

"I don't have anything else," Peniel protested.

"Then stay back," Amos concluded.

The conference Peniel insisted on conducting took place while the participants were half a city block apart.

"Thanks for not giving me away," Peniel said.

"What kind of friends would we be?" Amos inquired. "Turn you in to torture or worse?"

Gideon sniffed. "Idiot of a guard captain! Fooling them is so easy. Expects beggars to be stupid, does he? So we just let him keep thinking that. Thieving vulture! Must think we were born yesterday. Offering to split a hundred denarii when he knows the offer is for three hundred."

Peniel wondered if this was reassuring or not. How much of Gideon's loyalty would remain if the officer had not tried to cheat him? How long would his allegiance to Peniel last if he were offered the whole sum?

Amos rounded on the cripple. "Who're you to talk about smart? Thought you said you sent the Temple Guard off after a wild hare. Off to Ashkelon, I think you said."

Gideon looked aggrieved at the accusation. "Did I talk to every squad of soldiers in the city? These were different guards. Can I help it if the high priest wants Peniel so much he sends patrols out in other directions?"

Amos processed this information. "Well, Peniel, you're blessed indeed. Only one God, but so many enemies."

Irritation reared up in Peniel. "Even a small man can have a big mouth!"

PART II

Yet we considered Him stricken by God,
Smitten by Him, and afflicted.
But He was pierced for our transgressions,
He was crushed for our iniquities;
The punishment that brought us peace
*   was upon Him,*
and by His wounds we are healed.

Surely He took up our infirmities
And carried our sorrows.

ISAIAH 53:5, 4

14

Lily could not weep. Tearless eyes were the first sign of approaching blindness.

She sat with the council at Rabbi Ahava's hut. The original nine of the chosen minyan were there as well. All downcast. Grieved. Frightened by Cantor's swift demise.

Carpenter stuck his lip out. "With Cantor flown away? Well, it's like this, Rabbi. Those of us with a few years on us—mind you, not these four youths, but the rest of the party—well, we're thinking maybe it's a sign. Maybe we're meant to stay Inside."

Other voices broke in.

"Aye."

"That's it."

"Thinking it's a sign we shouldn't . . ."

"Never was too keen on the idea of leaving the Valley."

Carpenter broke in, "So, if your honor agrees with what we're saying? Well, Rabbi, we'd rather just . . . you know."

Rabbi Ahava frowned. His head bobbed as he considered their reasoning. The old man studied Lily. She knew he saw the redness of her eyes. "What do you say, Lily?"

Lily's heart wept silently. They could not hear her sobs or taste the salt of streaming tears. "I didn't want Cantor to leave the Valley. But it seems to me he wouldn't have wanted the rest of you to give up the quest just because he's not here to lead you."

Carpenter shifted uneasily. "I'm not as young as I used to be."

The four hawking boys sat forward eagerly. Their leader proclaimed, "But we're young! Still strong! Ah, Rabbi! We've never been Outside since we were small. Since we entered. Let us go! We'll go! Let us go Outside on our own! If there's a Messiah, we'll find him!"

Rabbi raised his hand for silence. "Fine lads, all of you. Cantor would be proud of your eagerness. You're sons of his brave heart, that's certain. But without a leader. Without Cantor or Carpenter . . ."

Lily grasped Carpenter's hand. "Carpenter! Oh! Cantor loved you so. Made you second in command in case . . . in case . . . something happened to him. He knew you could lead the others. Would you have turned back if he had died on the road?"

"I may well have done so," Carpenter admitted.

"And if the Messiah was just over the next hill? If hope was within reach! Just a mile away. Would you have turned back?"

"Well, now . . . well, now . . . that's altogether another story."

Lily held up her clawlike left hand. "And if you knew a touch or word could restore this? And the One we've all been waiting for was close enough for you to shout to him? to run to him? to grasp his knees and not let him go until . . . until . . ."

"If you put it that way, Lily, of course we'd go on."

"Yes. Yes, Carpenter! Cantor would expect it of you. Expect you all to be brave!"

The hawking boys rallied behind her, cheering her on.

"Sure. Sure. That's right. Just what Cantor would say, I suppose, if he could speak. Well spoken, Lily," Carpenter said approvingly.

Rabbi nodded.

Lily sat back and gazed down at her hands. Now she had no feeling in her right index finger. Bite by bite she was being devoured. She longed for physical pain. Pain to mask the deep internal ache that throbbed in her. But she felt nothing. Nothing where the sickness consumed her.

"I know!" Carpenter exclaimed. "Lily can go with us! Lily can be the tenth in our minyan!"

Hopeless thought. "The baby. I can't. Deborah is my sister. My mother. As she grows weaker, she's becoming my child. I have no one left now but Deborah and the little ones. I can't leave them."

I'm crying out to you, Unhearing One! Who among men and angels will hear my cry now that Cantor's gone? No one. No one. And so I hold back my dark sobs and look them in the eye and speak rationally when I'm shattered like a tree blasted by a bolt of summer lightning. I will not leave Deborah. Though the hours are coming soon when she, like Cantor, will leave me.

And so it was settled. Carpenter and the other eight men and boys marched out of the Valley of Mak'ob as those who remained Inside gathered on the Valley floor to cheer or shake their heads or tap their temples . . . because not everyone believed. Not everyone still had strength to hope.

And before the end of the day, nine new lepers from Outside had descended into Mak'ob to fill the places of those who had gone in search of Messiah.

Each who entered brought with them a new story of the prophet Elijah returned to earth, or of King David's long-awaited son, or of Mosheh the righteous lawgiver raised up from the dead . . . whose touch could cure any ill.

None of them, however, had ever come near enough to know if these rumors were myth or reality.

Lily tried not to think about what was coming as she worked through the day.

I'm praying again, Silent One. I am the tree. My roots are here . . . now. These, my dear ones, are the dusty soil where my heart grows. The winds are coming. I feel it. Must I live on through the tearing? Why don't you answer? Heal little Baruch! Make Deborah strong again! Save this baby!

The Hawk had hunted and brought back three pigeons this morning. Lily made soup. A pinch of salt, a little cabbage, a handful of lentils. It tasted almost as good as Mama used to make. Almost.

That evening Lily fed Baruch first, sang to him, prayed with him, told him a story, and tucked him in.

Deborah looked on through fevered eyes. The baby nursed quietly. A whisper. Almost inaudible. "What would I do without you, Lily?"

"You're my family." Lily ladled soup into a cup and brought it to Deborah's bedside. The baby was dozing but still contentedly attached.

"God knew we needed you."

"I'm just Lily. No one's answer to prayer."

"Since Jekuthiel left, you've been taking care of us all. All the work. The garden. The hawking. Chickens and goats. Baruch. The baby. Me."

"My family." Lily waved her hands expansively at the interior of the cave. "What else? It isn't so bad."

Two wooden chests of belongings had been carted down from the Outside. Once a month, meager supplies arrived from Jekuthiel's father. A basket of salt, oil, grain, a jug of wine, seeds for planting—all were dropped off at the top of the cliffs. Lily hiked up, retrieved the delivery from the barrier wall, and carried it down.

Deborah told her, "Last month I wrote Jekuthiel's father. Asking if Jekuthiel had come back to him for help. I told him about the baby coming. Asked if he would take in a healthy baby. His grandchild."

Lily glanced up sharply. So, they would talk about it now. "And?"

"No. No about Jekuthiel. I'm afraid. If Jekuthiel didn't go home to his father for help, then . . . I'm afraid."

"Jekuthiel wouldn't have gone to that old jackal. There's no help from the likes of him. Every month for years he's sent just enough supplies to the top of the cliff to pay off his conscience. Less and less as time passes."

"He said no . . . about the baby. Doesn't want him. Said he'd keep sending supplies until we don't need any more. Until we're all dead, he means. But he wants nothing to do with *tsara'im* or the child of *tsara'im*. The shame of it. Disgrace. Even though he's a healthy baby . . . I suppose he's afraid. You know?"

Lily touched the baby's soft head. "Who could be afraid of this?"

Deborah stroked the infant. "Jekuthiel tried to leave the boys behind with his father when we were exiled . . . but . . ."

"No mercy."

"Why, Lily? They don't see us as we are, I suppose."

"Don't see that they are us. On the inside they are what we are. The same. Needing mercy. No different . . . wounded. In different ways. But still wounded. All of us. They want to forget. Not think about it. Get on with their lives."

"I long for that oblivion sometimes. The days when I cheerfully dissected and diagnosed the problems of everyone who wasn't me." A bitter laugh. "If the ones I injured by my gossip could see me now!"

"Eat, Deborah. You're melting away to sticks and straw while the baby gets fat."

"They were healthy boys until we came here. Both of them. They could've lived a life without Jekuthiel and me . . . Outside. Lived. Grown up. But their grandfather couldn't be bothered. Didn't want the family disgraced." She cast a sorrowful look towards Baruch. "First Hosea. His lungs filled. Less than a year and Hosea was gone." As if to emphasize her point, Baruch coughed in his sleep. "Soon Baruch. The baby eventually unless . . . unless . . ."

"Here. Soup. It's good. Three pigeons the Hawk caught today. I cleaned them. Fed the Hawk what we couldn't eat. He was very happy to have it too. He's a useful bird."

"Good." Deborah sipped gingerly from the spoon. "Good."

"Like home," Lily agreed. "Mama always thought I'd make a good cook."

"Your mama. Ever hear from her?"

Lily shook her head. She did not want to talk about what was past. "Never."

She held another spoonful of soup out for Deborah. "Here. Eat. You've got to get strong again. You must. You . . . must."

I'm praying again, Uncaring One. Can you hear my groaning from your distant outlook above Mak'ob? I'm the tree. Things are calm again, for the moment. My branches don't yet tremble. The dust sleeps quietly. See? But the winds are coming. I sense them. My heart fears their approach. The winds. They'll tear us apart. Blow away the only ones who love me. I've seen it before. I recognize the signs. You've already taken Cantor. And when it's finished I'll be the only one left. Alone! The tree, alone!

The rest of Simon's household was still asleep. In minutes the sun would peep over the eastern horizon, bringing a new day to the Galil . . . and a restored life to Simon.

Ten pounds of the bitter black chaulmoogra seeds cost Simon more than a camel-load of frankincense—almost as much as a whole field of saffron. To complete the purchase he'd borrowed the cash against six months' income from his wine sales. Judah of Bethsaida, the money-lender, had advised against it.

Of course he believed Simon's story: The denarii would be used to expand Zeraim wine and fish sales into Damascus. "Things are very un-settled right now," Judah warned. "Passover riots, the Roman governor pulled this way and that by the high priest and Herod Antipas. Lots of would-be liberators running around the countryside and half the *am ha aretz* running after whoever will promise them bread. It's a bad time to be overextended."

Judah was a fellow Pharisee, a good friend, and a wise counselor. His cautionary opinion was well meant, and in ordinary matters Simon would have acquiesced to it.

But not in this instance. It didn't matter. Nothing compared with reaching Simon's goal and achieving the release from the burden that haunted his every moment.

Crushed and then squeezed for seventy-two hours between the heavy granite stones of a small olive press, the chaulmoogra seeds had yielded up their secret. The process produced murky, pale yellow oil that hovered above the black crusts and had to be skimmed off with a silver spoon.

It was now easy to see why it took its name from the Hebrew words *khalav mooglah*, "pus milk."

It smelled bitter. Simon dabbled the fingertips of his left hand in the fluid, then massaged it into his right palm. Almost at once he could feel a tingling sensation.

His excitement mounting, Simon smeared a dollop of oil across his forehead and scraped it into his scalp behind his ears. A stinging, burn-ing feeling followed.

He was exultant.

But the ultimate test was yet to come.

The scroll was very explicit. Simon had already completed the chalk inscriptions on the floor of his study. He had practiced the unfa-miliar Egyptian words until they flowed from his lips as though he'd been born to them.

The image of a hawk-headed god drifted across Simon's thoughts.

Angrily he rejected the self-accusation, but he could not fully eliminate the fear.

Was he playing with fire? Stories from Torah arrived unsummoned for his consideration: Jews from ancient times falling under Elohim's wrath for associating with foreign gods.

The Pharisees scrupulously observed 613 regulations so as to please the Almighty. What lightning would strike Simon for violating the one that read *"You shall have no other gods before me"?*[28] Wasn't that the first of all the commandments?

Simon forcibly rebuffed his dread of a possible curse by reminding himself of his present reality. He stood within the geometric device drawn on his floor and lifted a beaker of chaulmoogra oil toward the rising sun. Reciting hesitantly at first, then faster and faster, Simon's words raced onward toward a climax.

Swept up by the momentum of the chant, Simon's crabbed right hand cupped the bottom of the flask. His left guided it to his lips. Holding his breath against the stench, Simon drained the cup of oil.

It burned his throat as if he had swallowed a stream of molten lead from a refiner's forge. The chaulmoogra landed in his stomach the same way. A cramp clamped around him from backbone to sternum, driving him to his knees. From throat to groin his body went into a spasm. It was impossible for him to breathe, let alone cry out for help.

I'm dead, he thought, just before his body slumped sideways. He struck his head on the table leg, then slid down to the floor.

From a great distance away Simon heard someone calling his name. He could not move, his eyes didn't focus, and his breathing roared, though his ears seemed stuffed with cotton.

Simon, an angelic voice summoned him.

He was dead, then. No doubt about it.

Unaccountably, since dead people feel no pain and suffer no sickness, Simon experienced a surge of nausea. Unable to turn his head, he vomited straight up, then panicked, lest he drown.

Someone gently pushed his head to one side, and he retched again.

Not dead then.

Paralyzed?

"Simon," Jerusha's voice repeated his name. "Come back to me, Simon. Don't leave me!"

He moaned. It was the only signal he could manage. When he opened his eyes, the world swam worse than on any trip across the Lake of Galil he'd ever experienced.

Simon tried again, opening only one eye this time. That was some better.

He looked up into Jerusha's upside-down face. Ignoring the stench of the oil and the vomit, she cradled his head in her lap. Dipping a cloth in a bowl of clean water, she sponged his forehead and his cheeks.

"I . . . I took sick . . . ," he managed to mutter. "Something I ate."

Jerusha said nothing, only wet the cloth again and, folding it into a square, placed it over his eyes.

How could he explain this? The oil press clogged with chaulmoogra seeds was still on his worktable; the enigmatic figures were still traced on the floor. Feebly Simon rubbed his left sleeve over the chalk marks, trying to erase them.

"Simon," Jerusha said firmly, "I know you are *tsara*. I've known for some time."

Simon stiffened, held his breath. Now she would call the priests to examine him and then reject him, as was her right. All his secrecy had come to nothing.

Then why was she still embracing him?

"You wanted no one to know . . . to heal without risking exposure. But oh, Simon! You might have killed yourself!"

"How . . . did you . . . ?" he mumbled.

"Do you think after our years together I've stopped looking at you? I noticed when your eyes were too bright, when your ears were too pink, when your hands weren't the same . . . your poor hands!" Jerusha picked up Simon's right hand, now more drawn into a rictus than before. Lifting it, she pressed it to her own cheek.

"Don't . . . Jerusha," he protested immediately, sweeping aside the cloth from his face with a clumsy gesture.

"Here's what we must do," she said firmly, without relinquishing his arm. "No one else knows. I'm sure of that. We'll hire a steward, place all the business under him. Send Jotham away to school, as you said. Then we'll go away together—someplace outside Judea. Damascus, perhaps, or even Rome. We'll try every cure till we find one that works. Perhaps this smelly oil is it, if you can keep it down! A smaller dose next time; build you up gradually. You'll see. We'll tackle this together."

She was rambling. Perhaps relief that Simon was still living had made this normally serene and subdued woman turn garrulous.

Simon's cheeks were now moist from more than the cold compress. His eyes overflowed with tears. How could he have been so stupid? This wonderful, blessed woman; this faithful, practical wife. They'd face this crisis together, find the solution together.

"Money . . . may be a problem," he said, remembering the cost of just one batch of chaulmoogra seeds.

"Then we'll sell this house. No need for it to stand empty, waiting for our return. When you're well, we'll buy another. Nothing matters except that you get well."

"Yes . . . yes," he agreed, strength finally returning to his limbs. He sat up so he could see Jerusha's face. "We'll find the answer . . . together. You and . . . I," he said. Then hoarsely, anger giving him momentary breathless vigor, "Already know the cause: that wretched harlot, Miryam of Magdala! Came to the supper here. She brought this scourge on me! Should have had her beaten . . . thrown out."

The false coin of energy fueled by resentment already spent, Simon leaned back against the wall and shut his eyes.

Jerusha cleaned him up but made no further comment.

15 | CHAPTER

"He'll come back," Deborah whispered to Lily. "I know he'll come back."

It was Shabbat. Just after sunrise on the eighth day the *chedel* people began to arrive outside the cave to await the circumcision of Deborah's son. Some carried gifts, precious momentos of their former lives, to celebrate the baby's *Bris Milah*, or circumcision ceremony: a square of fabric that had been squirreled away, a coin, a small silver rattle in the shape of a bunch of grapes. Others brought bouquets of wildflowers.

Young and old had come to see this wonder!

Who could imagine this?

A perfect human child born in the Valley of Mak'ob!

Those newly scourged by disease and still somewhat intact stood among those so horribly ravaged they no longer seemed human.

Chedel arrived in twos and threes, the strong assisting the weak. Some were carried on stretchers. The crowd grew to one hundred. Two hundred. By midmorning a semicircle of nearly four hundred were gathered in reverent silence.

There were, of course, others in the large cave who could not come. Some on the outskirts of the settlement who would not come.

But those who still believed that life was possible waited in the hot sun until Rabbi Ahava hobbled out from his hut and called the congregation to order.

All was prepared for the circumcision and naming of the baby, but Deborah was not yet willing to present him. She remained in the shadows of the cave, watching, waiting as the sunlight shifted on the hillside.

Lily did not speak up, but she knew what was on Deborah's mind. *Where is Jekuthiel? Why hasn't he come back?*

Deborah was dressed in the same brightly colored linen gown in which she had been married. She had taken it from the great wooden chest once used for storage when they lived in a home like real people. She stood feebly framed in the light. Her hair was plaited with yellow ribbons and with blue lupines gathered from the hills.

Lily stood just behind her, like a servant, holding the precious infant. Waiting. Waiting for Deborah to accept the fact that Jekuthiel would not be coming.

Lily's heart ached for the young mother and the newborn.

I'm praying again, Unhearing One. Words pour out from the depths of me, asking only one question. . . .

Little Baruch, bathed and dressed, bored with his mother's preoccupation, nodded off on a mat in the corner.

From this angle it was hard for Lily to see that Deborah was *chedel*. *No, no*, Lily thought, Deborah was more like a princess in a legend who had been cursed and exiled to a desolate underworld until a warrior would arrive from heaven to rescue her!

But still Jekuthiel did not come.

Deborah held her head high as she surveyed the silent assembly. Lily was certain she was searching the hills and switchback trails that surrounded Mak'ob for some sign of Jekuthiel's arrival. But he did not come.

Lily questioned heaven. *All these, your castaways, heaped together to honor her and the child. A bonfire on this forsaken shore. Lord! From the shadows of the deep ravine do you hide from us? Do you watch as we raise our half hands to you? Our hearts are eaten away by grief. They are gaping wounds where hope has been torn out by the roots of our souls. Do you hear? Perhaps. Yet you dare not come among the unclean! Do you have eyes that see even those of us who are unclean? Then look at her, Lord. Standing there, waiting for him when he's never coming back. Have mercy!*

Rabbi Ahava, prayer shawl wrapped to conceal all of his face except his eyes, came forward to the opening of the cave. His words were gentle but firm. "It's time. Deborah?"

"Jekuthiel isn't here yet," Deborah argued from the shadows.

"My dear girl—" the old man's voice quaked—"so many good men of Israel have come here to stand in for him. They've been waiting many hours on broken feet. Some can stand no longer."

Deborah pleaded, "Oh, Rabbi! But he promised! Here is his son! He'll come soon. Please, Rabbi."

The old man did not step into the dwelling. He fixed his rheumy eyes on Lily, then made a gentle inquiry. "Is the baby sleeping, Lily?"

Lily looked down into the peaceful face of the infant. "Yes, Rabbi. Fast asleep."

"That's fine. Fine. Nothing in the world so beautiful as a baby sleeping peacefully, eh? The sight makes even a heart of stone melt." Then, to Deborah, "Well, yes. We can delay the *Bris* awhile longer. In case your husband comes back. Yes. Until the sun is setting. But . . . dear girl . . . will you let people see him? The baby, I mean? Not all of them can remain. The sun. So hot. And they all came just to see the baby. Such a treat. Such a sight will never come again for many of us here. They've been planning this for days, you know. There's food. Gifts. Maybe we celebrate before, eh? And circumcise him later? Planning since before he was born even. Will you walk and carry the baby among the *chedel* and let them see how beautiful . . . how beautiful life is? Even here."

Deborah nodded.

By her sigh, Lily knew she was relieved. Deborah turned and took the baby from Lily's arms. Adjusting the blanket, which was adorned with the pattern of Jekuthiel's tribe, Deborah called Baruch to wake up and come walk by her right side. Lily remained close in case Deborah needed to lean against her.

"Are you ready then, dear girl?" Rabbi Ahava swept his arm toward the gathering.

"Yes," Deborah said. "Yes."

And so they emerged, shuffling with the broken-footed walk of lepers, from the darkness of the cave into the light for all to see.

Sunlight shone on Deborah's mustard yellow robe, shimmered on the bands and flowers in her hair. Tiny, uncertain steps on bandaged feet. No one seemed to notice the hideous lesions on her face. No, Deborah was beautiful again.

A collective sigh of wonder rose.

The rabbi laid his cheek against his hand as a warning that the baby was sleeping and they must not wake him. And then the old man made a blessing: "Blessed are you, O Adonai, who has preserved us and allowed us to see this . . . baby . . . which you have formed and made in your image."

Absolute silence descended and covered them like a blanket. There was a hushed shuffling as those in the back tried to move forward to get a better look.

Deborah steadied herself against Lily. So fragile. So near to collapse. Lily braced her up with a strong right arm.

I am praying again, Dormant One. Here they are, gathered, swept together like broken pottery. I'm one of them. What would my other life have been today if I had not been condemned? Ah, well. I'm a clay pot too, shattered in pieces. Some slight recognition of what I once was, what might have been . . . but useless now. No putting me . . . us . . . back together. This baby. A reminder of wholeness. Our prayers are wind beating against your stony face. Nothing. Nothing now. You do not move or speak to me, no matter how I wail.

A trio of *tsara'im* approached. They were those who had been in the Valley of Mak'ob the longest time, cut off from family, friends . . . virtually all contact with the Outside. They were *chedel*, the living dead, in the fullest horror of all that phrase implied. By common, unspoken consent, these three had first right to see the miracle of a perfectly formed baby.

One was a man whose hands were stumps—his feet also. He walked on a pair of sticks tied to his forearms. His brows were swollen: hairless ridges that overhung his eyes. His misshapen head was a ponderous mass, far too great for his spindly neck to bear much longer.

Beside him was a woman. She was blind, her eyes frosted over and opaque. Her face and hands were smooth and unmarred except for her ears and lips. These protruded from her head like strangely coiled hoops of copper wire. Mother of seven children, she had neither seen nor heard from any of her loved ones nor her husband in all her residence in Mak'ob.

At the front of the queue was the longest living resident of the Valley. In the cruelest irony leprosy inflicted, some of the stricken lived unnaturally long lives. The Pharisees declared that sins of those who lived on and on in suffering must be especially egregious for Elohim to lay on them such a scourge.

No one now living in the settlement even knew the name of the old one; no one Outside cared. He was simply called Choly—"Grief"— because he embodied every sorrow, every fear, every sense of abandonment by man and God alike.

His visage was fierce. Hell had etched its image on his features, erasing all semblance of humanity.

The stench of his flesh was like an open grave. Lily covered her nose with her hand. She tried to turn her eyes away yet could not help but stare and wonder if she was looking at the future reflection of her own face after the disease took hold.

Choly resembled someone who had been burned. Ears gone. Brows, nose, cheeks, and chin all melted together in a horrifying parody of a human being consumed by an inner flame.

He shambled forward and bowed his head in deep reverence. From the hole where his mouth had been came this most human entreaty: "Lady . . . dear . . . lady . . . may we who are dead . . . see . . . see . . . this . . . this beautiful . . . miracle . . . this precious . . . life?"

What longing there was in the old one's request, Lily thought. And for a moment, just a moment, she thought she heard a whisper. For a moment, she set aside doubt. Maybe God *was* watching. Maybe he *did* care.

I am praying again, Eternal One! This is myself! With my half voice I sing to you! Oh, Adonai!

What heartache! For this distorted creature to see this infant and remember. . . . What did he see when he looked at the baby in Deborah's arms? Was it the memory of his own child, perhaps? his own son? his baby presented to the Lord for circumcision long ago when his world was still filled with hope? before he had awakened to this living nightmare?

Deborah could not reply. Profound sadness flooded her eyes as she granted the old man his wish. She turned back the fold of the blanket.

"*Ahhhhhh!* Oh! Look!" Choly raised his stump and exclaimed to his blind companion in an earnest whisper. There was a smile in his voice. Yes! No lips, but Lily heard the smile! Choly's soul was smiling! "Perfect. Ah! Perfect! The mouth of him, *ahhhh!* Look! His tiny mouth! Remember? Smooth . . . cheeks, tiny lashes . . . oh! His hands! His hands! Fingernails fragile as a butterfly wing!"

I am praying again, El Olam, Eternal God! This is myself! With my half mouth I praise your wonders, O Lord!

The woman who had no eyes began to weep at the beauty of Choly's description.

"*Baruch atah Adonai elehaynu* . . . blessed! Blessed art thou! O Lord, God! Blessed King of the Universe! Blessed . . . who has preserved! Blessed us till this day, and blessed! Allowed us to see! Blessed! Such wonder and miracle in the world."

I am praying again, Living Light! This is myself! With my half sight I see you shining in the face of a newborn!

Choly said, "Once we were like this baby boy! Once we were . . . I was! Even I! I was once . . . and once I was a father of such a perfect baby boy! Once! Oh, once I was a father!"

Rabbi Ahava cried in a loud voice, "And so your soul is still this child cradled in the arms of the Almighty! The Almighty remembers the day of your dedication! He sees your suffering!"

Are you watching, Lord? Good Shepherd? While you stand back from us and wait in the shadow of the ravine? Do you see us down here? Pathetic creatures. Are we still your flock? Am I your lamb?

Choly began to weep. Soon the entire congregation sobbed, each man and woman mourning for the child they once had been—for what had been lost.

"Oh, Lily! Lily!" Deborah also was clearly in agony. She passed the infant to Lily. "Take the baby up to the platform! Let them all see him! How beautiful he is!"

Rabbi Ahava cried, "Yes! Let them all see that the Lord is good! Let them see that the Lord hasn't forgotten us. That he still has hope for us! Go there, Lily! Yes! Yes! Take this newest son of Avraham! This miracle! Take him up on the boulder. Quickly, Lily! Hold him up. Our blessing! Our reminder!"

Baruch, troubled by the tumult, clung to the skirt of his mother.

Lily took the baby and climbed onto the flat rock that served as a platform for Rabbi Ahava's Shabbat teaching.

Draping the blanket over her shoulder, she held the naked child high for all to see.

Rabbi Ahava called out to his congregation. "*Chadel!* You who are rejected and despised by your families! *Chedel*, you living dead. Look at him! Look at him! Every baby is sent so we can see our souls as the Eternal One, El Olam, sees us!"

Yes. Yes! Lily thought, understanding the lesson.

After a time the mourning subsided. Lily wrapped the baby in the shawl and carried him back to Deborah.

Deborah's expression betrayed her exhaustion. "I have to go back. Lay down. Think awhile what I should do. What will I do if Jekuthiel doesn't come back?"

"Do? What should you do?"

"Jekuthiel isn't back. I hoped he'd be here to help me decide on a name. But he hasn't come, Lily. I have to reason it out alone."

Deborah returned to her bed in the cave. Lily helped her undress. The cheerful sunny gown was returned to the chest. The baby awakened and nursed while the *chedel* celebrated his circumcision, though it had not yet taken place.

Outside there was music and dancing. The aroma of food and campfires. Laughter. It was a fine party, Lily thought, almost like real people who lived outside the Valley of Mak'ob. Joy. Even here. Well. It was a good thing.

"Jekuthiel will come." Deborah stroked the baby's head. "Your papa would not miss your *Bris*. Your naming. He'll be here. They'll see."

Jekuthiel did not come back.

Deborah did not get up even when Rabbi Ahava entered the cave just before sunset.

"The eighth day is almost gone." The rabbi tugged his beard. "Circumcision is so important we perform it even on Shabbat. So. The day is going . . . Deborah?"

Lily knew Deborah had lost hope. She was dying.

Little Baruch grew weak. He lay coughing on his pallet.

In the darkness of the place, with the help of Lily, the old man came to circumcise the boy child. As the rabbi stood with knife at the foreskin, he said to Lily and Deborah, "As you know, circumcision is a future sign of what Messiah will do for us. The letters of the Hebrew word for covenant total only 612. There are 613 laws in Torah. One more than the number for covenant. The Hebrew word for The Light totals 613. Only when Messiah, The Light, is revealed to us will all the Law be fulfilled." Then he asked Deborah, who seemed disinterested in the ceremony, "And what is his name, my daughter?"

It was customary to name a child for some circumstance or event or deliverance. Deborah was at a loss. She raised her head and managed a hoarse whisper, "He is . . . born in exile. To . . . prisoners. Those who are banished to this place don't ever return to the Outside. This is a grave. If they go . . . try to go home again . . . they're stoned. Rejected. Despised."

The rabbi dismissed her morbid reverie. "True. True. No one likes us. Everyone fears us. Blames us for our affliction. True. We're all sure to leave our bones here. But the sun is setting. What's his name, woman?" The kind rabbi was growing impatient. It had been a long day. The baby needed to be circumcised; the rabbi needed sleep.

"How can I name my baby *Exile*? Or call him *My Sorrow*? That's what he is. But how can I name him that? Let Lily chose a name. I can't. Jekuthiel didn't come . . . and I have no hope."

The old rabbi narrowed his eyes and addressed Lily. "All these things? What his mother says? True. Everything his mother says. Terrible days, these days. Dark and hopeless days for us who are in Mak'ob. We are like Job. None of us understanding our suffering. But even with all this, the child is a son of Avraham, Yitz'chak, and Ya'acov. And he must have a name. Let's get on with it. Maybe you should call him Job. I always liked the name Job. Especially after I was stricken."

Lily shook her head and closed her eyes.

I'm asking you, Namer of Stars. What shall we call this baby? Rejected. Despised. Exiled. But also, you know, Lord, you know, he's just a baby. Not his fault, all this. Just the same he's beloved by you. What should I name your baby, Lord? He's yours. You created him. Love him. What should we call him?

The answer was not a voice, but a thought—a certainty that this baby was important to the Lord, wherever He might be hiding. Lily replied quietly, grieving at Deborah's hopelessness. "It's true. I feel it. Yes. In spite of everything, he's beloved."

"Yes. Yes. True. True. Beloved," Rabbi Ahava agreed. "Who would not love such a baby? So I'll circumcise him. He'll suffer. That's true. He's beloved by Adonai. Also true. So what will you call him?"

It seemed to Lily that there could be only one name for a child born in such a cruel world.

Exiled? Despised? Rejected?

Only one name for one so small.

One whose people face endless trials.

One who, in spite of the obvious fact that the Outside world hates him, comes from a race often surprised by divine deliverance!

"Well? I'm waiting." Rabbi Ahava wiped his brow and waved the knife.

"His name must be Isra'el!" Lily kissed the crown of the baby's head. "Yes. He is Isra'el!"

The rabbi pronounced the blessing. The foreskin was sliced away. Blood spurted. Isra'el's unhappy wail announced to the world that here was one more son of the covenant to deal with! As if to protest this indignity, the baby urinated on the rabbi's sleeve.

"Yes. Well, I've had worse done to me in this place." The old man laughed.

Lily felt faint. How strange it seemed that in a society where horrendous torment was commonplace, she agonized over the injury done to the baby's unmarred skin. His thin bleats tore her heart.

Poor Isra'el. Poor baby!

"As if being born isn't hard enough, eh, little one? From the eighth day on, we Jews suffer!" The rabbi wiped blood from the knife. He blessed the cup of wine and touched a drop to the trembling lips of the infant. "*L'Chaim!* To life, little one!" Rabbi Ahava spoke so quietly Lily had to strain to hear his benediction. "You're part of the chosen people now. So we Jews often ask God why he couldn't choose somebody else to suffer for a while? Get used to it, little one. Isra'el. Well named."

16

eniel lay down in the shelter of a large boulder to sleep. How many stars shone in the high desert sky above his head? Innumerable. Displaying all the wealth and extravagance of the El Olam, the Eternal One. A meal for the soul.

Peniel feasted on it, reveled in it. To have eyes! Such a wonder. Such a gift. He considered that being allowed to glimpse creation should have been enough to feed him for a lifetime. How could anyone look up and doubt that a God of mighty power had set everything in the universe in place? He considered the children of Israel looking up at this wilderness sky every night for forty years! Their clothes did not wear out. Their shoes remained like new. And the Lord had provided bread for them every day. What else could they have wanted? How could they have grumbled against the Lord? How?

And then Peniel's stomach rumbled.

Three days had passed since their last fragment of bread had been eaten. Only three days. The pain of hunger gnawed at his belly. He felt sick. Not even the vision of spiraling galaxies and distant pink clouds of creation embedded with new stars could assuage the ache of starvation.

Crickets chirped. The dwarf moaned softly in his sleep.

Peniel closed his eyes, hoping to sleep. Against his wishes, ungrateful thoughts tumbled through his brain: *I'm hungry, Lord. Hungry. Have you let us come out here in the wilderness to die of starvation? Maybe Gideon is right. Maybe I should let them turn back. Go home before they starve. What am I to do? What?*

Silence. Silence. Would the Lord not answer? Peniel faced the worst crisis of his life. Three other lives were dependent on him for sustenance. Would the Lord offer no solution? Could the One who splashed His wealth of stars like jewels in the night sky and poured out blessings like rain upon His people not find a morsel of bread to spare this pathetic little band?

At last exhaustion overtook the pain in his empty stomach. Peniel slept.

The rush of rain, gentle rain, comforted him. No thunder tonight. No flash of lightning. Just a single, gentle word followed by other words. Words like rain pouring out. Peniel strained to hear them all but could not understand their meaning. Too many words. Too many. All pouring out like raindrops from heaven.

And then someone spoke his name. *Peniel! Peniel!* It was Mosheh.

"*Ulu Ush-pi-zin.* Welcome, exalted wanderer. I have no bread to offer you. No shelter either. But you are welcome to share my misery."

Ah, the bread of misery. Enough of that to go around, eh? Better if it is shared. Easier to digest if it's divided. Mind if I sit with you awhile?

"As long as you like. You're good company. Take my mind off my stomach."

Hungry, Peniel?

"Starving. Three days without bread. I don't care so much for myself. But the others. They're not as strong as I am. Gideon the lame man. Amos the dwarf. They're growing weaker by the day. Thinking about turning back. But Jekuthiel the leper? He'll die soon if I don't get bread for him. I'm scared."

I know what you mean. The same sort of thing happened to me when I led a million or so people out into the desert of Sinai. Yes. We ran out of provisions after a few weeks, and that's when the trouble started.

"What did you do?"

Me? What could I do? I was as hungry as they were. We had only just left a camp where there were twelve springs and seventy trees.

"I know this story.[29] The camp was Elim. The seventy trees symbolize the seventy elders of Israel. The twelve springs of water symbolize the twelve tribes."

Well spoken, Peniel. But man cannot live by symbols alone. We needed food. Real food. And there just wasn't any.

"Like us."

Like everyone who lives in this world. Staying alive has some basic requirements. I was worried that perhaps Adonai had forgotten that we were flesh and blood and needed to eat. I told Him as much. Asked Him about it. Explained to Him that these people He had sent me to were looking back toward the green valleys of Egypt and considering stoning me and turning around.

"Sure. I remember this story.[30] Every morning, six days a week, Adonai sent down bread from heaven. Manna. Like rain. Looked like coriander seeds. Tasted like wafers made from honey. You told the people to collect the day's portion in a jar called an omer. On the sixth day every week there was enough to last through the Shabbat. So no one had to gather food or work on Shabbat."

You know about manna.

"A good story for a beggar to know backwards and forwards. It cheers a person up to think that bread could rain down from heaven like that. Every day for forty years. Enough food to feed everyone."

Should I go now? Since you already know the story so well?

"No! Please, no! Forgive me. Don't go. Stay awhile and talk to me. You always have a way of pointing out new little details in what I thought I knew. Explaining what the story really means."

It is written that man does not live on bread alone but on every word that comes from the mouth of El Olam, the Eternal One.[31]

"Every word?"

Every. Yes. Every word written in Torah and Tanakh. Those words which seem small in Torah and those words which seem large. Every word points to the One: the Alef and the Tav, the First and the Last. The Beginning and the End. The descending of Messiah from heaven to redeem the world.

"You must admit, tonight I have reason to dream about manna, the bread which came down from heaven. I'd like a bit of it, if there's any left."

Manna. Yes. Now there's a story. A wonder. A miracle it was. Unending. Shall I begin there, even though you think you know it all?

"Please. Since there's no fresh-baked bread tonight, feed me with words spoken from heaven. I promise I'll listen quietly."

From far away came the harmony of two voices, a man and a woman singing together.[32]

"I will sing to Yahweh, for He is highly exalted!
The horse and its rider He has hurled into the sea.
Yahweh is my strength and my song;
He has become my salvation.
In Your unfailing love You will lead
The people You have redeemed.
In Your strength You will guide them
To Your holy dwelling."

Mosheh said, *And so it was that after all the children of Israel had passed through the midst of the sea on dry ground that I and my sister Miriam stood on the far shore of freedom and sang this song of victory to Adonai. This very song is repeated every Shabbat in the Temple when the drink offering of the festive sacrifice is poured out. By its words Israel is reminded that until the end of time the people of Yahweh will be surrounded by the hostile powers who rule this world. Until the end there will rage a battle between the Kingdom of Yahweh and the powers of darkness, and yet, Yahweh will Himself intervene to destroy His enemies and save His people!*

We departed the sea as the bodies of our enemies washed into the shore behind us. We were a nation, created by Yahweh for Himself! It remained only for us to be consecrated to Him on the Mountain of Sinai, where He first revealed His name to me.

We left the seashore singing! Rejoicing! Believing! It should have been enough proof for us of Yahweh's love. But it was not.

The wilderness ahead was called Shur, or "the Wall," because of the bare limestone hills that rose before us like a wall. In the shadow of these rocky peaks and through the dry ravines we traveled the desolate road toward Sinai. From the watering places of Marah to Elim we rested, then traveled on until at last we reached the Wilderness of Sin. Hot. Dreary. A seemingly endless tract of sand and chalk hills. It was here that the provisions we had brought from Egypt began to fail.

Near us were the high purple mountains of the Sinai range. To the west was the sea we had traversed. On the other side of the water, through the veil-

ing mist, we could just see the green and fertile land of Egypt, which we had left behind forever.

It was the fifteenth day of the second month since deliverance that the people looked back to Egypt and forward to the sandy wasteland.[33] *Then the first murmurings of discontent broke out against me and my brother Aaron. "If only we had died of old age in Egypt! There we sat around pots of meat and ate all the food we wanted! But you have brought us out into this desert to starve all of us to death!"*

Peniel interrupted. "They sound like me . . . or maybe me like them. Like I wanted to go back to the home of my parents. Unpleasant as it was there, it was familiar."

Mosheh nodded and continued. *In my tent I called out to Yahweh, "Hear them? See them?"*

And Yahweh spoke to me. "I will rain down bread from heaven for you. The people are to go out each day and gather enough for that day. In this way I will test them and see whether they will follow my instructions. On the sixth day they are to prepare what they bring in, and that is to be twice as much as they gather on the other days."

So Aaron and I went out to the people and told them, "In the evening you will know that it was indeed Yahweh who brought you out of Egypt! And in the morning you will see the glory of Adonai, because He has heard you grumble against Him. You will know it was Yahweh when He gives you meat to eat in the evening and all the bread you want in the morning!"

And it came to pass that evening as we were gathered in the camp that the sky was darkened by a flight of quails. They dropped down into our midst, and the people ate and were satisfied. And in the morning, when we rose, there, like frost on the ground, was our heavenly bread. When the people came out of their tents, they called out, "Manna?" Written in Hebrew letters Mem-Noon. *Pronounced: "Mawn!" Amazing stuff it was. The food of angels. "What is it?" the people asked. So this is the meaning of manna in Hebrew.*

Peniel asked, "What?"

Yes. What? The name of the bread. What? The word can also mean "Who?" As in "Who did this?" But that's the part of the story everyone knows. Or at least they think they know. Manna means "What?" and also "Who?" But there's so much more to it.

"Tell me then. Tell me what I don't know."

Yes. Well. You remember the people were instructed to gather the manna in jars. One omer for each person in the tent. Now an omer was a measure-

ment, about the size of half a pitcher of milk. Not much, but sufficient to feed one person for an entire day. While there are other meanings of the word, there is no other place in all of Torah and Tanakh where this ancient measurement of the omer is used. For centuries ever after the size of an omer measurement had to be explained to Torah schoolboys. The very obscurity of this word is a hint that it must be important. That it must have some significance not only to the story but also to Messiah and prophecy. Can you think what it might be?

Peniel sighed and considered. "It was the measure of bread from heaven. That seems important, doesn't it?"

True. True. Later Adonai commanded that we make a golden vessel and gather up two days' ration of manna and place this before Adonai in the Tabernacle. Two omers of heavenly bread given by Adonai as a memorial of His provision for His people. But there's more.

"Speak. I'm listening. I'd rather dream this dream than sleep."

All right, then. Listen closely. This Omer is spelled Ayeen-Mem-Resh. Adonai said He would send bread like rain from heaven. And so He did. From heaven He sent down What? and Who? to nourish us day after day for forty years.

Now here is the secret of the Omer and the bread sent down from heaven: Omer has a second meaning. Spelled with a slight difference, Alef-Mem-Resh is also pronounced Omer. It means "Promise! Speech! Answer! Word!"

Listen! See the meaning in your heart, Peniel! Every day Adonai was saying to the people of Israel as they gathered an Omer of manna, "This is My promise to you! I AM speaking here! My Word is the true bread from heaven! My Word will feed your souls as you cross the wilderness of life! Until the end of time there is a battle raging against you, but I, Yahweh, will win the battle for your souls! I, Myself will lead you and provide for you, if you will only trust Me! My Word sent from heaven is your salvation!"

Maybe they learned; maybe they didn't. But this is the lesson: This small truth speaks to us in a big way of Messiah. He is the WHO, the Messiah! He is also the WHAT, the Bread of Life sent from heaven! He is also the WORD, the OMER, the full measure of truth that feeds men's souls. There is always enough to meet our needs and to satisfy the hunger of our hearts.

It is written in Deuteronomy: "Let My teaching fall like rain and My words"—Omer—"descend like dew."[34]

It is written in the Psalms: "The heavens declare the glory of God;

the skies proclaim the work of his hands. Day after day they pour forth speech"—Omer. *There is no speech, no language, no Omer, where their voice is not heard.*[35]

Forty-four times in Torah and Tanakh, the word Omer *is used to convey Yahweh's speech, His promises to His people. Omer! His teachings. His revelation! His answers! His blessings poured out, rained down on mankind from heaven!*

Bread sent from heaven to give life to all who needed it. Manna. The people asked, WHAT IS THIS? WHO IS THIS? These questions were asked every day by those who gathered Yahweh's blessings and ate the bread rained down from heaven upon them.

The answer to our questions is found within the Omer, like gathering a container of miraculous bread. More than just a measurement of man's physical need, the Omer—the Word, the Answer—is the daily ration of Yahweh's voice, revealing eternal answers to our souls. The Omer of Yahweh's revelation never runs dry. There is always truth to nourish us!

Who is our Messiah? That is the question. Yahweh's speech, Yahweh's words—the Omer—contains the answer! The heavens declare the glory of God. The skies proclaim the work of His hands.

Peniel looked up at the stars. "Yes. I understood what that meant when I looked up tonight. Beautiful. He is a joyful, wonderful, creative God to share what he has made with us. Loving. I feel his love when I look up. I'm blessed. Blessed that I can see it all."

Day after day the heavens pour forth speech like manna, raining Yahweh's answers like bread from heaven. There is no language in which God's words are not understood. We in the wilderness ate bread from heaven . . . and yet we died! I tell you the truth: One is coming—no, He's already here living among you—He is the true bread sent down from heaven! He is the WHAT! He is the WHO! Those who eat this bread will have eternal life. For God so loved the world He gave His only Son that whoever believes in Him will never die.[36] *Do you understand what I'm telling you, Peniel?*

"I think I do. I hope so. I've seen his face. I believe he has come down to give us eternal life."

One last thing, and then I must go. Strange, is it not? When Yahweh promised to give bread from heaven, the Hebrew word for give is a palindrome. It is spelled the same backwards and forwards: Nun-Tav-Nun. *It reads the same from either direction. Give is a word that never ends. Never runs dry. An eternal word. Past and present and future. God gives His only*

Son as living bread, so we may feed on every word and live with Him for eternity. God's love for us is a palindrome.

Think about it, Peniel. Meditate upon even the small things in Torah. Everything means something.

"I will. I will. Thanks. And if you see Messiah tell him where we are. Tell him we're looking for him. And if you don't mind, tell him we're hungry."

I'll tell him! Shalom! Shalom!

Silence. Silence. The sounds of the night swirled around him.

Peniel did not know how long he slept. Dawn was breaking when he opened his eyes.

Jekuthiel sat at a distance on a rock. His face was covered. "I've . . . been . . . waiting for you . . . to wake . . . up."

"Shalom." Peniel greeted the leper.

"There's . . . a nest of . . . quails . . . just there . . . beneath that bush. Yes . . . eggs for . . . breakfast."

"Tell me about your life, Lily," Deborah whispered in the dark as the embers burned low. "Your parents. Your mother. Tell me . . . again. What was she like? Your mother."

So it had come to this. Deborah had spent the day talking about her family. Brother. Sisters. A mother who had wept at her banishment. A father who had turned away when she returned. And now Deborah wanted Lily to remember Outside.

Remembering the past was a way of denying the present, of letting go of the future. Lily had seen it a hundred times among those waiting in the dying cave. Talk. Talk about what was. To make you forget that what-will-be was out of reach now.

Cantor was dead. Deborah and Baruch were dying. The baby would die soon after that, since there would no longer be nourishment for him. All hope was gone, Lily knew. All. Gone.

"My family." Lily turned her face to the cavern wall. Images of Mama and Papa and her brothers were clear before her. As clear as a painting. They smiled at her across a Passover table. All of them leaning forward as Papa unwrapped gifts he had brought from

Yerushalayim. A new dress for Mama. Candlesticks. Slingshots for the boys. A wooden box inlaid with lilies for Lily.

"Mama? She looked like me, I think. Her hair was gold. Eyes blue. Taller than me. But maybe I just remember her being taller because I wasn't grown."

"And your father. A good father was he?"

"He loved the boys. Brought them slingshots from Yerushalayim. Taught them to kill crows in the fields. Yes. Papa was . . ."

"And your mother? She'd hold you when you were frightened?"

"Tell us stories before bedtime. Sing to us. Brush my hair. Yes. Brush my hair." The words clearly choked Lily as she tried to capture the flood of memories that startled her like a bird rising up from a long-fallow field.

"More. Tell me, Lily."

"Please, Deborah. I can't. It's like losing them all over again. I can't!"

"But your mother is kind? She's good with children? with boys?"

"Yes. Yes."

Deborah's mind wandered. "We were once part of a great clan, Jekuthiel and me. Once we were. Our fathers were masons. Men of the quarries. Carvers and foremen at the Temple. Strong hands. Men of strong hands. We were rich once . . . Jekuthiel a journeyman. An artisan, they said, until . . ."

"Yes. Yes." Lily had heard it all a hundred times before.

"But your mother. She would take in a baby boy? Child of a mason? Of a great clan?"

So this was it. "You're giving up."

"He's not coming back. Jekuthiel and Cantor are both . . . somewhere else. God has forsaken us. We are the ones who are Outside. Outside the love of God. How can we think otherwise? Rabbi Ahava? He's lying to us. We aren't loved by God! He has . . . forsaken us! Listen to Baruch breathing there. How long do you suppose he'll last? A few weeks. I'll try to live until he goes but then . . . and the same fate awaits the baby if . . . if . . ."

"Your own family? Outside?"

"Turned us all away. The great clan. Wouldn't take in my boys. No. No. But your mother . . . a good person, you say? Would she?"

"How?"

"You'll take him. Carry him alone."

"Deborah . . . how?"

"You'll get up one morning and you'll go. Outside. You'll just carry my baby Outside. Carry him home to your mama, where he'll have a life. She'll rock him to sleep like she did you. She'll sing to him. Let him lick the bowl when she makes honey cakes. And you'll see your mama one last time."

"What makes you think I want to?"

"Because . . . because . . . you've been talking in your sleep. Talking about her. Oh, Lily! Please! There's no other way for him to live."

I'm praying again, Silent One. How can I look past my own grief to see if perhaps this might end happily? And in the seeing find the light of hope that could keep my broken heart beating?

I am a tree, tangled in a dense forest of others like myself. Branch intertwined with branch. All of us stand together. Evergreen. Seasons come and go. Living. Longing. Dying. Never changing. One falls and another sprouts to take its place. Evergreen, tangled, sorrow thrives in the soil of our hearts.

Simon carefully folded the latest communication from High Priest Caiaphas and tucked it into his pocket. He was aware of Jerusha watching him from the doorway. The servants were off to market. The house was empty, except for the two of them.

"You're going out to hear Yeshua today?" she said quietly, hopefully. "You'll ask him? Ask him to help you?"

Simon drew himself erect and snapped, "Ask him? Never! I'll be there in an official capacity. A representative of the Sanhedrin. To interrogate. To observe."

"But, Simon!" Jerusha pleaded. "What if? What if he could help you? Help . . . us?"

"If he could have helped me, he would already have done so. If he was who he claims to be, then he would take one look at me and . . . and . . ."

"And know how you're hurting. How desperate, how afraid you are."

Simon's fist crashed down on the table. "Enough! I will not hear more about it. The oil is helping. I'm better every day! I'll never ask that charlatan for help! Not ever! Or don't you know? Have you forgotten? There's an edict against him issued directly by the rulers of Israel! You think I'd approach Yeshua for help and risk being cast out by our own authorities? Look at those who have been banished! Look . . . even Zadok . . . Zadok is among the outcasts now! He follows Yeshua openly."

"Many others follow him as well. Oh, Simon! Let *me* go! Let me go to Yeshua. Ask him on your behalf! Ask him to meet with you in secret!"

"Never! You'll not go near him or his little band of fishermen, Jerusha! Do you understand? I'll lock you away before you disgrace the House of Zeraim by approaching a false prophet in public! You go against the Sanhedrin's edict, and we'll be dragged before the rulers in disgrace! The Law is the law!"

She lowered her voice to an urgent whisper. "And how long, Simon . . . how long until these laws, which are the very god of your idolatry, command that you be cast out from Israel? How long until you're discovered and . . . and . . ."

Simon roared and leapt to his feet. "You dare to challenge me in this? You dare?"

"I love you!"

"If you love me, you'll keep silence. And if Yeshua is anyone . . . any sort of prophet, he'll look at me and know. He'll do something without my having to ask or grovel! I'll wait and see what he does. I'll know if he's a man from God by how he treats me, a respected ruler of Israel. By what he does! Hear me, Jerusha! I'll not bend my knee to him! I will not beg! I'll rot away before I ask Yeshua for help!"

17

CHAPTER

It was unseasonably hot on the north shore of the Sea of Galilee. Perspiration dripped from Zadok's brow. The old man wiped his face on his sleeve and urged Avel, Emet, and Ha-or Tov ahead through the packed crowd. Red Dog pressed himself hard against Avel's left leg.

Avel clung tightly to Zadok's belt as the shepherd cut through them. Ha-or Tov hung on to Avel's tunic. Emet hooked his fingers in Ha-or Tov's sleeve.

Outside the village of Capernaum, beside the main highway, was a disused winepress. Around it a large congregation gathered. On one side of the road, stretching from it down toward the lake, was a vineyard. Neatly strung vines hung heavily with ripening clusters. Opposite the grapes, an olive grove marched in orderly precision up and over a nearby hill.

Zadok and the three boys caught up with Yeshua and those who flocked to hear Him teach.

From far off Ha-or Tov, who once had been blind, spotted Yeshua, seated on the stone ledge bordering the winepress. "There he is!" shouted the boy. Ha-or Tov's joyful cry matched the exuberance of his curly, red hair.

Avel focused where his friend pointed. Yes. Yeshua. The Teacher was deeply involved in a discussion. Most of His audience were *am ha aretz*. A few were richly dressed Pharisees.

"We won't interrupt him, boys," Zadok warned as they approached near enough to hear the discussion.

Avel tugged Zadok's sleeve. Though everyone else's attention centered on Yeshua, Judas Iscariot fixed his focus on Avel and detached himself from the group around the Teacher. It was clear Judas had not noticed Zadok, only the boys.

"Master Zadok," Avel said urgently. "That man—Judas—was with bar Abba. Before we came to live with you, we saw him with the rebels."

"Aye?" Zadok sized Judas up. "He looks too soft to be much trouble."

"He . . . he scares me!"

"Us," Ha-or Tov corrected. "He scares us."

Emet nodded vigorously.

"Only way to meet trouble," Zadok instructed, "is head-on. But y' boys just stay here beside me."

Red Dog bristled and growled as Judas came near.

"Get by, dog," the old shepherd instructed the animal. "I can handle this fox without your help."

Red Dog stood down, taking his place close at Avel's heel.

Judas' jaw clenched as he neared the boys. He stopped short as Zadok stepped between him and Avel.

"Looking for someone?" Zadok challenged.

"Shalom." Judas cleared his throat nervously. "Chief Shepherd Zadok, aren't you?"

"Was. Was Chief Shepherd in Beth-lehem." Zadok peered at the well-groomed disciple in warning. "Now me and my boys, we've come to join Yeshua. Aye. Me *and* my boys." One of Zadok's brawny hands rested on Avel's shoulder and another on Ha-or Tov, while smaller Emet was sandwiched in between them. "But then," he added, "y' have met my boys before, haven't y'?"

"Yes, well . . ."

"They tell me y' were in the camp of bar Abba. Hadn't heard that before."

Judas stammered again. "I-it's been a while."

Zadok continued, "Makes no difference to me . . . so long as a man's true and trustworthy. There's many who want the kingdom restored to Israel. My boys were in bar Abba's camp themselves before they came to their senses."

Judas began again. "Bar Abba wanted to force Yeshua to proclaim his kingship. I was . . . a sort of go-between. Nothing more. A messenger boy. But of course Yeshua won't hear of it. And since the violence, I won't have anything to do with bar Abba anymore."

Zadok glared into Judas' eyes. After a moment Judas turned his gaze away.

"Just so y' heard me," Zadok added. "These boys are mine, eh? Yer background's yer own affair. But trouble these little ones and y' answer to me."

"Trouble? No!" Judas protested. "I recognized them. Just wanted to say it's fortunate they escaped bar Abba's men unharmed. Some of the rebels are utterly ruthless and bloodthirsty, not to be trusted." Judas glanced at Avel. "That's all. Not to be trusted . . . some of them."

"Thanks for the warning," Zadok drawled. "Come on, boys." Zadok herded the trio closer to Yeshua.

The ongoing discussion bordered on hostility.

"You must show us a miraculous sign," prompted a Pharisee whose leather gloves were a clear enough sign that he did not wish to be contaminated by those he stood among.

At the sight of the Pharisee, Zadok halted mid-stride and blanched. "So, Simon ben Zeraim has found his way to the Teacher. It's certain he's not here to be taught."

Avel glanced up at the old man. Was that anger in his voice?

"Yes," a sturdy farmer agreed with the Pharisee. "If you want the people to believe in you, show us a sign. What'll you do for us?"

With a hint of slyness in his manner Simon suggested, "After all, our ancestors ate manna while they journeyed through the wilderness! As the Scriptures say, *'Mosheh gave them bread from heaven to eat.'*"[37]

"I know what he wants," Avel hissed to Ha-or Tov. "We saw Yeshua feed all those people with our barley loaves and dried fish. They want him to feed them again."

"Shh!" Zadok cautioned. Then, bending near Avel's ear, the old shepherd admitted, "Some folk want him to feed them *every* day. Back to the wilderness, ha! Never work again, they mean! Paradise on earth."

Yeshua spoke. "I tell you the truth. It wasn't Mosheh who gave them bread from heaven. Manna was a gift from my Father. And now he offers you the true bread from heaven."[38]

"What's this? What's this?" challenged the Pharisee.

Yeshua replied, "The true bread of God is the one who comes down from heaven and gives life to the world. To life!"[39]

A ripple of confused questioning ran through the crowd, mixed with appreciative laughter. The word for bread, *lechem*, sounded very much like the toast *L'Chaim*, "to life."

"By the *lechem* of God, God offers *L'Chaim* to the world," whispered Zadok admiringly. "A wordplay. Quite a good one. He's tying the opposition in knots."

Simon the Pharisee continued the discussion. Undisguised disgust was in his eyes. "What do you mean, 'The bread of God is the one who comes down from heaven'? What's that supposed to mean?"

It occurred to Avel that the Pharisee wanted to goad Yeshua into performing a magic trick.

The second interrogator continued, "Sir, give us that bread!"

The farmer concurred. "Yes! Give us that bread every day of our lives!"[40]

Zadok nudged Avel, and when the boy looked up, the old man gave a solemn wink.

But Yeshua had His own agenda for this debate, Avel noted. Continuing, the Teacher stated, "I am the bread of life. No one who comes to me will ever be hungry again. Those who believe in me will never thirst."[41]

Yeshua continued to expound on this theme, but only the nearest rank of His audience heard Him because of the muttering of the rest. The uproar that followed Yeshua's connection of Himself to the bread of life included angry shouts.

Simon, the well-dressed Pharisee, said loudly enough for everyone to hear, "Who's this? What? Does he think he's Mosheh leading us through the wilderness? He's a nobody! Yeshua, the son of Yosef the carpenter. We know his father and mother. How can he say, 'I came down from heaven'?"

Avel studied the features of the obviously wealthy Pharisee, noting again that Zadok continued to pay particular attention to the same man.

Raising his voice to be heard over the tumult, Yeshua added, "I assure you, anyone who believes in me already has *eternal* life. Yes, I am the bread of life. Your ancestors—" Yeshua confronted the Pharisee again, head-to-head—"yes, your ancestors ate manna in the wilderness, but they all died! Only the true bread of heaven gives eternal life to everyone who eats it. I am the living bread that came down out of heaven. Anyone who devours this bread will live forever. The bread is my flesh, offered so the world may live."[42]

"What?" the Pharisee demanded in outraged tones.

"What's this?" the farmer asked a Torah scholar. "How can a man give us his flesh to eat and call himself bread?"[43]

"Don't be daft," another observer interjected. "He doesn't mean his body. I mean, I don't know what he means, but he doesn't mean that!"

"Another wordplay," Zadok explained to the boys. "Listen to his words. *Lacham*, 'devour.' Yeshua doesn't just say 'eat.' *Lacham—lechem—L'Chaim*. Devour the bread in order to have eternal life. But he also means *his* life," Zadok rumbled.

Yeshua elaborated, "For my flesh is true food, and my blood is true drink. All who eat my flesh and drink my blood remain in me, and I in them . . . those who partake of me will live because of me."[44]

"Drink his blood!"

"Pagan evil! Grotesque!" The Pharisee pushed angrily through the crowd and set out down the road, shaking his head and waving his gloved hands in an elaborate show of exasperation.

The cloth dyer and the farmer likewise backed away from Yeshua. The size of the crowd shrank, as from the outside knots of two and three melted away.

"Drink, yes, but not just a hasty swallow," Zadok mused. "Not *shaqah*, but *shathah*—drink deeply, fill yerself up completely with his life."

Avel heard John, Yeshua's coarse-bearded, broken-nosed talmidim, say to his stocky, quieter brother Ya'acov, "What's he talking about? This is very hard to understand."[45]

"How can anyone accept it?" brawny, bull-like disciple Shim'on added.

"What's the problem?" Emet asked Zadok. "Why's everybody leaving?"

"Those who don't care what he says are disappointed because he won't feed them for free," Zadok explained as they moved forward against the retreating flow. "And those who actually listen to him don't like it because he's made himself greater than Mosheh. The lawgiver never claimed he came down from heaven, only that he was sent. But Yeshua just did. Said he descended from heaven like manna to feed our souls. Called himself manna, the bread from heaven that fed the children of Israel for forty years in the wilderness. They judge him badly because of something they don't understand. When he says 'eat his flesh and drink his blood,' he means to fill yerself up completely with him . . . his life . . . his teaching . . . his Spirit. Aye. He's telling them plainly who he is. The Anointed One of Adonai. Born in Beth-lehem, the 'House of Bread.' He is the Bread of Life. But they'll have none of it."

Zadok halted, waiting for Yeshua to see him.

Turning to the brawny fisherman Shim'on, Yeshua asked, "Are you going to leave too?"[46]

Frowning around at the others, as if daring any of them to challenge him, Shim'on said forcefully, "Lord, who else would we go to? You're the only one who has words that give eternal life. We believe"—the burly fisherman stopped, then corrected himself—"we *know* you are the Holy One of God."

Avel saw Yeshua nod and clap Shim'on on the shoulder.

Then Yeshua said, "I chose the twelve of you. But even so, one of you is a devil." The last phrase was said lightly, casually, and Shim'on and the Zebedee brothers laughed as if it were a good-natured jest.

But Avel noticed that Yeshua's intense gaze rested briefly on Judas. Judas looked quickly away, then raised his hand as if greeting someone across the field. A flash and he melted into the crowd.

Avel shuddered, wondering if Judas was hurrying off to meet someone. Perhaps a member of the rebel band?

"Come on, boy," Zadok comforted Avel. "It's not polite to stare."

"Even if you're staring at a snake?"

Zadok chuckled. "You're safe. I've got my eye on him. Even if it's only one eye, I'll keep sharp watch on that one." His gaze followed the retreating Pharisee. "And I'm watching others as well."

And then Yeshua's face broke into a smile. He rose and called out as He advanced through the group with His hand extended, "Zadok! My friend! You're a long way from home. You and the boys!" He mussed

Avel's hair and tapped Ha-or Tov and Emet each on the shoulder affectionately.

Zadok smiled with relief for the first time in days. "I've left Migdal Eder at the urging of Caiaphas and with the sword of Eglon at my back. Y' have powerful enemies. They hate even the sound of yer name. I spoke yer name boldly. Told of the night of yer birth. And so, here we are. Like yer talmidim, I didn't know where else to go but here. To y'."

Yeshua embraced the old man. "Zadok. I'm glad you've come. Yes, old friend. I am glad to see your face again."

Avel lay near the fire, his arm encircling the ruff of Red Dog. There was comfort in the nearness of the animal. Somehow Zadok sensed the boy's need for that comfort and allowed the creature to remain close by.

That night, around the campfire, word came that Yeshua and the talmidim, as well as those of His other followers who remained with Him, would leave on a journey out of the Galil and into Gentile territory. Avel wondered if the change of location was prompted by Zadok's warning about Caiaphas and the possibility of Eglon's pursuit. Did the challenge of Simon the Pharisee have anything to do with it? Avel had heard that there were many who reported directly back to the high priest. And now Herod Antipas had also returned to his palace in the Galil. Slipping out of the Jewish province altogether seemed to Avel like a good idea.

The trio of boys snuggled near to the campfire. Firelight deepened the scars on Zadok's weather-beaten face. The old shepherd stirred up the embers and stared in silent contemplation at the orange glow.

Avel ventured, "Why do so many people hate Yeshua?"

Zadok shook his head. "Never mind. Aye, boy. It's all coming to pass as it was written in Torah long ago. What will be is written. And them as seek to silence Yeshua may as well throw stones at the sun to keep it from rising."

"So many left him today. They won't follow him again, will they?"

"Not surprising. Aye. Caiaphas and his band don't believe in life after this life. And all Herod Antipas can think about is his own power. To that end both factions are bound by oath to trap Yeshua. Or to kill him. To do harm to his reputation. Yeshua has said now, straight-out, that he's the Bread of Life. So he is. And also the Lamb of God. He'll feed all who call on his name. We shepherds knew the meaning of it from the first night. He is the true Manna from heaven."

"Why does that make them so angry?"

"Because he is not only our Manna; he is the Omer, the full measure of Yahweh's truth offered freely, like manna, to feed mankind. He alone can fill our hungry souls. All truth and righteousness in this life and the life to come must be measured by Yeshua's life and words. He is the full Omer of spiritual manna come down from heaven. Anything less than his righteousness is a counterfeit. Those who live for themselves and not for God can never measure up. Yeshua is a reminder of how empty our hearts truly are unless God fills them."

"It seems like they would want to be like him."

Zadok tossed another stick onto the flames. "Aye. So it would seem. But these fellows serve no god but their pride. They make a big show of their religion so everyone can admire them. They heap rules upon rules when the truth is, the true bread God offers mankind is a simple fare. Humble. *'Love the Lord with all your heart . . . and your neighbor as yourself.'* [47] Aye. If we all followed that command with all our hearts, minds, and strength, that's bread enough to feed the whole world every day. No one on earth would ever go hungry or live out a life of loneliness if this was the bread we broke and shared together. That is what Yeshua is. Manna from heaven. Enough love and mercy for everyone. Enough to go around. Those who gather much have just as much as those who gather little."

"When I was a beggar I was happy to have bread three times a day. Just bread." Avel remembered hoarding a loaf, making it last because he did not know if there would be enough for tomorrow.

"Aye. Just so," Zadok praised. "The Lord nourishes the humble soul with the simple bread of his love. The proud man, like that Pharisee we heard today, feasts on other things. Aye. I know that fellow. I wonder what sort of sign he wanted from Yeshua. Something to do with himself, no doubt, for that's the only petition a man like him knows how to present."

Avel considered Zadok's words for a time. "What should we ask for? If we ask anything at all?"

"That the will of the Lord will be done in our lives. Aye. God's will for us is never wrong. Never. The Lord feeds the humble man because he loves us. If we make the Lord as much a part of our daily lives as eating, then truly he is our 'bread of life.' Y' heard Yeshua apply that name to himself. Has he not proved the truth of it by the Omer, the measurement of his words and deeds? Anyone who calls himself 'the bread of heaven' must be measured, judged, by the Omer, the standard of God's Word. That is what the Torah scholars in the crowd objected to . . . and so do Herod Antipas and Caiaphas and the Sanhedrin: Because, in every way, Yeshua measures up! Yeshua is truly the bread sent down from heaven. His words spoken to us are the daily Omer, the exact measure that feeds our souls. It doesn't take a doctor of the law to understand what Yeshua meant. Now, get some sleep. There's a long road ahead of us."

It seemed to Avel that it might also be a difficult road. Dreams of Eglon, the high priest Caiaphas, and Judas Iscariot tumbled together through Avel's sleep.

It was not a restful night.

It was no good trying to go farther. Jekuthiel was exhausted, barely able to put together three steps in a row without stopping to rest. Nor was he the only member of Peniel's straggling band to feel a need.

"What about food?" Gideon yelled from a hundred yards back.

"Don't have any," Peniel returned. "You?"

"How'd you expect us to eat?" Amos challenged in his implausibly deep voice coming from his child-sized body. "No place to buy from if we had money, which we don't! No one to beg from! God should bless me so I don't need to eat!"

Since turning aside from the main road in fear of the guards' return, the quartet of beggars had seen no other travelers on the chosen byway. Recent rains had muddied the path, and it displayed no footprints.

"So this miracle worker of yours can make bread?" Gideon challenged. "You didn't make him show you how? You bring us out here to starve?"

"I . . . think," Jekuthiel observed, leaning on his staff, "there's an orchard down . . . there." He gestured with his walking stick toward dark green treetops just visible above a neighboring ridge. "Maybe . . . we can . . . find something."

Just where the footpath negotiated a horseshoe bend around the slope stood a massive fig tree. It loomed large against the hill, away from the other trees, as if planted as a representative—a model of how fig trees were supposed to look.

Peniel ran toward it, passing Jekuthiel. Here they would find food! The tree was rounded, in full leaf, possessing the glory of early summer foliage . . . and bare of any fruit.

Peniel was bitterly disappointed.

"Don't . . . worry," Jekuthiel puffed, coming alongside. "Trees off . . . by themselves . . . often . . . don't bear fruit. The others . . . will have."

How did a leper know that? Peniel wondered. What chance did someone who slept in graveyards have to learn anything about farming?

But Jekuthiel was right. Below the brow of the knoll were orderly rows of trees. The thunderstorm had battered the orchard. The ground was littered with greenish purple figs and a swarm of rust-and-orange butterflies. Disturbed by humans, insects fluttered aloft, like a cloud of fallen leaves trying to reattach themselves to the trees.

Gideon arrived, scooped up an armful of figs, and bit down on one. "Ha!" he shouted.

"Good?" Amos selected one for himself.

"Terrible! Hard! Sour!"

"Wait . . . watch a . . . minute," Jekuthiel instructed.

"Watch what?" Gideon asked doubtfully.

"Watch."

Presently the flock of butterflies settled to the ground again, flitting amongst and bouncing up and down on the fig bulbs. "Watch . . . them," Jekuthiel said. "If they . . . come back . . . to the same fig . . . more than once . . . it's ripe."

Amos brushed aside two sets of russet wings to pluck a piece of fruit from the ground. Sniffing it suspiciously, he took a bite. "Right!" He stuffed half in his mouth and reached for another. "Where the flies swarm there is honey . . . well? True with figs and butterflies, eh?"

"How does a . . . I mean, how does a . . . a . . . a . . . ," Peniel stammered.

"A leper," Jekuthiel finished.

"Right. How do you know about . . . that sort of thing?" Peniel asked.

"My friend . . . Cantor . . . showed me," Jekuthiel explained. "There are . . . fig trees . . . in our Valley."

This was another new thought. It had never occurred to Peniel that lepers had friends. Companions in misery, perhaps, but friends who spoke of commonplace wisdom like figs and butterflies?

Jekuthiel sat some distance from the others. Resting against the trunks of trees, the beggars ate their fill of windfall figs, then stuffed their pouches full of fruit.

Jekuthiel fell asleep.

Amos nudged Peniel, "Here's our chance! He's sleeping."

From the look on his face, Gideon was clearly tempted.

"Leave now and you're on your own," Peniel warned.

Amos pouted then conceded. "If you'd stick with a leper you'll be loyal to a small man too. There must be merit in that. It'll come to me."

Amos did not leave. Nor did Gideon. After a time they slept at the base of a tree. Butterflies lit on them, checking for ripeness, Peniel mused.

Peniel was drowsing when a lean, sun-darkened man yelled at them from the trail: "Hey! Get! Away from here! You! You! Stealin' fruit, are you? From my master?"

Peniel jumped up quickly; Amos and Gideon more slowly. Jekuthiel remained asleep. The farm steward bustled up to them, brandishing a stick.

"We're not," Gideon argued. "Just gleaning. Our right, it is! We know the rules about gleaning! We haven't picked any except what's on the ground! Isn't that right?" The cripple got agreeing nods.

"Go on! Go on! See for yourself," Amos blustered up at the fellow. "All over the place, they are!"

"Well—" the steward sniffed—"all right then. Enough! On your way now."

"We've traveled far. Could we rest a bit?" Peniel asked. "Our friend there. Done up."

The steward, who had not noticed Jekuthiel before, strode closer to the sleeping leper and inhaled sharply. "Lord have mercy! One of *them!*" he cursed. "Lepers! You! Lepers! Out! The stink of it! Out of my orchard with you! Unclean!"

"We're not . . ." But Peniel's protest went unheard as the steward's stick whistled through the air, hitting Peniel on the arm.

Amos took flight, spilling figs from his sack as he scurried toward the path.

Gideon backed up into the trees, put a row of trunks between him and the steward, and scraped away in retreat.

"Clear off!" Another blow, aimed at Peniel's head, missed as he jumped aside. "The trees! The crop! The stink of it! Clear off!"

Jekuthiel woke up, struggled to hoist himself upright. "We're . . . going."

The steward grabbed up a handful of figs, throwing them at Peniel. One hit him in the face. Another bounced off his chest. "Too bad they're not rocks!" the steward shouted. "You! You! Clear off! Hear me? I'll set the dogs on you! Clear off!"

The hut of Rabbi Ahava was one of the few semipermanent structures in the Valley of Mak'ob. It consisted of a single nine-by-nine-foot space cobbled together from the ruins of an abandoned Canaanite building. The bottom half of the house was stone wall. The top was a concoction of poles tied together for support and covered over with palm branches. The floor was packed dirt beneath a scrap of reed mat.

Lily approached the hut quietly, not wanting to disturb the old man, and yet she had to speak with him! She hesitated as her shadow fell across the open threshold. A mezuzah was in place on the doorpost, as if this was a real home instead of the last refuge of a leper.

She could hear Rabbi Ahava murmuring, as if he was speaking to someone within.

And then his voice addressed her. "Well? Are you standing out in the hot sun all day?"

"Rabbi, it's Lily."

"How's Isra'el? Baruch? Deborah?"

"Am I disturbing?"

"Yes."

"Should I come back?"

"No. No. Studying. Welcome. And come sit at my threshold."

She bowed slightly, approached, and sat down in the shade outside the doorway. Inside, sunlight seeped in through the thatch and cast a dappled pattern of light on the ravaged skin of the rabbi in contrast to the smooth lambskin scroll that lay open before him.

"There's water." He indicated the jar and drinking gourd beside her.

She dipped out only a spoonful to drink, knowing how difficult it was for him to refill the container.

And then he asked again, "Well?"

Lily fought to control the emotions that had been pent up these days. "Deborah has given up. Jekuthiel is not coming back. She thinks he died on the road somewhere. So she's stopped wanting to live."

The old man nodded once, indicating he had suspected as much. "Yes. The children?"

"Little Baruch is the same. Feels her gloom. I can't make him smile. His cough grows more fierce every day. I'm afraid he's dying."

"The baby?"

"Isra'el thrives."

Softly the rabbi said, "Praise to Adonai."

"As long as Deborah lives, her body gives him milk. She's melting away as he grows stronger. But I'm afraid for him. Afraid! Oh, Rabbi! He's so perfect! Untouched by our scourge! He's smiling, Rabbi! Looks into his mama's face and doesn't see . . . her wounds. He smiles at her. Smiles at me too. My heart will break if he dies! And if Deborah dies, he'll die!"

The rabbi answered in a distracted voice, as if something else was holding his attention. "You must speak to her about this. Tell her she must go on living for the sake of her children."

"I hoped you'd tell her," Lily said anxiously. "Who am I? I'm *tsara*. Just like her. But you. You're the rabbi. You can order her to live."

He did not reply. His arm lifted, displaying fingers newly ulcerated. At this slight gesture the aroma of decay filled the air.

Staring down at the scroll, he countered, "I can't add one minute to anyone's life, dear girl." Then, "Lily, do you know how many *tsara'im* we are in this Valley?"

"No. Not exactly."

"Six hundred and twelve. Exactly."

"A lot of us."

"I have lived here seventeen years."

"A long time."

"Yes. A long time. A lot of people have come. Many times that number lie in the graveyard outside the Valley."

What was he getting at? Lily wondered. His voice was so sad. She attempted to comfort him. "Everyone loves you, Rabbi. Before you came they say there were no gardens planted inside King David's fences. No Torah. No synagogue . . . even if the bema is a flat stone in the clearing, it's still someplace for us. No one remembered Shabbat anymore before you came and reminded them."

"Well, then. Do you know how many lived here the first day I entered?"

"No, Rabbi."

"I'll tell you then. Six hundred and twelve souls were alive when I first arrived in the Valley of Mak'ob."

"The same as now."

"Yes. The same as always. The number has never changed. I've been puzzling over it for some time. One dies in the night, and the next morning another straggler enters the Valley. Two die in the afternoon, and by nightfall two more exiles beg refuge. In all my years, in all these years, it's always been the same. Six hundred and twelve of us living in a state of perpetual dying. What do you think of it, child?"

Curious. Terrible. As if the cup of Mak'ob never emptied. Pour suffering out and there was always more to fill it. She shrugged. "I don't know."

"Six hundred and twelve of us. Always. Different faces. Yes. But always the same number of *tsara'im* in this place. The records show—" he tapped a stick on the parchment—"it has never varied. Always the same number."

Back in the cave, Lily thought, three were in danger of perishing right now. Those three were far more important to her than unknown hundreds. "Will you speak to Deborah?" she reiterated.

He stroked his beard and did not reply to her question. "Jekuthiel left four months ago. And that evening his place was taken by a woman from Joppa. That very day."

"Is he coming back? Can you give Deborah any hope?"

"The baby was born to Deborah and on that same morning Cantor perished. Six hundred and twelve."

"Yes. Yes." A chill coursed through Lily. "One who is living seems to take the place of another who has died or gone away. Does it mean something, Rabbi?"

"Everything means something." The old man sighed and shook his head. "But what? There are 613 laws in Torah. We who are gathered in this place, waiting in sorrow, are 612—not thirteen—twelve. Incomplete. The same number as the word *covenant*. Waiting for one more to arrive here and join us so our number will be fulfilled like the commands of Torah. I've tried to reason it out. Make it fit some pattern. What's it mean? Who can say?"

"Where's Jekuthiel, Rabbi? Why did you send him Outside?"

"Some months ago there was a rumor of a prophet, a wild man. Name of Yochanan the Baptizer. Preaching and baptizing for the forgiveness of sins at the Jordan in the wilderness. Some said he could be the one we are looking for."

"Messiah?"

Rabbi Ahava shrugged. It was as unclear to him as it was to Lily. "I sent Jekuthiel Outside to seek the answer. To see if this Yochanan is the Man of Sorrows the prophet Isaias wrote about . . . rejected by the world . . . like us. To see if Yochanan is the One we've been waiting for."

"Jekuthiel's been gone so long. He promised by the feast of Shavuot, he'd be back. He promised Deborah. But he didn't come back."

"I no longer believe Jekuthiel will return to Mak'ob."

"He's dead then."

"The Eternal One knows."

"But what about Deborah? Without him she won't survive. What can I do to make her want to live again? Rabbi! I don't have any family but them! Nobody. They're my family. And little Baruch! No joy in him. You've seen it all before. With others. The despair kills them. Time's running out!"

The old man did not have an answer. "We must think about the only one among us who isn't sick. Put his welfare before our own."

"The baby!"

"Baby Isra'el will perish if he stays in our camp. He'll sicken and die," the rabbi said bluntly.

"What can we do?" Lily asked in despair.

"I'll pray. I'll fast. It'll come to me. We'll reason together. Discover what must be."

Jekuthiel spoke less and less as time went by. Peniel noticed the leper no longer had breath for both talking and trudging along the dusty paths.

It was now either one or the other.

Perhaps it was just as well. The shouted complaints of Amos and Gideon more than made up for Jekuthiel's lack of conversation. The three beggars got along like a cat and a dog and a pigeon, Amos kindly pointed out. Peniel felt like the pigeon. He wished he could fly away.

"This trail! Much steeper than the other."

"Should've taken the other fork!"

"Should've gone by way of Ephraim. Good begging around Ephraim! Treat beggars good there!"

Because of the danger to Peniel from the Temple authorities and the universally harsh public treatment of lepers, the journeyers kept off the paved Roman highways. What remained to them were rutted tracks, little better than trails, through the canyons and weeds. Such villages as had once existed along these roads were decayed and largely abandoned in favor of more profitable locations.

It made travel safer but more troublesome for food and water.

"Got any figs left?" Amos asked.

Peniel left Jekuthiel against a boulder in the shade and plucked three of the remaining figs from the depth of his pouch. "Take them," he said to the dwarf and Gideon.

"No, thanks," Amos returned. "I'll eat anything! As long as it's not figs."

"What I wouldn't give for a nice, hot loaf of bread," Gideon mused aloud. "You know Reuven, the baker by Damascus Gate? Has a son with a club foot, he does. Every Sabbath he passes out bread to cripples."

Peniel's stomach rumbled.

"Skewer of lamb chunks'd go nice right now." Amos rubbed his chin, as if wiping away imaginary grease. "How'd you figure on feeding us out here, anyway?"

Peniel had not figured on feeding them at all, had not thought past the necessity of getting to wherever Yeshua was. Since he had never lived outside the circumference of Jerusalem, Peniel had no concept of distance. He'd heard pilgrims speak of a five-day journey from Caesarea on the seacoast or of a week's travel to reach Capernaum, but Peniel had not thought about the practical side of needing to eat every day.

"Well?" Amos queried. "Did you bring us out here to starve? Why'd we leave Yerushalayim, anyway? What good's it do to go wandering around looking for Messiah if we die before we find him? If it doesn't get better soon, believe me, it'll get worse!"

"I've got an idea," Gideon suggested. "Just over the hill is Tappuah. Let's leave the leper here and go there and beg. Then we can buy food, come back, and share it."

Amos muttered, "With our luck? Don't sell the skin of a bear that's still in the forest."

"Shut up." Gideon glared threateningly at the little man.

How did Gideon know the location and name of the next village? Peniel mused. Why wasn't the cripple leading this journey if he knew so much? Maybe because Gideon would only have himself to blame for whatever went wrong.

Peniel discovered the others looking at him, waiting for a decision. "We'll do it that way," he concluded. "Jekuthiel will wait here, and we'll bring back supplies."

The last of a pair of pigeons had gone into the pot a day earlier. Deborah needed fresh meat to keep up her strength. Today Lily would make the Hawk earn his keep. On this outing Lily allowed only Baruch to accompany her.

It was late afternoon, past the heat of midday. The lengthening shadows within the Valley encouraged quarry animals to be more active and birds flew home toward nests.

Another path wound across a cliff face in a narrower part of the Valley. It was steeper than the main route and not one Lily had ever before attempted without Cantor. Lily had previously marked where pigeons roosted in crannies on the rock face of the gorge. She had also seen rabbit droppings along the track.

Trying to remember exactly what Cantor would say and do, she cautioned Baruch to keep well back. They must not flush the quarry too soon.

The duo made their way out of the Valley and into the more constricted part of the canyon. The hunt took longer than Lily hoped, carrying them farther away from the settlement. Soon they struggled painstakingly around boulders too big to climb over. Lily had to help Baruch past the tougher spots.

The wind was rising. Funneled by the ravine, the breeze ruffled the Hawk's feathers and Lily's nerves. Though never voiced aloud, in Lily's mind was a lingering concern that the Hawk would sometime leave her fist, never to return.

As Lily and Hawk played or hunted amid the groves and vineyards, she could set aside this fear. Outside the settlement, the wildness of the place and untamed nature of the breeze transferred to her hunting partner.

Then Lily knew fearsome anxiety.

Unlike the human inhabitants of Mak'ob, the Hawk remained by choice. He was perfectly capable of soaring up and out of their lives forever.

He was her only remaining link to Cantor, the surviving member of her now never-to-be family. The thought of losing this creature in whose noble bearing and watchful eyes she recalled Cantor's presence was agonizing.

She very nearly remarked to Baruch that conditions were too dangerous. Lily could make it sound as if she was worried about the hazardous ascent.

Yet Lily knew Deborah was depending on her to be the provider for their little clan. Deborah often remarked what incredible grace the Almighty showed in letting them have the Hawk in Mak'ob. He would not take that grace away on a whim, she said.

But what of the grace that gave Cantor to Lily and then took him away?

The wind, though not fierce here on the trail, could be heard howling on top of the ravine.

If you're listening, O Aloof One, hear me, Lily prayed. *Not today, not today*.

A rabbit darted out from beneath the next boulder before Lily had her feet solidly back on the path. Shouting. "Ho!" to let the Hawk know of the quarry, she made an awkward cast, more sideways than upward.

Like a twig in a rushing stream the bird was swirled away downwind, away from the rabbit and away from Lily.

Terrified that her worst fear had just become reality, Lily whistled frantically. She spilled the pouch of reward bits on the ground while trying to lift her glove to call for the Hawk's return.

In the confusion she had taken her eyes off the darting raptor. Where had he gone? Was he even now above the heights, tasting new freedom and vaulting into an unfettered sky?

"There he is," Baruch said, pointing across the canyon toward the opposite rim.

Would he refuse the command to return? Would this faithful companion choose today to be incurably disobedient? Lily spotted the Hawk just as he dove out of sight into some brush.

She whistled again. Did her signal carry far enough to reach the bird's hearing? Had he already decided to part company forever?

It would be too dangerous for her and Baruch to retrace their steps when it grew dark. In any case, there was no point in remaining on the opposite shore of a quarter-mile-wide river of air. Tomorrow Lily'd go in search of the Hawk, climbing laboriously up the other side of the ravine.

Tonight she'd have to tell Deborah that there was no meat . . . and no longer an easy way of providing any.

And tonight Lily would surrender the last bit of her connection to Cantor, say an aching last good-bye.

"He'll be back," Baruch remarked with assurance.

Nothing further was said on the long hike back to the settlement. Lily's grief was so palpable that even her youthful companion respected the silence.

Jekuthiel remained outside the town as the other three approached it.

The tiny village of Tappuah was midway between Shechem and Bethel. At one time it had been an important commercial center, provincial capital of one of King Solomon's administrative districts. The presence there of copper ore, used in the manufacture of bronze tools, had enhanced the fortunes of Tappuah, but the ore was played out.

Now the village was a sleepy hamlet, home, from Peniel's vantage point, to a dozen families, three donkeys, a score of chickens, and one very obnoxious yapping dog.

"This place is proof that four times a year the poor are bad off. Summer. Winter. Fall. And spring," Amos said scornfully. "They may beg from us!"

"A coin or two," Gideon assured him. "We'll get something, I promise you."

"If your promise was a bridge, I wouldn't cross over."

"It looks safe enough," Peniel observed. "No soldiers about."

"No," Gideon noted. "No, I don't see any either."

In the center of Tappuah was the one structure large enough to be its synagogue. It was toward that building that Gideon led the way, showing more confidence than Peniel was used to seeing in his companion.

Just as the beggars reached the bottom of the slope four men emerged onto the porch of the synagogue. Sunlight glinted off bronze helmets.

Soldiers!

Peniel dropped to his belly, clutching the spiny base of a seven-branched sagebush. Amos almost disappeared into a badger hole. Gideon dropped to his knees behind a boulder. "Thank Adonai they came out just then," Peniel breathed. "We might've walked right into them."

"Sure might," Gideon drawled.

"When they leave we'll sneak back up the hill," Peniel suggested.

"Still no food," Gideon pointed out.

"What do you expect me to do?" Peniel snapped. "Put my head in a noose so you can have supper?"

"No," Gideon responded. "But I can go. After all, you're the man with the price on his head. Amos and I can still go in and beg while you wait here . . . or go on back to the . . . to your friend."

"Not me," Amos protested. "I don't care for soldiers either. You know that. They like to drop me headfirst into rain barrels or make bets on how far they can toss me. I'll stay here too."

"Suit yourself," Gideon replied scornfully. "But if I do all the work, I get more than one share of the food."

Gideon waited only until the soldiers had moved from the synagogue steps to what appeared to be an outdoor market of canvas-covered stalls.

Rising from the ground and dusting himself off, he limped confidently toward the town. Gideon whacked the yapping dog with his crutch when it snarled at him before he turned brazenly into the marketplace.

"Gideon. There goes living proof that the stomach swallows the brains of a poor man." Amos shook his head.

Peniel shrugged. "Come on. Let's go back to Jekuthiel and wait for him."

When Gideon did not return to their camp by sunset, Peniel worried aloud. "Arrested, maybe? Somebody saw us together? Maybe they're torturing him right now! Maybe I should go!"

The beggars sat in darkness, fearing a fire would give away their location. Jekuthiel rested some distance away.

Halfheartedly they gnawed on wizened figs.

Amos, standing alongside where Peniel sat on the ground, slapped him lightly across the face. "Don't be daft," he warned. "Gideon tortured? He'd sing any tune they played before the first lash went across his back! No, if he was captured you'd have a soldier boxing your ears right now instead of me."

"Right you are," came Gideon's voice from the darkness of the hillside. "Shalom the camp. No fire? How can we roast our chicken then?"

Whistling, the cripple strode into the site. Slung across one shoulder was a sack that bulged and squawked to prove the aptness of his inquiry. Tied to the fork of his crutch was another bag, manifestly heavy from the way it hung and resisted moving when Gideon stomped into view.

"Bread! Dates! Olives! And . . ." Gideon reached into the wriggling pouch and extracted the promised fowl. "Fasting will be easier now with a chicken leg and a half bottle of wine, eh?"

"Are you crazy?" Peniel yelped. "Stealing a chicken will land us in prison and me dead!"

Amos took the sack and peered into it. "Tasty is the chicken from someone else's pot."

"Not stolen," Gideon replied. "I told you I could get anything we needed. Now, who's cooking? I did all the work so far."

Later, while the companions let hot chicken grease drip onto chunks of fresh bread, Gideon looked across the clearing to where Jekuthiel leaned against a boulder. "Tell him to stop staring at me," the cripple demanded. "I don't like the way he watches me. Gives me the chills."

"He's hungry," Peniel replied curtly.

"Hungry? Yes," Gideon grumbled. "Stares at me like a stray dog hoping for a bite of food. Well, he's not getting anything from me."

Wordlessly Peniel gathered the scraps and carried them to the leper. "Supper. Smell of cooking driving you crazy?"

Jekuthiel examined a crust of bread. "No . . . can't smell . . . anything."

"There's a mercy anyway." Peniel almost blurted what he had been thinking: that the leper seemed to smell even worse today than yesterday.

"There's . . . no . . . mercy for lepers." Jekuthiel took a cautious bite.

"No. I suppose not. But try not to stare at Gideon, will you?"

"He's a . . . curious . . . sort. I've been . . . watching him. You . . . trust him?"

Peniel frowned. "Trust Gideon?"

"Just asking. . . . He's . . . something . . . something. Can't put my . . . finger on it."

"I don't care what he is. Just don't stare at him. Or I'll have a revolt on my hands."

"Don't trust . . . him . . . too much."

"You talk like that, he's likely to knock off one of your body parts with that crutch of his."

"Just . . . listen. You be the one . . . to decide . . . which road . . . we take, eh?"

Little Baruch went to stay in the camp of children. Deborah thought it best.

"No use." Deborah turned her face away as baby Isra'el struggled in frustration against her breast. "Lily, take him. My milk's dried up. No use. No use."

Lily took Isra'el from his mother and painstakingly fed him goat's milk from the tip of a leather glove. An hour later the infant, half filled and exhausted from the effort, fell asleep in Lily's arms.

Only then did Deborah speak again. "He'll learn. Goat's milk will keep him alive."

"Tomorrow. You'll see. Your breasts will be full again."

"He'll die if he stays with me."

"You must keep trying to nurse him," Lily encouraged.

"The black sores cover me now. My eyes are going. Soon they'll take me to the dying cave."

"Don't!" Lily commanded.

"It's true. True."

"You'll get better . . . you will. Sometimes, you know. If you just rest. That's all! You'll get better."

"Jekuthiel is dead. I'm sure of it. Or he would have been back. And unless the baby is taken Outside, he'll catch this scourge from me and die."

Lily cradled Isra'el in her arms.

I'm praying again, Heartless One. Desperate! Desperate! Oh! Do you hear this? Where are you? How can this be? Not a drop left for Deborah to nurse this beautiful baby?

"You have to hold on, Deborah! Good food. Rest. Your milk will come in again. You'll get better and . . ."

Wearily, as if she had told herself the same thing, Deborah replied, "No. No. Can't you see what's happening, Lily? Cruelest thing I can do is keep him here. Selfish love will kill him . . . no. No. You take him."

"Me? Take?"

"Outside, Lily! Carry him home."

"Home? This is my home. What do you mean?"

"Your village. Your mother and father! They are kind folks. You said so yourself. Said you reckoned it nearly killed your mother to give you up. Oh, Lily! Wouldn't she take him in? My little boy? Raise him?"

"The only road out of Mak'ob for us is the road to the grave!"

"My baby can have a life . . . if only . . . if you will only . . ."

Lily traced the image of the sleeping child with her eyes. "Oh!" she cried, as she imagined placing him in the arms of her mother, yet not being allowed to embrace her. "Oh, Deborah! I can't! I can't go back there! Never again!"

"He'll die if he stays with me. Can't you see the truth of it, Lily? I can. Please. I have nothing left to give him now except life. You must . . . help . . . me let him go."

19

The Galilean villa of Herod Antipas overlooked the Sea of Galilee and the Roman city of Tiberias.

Eglon spurred his mount up the long curving road leading to the gates of the tetrarch's northern palace. Admitted to the grounds, he was taken immediately to the courtyard. Herod and Herodius were entertaining twenty Jewish magistrates of the province.

As Eglon entered, Herod rose at once and hurried to meet with him privately in a side chamber. "Well? What news, Eglon?"

"We're proceeding, Lord Antipas."

"Proceeding. Proceeding? What's taking so long?"

"The beggars make slow progress."

"They make no progress at all, it seems!" Herod was clearly angry that Yeshua still lived.

"I'm in close contact with the one called Gideon."

"The lame beggar?"

"That's the one."

"Can't he walk any faster?"

"It's the leper holding them back."

"Leper!"

"Aye. They've picked up a leper along the way. He can barely move. A snail's pace, the cripple says. And Peniel will not leave the leper behind. Says he'll take them all to Yeshua or else he threatens to leave Gideon and the other one behind."

"Tedious! Tedious! Why not just storm the camp of Yeshua and be done with it?"

"As ever, my lord Antipas, Yeshua is surrounded by a core of loyal followers. Twelve close by him always. About a hundred more men in the outer circle. And thousands of common folk. There's only a handful of us with swords, counting myself. Without using these beggars to get close to Yeshua, I wouldn't stand a chance."

"Can't you get rid of the leper? Baggage! Slowing the whole thing down. I want it finished! Caiaphas sends me letters from Yerushalayim! The high priest and the Sanhedrin are counting on me to settle this here in the Galil before Yeshua can stir up an army and take Yerushalayim! Do you understand? They're looking to me to handle it. And I'm depending on you!"

"I've found a way to separate the leper from the group. The next village. The group'll move along better without him."

"But, Eglon, how long must we wait before this matter is settled? My wife grows impatient. She will not stop harping on the matter. You would think that by killing the Baptizer she'd have been comforted. But no. Now she wants the head of the Baptizer's cousin. Women! No matter what you give them, they want more!"

"I've got to play it carefully. Aye. The one called Gideon says Peniel is dedicated to Yeshua. If Peniel caught wind of what we're about, no doubt he'd lead us entirely in the other direction. Away from Yeshua."

"Why not just . . . threaten to put his eyes out! That would bring him into line."

"It may come to that. Meanwhile, your honor, leave it to me and my men. We'll handle it so the matter is over and done with."

"Tell that to my wife."

It was hot and dusty. The sun was high.

The main caravan route followed the Jordan River Valley, where there was plenty of water for thirsty travelers.

Not so on the secondary route traced by Peniel and his company. Despite the recent storm, ravines were dry. Springs nonexistent. Hill-country wells were few and far between. The need for water was exaggerated by their pace, excruciatingly slowed by Jekuthiel. The sun's early rising and relentless, cloudless pursuit, quickly parched moisture out of everything.

"Anybody got water?" Gideon inquired as they paused for a noon-time break. "Mine's gone."

Amos turned his waterskin upside down to show that he was also out. He worked his mouth, smacking dry lips as proof that not even a single proverb or a drop of spit was left.

Peniel's jug had about a cup left. He shared with the other two beggars, keeping none for himself.

Jekuthiel offered his waterskin. No one accepted.

"What'll you do about it?" Gideon challenged. "Can't go on without water."

Amos gestured at a camel skeleton lying on the ground. "Don't see what he's got to grin about," the dwarf quipped. "He's dead."

"He's laughing because if a camel dies out here for want of water, what chance have three beggars and a leper got?" Gideon retorted.

"Ah, Gideon, if your grandmother had a beard, she'd be your grandfather," Amos said. By the way of stating the obvious, he showed his agreement with Gideon. "So we're thirsty. What are you going to do about it, Peniel?"

Once more Peniel wondered why it was *his* duty, *his* responsibility, to do anything about it at all. He almost said as much, drawing back only when he remembered that his report of Messiah's ability had started this quest.

"Can your Messiah bring water out of a rock by hitting it with his staff?" Gideon waved his crutch in the air.

"I'd like to see that." Amos tugged at his eyebrow.

Gideon struck the camel skull with his crutch. The top half of the desiccated, porous bone shattered into powder, leaving only the grin. "Mosheh could. Can your Messiah manage that?"

Amos agreed that the challenge was fair. "If there really is a Messiah. Are you even sure he likes beggars? Maybe he's working for the Romans. Wants to lure us out here to die. That'd be one way to get rid of our beggar army."

What beggar army? Peniel wanted to shout. It wasn't possible for these two comrades to go more than a hundred yards without grumbling. How could they ever expect to be an army?

"Can't go into a village in the company of that." Gideon jerked his thumb over his shoulder at Jekuthiel. "Can't draw water from a public well with a leper within a mile of us. They'll smell him."

"Leave me . . . here," Jekuthiel suggested. "Go . . . get water."

As with the provisions obtained from Tappuah, Peniel reluctantly agreed.

"Abel-Meholah's just up ahead," Gideon suggested, squinting at the remaining lower jaw of the now vanished camel. "Plenty of water there."

Amos shrugged. "It costs nothing to look."

Just how did Gideon know anything about Abel-Meholah? Peniel wondered.

Abel-Meholah, whose name meant "brook of dancing," was located on a tributary of the Jordan. The creek bed was dirt this time of year, but there was plenty of water in the town well.

Olive trees grew on the terraced hillsides. Bees buzzing around the meadow south of the town gave evidence of the honey production for which the area was known.

"You wait here," Gideon suggested. "I'll go ahead and scout. Make sure it's safe."

Touched by this offer, Peniel regretted his earlier harsh judgment of Gideon's griping. "Sure."

"I've known Gideon a long time," Amos pondered when Gideon was out of sight. "He's a coward to the bone. Meaning no offense. Just a fact. Now look at him. Hobbling up there. Scouting out the place. Like a spy in old Canaan he is. Bold as brass. God watches over fools."

Peniel composed himself behind a screen of elderberry bushes to wait.

Gideon returned within minutes. "All clear. Come on! Plenty of water." The cripple unslung the waterskin from his back to show that it was full to bursting.

How did he have time to look around for soldiers, visit the well, and return that quickly? Peniel wondered. "Sure it's safe?"

"You think I didn't look? Stay here then. Make me do all the work."

Peniel shook his head. He would not ask a man limping on a crutch to carry water for him. "We'll go."

The town water supply of Abel-Meholah was in the center of the market square. It was paved around with limestone slabs. Along one side was a deep trough for watering livestock while the well itself was surrounded by a circular stone wall high enough to keep sheep from falling in.

A young woman was ahead of the three beggars at the well. She looked with curiosity at Amos. Averting her gaze from the dwarf, she smiled shyly at Peniel. "Shalom. You've come far?"

"From Yerushalayim," Peniel replied.

"Looking for the Prophet from Nazareth," Amos rattled. "Earn favor with the Almighty by me. For a coin I'll mention your name to him when we meet him."

"I don't have money," she explained. "But the Prophet's been here."

Peniel and Amos exchanged startled glances. "Who do you mean?"

"Yeshua." She shifted the burden of the clay amphora of water from one shoulder to the other. "He healed Issachar, my uncle from Abel-Meholah. My mother's younger brother from her father's second wife. Born with a crooked spine. Lived in pain for thirty-six years and Yeshua healed him, just like that. Others too. The village was packed. People from everywhere. Never been like this before, my father says. Not since the days of Elisha."

Peniel exclaimed. "When? Yeshua? How long ago?"

Thinking for a moment, the girl replied, "No more than three . . . no, that's it exactly. Three days ago."

Peniel calculated the ponderous progress imposed by Jekuthiel. If they had abandoned the leper, they would have caught up with Yeshua.

"Heading north?" Peniel queried. "I need to find him . . . to warn him. Soldiers from Yerushalayim are—"

Nervously Gideon jerked his head toward Jekuthiel's hiding place. "Peniel! Our friend is waiting for us. Can't talk here all day, eh?"

The girl prated on proudly. "We're blessed by the Almighty here. Abel-Meholah is the birthplace of the prophet Elisha. Pay Father a penny and he'll show a pilgrim where the foundation of the old meeting house is. The prophet was staying here when he healed a Syrian leper."

"Yeshua?" Peniel inquired.

She glared at him. "No, Elisha. Nobody's healed a leper since Elisha. And nothing exciting's ever happened here since then. Until now. Now we've had another prophet pass through our village."

At that a hawk-faced woman shouted at the girl to hurry. She packed up her jar and, without another word, scurried back into the village.

"The prophet Elisha, eh?" Amos mused aloud. "Healed a leper, eh? We can leave Jekuthiel here and—"

Gideon thumped him on top of the head. "Keep quiet about that!" The cripple glanced over his shoulder. "If people hear we're traveling with a leper, they'll run us all out of town."

Gideon lounged on the rock wall. Peniel did the work of dipping, filling, and hoisting. Amos tied the mouths of the waterskins closed. The streets emptied as commerce came to an end.

Peniel glanced up a lane of shops. A flash of sunlight glinted off something that gleamed bronze in the sun.

Gideon stared in the same direction.

"You saw it too. A sword?" Peniel inquired.

"Here? Not likely." Gideon shrugged. "But say! So we're that close behind the Messiah, eh? So what are we waiting for?"

"Three days behind is not a short walk," Amos chided. "No point in rushing about in the heat."

"Here's a plan." Gideon beckoned for Peniel and Amos to come closer. "You know why we're three days behind, eh?" He gestured with his crutch in the direction of Jekuthiel's hiding place. "We treated the leper all right . . . better than he deserves. Amos is right. Let's leave him here. We'll go twice as fast."

Amos' chubby hands grabbed a double handful of his wiry beard in thought. "It's true what he says, Peniel. Nobody ever even talks to a—" the dwarf lowered his voice to a conspiratorial whisper—"a leper. He'll just have to understand."

"I promised," Peniel argued. "Promised to take him. That's it. You two go on if you've a mind. But I'm going back for him."

Amos bristled before Gideon cut him off.

"Wouldn't think of it. Only a suggestion," Gideon said. "You're the captain. But we're wasting time. Let's pack up and get going."

"Hawk's still gone," Lily commented when Rabbi Ahava settled himself. The sun was nearly straight overhead, the shade meager.

"I heard," he replied.

She sat beside a lone broom tree on a promontory overlooking the settlement. The thick cluster of the shrub's spindly branches bristled upward from its base in the shape of a hand. This was a hot, bare, lonely place, difficult to reach. The struggle required to get here meant Rabbi Ahava had something on his mind, something to say to her, but for Lily no words of comfort would help. She would stop him before he got started.

Pent-up bitterness foamed out of Lily like a jug of vinegar to which soda had been added. "He took everything. He takes everything. You can have almost nothing and still lose it."

The rabbi knew who it was Lily accused.

She went on. "He's cruel. Why else *give* hope, then . . ." She wiped her nose on her sleeve. "Can't take care of Deborah. Barely fed her and Baruch and me before. Now Hawk's gone too. Why? Just cruel."

Lily expected Rabbi Ahava to interrupt her diatribe, to denounce her for blasphemy, to call fire down on her head, to say something.

He remained mute, forcing her to continue.

"I have nothing left to care about . . . or won't soon. My family first. Then Jekuthiel . . . that'll kill Deborah. Cantor . . . my life, my hope! Now the last . . . punishment! Isn't there a limit? Isn't there?"

"And little Baruch?" Ahava prodded gently. "And baby Isra'el?"

Lily nodded, gulping, but still refused to admit any remaining ties. "Better off with someone else," she asserted, reaching up to snap an overhanging limb off the thumb of the broom shrub.

"Is the journey too hard for you?" Ahava asked.

"Beyond hard. It's impossible!" she said savagely, with a look daring him to contradict her.

Ahava reached out for the sprig of juniper, and Lily passed it to him. She imagined him whipping her with it, but instead he twirled it in his fingers and said, "I've known a time here when crops failed, and we ate the roots of broom trees ground into a kind of flour. Bitter, they are, but keep you alive. Use the roots for charcoal too; bake a cake of juniper roots on a fire of juniper roots."

What was this about? She was no Torah schoolboy to puzzle over wordy and complex questions of Scripture lore.

"I don't understand you," she said.

"You know Elijah? The prophet the ravens fed, like the Hawk fed you?"

Lily nodded.

"When Elijah ran from Queen Jezebel, he fled into the wilderness," the rabbi went on. "Rested under a broom tree—prayed he might die."[48] Rabbi Ahava gazed into Lily's eyes and lifted the scaly patches of skin where his eyebrows had been.

Lily ducked her head. Of course he knew she wanted to die! Who wouldn't?

"This isn't about guilt, Lily," the rabbi said kindly. "Elohim told Elijah, *'The journey is too hard for you.'* And Elohim baked Elijah bread and brought him water and told him to rest."

"How will I ever rest again?" Lily cried. "How?"

Ahava did not respond to the desperate plea and continued the story. "After the prophet had rested more and then journeyed more, Elohim asked what he was doing out in the wilderness, running away. Elijah didn't hold back: told God every difficult duty he'd ever performed for God. Complained how alone he was, how terrible his life was. On and on, even in the very presence of El Olam, the Almighty, the Eternal, Elijah complained and complained. And did Elohim strike him down?"

Lily shook her head. She knew this story, even if she still didn't understand what it had to do with her.

"No, he didn't," Rabbi Ahava agreed. "He patiently let Elijah pour out all his complaints, and then he gave him hope. Gave him hope and a new mission. Gave his life purpose again."

"But all my life's purpose is gone, buried over there," Lily said sharply, pointing toward the visible heap of earth and the dead, dried-up flowers over Cantor's grave.

"Lily," Ahava said, "I sometimes wonder if the bread Elohim baked for Elijah wasn't broom roots. Keeps you alive, but oh, so bitter! You can go on in bitterness, but why not ask Elohim for new purpose instead? Even if you submit to the will of Elohim, if you submit without believing in his love, all your life will be is bitter."

A tinkling bell, followed by a piercing scream overhead, made both Lily and Rabbi Ahava look up. The Hawk, veering from side to side as he struggled to balance his burden, swooped toward the broom shrub. With difficulty he flared to stop his dive . . . and dropped a pigeon almost as large as himself at Lily's feet.

The three beggars rejoined Jekuthiel outside the village.

Gideon was suddenly on fire to catch up with Yeshua. In place of his customary pugnacious griping, the cripple brimmed with cooperative energy. "Let me carry two of the waterskins," he offered. "Peniel can help the leper. We'll move faster."

The thought of Jekuthiel leaning on him, putting a hand on his shoulder, breathing the same air, was almost more than Peniel could bear.

Jekuthiel took a long draught of fresh water and wiped his mouth. The leper refastened the obscuring veil over the ruins of his face. He eliminated the dilemma by saying, "Let . . . Peniel . . . take . . . my . . . water and . . . provisions. I can . . . manage."

At the edge of the meadow Peniel located a stout tamarisk limb. Trimmed of leaves, the pole was straight enough to tote waterskins and pouches on the ends. Peniel carried it across his shoulders. "Now," he said, "better the long way around the meadow."

"Not at all," Gideon argued. "Town's quiet. Seen us already. Nobody's worried about strangers. Go straight through town."

"Through the village?" Amos said doubtfully. "Walk with a leper? What a man thinks up for himself, his worst enemy couldn't wish for him!"

"No," Gideon admitted. "Jekuthiel follows behind. We wait for him at the other end. Easy."

Peniel studied the hummocks and thick overgrowth of the meadow. He considered the shallow but steep ravine of the creek bed and compared it to the level expanse of roadway.

In a low wheeze Jekuthiel warned, "Told you . . . you pick . . . the route."

"It's all right," Peniel decided. "Easier and quicker on the road. We'll cut through the town. Let's go."

The main street of Abel-Meholah was deserted. Strange for the time of day, it seemed to Peniel. Despite the quiet of the place, something was amiss.

Gideon kept well out front of the trio, urging the others to hurry up.

Peniel was uneasy. Several times he looked around to watch Jekuthiel's halting progress.

"Unclean!" came the leper's required warning as he entered the village. "Unclean!"

There was no one around to hear him. The town seemed empty.

Jekuthiel was just passing the well. Peniel was at the opposite end of Abel-Meholah when a gang of toughs burst into view. Five rough-looking men, cloaked despite the heat, appeared from an alleyway. Their fists were clenched.

"Get! Hey, you! *Chedel! Tsara'at!* Get out of here!" one bellowed, throwing the first stone.

"No scum allowed here!"

The first rock sailed over Jekuthiel's head. He ducked to escape the second.

"Clear off!"

The next pair of stones struck him, one in the leg and another in the back as he turned away. The attackers formed a screen, blocking Jekuthiel's advance down the street, separating him from Peniel.

"Let's get out of here," Gideon urged.

Peniel dropped water and food from the carrying pole. Bracing it in both hands like a club, he started forward.

Gideon grabbed him by the arm. "Whatever you're planning, don't!"

Jekuthiel's tormentors kept their distance . . . circling . . . circling. Flinging clods and laughing as he flinched and ducked. Their backs were to Peniel and the others.

Amos cowered behind a tree stump.

Peniel shook off Gideon's grip.

"Not for a leper!" Gideon shouted. "You'll get killed!"

Whirling the pole overhead, Peniel charged into the fray. "Leave him be!" he cried.

Peniel's assault, coming from behind, took Jekuthiel's assailants by surprise. The first swipe of the tree limb battered two of the enemy apart and opened a route through to Jekuthiel. "Let him alone!" Peniel insisted again. "Stop it!" He stood defensively in front of the leper, facing the foes.

Peniel had no time to consider it just then, but one of the cloaked attackers looked very much like one of the Temple Guards: same inadequate chin, same bulging eyes, exaggerated throat.

Another rock hit Jekuthiel in the head. He moaned and stumbled over the watering trough, then fell to his knees.

Peniel rushed at the thrower, slashed downward with his stick but missed. A fist crashed into Peniel's ear. His pole spun away, clattering onto the mouth of the well. It teetered on the brink of the cistern, then rolled into the stone basin beside it.

Villagers appeared at windows and doors to view the disturbance. "Lepers!" someone called. "*Chedel* drinking from our well! Polluting our water!"

Suddenly the street was filled with people, all shouting and gesturing. A stone struck Peniel in the knee.

Gideon rushed up. "Not him," he yelled. "We're not lepers." A clod the size of a hen's egg bounced off Gideon's nose, making it gush blood. "Not me, either!"

"They're lepers," another villager bellowed. "Drank from our well! Stone them all!"

Amos bustled into the conflict, adding his screech to the pandemonium. A rock bounced off the top of his head, stunning him before he struck a single blow.

Jekuthiel grasped Peniel's tree branch and levered himself upright. His veil was gone, revealing the gaping wound where a face should have been. As if meeting an apparition rising from the grave, the crowd groaned and drew back a pace.

Peniel grabbed Amos. He tried to lift the dwarf but failed, then took the small man by both arms and dragged him. "Stop!" Peniel yelled. "We're going. Come on, Jekuthiel."

Rocks continued to shower around them until the four beggars passed the boundary marker of Abel-Meholah. The quartet did not stop their retreat until a cave in the ravine provided a shelter out of sight of the road to dress their bloody wounds.

Peniel's ear was split from the clout he received.

Blood matted Amos' hair and beard from crown to chin. The dwarf was near hysteria. "What! What was that, Peniel? You want to die? Those who can't bite shouldn't show their teeth!"

Peniel shrugged and muttered, "When one has nothing to answer, it's best to shut up."

"That's right!" Amos shook his finger at Peniel. "Well spoken! Yes!"

Gideon's nose was swollen to twice normal size, and he had two black eyes.

Of all the companions, only Jekuthiel's injuries were unseen and unremarked on. Peniel wondered whether under the concealing robe Jekuthiel was a mass of bruises or open sores. The phlegmatic leper, seated some distance away, gave no sign he was any worse off than he had been before the attack.

"Those men," Peniel remarked. He held a dampened fold of his cloak as a compress on the side of his head. "The first ones. They already had rocks in their hands."

"So?" Gideon queried, tying a strip torn from the bottom of his tunic around Amos' head. "They came to stone a leper."

"But they'd already picked up the stones. Before Jekuthiel was in sight," Peniel objected. "How'd they know he was coming?"

Gideon made a dismissive noise. "Want to go back and ask?" he sneered. "Men throw stones at lepers. No explanation needed."

"Yes! When you want to beat a dog, be sure to find a stick! What else are they going to stone a leper with? Bread?" Amos dabbed his brow, examined his own blood. Dabbed and stared. Dabbed and looked.

Peniel ignored him. "But it's like they intended to drive him back, away from us."

"You're imagining things," Gideon scoffed. "We're just lucky we weren't all killed. No thanks to that one—" he flipped his hand at Jekuthiel—"that we weren't. I warned you to leave him."

"You're also the one who said going through town was faster," Amos put in. "Man thinks and God laughs."

"You keep out of this!" Gideon warned, yanking on the knotted bandage and wringing a squawk of protest from the dwarf.

Minutes of silent, mutual recrimination passed and then Amos said, "Maybe they failed to turn back the leper, but it worked on me."

Peniel passed a waterskin to the dwarf and asked what he meant.

"This looking for Messiah," Amos explained. "It's not worth it. I mean, maybe he is and maybe he isn't. But sleeping under bushes . . .

going hungry . . . now being nearly killed. In Yerushalayim I was never once stoned . . . oh, kicked and cuffed, of course, but that doesn't count." The dwarf shrugged. "Nobody ever tried to kill me. What I'm saying is, I've had enough. I'm going back. A man should stay alive, if only out of curiosity."

"But we've come so far," Peniel protested. "And we know he's just up ahead. Don't quit now."

Amos shook his head and winced. "Don't you think every town we come to now will know that a dwarf and a cripple are traveling with a leper? It'll get worse, not better. Sometimes the remedy's worse than the disease. No, my mind's made up. I'm leaving in the morning."

"He's staring at me again," Gideon said, pointing at Jekuthiel. "I tell you, he's bad luck. Better get rid of him soon, or none of us will make it to Messiah."

"Listen, Amos," Peniel said. "Think it over. Sleep on it. If you can't endure the bad, you'll not survive to witness the good, eh? Well spoken?"

Amos screwed up his bloodied face. "Survive. Better a live dwarf than a tall dead man. That's what I'm talking about."

PART III

We all, like sheep, have gone astray,
Each of us has turned to his own way;
And Adonai has laid upon Him
The iniquity of us all.

Surely He took up our infirmities
And carried our sorrows.

ISAIAH 53:6, 4

20

"Let me hold him one more time," Deborah rasped as Lily finished packing. Food enough for the journey home.

Baby Isra'el, belly full from a supper of goat's milk, slept in a woven basket opposite Deborah's mat.

Lily scooped him up carefully and placed him beside Deborah.

He did not awaken but instinctively turned his face toward his mother's breast.

"He's perfect," Deborah whispered. "Isn't he, Lily?"

"Perfect. Yes." Lily could not look at her. She resumed the task of preparing for the journey.

"We were all like this once. Look at his skin. Perfect. Little ears. His eyelashes. Oh, look, Lily! Once I was . . . beautiful . . . once."

"No use thinking about what was."

"Your mother will love him."

"Yes. Mama will."

"Tell me again, Lily. Tell me about her. About your mother."

"Her hair was gold. Like mine. Eyes blue. Like mine. She had a bright and happy laugh. Loved to sing. Always she was singing around the house and . . ."

"You're a lot like her."

The thought of such a thing made Lily stop, raise her eyes, look at the cloudless sky beyond the Valley. Was Mama thinking of her at that moment? Somehow knowing Lily would return? What would she do after so many years? So many silent, lonely years? "I suppose I would have been like her. If things had been different."

"And she'll rock him to sleep at night. Tell him stories. She'll love my baby boy, won't she, Lily?"

"Yes. Yes. Mama will . . . she'll love . . . him."

"Look. Look, Lily. He looks so much like his father, don't you think? So much like Jekuthiel? He'll grow up to be strong and handsome. He'll marry and have children. Our grandchildren. And . . . won't he, Lily?"

"Yes. Yes. Deborah."

"He'll never know. Never. Never know about us."

"No. Never."

"Well, then. Well . . . then. Farewell." She kissed his silken skin with ragged, blackened lips. "Farewell, my little boy. Someday. Someday. Oh! Take him, Lily! Take him now! Now before I change my mind! Go! Take him away! Away!"

The child began to wail. Lily took him from her arms. Deborah turned her face to the stone wall and sobbed quietly as Lily left.

A final farewell.

Lily climbed the path to Cantor's stone for one last look over the Valley of Sorrows, which had been her only home since she was rejected.

She knew as she looked down that she would never return. What use? Cantor dead. Deborah and Baruch slipping from life. She would carry baby Isra'el back to Mama. Leave him, whole and beautiful, in her care. A parting gift of life to say, *Here, Mama. A child for you to love . . . a life for the one taken from you. . . . I always loved you, Mama.*

And then Lily would die content . . . die Outside.

There, among thousands of graves, was the mound of Cantor's grave.

Smoke spiraled up from the cook fires. Her people, the half

people—people of half hands and half faces—had loved her with whole hearts. The chains of suffering had bound them to one another.

How Lily loved them as they lived out their dying lives! Hideous faces. Marred beyond human appearance. Those Outside could not look upon them without terror. Despised. Rejected. Acquainted with grief. And yet how Lily loved the people of this Valley!

I'm praying again, God of Suffering. Someday when I'm freed from this grim vision of life on earth, let my soul unite again with their souls, whole and beautiful! And let us who die without tongues sing praise in the presence of assenting angels.

For now? Against my will my heart beats on between the hammer blows of grief.

My hope? That someday every stroke drummed on my spirit will be music for some great chorus sung before your throne!

And then? Will you smile then, God of My Anguish?

Will you turn your eyes on me then . . . and clap your hands in pleasure of my part?

Then . . . then, how I will cherish this long night of my affliction! And I will regret the hours I could not bend my knee and bow more deeply and thank you for my suffering!

Slowly the long shadows of early morning rolled back from the deep Valley of Mak'ob.

Halfway up the steep climb Lily paused and took a final look at the place that had been her home for so many years. She was afraid. More afraid to leave than she had been to enter. She knew firsthand how those living in her village treated *tsara'im*. They killed the wounded and called the judgment righteous!

I'm praying again, Unyielding One. Even if I die for daring to come back from this grave into their world, have mercy on Isra'el! Save this baby!

Everything familiar seemed so insignificant, so toylike from this high vantage.

The rabbi's house. The stone bema where even now a few limped out for morning prayers. The well. Groves of ragged trees. Shacks, shanties, hollow shelters scratched out from the sides of the cliffs. The cave where Deborah lay dying. The larger cavern where those severely crippled were laid. The vast, crowded rubble of the graveyard, where so many more would likely be buried before Lily would return to the Valley.

Only 610 souls remained below now as Lily and the baby climbed out. And yet the rabbi had told her there was always enough to refill the cup of suffering in the Valley of Mak'ob.

Who would descend into the colony and replace Lily and Isra'el by the end of the day?

The bell of the Hawk tinkled as he swooped from rock to bush to outcropping. The bird kept a constant pace as he followed Lily up and up the switchback trail leading from the Valley.

The rope of the milk goat was secured around Lily's waist. The creature, undaunted by the steep climb, nipped at stray blades of grass along the way. Baby Isra'el was asleep in the sling that hung from Lily's neck.

From the switchback above her sounded a warning.

A battered, filthy woman cried out from behind her veil, "Unclean!"

"Shalom," Lily replied, smelling the decay of number 611. So Lily met her replacement at the hairpin turn. "I'm also a leper."

Relief and terror mixed in the woman's question. It was clear to Lily this one had not yet accepted her fate. The filth-caked garment showed some remnant of flowers embroidered on the hem. It had been a pretty dress, Lily reckoned. And maybe this leper had also once been pretty.

"This is it then? The Valley of Mak'ob? The colony for . . . for . . . *tsara'im?* But you aren't . . ."

Lily presented the remnant of her left hand. "Yes."

Desperation gushed from the wild-eyed stranger. Unconscious, babbling near to madness. "I've been wandering. Wandering. Driven out from every place. Weeks. They threw stones at me! Drove me out! I'm half starved! Weeks since I left home. Weeks!"

So. The Outside had not changed in the six years since Lily had been cast off. Lily averted her gaze from the haunted eyes. The newcomer's feet were bloody stumps. Worms wriggled in the flesh of her toes. She would not last long, this one, unless the feet were amputated. Fingers too. Rabbi Ahava would have a job to save this one from her neglect.

"Home?" Lily asked.

"Gaza. My family. My husband and . . ."

"You've come a long way."

"You're just a girl. Is that a baby in the sling?" The woman leaned forward and reached out as if she would touch Isra'el with a gangrenous claw.

Lily drew back. "He's not sick."

"He? I have three boys at home." The voice of the woman broke. Then she remembered herself and pulled the veil close over her mouth. *Hiding what she has become behind the memory of what she once was.*

"Why is he here? A baby! In such a terrible place?"

"I'm taking him Outside. Born here. Mother and father both *tsara.*"

The outcast began to sob. "I didn't know. How can this be? Children here! I have three boys . . . three sons . . . at home."

Lily had heard it a hundred times before. She lowered her head and tugged the rope of the milk goat. "I've got to go. Let me by. I'm taking him up from here. Outside."

"I . . . didn't know. Children!" The stranger stepped aside, clinging to a sagebush for balance as Lily passed.

Then, a reprise of terror. "Tell me, girl!" she called after Lily. "What are they . . . like? Down there?"

Lily kept her eye on the Hawk as he flitted to a fallen stump. She was just as frightened to be leaving the familiarity of Mak'ob as this woman was to be entering it. Lily focused on the Hawk's bell. Guiding her up and up, away from her home, her people.

She trudged on. "We're just people. Like you. Go on. There's a good rabbi named Ahava. Expecting you. At this hour he'll be making morning prayers with his congregation."

"Where?" she called.

"The flat rock. The bema of our synagogue."

The sky seemed no closer at the top of the precipice than it had from the bottom of the Valley of Sorrow.

Blue. So blue. Yes. Wide and deep like the Sea of Galilee. Unbroken blue except for a few clouds in the west.

The west. Where Lily's home had been so long ago.

Home. Where Mama lived. The little house Papa had built with his own hands the year of Lily's birth.

Home. Where Papa farmed his patch of earth for the great landlord of Capernaum.

Home. Her brothers would be nearly grown now. Like young trees with thickening trunks and hardened bark.

Home. The sky seemed no closer, but memories tumbled down on her with an avalanche of grief. She remembered everything! *Mama! Papa!*

Lily ached for what was as though it were yesterday when she had lost her life!

Step followed step. Certain. Unhurried. The bell of the Hawk preceded her, announcing her return from the tomb of Mak'ob.

The milk goat behind. The baby in her arms. She approached the stone cottage of the Overseer, who guarded the entrance to the Valley.

The gatehouse was ancient, built between the two enormous boulders that served as the upper entrance to Mak'ob. It was outside this station that charitable supplies were delivered. Overseer took a cut of everything for himself before he allowed the goods to be retrieved by the lepers and carried into the Valley. No one entered or left without his permission.

Overseer was a large, heavyset Samaritan with a bulbous nose and eyebrows that sprouted like miniature broom trees above his black, dead eyes. He had deserted the Roman legion, it was rumored, and had fled to the wilderness for refuge. He got no farther than this gatehouse, where he lived for twenty years with the old man who had preceded him in the post.

Sometimes young women from the Valley whose disease was not far advanced made trips to his hut by night. They returned in the morning with food or clothes. Lily had never before known what the women had exchanged for these gifts. Now, after her one night with Cantor, she guessed.

How would she get past him?

I'm praying again! Praying . . . Oh! Please!

The Overseer sat in a chair beside the entrance to his hut. Sausagelike fingers curled around the neck of his wine jar. His head lolled to one side.

Sleeping!

A half-jackal dog slept at his feet.

Lily hung back a moment, like a deer trembling at the edge of an open meadow. Waiting. Watching. Fear made her mouth dry.

I'm . . . praying . . . how? Show me! Invisible One! I'm praying!

Hawk launched from the branch of a bristlecone pine. His bell tinkled as his shadow traced a path directly in front of the Overseer. The Samaritan did not awaken. Hawk passed beyond the barrier, flared, and landed Outside on the flat table rock where supplies were deposited.

Lily took a step forward. Then another.

I'm praying again, God Who Soars. Give me wings! Like Hawk!

Lily followed the path of the shadow. She approached Overseer. The stink of wine and urine was heavy in the air.

Baby Isra'el stirred and whimpered. The goat bawled and pulled against its rope!

Suddenly the dog leapt up! Snarling at Lily, it blocked her path! She froze, her heart beating like a small bird.

Praying! God of . . . Unseen . . . !

Hawk launched again, swooping just above the hut.

Overseer awakened with a start. His grizzled head jerked up in drunken irritation. "What? What?" He slapped the dog and gazed around. His eye passed by Lily as though she was not there, then caught sight of the Hawk. "Just a shadow! Look there! A hawk! What now? You! Shut up! Shut up! There's nothin' there! Nothin' there a'tall. A shadow on the ground! Daft!" Another blow cowed the creature. It slunk back to its place, where it glared sullenly at Lily.

Hawk swooped over her again, brushing her head with his wing tip. His shadow urged her forward.

Lifting her chin, she fixed her eyes on the way. She took a step. Overseer did not seem to notice her.

Praying again! Frightened! How could this be?

The dog growled, low and menacing. Its master slapped the creature to silence, took a draught of wine, and wiped his greasy chin with the back of his hand. He leaned back, closed his eyes, and covered his face with his keffiyeh as Lily walked, unseen, within two yards of him.

Outside!

The dog sprang to its feet in a fit of wild barking at her back. She whirled around as Overseer stood and glared at her.

"You! Hey! What're you here for, miss? Delivery day isn't till next week. New moon. That's the rule."

So he thought she had come to the Valley to make a delivery.

"I've come to . . . to bring this goat. To my . . . my sister."

He eyed the milk goat with interest. "Nothing goes in to them dead ones without my say-so. You can leave the goat. I'll see she gets it."

"No . . . I'll come back." She turned from him. Would he recognize her as one of those who had carried loads of supplies down the switch-back trail to the Valley? Would he remember she was one of the dead who inhabited Mak'ob?

"What's that you got there?" he demanded gruffly as he strode un-steadily toward her. "An infant is it?"

"My baby."

The shadow of Hawk touched her face as he circled restlessly above her.

"A baby is it?" He reached for Lily. "Newborn, eh? Well. You're a pretty young thing. Pretty. Yes. Care to come inside and rest yourself awhile?"

"No!" she shouted as he grasped her arm.

At her cry the Hawk shrieked and swooped, flashing between Over-seer and Lily.

The Samaritan cursed and lashed out as sharp talons lacerated his scalp. Hawk careened to the side, hitting the dog with a loud crack on its skull, sending it yelping toward its master.

"What's this? What's this!" The Overseer stumbled over the dog. Kicked at it. "Get by, you! What's this!" The Overseer shielded his face as Hawk dove a second time, then a third, and fourth.

The Hawk flailed at the Overseer's head, his neck, his ears. Each pass brought a hiss of wings like a flying serpent; each screeching plunge and stab came nearer the Overseer's eyes. He flung up his hands to shield his face and lurched blindly toward his house.

Lily ran from the struggle as the guard took shelter inside.

Overseer roared after her, "You! You! Woman! What are you do-ing here? Go on with you! Nobody gets by without my say-so! You hear me! Nobody!"

21

CHAPTER

The dusty band of talmidim sat under the shade of a stand of fig trees to eat a midday meal. Avel shared his food with Red Dog. The animal had become attached to the boy. Protective. Perhaps it was because there were no longer lambs to guard that Red Dog turned all his attention to herding children.

The pace of the journey northward was not punishing, and they were still within Jewish territory. Yeshua continued to attract new listeners to replace those who left, but with each gathering Avel thought he heard more open hostility. But maybe he imagined it.

Today a brace of Pharisees, including Simon ben Zeraim, the one Avel had noticed in Capernaum, approached. Yeshua greeted them, asked them to join in the food.

"That one won't," Zadok growled, indicating the same man Avel already spotted. "Simon of Capernaum."

None of the religious fraternity accepted, but they stood by, as if waiting for something to happen.

Yeshua made the *b'rakhah* over the bread and divided a loaf.

John broke off a chunk and passed it to Shim'on, who stuffed a corner in his mouth while wiping his hands on his tunic.

As if that action were a signal, Simon demanded, "Why do your disciples disobey our age-old traditions?"

Zadok snorted. "That Simon. Six thousand Pharisees in this land and he aspires to be the most righteous of them all. Won't go into a Gentile's house. Won't sell to a Gentile. Won't have anything to do with anyone not upholding their standards. In all this land only they are holy."

"Your disciples ignore our tradition of ceremonial hand-washing before they eat,"[49] Simon persisted. His hands, encased in doeskin gloves, gave every evidence of being especially fastidious about cleanliness.

Yeshua looked around at His friends, then up at Simon. "And why do you, by your traditions, violate the direct commandments of God?"

Simon puffed up like a toad, Avel thought. His cheeks quivered, and his frown devoured his eyes.

Yeshua stared at Zadok for a long moment before continuing. "For instance," the Teacher resumed, "God says, *'Honor your father and mother,'* and *'Anyone who speaks evil of father or mother must be put to death.'*"

A pair of Torah scholars standing behind Simon indicated their agreement with His words.

"But you say," Yeshua declared, pointing at Simon, as if this example was meant especially for him, "you say you don't need to honor your parents by caring for their needs if you give the money to God instead."

Simon looked uncomfortable, shuffling sideways.

"And so, by your own traditions, you nullify the direct commandment of God."

"Aye, that's poked him right where he lives," Zadok noted.

Yeshua paused to let the import of His words sink in. Avel knew Pharisees loved to make a big show of giving to the Temple charities. Yeshua made it clear that some of that show was really not holy at all. The same self-righteous Pharisees failed miserably at caring for their own aging parents.

"You hypocrites!" Yeshua shook His head in amazement at them. "Isaias was prophesying about you when he said, *'These people honor me with their lips, but their hearts are far away. Their worship is a farce. They replace God's commandments with their own man-made teaching.'*[50] Listen." Yeshua hailed the crowd. Some now smiled their enjoyment at seeing the Pharisees embarrassed. "Listen closely and you'll understand. What goes into a man's mouth doesn't make him unclean. But what comes out of a man's mouth. That's what makes him unclean."[51] Yeshua stared openly at Simon's gloved hands. He took a bite of bread and asked the Pharisee quietly, "Ah, Simon. Why do you worry about polishing the outside of the cup, you know? When it's the inside of the cup that's so unclean?"

At this final insult, Simon gathered up his brother Pharisees. With a sweep of robes they stormed from the argument.

"Do you realize how badly you offended the Pharisees by what you just said?" John asked.

Avel watched the rigidly straight back of Simon's retreating form. "If Simon's from Capernaum," the boy asked Zadok, "how do you know so much about him?"

"Because," the stern-faced shepherd replied, "he's my son-in-law."

"The Pharisees? Ignore them!" Yeshua replied to His talmidim. "They're blind guides leading the blind, and if one blind person guides another, they'll both end up in a pit."[52]

Avel pressed Zadok for an explanation. "Your son-in-law?"

"Aye. And it's clear Yeshua knows it. Yeshua's hit him where it hurts."

Avel asked, "You have a daughter?"

"Simon married my only daughter. She was born after my sons were killed. Yes, a beautiful girl. Looked like her mother. Her name is Jerusha. Sweet spirit as well. Married Simon many years ago. Loves him well, I hear. Obeys him. As for me and my wife, Rachel? We had some hopes of filling our house again with the sound of children's laughter. Grandbabies. Dreamed of grandchildren. That joy was denied us by Simon. And Simon's declared me dead to his family."

Avel repeated, "I didn't know you had a daughter."

"Might as well not have," Zadok admitted. "She can't have anything to do with me. I've been too blunt in my opinions about the religious rulers. Simon won't let me see my daughter or grandson. I haven't seen the boy ever. And as for my daughter? Well, not in years. I tried to contact her when her mother died. But it made trouble."

As the Pharisees stalked away, Yeshua's talmidim persisted in the discussion. "Explain what you meant when you said people aren't defiled by what they eat."

"Are you so dim?" Yeshua seemed amused. He tossed a piece of bread to John. "Anything you eat passes through the stomach and then goes out of the body. But evil words come from an evil heart and make the person who says them unclean. First from the heart come evil thoughts. Then following that are evil actions: murder, adultery, sexual immorality, theft, lying, and slander. An unwashed heart is what defiles you. But eating with unwashed hands? Put it in perspective." He laughed. "Come now! A little dirt under the nails is not what makes you unacceptable to God!"[53]

Zadok stared at the Pharisee's back for a long time. "Aye. There goes a man who's got it all turned round. Well. Perhaps if he comes near Yeshua enough to understand him, he'll get the message right at last."

Simon ben Zeraim trembled with rage. From head to toe he quivered like the topmost branch of a sycamore tree in the path of a Galilean gale.

"I hate him!" he announced to Jerusha. "He's evil. Maliciously evil."

There was no need to repeat Yeshua's name as the subject of the diatribe. Since returning home from his last encounter with the Teacher, Simon had spoken of nothing else.

Simon's face was covered in fiery red blotches, which he attributed to his wrath. "Criticize me, will he?" the Pharisee demanded rhetorically. "Call me an 'unwashed cup'? That charlatan! That heretic! He deserves to be stoned to death!"

"But if he could help you . . ."

Simon rounded on Jerusha savagely. "He *can't* help me!" he stormed. "If he were *really* a prophet, he'd know what was wrong without my saying a word, wouldn't he? Wouldn't he?" he challenged. "No, he's a false prophet, and the Law requires that a false prophet be stoned."

"But . . . if you *asked* him to help you?"

"Never!" Simon boomed. "He's cruel, he's evil, he's a fraud, and I hate him! The sooner he's brought low, the better."

Simon caught his reflection in a glass. After a sharp intake of breath, he gave a slow, deliberate exhale. "It's not good for me to get excited," he concluded. "Counteracts the benefit of the oil. You see how evil he is? Just speaking about him produces a bad effect. I insist: Don't mention him to me again. Ever!"

Peniel sank down in misery and fell asleep almost immediately.

What was the truth here?

Peniel was lost. He had no idea where he was going. Like the Israelites of old, wandering forty years, he was taking his companions through the wilderness. Only Peniel was no Mosheh!

The truth?

Peniel had no staff with which he could lead a people free after four hundred years of slavery or part the Red Sea or cause water to come forth from the rocks!

Truth?

Peniel was only Peniel. He was more comfortable in darkness than in light. He had liked his life beside Nicanor Gate. Had enjoyed a life without adventure. Who was he to lead anyone anywhere?

The truth? Peniel could not tell them exactly where Yeshua was. So how could they expect to find Him?

Peniel breathed a sigh. In his dreams he heard the distant whisper: *Peniel, always speak the truth. It is the only defense your soul will have when you stand before the Almighty!*

"But what is truth?" Peniel asked.

The voice, familiar and amused by the question, replied, *Peniel.*

"Mosheh? *Ulu Ush-pi-zin.* I'm dreaming again. I know. I need a good dream to help me face tomorrow."

Trouble sleeping, Peniel?

"Here's the truth of it. Troubling dreams. Too many questions. And I'm making up the answers. As if I know. And the truth is I know nothing at all. Except what I've heard."

A truthful answer. Tonight I'll remind you of things your heart knows and yet has never fully understood before. Yes. Just listen. What I tell you is the truth.

"I'm in need of a good story. Will you tell me about plagues and crossing the Red Sea and drowning Pharaoh's charioteers?"

Not tonight. Tonight I'll tell you a little something about Truth. About finding your way when you think you're lost in this eye blink of time you call life.

"At least you had pillars of fire and heavenly clouds and the Lord telling you what to do and where to go. Here I am, pursued by assassins. Two stubborn beggars from under the viaduct and a leper who stinks so bad he draws flies. What good can come of this?"

Nothing is impossible with God.

"It feels impossible."

Just listen. Open your heart. Your mind. Everything means something. Every word, every number in Torah speaks about God's love for us. About the redemption of our souls from the power of a terrible master who seeks to destroy our lives.

Peniel exhaled. "Tell me, then. Teach me about truth. My heart longs to know."

The word truth *is a tiny word in the Hebrew language.* EmeT. *Three letters. Spelled like this:* Alef. Mem. Tav. *Who would think that the story of eternity; of Messiah; of love, redemption, life, and death could all be contained within that one word? And yet within* EmeT, *all the truth of eternity exists.*

In the Hebrew Torah, as given on Mount Sinai, important phrases are all bracketed by a two-letter combination: Alef-Tav. *The Greeks would call it Alpha and Omega. The Beginning and the End. Another name for the Lord. You see, Adonai inhabits all eternity. So we will begin with* Alef-Tav, *or eternity, shall we?*

Peniel agreed. "The beginning and the end. Eternity? Forever? It's much bigger than here and now."

Mosheh laughed. EmeT, *the word for truth, begins with the first letter of the Hebrew alphabet:* Alef.

"The One," Peniel interjected.

Well done. And the last letter is also the last letter of the Hebrew alphabet.

"Tav."

You know your Hebrew, Peniel. And so now you see that Truth begins and ends with the Alef *and the* Tav. *The Lord, Yahweh, the Almighty, and Eternal Father contains all Truth.*

"But what about the middle letter?"

Think of what you already know, Peniel. There are twenty-two letters in the Hebrew alphabet, but twenty-seven when the variant endings are included. What is at the exact center of those letters?

Peniel counted on his fingers. "The *Mem!* The *Mem* is in the center!"

The Mem, *the middle letter between the beginning and the end, represents man's life in this world. So the word* EmeT—*truth—and* Alef, Mem, Tav—*beginning, middle, and end—tell us that Adonai our Elohim is truth from beginning to end and also inhabits everything in the middle. He is with us even in our lives on this earth.*

"Well, I never thought of it before!" Peniel declared with satisfaction.

But there's more. So much more!

"Yes, tell me! Teach me! I want to know it all!" Peniel felt immensely cheered. "I've missed my studies of Torah at the gate! They didn't know I was listening."

But your heart heard it all as you sat beside Nicanor. And so now I'll offer you another layer of truth that they did not teach and did not speak and did not understand. I will tell you about Truth and the Messiah, the One who has come down from heaven to dwell among men on earth. He has said, "the Truth will make you free!"[54]

Peniel smiled in his sleep. "Catchy phrase, but what's it mean? Tell me! Tell me everything, Mosheh! Everything you heard on the holy mountain when the Lord taught you for forty days and forty nights!"

At these words Peniel heard a sound like distant thunder and a howling wind. Mosheh lifted his chin, as though he was listening to a voice.

Now there's a story. The meaning of those numbers found in the word Truth. *All recorded in Torah! Four hundred years of bondage for the children of Israel. Yes. Four hundred years waiting for the One who would deliver them from slavery. And then the years and days of my life. Count them. Forty years a prince of Egypt. Forty years of obscurity living as a shepherd in Midian. Forty days on the mountain of Sinai as I was given the Law directly from Adonai. Forty years of wandering with the nation of Israel in the wilderness because of their disobedience.*

And then, me, Mosheh. Forbidden by God to be the one to lead His people into the Promised Land. No. After forty years I failed. I failed, so I was not allowed to enter the Promised Land. Israel followed another leader across the river to enter Eretz-Israel.

Peniel queried, "But what can all these forties and four hundreds in the Scriptures mean? They keep showing up. So many. I've always wondered. Nobody ever could explain."

I'll tell you plainly so you'll never have to wonder again. All the explanation is found in the word Alef, Mem, Tav. EmeT, *Truth. Hebrew words have numerical meanings as well. The letters of Truth add up to the number 441. The same number used to describe Israel's deliverance from slavery. Four hundred years in Egypt. Forty years in the wilderness. One Deliverer to lead them out. 441. Remember this. It means something.*

The first letter of Truth is Alef. Alef *is the number One. Every Jew knows* Alef *stands for the Eternal One. Hear, O Israel, the Lord our God is One!*[55]

The middle letter of Truth is Mem. *This is the number forty.*

How many times is forty found in Scripture? The children of Israel wandered in the wilderness for forty years. And when you see this number it is always associated with testing, with trials, with going through a time of learning. Just like our lives in this world.

The last letter of Truth is Tav.

Tav is the number four hundred. The children of Israel were in Egypt four hundred years before their deliverer came to them to set them free. Are you following this, my friend?

"I think so. Yes," Peniel answered. "So much in one little word."

Much more than what I can teach you in a dream. But this will be the first lesson. The first of many about the meaning of truth. Four hundred years of captivity and then freedom! Forty years of wandering and testing in the wilderness of this world! And only the One true Elohim can lead us home. Truth!

Between the Alef *and the* Tav *of eternity, our life on earth is the* Mem, *the forty years of trials and testing.*

I tell you the Truth! There is coming a moment which will stand forever in the center of all eternity! The Mem of forever!

Messiah will be lifted up as the Light to the nations. He will draw all men to Him. And all those who call upon His Name . . . those who acknowledge that He is the Way, the Truth, and the Life[56] *. . . will hear His voice cry out to them, 'I AM the Truth! I AM the fulfillment of all* EmeT *as written in the Torah and Tanakh! I AM the Alef-Tav! The Alpha and the Omega! The beginning and the end! I AM the One who will enter the Mem of your time on earth and walk with you through your wilderness! I will endure the trials and testing of life with you! I AM* EmeT! *I AM the One who will deliver you from bondage. I AM the One who leads you and brings you home to eternity!'*

Peniel nodded, understanding. "Yes. I get it. A lovely little word, *EmeT*. A big word. Now, tell me plainly, Mosheh. What does Torah tell us about the name of the One who will lead us out of this wilderness called Life and into the land of Promise?"

The rumble of thunder grew more distant.

It is written that after my day the one who finally led the children of Israel across the Jordan and into the land of milk and honey was called by the Hebrew name, Yeshua. Joshua, the Greeks call him. Some call him Jesus.

Yes. So it was in my day. So it is in this time. That is the Name. So it will be in the future. Yeshua! God is Salvation! He is the Truth! He is the Life! He is the Way! Listen to Him and be saved!

"Things are bad for Yeshua now. So many enemies. Even those of us who know him doubt sometimes. How can he set up his kingdom in such a world as this?"

Mosheh's voice was a sigh. *Nothing is too hard for God.*

Thus ended the lesson. Peniel opened one eye. The fire had died to embers. Gideon and Amos snored loudly. Jekuthiel was off somewhere, but near enough so Peniel could still smell the dying flesh of the outcast.

"Nothing is too hard . . ."

The goat provided ample milk for Isra'el's needs, but Lily's limited store of provisions was exhausted. She feared entering a town to beg. If her *tsara'at* was recognized, she'd be stoned. What would happen to baby Isra'el then? She could not risk it.

Lily placed Isra'el in a shawl tied around her shoulders. Leaving the goat tethered to a shrub, Lily took Hawk hunting.

Hawk darted from sage to broom tree to gnarled, lonely oak as Lily followed the barest trace of a path.

Time passed without result. The countryside was desolate. No game appeared.

Once, in the distance, Lily spotted a pair of foxes slinking around a gully. Though of no use to her, at least their den proved game existed. If foxes found sustenance, so would Lily.

That bit of encouragement kept her moving forward, but still without success.

At length Lily decided to give up and try again the next day. She feared to leave the goat alone too long. Likewise she must not go too far from her camp, lest darkness make it difficult to find the route back.

Can you hear me, Distant One? You fed your people in the wilderness. Can you feed me too?

The return trek led her past a dense thicket of brambles. As she drew near it, she heard a low chuckling sound from the midst of the brush. Stopping dead still, Lily spotted Hawk. The bird was poised at the edge of the briars on a tamarisk snag.

What had Cantor taught her? Quail, Lily decided. Quail go into thick cover toward late afternoon to hide themselves for the night. There might be fifty or a hundred sheltering under the thorns.

But Hawk could not operate in such impenetrable cover. She'd have to work as Hawk's partner, flushing the birds from their refuge. Perhaps then he'd have a chance to seize one.

Locating a broad, flat rock, Lily unwound sleeping baby Isra'el from the sling and placed him in the thicket's shadow. Wrapping her cloak tightly about her for protection, she advanced toward the brambles.

She whistled to get Hawk's attention.

Instantly the chatter from the undergrowth ceased. The patch of briars took on an alert quality, as if the thicket itself were being stalked.

Lily plunged into the thorns. Heedless of the snagging of her clothes and legs, she ripped her way in toward the heart of the plot. Beyond this first tangle was another even larger area of brambles. If the covey made it across the open space, there was no way Lily could pursue them farther.

At the halfway point of her passage there was an angry outburst of sound. A frantic clatter of wings erupted from under her feet. A dozen birds broke free of their haven, splitting the silence as they battered the air in all directions.

"Ho!" Lily yelled. "Ho!"

Hawk launched himself at a pair of quail flying in tandem formation. Just before his impact they split radically apart and Hawk flew between them, missing both. He circled, regaining altitude.

Lily pushed forward.

Baby Isra'el awakened, began to cry.

A second score of birds burst from the thorns and took wing.

Hawk pounced.

Feathers exploded as Hawk and a quail collided in midair. Hunter and prey tumbled to earth. Hawk remained where he landed till Lily approached. Hawk instinctively mantled his wings over the carcass. She praised him and he stepped down, relinquishing the prize. Training had taught Hawk that Lily would reward him for his work with a portion of the kill.

I'm praying again, God of the Wilderness. One quail. A single quail. I am small. I will eat and be glad for what you have given.

Baby Isra'el was full to bubbling.

Hawk contentedly gnawed his reward: quail head and entrails.

Lily had a finely plucked and dressed quail carcass prepared for her supper . . . and no fire to roast it.

Her left arm was useless. She had always relied on the right . . . until now. Her right hand had chosen this moment to lose all remaining feeling. Try as she might, Lily could not grasp the pieces of flint firmly enough to draw sparks to start her fire. Even while Lily stared at the operation, the flint stone turned in her grip. Her hand refused to cooperate.

Lily was faced with the choice of eating the quail raw or going hungry.

Or perhaps there was a third option.

A faint glow from the opposite hillside, nearer the main road, indicated the presence of other travelers. Lily could obtain fire from them. With the baby once more secured around her neck, Lily left Hawk sleeping on his perch. The goat she staked in a patch of grass. Afraid some night-roaming creature would steal her supper before it was cooked, Lily tucked the cloth-wrapped quail carcass into the sleeve of her robe.

Nearing the camp Lily moved softly, ready to bolt at any sign of danger. From behind a screen of bushes she inspected those she saw around the flames. A man and a woman were there, and nearby a pair of smaller shapes bundled in blankets—sleeping children.

A family with children. Lily sighed with relief. "Hello, the camp," she called.

The man snatched up a brand from the fire and held it defensively between his family and the noise in the brush. "Who's there?" he demanded. "Keep back, Hannah, till it's safe."

"I . . . I'd like to use your fire," Lily pleaded. "Use it to start my own, I mean. May I come closer?"

"Nahum," Hannah said kindly, "it's a young woman." Then louder, "Come to the fire and welcome."

Lily advanced into the circle of light. When Nahum saw the child she carried, he relaxed slightly. Then, "Are you alone?" he said suspiciously. "Traveling alone?"

"Across the ravine," Lily explained truthfully. "My party's there. Trouble getting our fire started. I saw yours."

"Of course, child," Hannah agreed. "Nahum, you must help her. Carry the fire for her."

"Oh no," Lily replied hastily. "I can manage. If I can just have a single stick . . ."

The man stepped toward her. Grasping the burning limb by its middle, he reversed it to present the cool end for her.

Lily reached out to take it from him with her right hand. When she closed her fingers around it, the torch fell from her nerveless fingers. She and the man both reached for it. In the illumination of the fire the unmistakable marks of *tsara'at* were revealed.

"Unclean!" Nahum shouted. *"Chadel!* Get back!"

Faster than before, he snatched up the blazing brand from the ground and thrust it at her face. Lily cried out, afraid for the baby. The package containing the quail fell unnoticed from her sleeve.

"Go away!" he ordered. "Unclean! Leave us!" Brandishing the fire like a flaming club, the man drove Lily away into the darkness.

22

"Here she comes again," Har-or Tov noted. "The Canaanite woman. Two days in a row."

"Three days," Avel corrected, tossing Red Dog a bite of his bread. The canine snatched it from midair, enjoying the game of catch the crumb. "She came once the first night, remember? Then several times yesterday. Now again this morning. That's three days."

"Why doesn't she quit and go home?" Emet whispered.

Zadok snapped his fingers and Red Dog came to his side. "Enough feeding him at table now, boys. You're teaching him bad manners. We've no flock to tend, but Red Dog must be patient. He mustn't beg nor expect to eat until I speak the word. So eat yer lunch and leave him to me."

Zadok surreptitiously slipped the dog a morsel.

Yeshua and His talmidim were in a region appropriately called "the borderlands." That expression was correct in several different senses. Up here north of the Sea of Galilee, farther north even than Lake Huleh, no one was exact about where the Galil ended and the province of Syria began. Besides that, the upper Jordan marked the boundary between the Galilean territory of Herod Antipas and Trachonitis, belonging to Herod's half brother Philip. The problem was, past Lake Huleh the river was not a distinct watercourse. Rather it was a series of rivulets and streams, forming a huge marsh but an indistinct boundary.

The village of Chadassa, on the heights to the northwest of Lake Huleh, might have been claimed by all three of the neighboring provinces . . . or none of them. Impoverished, nestled in the windswept amphitheater of a basalt plateau, Chadassa was remote from everything else in the world, Avel thought. The residents of Chadassa were regarded as illiterate country hicks by the richer Greek-speaking residents of Tyre and Sidon. They were treated as apostate mixed breeds by the citizens of Israel proper. In marketplace conversation the children of Israel were referred to by the Roman overlords as "dumb sheep." The Canaanites were referred to as "canines."

Even the name of the place reflected this ambiguity. The Jewish residents claimed it honored Hadassah, the biblical heroine also known as Esther. The pagans translated the name as that of an ancient Syrian king.

The village was built on the site of a settlement dating back to the days of Solomon, one of the northern cities awarded by him to his friend King Hiram of Tyre. Hiram was so unimpressed with the whole region that he referred to it as *Cabul*—meaning "obscurity."

The people of Chadassa made their meager living by collecting papyrus reeds from the swamps. Down in the mud and stagnate pools, the shoots valued for making writing material grew in great profusion . . . and so did fevers and diseases of all kinds.

Chadassa's placement represented relief from the worst of the humid heat and noxious fumes. Still, its situation overlooking the marshes was a constant reminder of where the residents had to venture to make their living.

Even then they did not receive the full value of their efforts. Cut and bundled, the papyrus reeds were transported to the coastal cities to be processed into writing material. Those who risked their lives to gather the raw material received barely subsistence wages.

This was the retreat to which Yeshua led His followers to escape temporarily from the crowds and the opposition around the Sea of Galilee. Even here the respite was not complete.

John and big Shim'on were conferring together. "Canaanite canine! The dog! Why doesn't Yeshua make her leave off nipping at our heels?!"

"Have mercy," the woman cried.

"Master," John begged. "Send the Canaanite away. Her barking is . . . annoying."

"By all means, somebody give the canine a good kick and send it to yelp somewhere else," Judas insisted.

Even though the demands of the two talmidim contained the same message, Avel recognized important differences. Judas had no use for a poor, illiterate Canaanite . . . and a woman besides. Why should they bother about her?

John, on the other hand, had a different motive, which Avel identified from his tone: *Send her away because her constant begging is embarrassing. She's hounding us!*

The twelve followers of Yeshua piled insult after insult on her. Yet the woman would not give up! Day after day Yeshua said nothing in response to her pleas, nor did He rebuff His followers as they railed against her.

And then she spoke the words that caused Yeshua to turn and look at her. "Have mercy on me, O Lord . . . Son of David!"[57]

Now something new had been added to the woman's plea. Today she addressed Yeshua by one of the titles of Messiah. Not as an itinerant healer or magician, but as the Good Shepherd, the Anointed One of God.

"Have mercy on me, O Lord, Son of David! For my daughter! My little girl! For the sake of my child! She is tormented by a demon! She's suffering terribly. Have mercy on her, Son of David!"

"Send the canine away," Judas urged again.

At last Yeshua responded. "Woman," He said, not unkindly, "I was sent to the lost sheep of Israel."[58]

Zadok nodded his understanding. Leaning closer to Avel, the old man remarked, "She called him Son of David. The shepherd. Yeshua speaks of the prophecy of Ezekiel: *'So I will rescue my flock. . . . And I will set one Shepherd over them, even my servant David.'*"[59]

The woman, haggard, worried, thin-faced, and stoop-shouldered, knelt at Yeshua's feet, close enough to touch Him. "Lord, help me!" she begged again.

Yeshua did not address her directly. Instead He turned to the band of talmidim. His piercing gaze withered John, Ya'acov, Shim'on, Judas, and the rest. He said to them, "So. First let the children eat all they want? Yes? It isn't right to take bread from the children and toss it to their canines, is it?"[60] Then Yeshua glanced toward Avel and Red Dog, as if to make a point.

To Avel's surprise the woman did not reel away from this apparent rebuff. Raising her eyes boldly to Yeshua's face, she lifted her eyebrows as if to instruct the men in the way of things in a woman's kitchen. "So the children are fed already! They're eating! The crumbs are falling! Even *house dogs* under the table eat the children's crumbs."[61]

"Now there's a wit." Zadok smirked and suppressed a chuckle at the chagrined expressions on the faces of Yeshua's inner circle.

The wordplay would have been funny if the subject had not been so serious. What would Yeshua do? Would He have the presumptuous Canaanite driven from His presence? Would He merely turn His back on her the way a Pharisee would have shunned the Greek canines of the north?

The tension disappeared as Yeshua smiled at her, gesturing for her to stand up. "Well spoken, woman. Yes. The children of Israel have been eating for quite some time now, eh? Crumbs are raining down from the table. Careless children. Careless. No need for those who are hungry to wait any longer. And so, for such a reply as yours? Your request is granted. Go on home now to your daughter. The demon has left her."[62]

Bowing again, laughing, crying for joy, believing, thanking Yeshua profusely, the woman scampered away. It was obvious from the change in her demeanor and energy she had complete trust that when she arrived home, she'd find her daughter completely delivered and healed.

"Well, she put us all in our places. And Yeshua let her do it, too. Set her up to do it, in fact. Aye. She knows a bit about shepherds and herding." Zadok guffawed at John and Ya'cov as they sulked at being shown up by a woman. Zadok scratched Red Dog's ear. "Aye, John! Dumb sheep and canines. Ask me! If it's a contest of wit between the sheep and the canine? Who'll win? Aye! Aye! And Yeshua let her nip the heels of his flock on this day!"

On a hill overlooking the Sea of Galilee, Lily milked the goat and fed baby Isra'el. When he was sated, Lily sipped a bit of warm, sweet liquid and felt grateful.

Late-afternoon sun hammered the silver sheet of water. Russet sails of fishing vessels scudded across the surface like butterflies skimming a pond.

Beautiful. Lily had almost forgotten how beautiful. Beyond the lake, the Galil was greening with new crops of early summer. Vineyards dressed the terraced slopes in a bright green cloak of perfect symmetry.

"Home." Lily inhaled deeply. The scents were so familiar to her even after all these years, it was as though she had never been away. "Home."

She reckoned she would be at the farm by twilight.

"Look, Isra'el." She held the baby face forward so he could see the land. "This is where you will grow up. Someday you'll be a man here. Their own dear boy. They'll love you. 'Such a quiet baby,' Mama will say. She always appreciated sweet little ones like you. Mama will sing to you. Rock you to sleep at night. Papa will show you how to plant and harvest. He'll teach you Torah. And with my heart, your voice will speak the words I long to say. You'll call them Mama and Papa. And they'll never know it's me loving them back from behind your eyes. Me there with you when you laugh. Me wishing joy for them through you. They are good folks, Isra'el. They couldn't help it that I had to go away. Mama said she wished it was her instead of me. But it wasn't. I pray for her every day."

Milk dribbled from his lips. He burped as she bounced him. Lily kissed the child on his velvet head. "It is a good place to spend a life-time, Isra'el."

Bean rows would all be planted by now. Tendrils climbing the beanpoles. The cow would be fat from the spring grass. Chickens in the coop would lay eggs enough for a good meal every day. And nobody in all the village made honey cakes like Mama!

Lily smiled as she pictured it all.

"Maybe there'll be baby lambs in the lambing pens. If it's a good year and Papa didn't have to sell them all."

Through the heat-induced haze Lily could almost see where their farm was situated. In a swale a half mile from Capernaum. Just behind the dark green of the landlord's walnut orchard. Yes. There was the swath of green. The orchard. Home was just there.

Hawk's bell roused Lily from her reverie. He flared and balanced on the thin branch of a sage. His golden eyes studied Lily, as if to ask what she was waiting for. He bobbed up and down on the limb in an almost impatient gesture.

"I see you," she acknowledged.

The bird mewed in response.

"Yes. You're right. It's lovely here. It's better here than our Valley. But we can't stay, Hawk. No. Just for a while. I wish . . ."

I'm praying again, Lover of This Land. Yes. I love it too. Home. Yes. You've carved it on my heart, I suppose. I just didn't remember how deep the etching. I didn't know that I would still bleed at the sight of it. Or at least I didn't let myself think about it. But the baby. He'll grow up here. You'll let him live. For all of us who won't. I'll think about him here and be happy. For Mama. Papa. For him. Yes. I won't mind dying if I can give them such a gift.

It was getting late. They would have to get going if they would make it home before sundown.

Avel was thankful when Yeshua completed His journey to the swamps of the north and returned to the Galil. His relief was short-lived, however, because the Teacher and His talmidim only passed through the Jewish territory. The little band pressed on into the Decapolis, the federation of Greek-founded cities that lay partly between Galilee and Samaria, but chiefly east of the Jordan.

Crowds of listeners, most Gentiles, gathered from all the cities of the region: from Hippos and Gadara, from Philoteria and Scythopolis, from Capitolias and even as far away as Philadelphia, way out on the border of Nabatea.

"Suppose one of you has a friend," Yeshua taught them, "and you go to him in the middle of the night and say to him, 'Friend, lend me three loaves of bread because another friend of mine who has been traveling has just arrived at my house, and I have nothing for him to eat.' Now the one inside may answer, 'Don't bother me! The door is already shut, my children are with me in bed—I can't get up to give you anything!' But I tell you, even if he won't get up because the man is his friend, yet because of the man's chutzpah he will get up and give him as much as he needs. Moreover, I myself say to you: Keep asking, and it will be given to you; keep knocking and the door will be opened to you. For everyone who goes on asking receives; and he who goes on seeking finds; and to him who continues knocking, the door will be opened."[63]

Among the thousands who came, there were few who openly opposed Yeshua. This multitude was not made up of Jewish Zealots looking for a Messiah-King to free them from the Romans. Also not represented in this semipagan country were Pharisees wanting a controllable prophet to validate their peculiar and restrictive brand of holiness. Nor were Jewish Temple authorities on hand, jealously guarding their privileges.

The people who followed Yeshua into the wilderness east of the Sea of Galilee were eager to see and hear the Healer and have Him touch their sick. Since the daughter of the Gentile woman was healed in Chadassa, the floodgates opened. Lame, blind, crippled, mute—all these physical ailments and more—were brought to Yeshua. He touched and healed them all.

As if trying to pack two years of His talmidim's training into the briefest space possible, Yeshua taught almost nonstop for three days.

"Is there any father here who, if his son asked him for a fish, would instead of a fish give him a snake? Or if he asked for an egg, would give him a scorpion? So if you, even though you are bad, know how to give your children gifts that are good, how much more will the Father keep giving the *Ruach HaKodesh* from heaven—the Holy Spirit—to those who keep asking him?[64]

"Don't work for the food that passes away but for the food that stays on into eternal life, which the Son of Man will give you. For this is the one on whom God the Father has put his seal."[65]

The location Yeshua had chosen was even more deserted than around Chadassa. The closest village was miles off. Nor was the hillside where He spoke especially hospitable. Unlike the lush grass of a few months earlier, the scene now contained sparse vegetation, brittle after more than two months of the dry season. The more exposed hillsides were bare rock or dirt.

Yet, as if His very words were food and drink, the crowds stayed. They acted unwilling to miss even half a day to trudge out to get provisions.

The first day they ate figs and boiled eggs brought from home.

The first night the assembly cooked over campfires. They prepared stews and soups and ate fresh bread purchased in Hippos.

The second day they ate leftovers and trail provisions: rock-hard barley loaves, dried fish.

The third morning they scrounged through knapsacks to find previously overlooked parcels of dried dates and fragments of matzah.

By noon all the provisions had been consumed.

Late in the afternoon on the third day Yeshua gathered His closest confidants on the hilltop. Avel, with Zadok, Ha-or Tov, and Emet, stood just outside this ring but near enough to hear the Master's words. "I feel sorry for these people," Yeshua said. "They've been here with me for three days and have nothing left to eat. If I send them home without feeding them, they'll faint along the road. Some of them have come a long distance."[66]

Avel's stomach growled. Ignoring it, he looked over the throng. His eyes lit on two sitting on the ground in the front row: the woman of Chadassa and a smaller version of herself, clearly her daughter. Both beamed at Yeshua.

"How are we supposed to find enough food for them here in the wilderness?" John asked, tugging anxiously at the knot of brown hair tied at the nape of his neck.

Yeshua spoke patiently, as if reviewing a lesson He'd covered before but which had failed to take proper root in His talmidim's understanding. "How many loaves of bread do *you* have?" He inquired.[67]

Shim'on and John took stock among the others. Zadok contributed one barley loaf—all that remained of his supply for himself and the boys. "Seven," Shim'on reported. "That's all—seven. And a handful of fish."

"Tell the people to sit down."[68]

The crowd did as they were told, but an air of expectancy ran through them.

"Blessed art Thou, O Lord, our God, King of the Universe, who gives us this bread to eat."

When Yeshua had said this blessing, He broke a loaf, passed two fragments to a waiting disciple, broke another, passed them, and then did so again.

Seven rivers of bread flowed down through the multitude like refreshing streams.

Avel watched Yeshua's hands.

He gave and gave and gave.

No matter how many times He broke a chunk of bread, another piece large enough to be broken again remained in His hands. It was not the amount of the bread that mattered.

It was the hands that broke the bread.

To this was added the dried fish, plentiful and to spare since it also passed through the hands of the Master.

Everyone tried to eat and talk at the same time. Some in the crowd remarked that now it wasn't only the Jews who could claim a story about miraculous bread being provided in a wilderness.

Avel himself carried two pieces of bread and two chunks of fish to the woman and her daughter from Chadassa. He could only imagine what went through the woman's mind as she compared her request for the crumbs from the Master's table to this ample, abundant, overflowing supply of rations.

"How many are getting their fill from seven little barley loaves?" Avel heard Ya'acov ask.

"About four thousand," Philip replied. Avel helped gather up the scraps after everyone had all that could be wanted. The leftovers filled seven large baskets. These containers were not small tubs but great wickerwork barrels—the kind used on board ships to carry provisions for long voyages to distant nations.

Yeshua blessed the crowd after that, then sent them home. He and His disciples hiked down the canyon, all the way to the shore. When they got there they found boats, arranged for by Miryam of Magdala. The vessels carried them across to her estate on the other side of the lake.

23

B eth-Shemesh, "the house of the sun," was a minor settlement on the Jordan near the Sea of Galilee's outlet. From there the river began a straight-line passage of seventy-five miles. In reality its course was nearly twice that length because of its meandering. Eventually water pouring from the Galil reached the Dead Sea.

The river called The Descender dropped to a quarter mile below sea level by journey's end. From bubbling, chattering, fresh and clean, the waters flowed downhill. It gathered volume on the way, only to stagnate and sink and come to uselessness.

Peniel thought he knew how the river must feel. They had come so far from Jerusalem. As they had entered the region of Galilee his sense of accomplishing his mission increased. So too his anticipation.

But now, on the very threshold of success, it seemed he was thwarted.

Beth-Shemesh was deserted. Chickens scratched and chuckled in stone yards. Goats bleated in pens. A wisp of smoke rising from a single chimney tantalized but offered no clues. There was no one left to either explain, beg from, or offer clues as to Yeshua's whereabouts.

"Plague, do you think?" Gideon muttered.

Amos had not deserted after all. He still had a flow of proverbs, but they came less glibly to his tongue. He glanced over his shoulder at Jekuthiel. Perhaps the leper was the embodiment of whatever dread disease had carried off the inhabitants of Beth-Shemesh.

"No," Peniel disagreed. "No dead bodies, no new graves. And look around you: The animals are all fed and watered. These people left in a hurry, but not in distress."

"So?" Amos challenged. "An example is no proof."

Peniel was too tired and too anxious to tell the dwarf to shut up.

It was important to make a correct decision here. They had expended a huge amount of energy over the past week, hurrying to catch up with Yeshua.

Jekuthiel was almost entirely spent. Long days of arduous tramping left barely enough recovery time before the next morning's demands.

Nor were Amos or Gideon in much better condition. The dwarf seemed shorter in stature, as if the inadequate, bowed legs he had were wearing down. Gideon appeared more crooked and more lame than at the beginning.

Up the east shore of the Sea of Galilee lay Bethsaida and Capernaum, perhaps another two days' travel . . . if they lasted so long.

If Yeshua had gone that way, then things might still work out.

But what if He had gone the other way . . . turned toward the Plain of Jezreel, or gone up the west shore of the lake? Peniel was convinced Jekuthiel would never live to see Yeshua if they guessed wrongly.

Gideon studied the cottage from which the tendril of smoke clung to a wall of cloud-trellised sky. "Food, anyway."

"You're stealing?" Amos chided. "Stealing to give away for charity is still stealing."

"Look at it this way," Gideon suggested as he barged into the hut. "I'm helping them perform a mitzvah. They'll be blessed for it, and they had no struggle achieving it."

"If my brother steals . . . ," Amos began another proverb, but then his stomach growled loudly. "Ah, well. When hunger comes in the door, pride goes to the dung heap. Wait, Gideon. I'll help you."

Jekuthiel was near a low rock wall. Instead of sitting and resting, he stood like a badly formed statue, frozen beside some marks drawn in blue chalk on the rough stones.

Gideon emerged from the farmhouse. His cheeks were stuffed with bread. Both hands were filled with barley loaves. Behind him Amos had an armload of dried fish.

"Has the leper finally lost his mind?" Gideon asked. "He looks stuck."

"Jekuthiel?" Peniel asked. "You all right?"

A slow nod in response. "Do you . . . know how to . . . read?" he inquired.

"Me? No. I can make out my name if I can feel the letters . . . but that's all."

"You?" Jekuthiel shouted to the others. "Either . . . of you . . . read?"

"What for?" Gideon replied. "What good is reading to a beggar? A vanity, that's all. Doesn't put one more copper in the bowl now, does it?"

"He's right," Amos concurred. "Give a pig a chair, and he'll want to sit at table."

Gideon thumped the dwarf on the head with a barley loaf.

"Then we'll . . . have to do . . . this the . . . hard way," Jekuthiel wheezed. "These . . . chalk letters . . . mention Yeshua."

"What?" Gideon demanded. "Where?"

"My eyes . . . too bad to . . . make it out. Describe each . . . letter to me. I'll see . . . what . . ." The leper wavered and staggered sideways.

"Quick!" Peniel ordered. "A stool for him."

A painstaking hour passed, full of descriptions like "The next one looks like three fingers of a man's hand and the one after that has a loop at the top and a straight line down on the left."

At last Jekuthiel asked for a drink of water. When he swallowed it, he took a deep breath and reported: "Yeshua . . . here yesterday. Tomorrow . . . near Shunem."

"Shunem? Which way? How far's that?" Peniel wondered. "Does it say?"

"Due west," Gideon offered. "If we climb the ridge tonight and camp, we can reach Shunem by noon tomorrow."

For fear of being spotted and recognized by old friends and neighbors or elders of the synagogue, Lily skirted the village of Capernaum. She waded across the shallow stream called Yismah. She stopped long enough to bathe, plait her hair, and change into the clean yellow gown she had worn on her wedding day.

In the last moments of daylight Lily glimpsed her reflection in the still water of the pool and remembered the meaning of *Yismah*, "He Will Rejoice." Once Papa had told her that the letters of the brook's name were the same as *Mashiyah*, the Messiah. And when, one day, Messiah washed His feet in this tiny stream, the waters would rise up like a great river and rejoice! And on that day all the people of the Galil would flow to Him as even the waters of a stream seek the sea!

It was a lovely memory. Papa had tossed a leaf into the current and taught her a verse from Isaiah. Often, in the hours of her greatest sorrow, she had recited what she remembered of the promise: *"There will be no more gloom for those who were in distress. . . . He will honor Galilee. . . . On those living in the land of the shadow of death a light has dawned."*[69]

I'm praying again, Light Who Will Come to Galilee. Will I someday, though I am dust, rise up with the waters of this brook and rejoice to see your day? Will I feel your touch? Will you restore the pain I long to feel again in my hands? Will I hear your voice with my desiccated ears? Oh! You've been silent so long in my life! If only! If only I could hear you speak! Feel your touch! My soul longs for you!

She waited, listening. There was only silence and the sounds of approaching evening.

The face looking back at her in the reflection was familiar, even lovely. "Mama?" Lily never before realized how much she resembled her mother: blue eyes, wide and friendly. Thick blond braid over her shoulder.

If Mama opened the door and saw Lily had come home, would it be for Mama like looking in a mirror of clear water? Would Mama cry out with joy? welcome her daughter home? enfold Lily in her arms?

Lily brushed a leprous finger through the image. It dissolved beneath her touch.

She tied the goat to the limb of a cottonwood tree. Hawk, sensing the end of his day, perched on a low limb above. Tucking her pack into the tree she explained to the bird, "I'll be back for you. I'm taking Isra'el home to the farm. To Mama and Papa now. But I'll be back for you and Goat before the sun rises."

Scooping up the baby, she set out along the familiar path. Night fell. Black. Absolute. A myriad of stars dusted the heavens. And one earthly star, embedded in a distant hill, guided Lily unerringly toward home.

Lights beamed from the windows of the farmhouse. Crickets chirped in the brush along the way. She passed the same berry patch where she had gathered blackberries her last summer at home. Tonight she recognized the scent of the tangled vines that grew wild on the gentle slope to her right. On the left were the pastures where Papa kept a few ewes and a ram. Beyond that was the walnut orchard of Simon the Pharisee, their stern and imperious landlord.

She walked the dark path as though a candle illuminated her way. She knew each step, each turning.

Isra'el was fast asleep in her arms, his face turned toward her breast. He would awaken tomorrow in the arms of Mama. Mama would feed him and smile down at him. In the clear pool of his innocent eyes there would be no difference between Mama's reflection and Lily's. And Mama would sing to him. Her voice so much like Lily's. He would feel no pain of separation from Lily. No. He would not miss her.

The reflection of Lily's love would stay with him. All his lifetime. When Mama turned to smile at little Isra'el, Lily's eyes would look gently at him too. Lily would be there, in Mama's voice, cheering baby Isra'el on when he took his first step. Spoke his first word. Held his own spoon. Grew and learned and became what he would be. Yes. As Mama loved him, Lily's love would be there too. Even though Lily would be dust by then, some part of her would remain. She had brought him here. Her final journey home.

"Home." She sighed, topping the rise. Now only the garden separated her from Mama's arms.

Light beamed bright from within the house as if to welcome her. As if nothing had changed. As if she had never left home or traveled to that far country called Sorrow. The melody, the perfumed scents of night, all sang to her, beckoning her to come closer.

She heard the sound of voices. A man. A woman. Discussing something . . . but what? She saw the silhouette of a male move across the open window.

"Papa?" she whispered.

Suddenly she realized this homecoming was also good-bye. She kissed the baby. Nuzzled her cheek against him. "You will live, Isra'el. Yes! You will . . . live."

The front door opened. Yellow lamplight streamed out, pooling on the path. A fire flickered on the hearth.

Lily strained to see within. Even a glimpse of Mama. But no. No. Not yet.

A man's voice said, "It won't take a minute: The old ewe's due any time." Carrying an oil lamp, he left the house and headed toward the lambing shed. The same place Lily had been quarantined. She inwardly groaned as that memory encroached upon her. She pushed it back. No! Not even that! Not even the recollection of those first agonizing days of separation would ruin this feast of joy!

She could not see his face. The light was too low on the path. Roses bloomed beside the walk. Mama and Lily had planted those roses together. Still there! Still there! The roses!

And, Mama, when you smell them in the summer, do you remember me? Do you remember who I was before? Before I pricked my thumb on the rose thorn and felt nothing, nothing at all? Not even remorse. Before the numbness of my illness overpowered me, forcing me to leave you? But I'm back, Mama. Still I bleed and don't know I'm bleeding. I hang in tatters on myself but live on, dying, unaware of pain. Oh! I know now. How much better it would have been to feel agony if only I could have stayed with you, Mama! Because you would have stayed by me, hurt with me! But now I'm numb, dead. There's nothing you can do but stand back from me. Give me up. Nothing you can do. And so tonight I've brought you this child. So you can rejoice again, although I'm gone.

All these thoughts were in her mind as she stood rooted like a tree outside the house. The wind of longing tore at her. All that had been familiar and beloved was once again there to touch. Not a dream. But if she stretched out her hand to Mama, Lily would feel nothing.

Separation.

The lamplight in the sheep pens moved about. Muttering to the animals, the faceless man finished his work and strode back toward the house.

Lily stood there. A tree. Rooted. Whipped by the storm. Unable to speak or go forward. The door opened. He entered. Then he closed it behind him. The bolt clanked into place.

I'm praying again, Unfeeling One. I'm Outside . . . Outside . . .

The clatter of crockery and bits of conversation drifted out to Lily from the farmhouse. Supper was over. Lily knew the routine. The washing up, prayers, and then bed.

Courage!

Lily bit her lip. Took a step forward. Stopped. Tugged the sleeve of her gown to conceal the claw of her left hand beneath the baby. She adjusted her veil across her mouth and nose.

I'm praying again, Silent One. Have I heard your voice since I left this place? Are you here? Did you stay behind when they drove me out? I'm praying again. Hear me. Please? If you are standing in the shadows, watching, please walk with me to the door of Mama's house.

Lily walked between the roses. Her slight limp seemed exaggerated by the crunch of gravel beneath her feet. The conversation within fell away. Did they hear her approach?

The scraping of a chair.

Lily stood before the wooden door. She glanced toward the mezuzah, by which the blessing of coming and going had been spoken every day in her early life. She resisted the desire to place her finger on it. She did not *touch* it but smiled at it as though it were an old friend.

May the Lord bless your going out and coming in.

Drawing courage from the memory of that blessing, she cradled Isra'el in the crook of her arm and raised her right hand to knock.

Quiet rapping. Three times only.

Absolute silence within.

"Someone at the door?" A man's voice called to her.

Lily's voice quaked. "Yes. Shalom."

The door flew open. A heavyset man of middle age with a frizzy red beard stood before her. He grinned curiously.

Not Papa. Where was Papa?

He bellowed pleasantly. "Why it's . . . naught but a girl." Then, "Shalom yourself, young lady! What're you doing out so far at such an hour? And with a babe in arms! Trouble on the road?"

Lily blinked dumbly at the stranger. "No. No trouble. I . . . I was looking for . . . Obed and . . . Abigail. Are they home?"

A woman called from behind the fellow. "Obed and Abigail did she say?" Footsteps. The thin, sharp face of the housewife peered around her husband. "It's been a while since I've heard their names spoken! Why would you be looking for them here, girl? And bringing a child with you? In the cold night air? Won't you come in?"

Mama. Papa. Not here! It was like a blow to Lily's stomach. She stepped back from the invitation. If they knew. If they saw her crippled hand or guessed . . .

"No. I can't stay. I . . . I was just looking for my . . . for Obed and Abigail. They live here. Don't they?"

"Used to," said the man. "That's been . . . what? How long, wife? Since they lived here?"

"Nearly five years. Landlord evicted them. Some trouble with one of their children as we heard. A daughter." The wife rattled on. "They had three boys, didn't they, husband?"

"Aye. Three boys and a girl they had. Then the girl . . . the girl was—" he lowered his voice—"stricken by the Almighty, as I remember it. You know what I mean. Aye. That's it. *Tsara.*"

Tears welled up. "But where . . . did . . . they? Where are Obed and Abigail and . . . their children?"

"Away." The woman made a motion with her hands like she was shooing birds from the garden.

"Aye," agreed the man. "Away. Simon, landlord, said he didn't want no trouble. And them as has kinfolk stricken with such a fearful thing must be under judgment of the Almighty. So he drove them away."

"But . . ." Lily stared down at little Isra'el. Poor baby. Poor Isra'el. *Mama! Oh, Mama!* She wasn't here to care for him. Oh, what now?

"And who are they to you, those people?" The wife narrowed her eyes and scratched her chin as she peered at the infant. "A relative, are you? Seems to me . . . yes . . . Abigail had flaxen hair. And . . . who are you, girl?"

"I . . . I'm no one." Lily stepped back another step into the shadow. So. Because of Lily, her family had also been exiled.

"But why've you come here after dark looking for them? After all these years?" The man tugged his beard.

The wife stuck out her lower lip. "You look familiar, girl. Familiar. Have you lived about these parts?"

Lily swallowed, fought the urge to run. Backed up. "Not for a long time."

The fellow emerged. Advanced toward her. "What'd you want coming here to our farm? Give me an answer, girl."

"This child. I heard . . . Abigail was a good mother. I heard she lost a child. I was bringing this little one to her in hopes . . ."

Husband and wife were dumbfounded. "Come to leave the child with that woman?" spat the husband.

"Couldn't have been much of a mother," declared the wife. "Her daughter was a leper, wasn't she? The whole family accursed by God."

Lily trembled. "Where are they?"

"How should we know such a thing?" The husband was irritated now. "Gone."

"And good riddance." The wife clucked her tongue. "So you've got a foundling child. Take it to the orphanage south a few miles over in Magdala, girl. If you've given birth to a child out of wedlock, they'll take it in, no questions asked. That's my advice. Get rid of it. But for mercy's sake, we'll do this much for you. You and the child can spend the night in our shed if you like."

Sleep in the lambing pen? The place her long exile had begun? Lily backed another step, heard tearing as the spines of the rosebush clutched her dress.

Mama! Oh, Mama!

"Careful there, girl! Those rosebushes!"

"The thorns have got your leg! Can't you feel that at all? Careful there! Look at the blood on your dress!"

Lily did not feel the thorns in her leg as she turned and ran from the place into the blackness of the night.

No.

Her flesh did not feel her anguish.

ily woke to the sound of baby Isra'el snuffling. He did not cry or wail, though he needed to be fed and changed. The goat grazed placidly under the cottonwood tree. Hawk still kept watch overhead.

In the depths of her despair and misery, Lily had thrown herself down on a mossy bank at the foot of the tree and slept all night.

All the thoughts of seeing home again . . . useless. All the miles had come to nothing. All the anxiety expended on what would happen, all the hope of a glimmer of joy at seeing Mama banished in an instant. Not even one moment to be loved.

Now they were dead to her, just as she had been dead to them. Gone. All these years she'd pictured them here. Her father toting her younger brothers on his broad, strong shoulders. Mama, brushing back a lock of stray hair from her forehead with the back of her hand.

The images of *who* they were inextricably linked with *where* they were.

Or where she'd imagined them to be. But now she understood fully the truth: Their lives, if they still lived, were elsewhere. Their memories were of other places.

The last point of contact Lily had clung to, the corner by the stove where she imagined Mama picturing her, remembering her, missing her . . .

. . . gone.

The wickerwork box of sewing things Papa had made for Lily in exact likeness of Mama's, the one that always rested on the mantel by the Sabbath candlesticks . . .

. . . gone.

The last vestige of home gone forever. No putting it back, ever. Not for an hour, not for a minute.

Shattered.

Lily sat up. Tended the baby.

Her gown was torn and bloodstained from the rose thorns. No longer cheerfully straw-colored, the dress was now the image of a field of hay stubble after being grazed by a flock of sheep.

Lily examined her legs. Some of the scratches were deep. There were many wounds; some were puffy and swollen with embedded, broken thorns.

There was no pain. Soon enough her feet and legs would succumb to *tsara'at*'s effects, leaving her a cripple.

She must go home, home to Mak'ob, while she was still able to travel.

Only one thing remained: to take the baby to Magdala.

There was no mercy for Lily. No mercy for the *chadel*.

Perhaps there was one drop of mercy for an innocent child? Mercy in Magdala?

O, Mute One, she prayed, *I have nothing left to ask except that you spare this child. He's done no wrong, has never injured another soul. Spare him from ever knowing the grief of being so . . . hopeless.*

The numbness of her hands and legs had spread inward as well. In place of Lily's anguish there was now emptiness. In place of her aching longing there was a dullness.

In place of her heart there was a stone.

Yeshua never escaped the crowds for long, Avel thought. Even here in Magdala, where the Master enjoyed playing with the children at Miryam's villa, the word quickly spread that He was present.

People came to be healed in their bodies and went away joyful, thanking God.

Others came, also requiring healing. The anger, hatred, envy, and jealousy bursting from them clearly showed their spiritual illness, but they would not admit their need. Anger made them blind to the mended lives all around them. Hatred stopped their ears to Yeshua's words. Envy stifled the taste of the bread of heaven that came through in everything Yeshua taught. Jealousy blunted their ability for Him to touch them and work any healing in them.

They were worse off than the lepers. Spiritual disease of the heart robbed them of all their spiritual senses. Pharisees, secure in their private club of self-righteousness, made common cause with the traditional religious party, the Sadducees, about only one topic: opposing Yeshua.

Simon the Pharisee was again in the front rank of the attackers. "Once more I challenge you: Prove you are who you claim to be by giving us a miraculous sign. If you let us suggest a trial and you complete it successfully, we'll have to admit there's some validity to your claim."[70]

Avel heard Yeshua sigh. "You know the saying, 'Red sky at night, sailor's delight. Red sky at morning, sailor take warning'? You are good at reading the weather signs in the sky, but you can't read the obvious signs of the times! Only an evil, faithless generation would demand a miraculous sign. But I tell you again, the only sign I will give is the sign of Jonah."[71]

Simon seemed almost disappointed. What was it he wanted? Why did he continue to demand a sign? The Pharisee cleared his throat, straightened his gloves and phylacteries, and left.

Yeshua announced that He was leaving there to again cross the lake, heading for the northeast shore en route to another preaching location.

Avel asked for and received a place for himself, Red Dog, Zadok, Ha-or Tov, and Emet in the Master's boat.

Yeshua rode in the bow, His face lifted to the spray. His eyes were closed.

He's praying, Avel thought. *If the one who can open blind eyes, unstop deaf ears, and fix broken hearts still needs to spend time praying, what does that say about me?*

Avel's mental soliloquy was interrupted by a controversy between the Zebedee brothers, John and Ya'acov.

"I thought you brought it," John suggested.

"No," his brother argued, "Remember? I told you to get the sacks off the porch of the caretaker's house."

"I don't remember that."

"What?" Avel asked.

John looked chagrined. "We forgot to bring bread for this trip."

After what they had recently witnessed Avel wondered why any of the disciples would ever worry about having enough bread![72]

Yeshua made His way back toward the center of the boat. Balancing Himself against the tilt of the crate and the roll of the waves by hanging on to the mast, Yeshua spoke loudly enough for all to hear. "Be careful of the yeast of the Pharisees, the Sadducees, and Herod Antipas."[73]

"He knows," John hissed to his brother. "He knows we forgot the bread."

Shaking His head with amusement, Yeshua said, "Why are you so worried about having no food? Won't you ever learn or understand? Are your hearts too hard to take it in? You have eyes—can't you see? You have ears—can't you hear?"

The same spiritual problems as the Pharisees and Sadducees, Avel thought.

"Don't you remember anything at all?" Yeshua continued. "What about the five thousand men I fed with five loaves of bread? How many baskets of leftovers did you pick up afterwards?"

"Twelve," John mumbled.

"And when I fed the four thousand with seven loaves, how many large baskets of leftovers did you pick up?"

Shim'on, hauling on a line, eyed the trim of the sail and replied with certainty, "Seven. It was seven."

"Don't you understand even yet?" Yeshua asked them.

"Everything means something," Zadok rumbled.

Yeshua applauded. "Just so," He agreed.

Avel approached Zadok with a question. "Yeshua mentioned all the numbers of bread and people and baskets as if it all meant something more. But what?"

Gathering his wards around him in a circle, Zadok posed a return inquiry. "Five," he said without prologue. "Who knows five?"

"I do," Ha-or Tov responded, waving his hand. "If you mean the same way the question is asked every Passover. Five is Torah, the Law, the books of Mosheh."

"Good," Zadok acknowledged. "Now, just like the Passover questions, boys. Think! Who knows twelve?"

Avel got it. His arm shot up. "The twelve tribes? The twelve sons of Ya'acov?"

Zadok nodded approvingly. "So. Five loaves, five books of the Law. Twelve baskets for the twelve tribes of Israel, eh? Y' boys saw Yeshua feed the five thousand back around Passover. He gave the bread of heaven to us Jews, eh? And there was plenty left over. But now, think: Now he fed the four thousand. Mostly not Jews. Who knows four?"

Frowns passed back and forth amongst the three students. "Four winds," Zadok prompted.

"To the four corners of the earth." Ha-or Tov caught the image.

"So. His words—his Omer—no longer just for us Jews, but he feeds all the nations of earth as well. Isn't that what we saw these days just past? And finally: Who knows seven?"

Avel scratched his head. Ha-or Tov sunk his chin in both hands.

Emet ventured, "Shabbat? Every seven days?"

"Good," Zadok praised. "Manna is given for six days in the wilderness and yet there was always provision enough to last for the seventh day. All creation—Jews and Gentiles—will be brought into the Sabbath rest and provision of the Holy One. Like manna poured down as bread from heaven, so Yeshua is poured out as *the* bread from heaven. But not just for us Jews . . . for everyone, everywhere . . . if they'll only receive him. For the twelve tribes of Israel *and* the nations of the four corners of the earth."

Avel was pleased with this explanation, but one thing still bothered him. "So, Master Zadok, what did Yeshua mean when he said, 'Be careful of the yeast of the Pharisees and Herod'?"

"That's where this whole discussion started, isn't it?" Zadok acknowledged. "It's this: Their pride, which is like yeast, makes these fellows all puffed up by their own importance, eh? In their pride they demand a made-to-order miraculous sign. They refuse the evidence of the powerful things Yeshua has already done. No wonder he calls them blind guides and warns us against being even the tiniest bit like them. And both Herod and the religious rulers have sent spies among the crowds. They plant doubts. They stir people up. Like yeast, it doesn't take much to ferment public opinion and turn it against the truth. Aye. Dangerous times."

The boat slid into shore, scraping its keel upon the sand. Avel raised his head above the rim of the boat and looked out at the harbor. Already there were hundreds gathered, waiting for the arrival of Yeshua. Surely the pride of the Pharisees was stung by all the *am ha aretz* who gathered on every shore to hear the teachings of Yeshua.

Had they all come because of a hunger in their souls? Or had they only come for bread?

The oil was working! Simon assured himself and Jerusha it was making a difference. Morning and night he rubbed the slippery yellow fluid into his neck, face, and hands. The tingling caused by the chaulmoogra reawakened places that had felt dead to his touch.

It had to be working!

Simon's right hand was still cramped. He stuffed the fingers of his right glove with rolls of linen to maintain a normal appearance. To any who inquired why he was so awkward with it he explained that it had been burned, which was true enough and deflected further inquiry.

Simon had also discovered he could tolerate swallowing a dose of the oil if he ate bread and drank a glass of wine first. Then he could safely bear a small spoonful of the mix, even though it still made him feel ill. But he kept the tonic down, and that was all that mattered.

Dressed in his Sabbath best, with Jerusha in the gallery looking on, Simon took his place at the front of the auditorium.

"Blessed art Thou, O Lord," Simon heard, "King of the World, who formest the light and createst the darkness; who makest peace and createst everything; who, in mercy, givest light to the earth and to those who dwell upon it, and in Thy goodness day by day renewest the works of creation."

No more darkness of fear in Simon's life. A few weeks' treatment and all would be restored. Simon would advance in honor and position and wealth, and no one would ever be the wiser.

A day of renewal, without question. A day of mercy for which Simon owed many lambs, many sacrifices of thanksgiving when next he went to Jerusalem.

At the back of the hall Simon spotted Levi Mattityahu, the former customs collector for the Romans and now a follower of Yeshua of Nazareth. Simon's eyes narrowed. A tax collector and a blasphemer! This was intolerable. Something would have to be done when Simon returned to Capernaum. In Simon's opinion, such a man should be politely but firmly told to go elsewhere to worship.

Now that Simon was on the mend he'd be even more forceful confronting Yeshua. He made a vow before the Almighty that he would.

"True it is that Thou art Yahweh our God and the God of our fathers, our King and the King of our fathers, our Savior and the Savior of our fathers, our Creator, the Rock of our salvation, our Help and our Deliverer."

Soon Simon would be able to give his *full* attention to dealing with the problem of Yeshua of Nazareth. Unless of course the cutthroats in the employ of Herod Antipas took care of Him first.

The service proceeded through readings and sermon and eulogies until the time for the final benediction was reached. The president of the assembly summoned Simon to the bema. As a special way of honoring Simon, he was invited to offer the concluding blessing.

"Thank you," Simon murmured, "but because of an injury I cannot remove my right glove. It's not fitting to lift up holy hands that way."

The chief of the gathering considered for a moment then said, "What if you remove the other glove only? We all know of your great attention to purity, Simon. Please oblige us."

Why not, Simon thought. *There's never been any mark or blemish on that hand. I only wear both so no one will be curious.*

He agreed to offer the final supplication.

Clearing his throat, Simon let the left glove fall to the ground and raised his hands beside his shoulders.

"May Adonai bless you and keep you."

A stirring ran through the audience. Not much, not loud. No more than the susurration of a spring breeze in the new foliage of the olive trees.

"May Adonai make his face shine on you and show you his favor."

Some in the congregation waved and gestured. Simon's sense of propriety was offended. What an affront to his dignity! What were these whispers that could not be restrained for a few moments more? Simon deepened the resonance of his voice, increased the volume.

"May Adonai lift up—"

Simon's left wrist was grasped by the president of the assembly. With shock and anger he stopped his recital.

"*Tsara'at!*" the leader muttered, wrenching Simon's hand downward. "Unclean!" Then louder, so the whole world could hear, he bellowed, "Unclean! This man is *tsara!*"

How could this be? What could it mean? Simon was baffled. "What?" He tried to wrench his hand away from the hostile grip.

A synagogue attendant grabbed his other shoulder, held him like a thief in the marketplace.

"What?"

The leader of the synagogue twisted Simon's left hand around so he could see its back.

A large white spot was emblazoned there. It was twice the size of a Temple shekel, swollen, and rimmed with an angry red border.

It wasn't there this morning, Simon thought stupidly. "It's just a burn," he yelled. "It's not *tsara*. I burned both my hands. Do you hear me? It's a burn!"

No one was listening. Grabbed by the other shoulder by another attendant, Simon was force-marched off the platform and toward the exit. His feet weren't moving fast enough to keep up. His knee slammed into a pillar as the guards swung him past it. Men crowded aside to avoid any contact, made the sign against the evil eye, shook their fists at him.

In their looks he saw fear, loathing, revulsion . . . scorn.

As Simon was hauled beyond the women's gallery he glanced up.

Only on Jerusha's face did he see sorrow. Then she buried her countenance in her palms.

"I don't know," Simon heard his friend Melchior say to someone as Simon was hustled outside. "Did he touch the scroll? We'll have to burn it, you know. It's defiled. Burn the bema cloth too, just to be safe."

25 CHAPTER

he action after Simon was dragged from the synagogue passed in a blur. The two attendants transported him by the sleeves, one on each side, as if he were an unruly goat between a pair of tethers.

Even worse, they shouted to everyone they saw, *"Tsara'at!* Unclean!"

"It's a mistake," Simon repeated, shrieking. "Why're you doing this? You're wrong!"

"Unclean!" they called still louder. "He concealed it! He even recited from the bema, knowing he was accursed!"

A crowd followed from the synagogue, joined by others in the street who heard the commotion. *Am ha aretz,* commoners too impious to even be in synagogue on the Sabbath, pointed at him and commented.

A swelling wave of remarks accompanied the flap of sandals:

"He's cursed for certain."

"A Pharisee? One of that holier-than-thou tribe?"

"He must have done something really awful to be smitten that way."

"It's always some sexual sin, I hear. Some perverted heathen practice, no doubt."

Simon blustered at them, "Don't you know who I am? I'll have you in court for this! I'll own you before I'm through! Your children's children will still be my slaves!"

His threats only made the attendants yank harder. At one point Simon's feet tangled in the hem of his robe and he fell. They hauled him along the cobbles of the market square, scraping his knees and the side of his face.

"Where are you taking me?" he demanded.

Where indeed? At the outskirts of town there was a primitive winepress cut out of solid rock, its floor twelve feet below ground level. Simon was rolled over the edge and tumbled in. He landed heavily, with a shock that numbed his right arm and his already bruised knee.

Simon tried to scramble upright but could not. He fell over again. "This isn't right!" he insisted, his emotions bordering on hysteria. "Why are you treating me this way? You're supposed to call a priest. I'm not *tsara* just because you say so. Don't you know it has to be a priest!"

The rim of the threshing floor was ringed with onlookers. The chief of the synagogue arrived in time to hear the question. "We've sent for the priest," he said. "But we're not taking any chances with the likes of you. You weren't treated this way because you're *tsara*; it's your arrogance! You knew you had something wrong, and you tried to hide it! You even sat in synagogue with all your neighbors, pretending, concealing the truth!"

Simon had no response. It was true. Anyway, he couldn't defend himself in front of this mob. But a priest would be a learned man—one who would know the force of law and the privileges of wealth and power such as Simon possessed. He could talk to such a man, reason with him.

"All right," Simon admitted. "But there's no reason to cage me here like a wild animal. Let me go home. I'll wait there for the priest. Let me go home."

One of the synagogue's wardens appeared with a winnowing fork in hand. "If you so much as jump up, I'll skewer you," he menaced, waving the wooden-tined tool in Simon's face. "Jepthah, you and Amnon get rocks. If he tries to escape, we'll stone him and bury him where he lies."

There was an intimidating murmur of agreement to this suggestion.

This couldn't be happening. It was a nightmare. Simon ben Zeraim was a model citizen, respected businessman, esteemed exponent of the purity of the Law. How could it be that Simon found himself in a pit? that he was surrounded by irate villagers who were prepared, even eager, to smash Simon's head like a melon?

It seemed like an eternity before the priest arrived. Simon sat on the rough foundation of the winepress. He rubbed his aching arm and leg, but every time the surrounding mob caught sight of the sore on his hand, there were repeated calls to just stone him and have done with it!

The appearance of the *cohen* was not as reassuring to Simon as he'd hoped. The man's name was Eli ben Sholom, and he was a Sadducee. He was one of the Temple officials who maintained a long-standing hostility toward the brotherhood of Pharisees. Moreover, he was a Jerusalem native, only in the Galil visiting relatives. Simon could not hope for any sympathy from him.

Nevertheless, Simon made his appeal. "There's been some mistake. I—"

"Take off your clothes," Eli ordered coldly.

Simon sputtered. "I won't!"

Eli shrugged. "*Tsara* who fail to obey the directions of the priest shall be stoned."

"But I'm not . . ."

Eli waved one finger.

A rock the size of an apple hit Simon in the back, making him duck and cradle his head in his hands. When no more missiles followed, he cautiously looked round to see Eli holding up a hand, ordering restraint. "Remove your clothes," the *cohen* said again.

Simon could not undress without first removing his right glove.

A groan of revulsion spread outward amongst the onlookers at the sight of Simon's crabbed right fist.

Embarrassment. Shame. Indignity.

Humiliation heaped itself on Simon's head. Every mark on his body was discussed in the company of strangers. In the bright sunlight flooding the pit there were no secrets. The thickening of Simon's earlobes was noted, the red marks at his hairline, the angry welts on his ribs and flanks. "From being dragged here!" he protested. "Just happened. It'd be the same for any of you!"

But there was no escaping the condemnation of the twisted right hand and the visible sore on the left.

"The Law," Eli ben Sholom stated, "is very clear. Book of Vayikra. Parashah 27: If someone develops on their skin a swelling, scab, or bright spot which could develop into *tsara'at*, he is to be brought to a *cohen*. If the bright spot is white and goes deep into the skin it is *tsara'at*; he is unclean."[74]

"Wait!" Simon begged. "You can't see how deep in the skin it is. There's a provision for waiting, checking again." If only Simon could get home. In a week more the chaulmoogra would have done its work. He'd be better. *All a mistake*, they'd say. *We wronged you*, they'd say. *Please forgive us*.

Eli interlaced his fingers across his belly. "Not in this case. The evidence is clear."

"No!" Simon protested. "Seven days! Give me my due! Let me out of—"

Hands holding stones reared up all around the pit.

In a tone that allowed no argument the *cohen* added, "Tonight you stay here." Then, to the chief of the synagogue, Eli instructed, "Guard him. Rig a shelter over his head and give him food and water. But he is not to be allowed out. Tomorrow he'll be examined again."

The village of Magdala was quiet in the sweltering heat of midday. Lily, carrying baby Isra'el, entered in search of the orphanage.

The milk goat was hungry, tugging at her rope as she lunched on bits of grass along the road. Hawk glided to perch on a rooftop—waiting, watching—as Lily limped slowly past. He followed in peripatetic flight.

Mama. Gone. Gone. Mama. Gone. Gone.

Lily had been so distracted by the joy of expectation she had not imagined that Mama might not be there. Lily would have been content just to see her. Content with just one moment. One word. Would have reached out, content, even without touching Mama. Content to lay the baby in Mama's arms. Content to watch Mama's lips brush the cheek of the baby and pretend that it was her cheek. Content as the door closed in her face.

Who could have dreamed Mama would be gone when Lily came home? Who could have imagined home empty of Mama? Not a day had gone by since Lily was forsaken that she had not pictured Mama there, smiling beside the hearth.

What now? What now? The face of Mama floated in a void before Lily as she trudged numbly forward. What now?

Lily's yellow wedding dress, caked with blood and dust, hung in tatters on her thin body. She took no pains to conceal her leprosy. What was the point? If anyone had bothered to look closely at her trembling hands or bloody legs, they would have seen that death, un-cloaked, was her close companion.

But no one who passed her on the road spared a second glance. She was simply another ragged beggar. Common as an earthenware cup with the word *hope* glazed on the rim. This was Lily. Between yesterday and today, *hope*, fired bright red in the kiln, was worn away.

A stone block used as a watering trough for livestock was near the well of Magdala. Lily stooped to drink from it.

An older woman with a water jug on the rim of the well studied Lily through dark, sad eyes. "I have fresh water. I have a cup."

"No. No . . . thank you."

"Where are you going, girl? You, and the baby?"

"I've come . . . because they said . . . they told me . . . there is a place in Magdala where I could leave the baby and someone would care for him and he would live."

"Yes. The villa of Lady Miryam. Not far. I'll take you. Your leg. You're bleeding."

"Come no closer. I'm *tsara. Chedel.* From the Valley of Mak'ob." Then quickly, "The baby is healthy. His mother's dying. I've carried him Outside. He's not sick. No need to fear him."

"I've never found a baby I was afraid of. What happened to your leg?" The woman left her water jar and came round the well toward Lily. Near enough to touch. She seemed unperturbed by Lily's confession as she examined the wounds.

"Thorns."

"What's your name?"

"Lily."

"Come on then, Lily. I'll pluck them out. Wash your wounds."

"You didn't hear me. Don't come near! I'm . . . untouchable."

"Is that so?" The woman reached out and put her arm around Lily's shoulders. Embracing. Comforting. "This way, Lily. Come along. You must be tired. Are you hungry? You've come a long way to save the life of this little one."

Lily began to weep. Her shoulders shaking beneath this unexpected first touch of kindness.

How long had it been? How long since anyone but another leper had dared to reach out to her, embrace her?

"Come along, Lily. To the house. I'll see to your leg."

"You can rest in the infirmary," the woman told Lily. "You'll have it all to yourself today. You can sleep there. Rest there. The journey is long."

The infirmary was a small stone cottage, built on the grounds behind the great estate on the shore of the lake. Young women, some clearly pregnant, others carrying tiny infants, came and went from the villa.

A red-haired young man spaded the garden as a trio of girls hung wash on a line. A number of residents looked on with mild curiosity as Lily and her guide entered through the gate in the high wall.

Hawk perched above the gate.

Lily's guide waved and called to the youth with the shovel, "Carta! Come take the milk goat to pasture!"

He obeyed, jogging toward them. "Welcome." He glanced approvingly at the infant. "Well this one's a boy, that's plain enough. Handsome fellow. I'm glad he's a boy. I could use some company. All girls this week."

"This is Lily." The woman touched Lily's shoulder.

Lily flinched, unaccustomed to being touched.

The youth bowed awkwardly. "Shalom and welcome."

Lily backed a step, looked away from his frank glance, and did not reply.

The woman instructed, "Carta, I've left the water jug back at the well. Please, would you?"

"Sure. Well, then . . . welcome to you." He wiped his hand on his tunic and led the goat away.

The woman watched him a moment, then said quietly to Lily, "You must be very tired."

"I'm not allowed to be here. You see. With people. Not allowed to be touched."

"Come. I'll take the baby inside to the nursery. Tavita will feed him. Wash him. While I work on your leg."

An edge of panic pushed at Lily's throat. So this was good-bye. Isra'el had found his place and now Lily would be sent away, never to see him again. "May I say farewell? hold him? one last time?"

The woman put a steadying hand on Lily's arm. "Let me wash and clean your wounds. Old Tavita will feed him. Watch him until you're rested. Then she'll bring him out to you if you like. That's all. That's all I meant. You may stay with him as long as you like."

"But. The others. Shouldn't be near me."

"You may stay here in the cottage until you're ready to travel. No one will mind."

"Why are you so kind to me?" Lily searched the gentle face for some explanation. Did this woman really fully comprehend what Lily was? An outcast?

"How far have you traveled, Lily, to save this little one? Tell me, why did you put yourself at such risk for him? suffer so much to bring him out of the Valley to safety?"

"It's not his fault the world is such a cruel place. He committed no sin. He's not to blame for his suffering. It's not his fault that his mother is a leper. Dying. Not his fault no one wants him. If I hadn't brought him out, who would?"

"Well spoken. Yes. My reasons are something like that."

Lily studied her for a moment. About forty-five years of age. Ordinary. Hands calloused. Knuckles skinned from pulling up the bucket at the well. Brown hair framed a round face made friendly by deep smile lines around her eyes. Yet such sad eyes. Eyes that seemed to see past everything and probe Lily's very soul. Deep brown eyes with flecks of gold.

"Tell me, please. Your name?" Lily asked.

"Mary, widow of Yosef, carpenter of Nazareth. Now wait inside the cottage. I'll take the baby in to Tavita."

Lily lingered in front of the cottage as Mary carried Isra'el up the steps of the villa. Surely Mary had not intended for Lily to enter the structure. Perhaps somehow she had misunderstood the seriousness of Lily's disease.

Mary returned a few moments later with bandages and a stack of clean clothes. "Come inside."

"I'm a leper."

"Tavita will send out something for you to eat."

"I haven't been inside a house in six years. Not in a real house. I'm forbidden."

Mary took Lily by the elbow and compelled her to enter the cottage. "Are you hungry? You must be hungry. Look here. Such a lovely dress you're wearing. The thorns have torn it just there. But we can wash away the blood and stitch it up. I'm sure of it. A little embroidery will close the tears, and no one will ever know it was damaged. Roses. Yes. If you like, I'll embroider roses just there and there. There. Along the hem where the thorns snagged it. Do you like roses? I've brought another dress for you. Not nearly so fine as yours, but put it on. You can wear it until we wash yours and repair the damage. My fingers aren't as nimble as they used to be, but still I can fix it good as new. Do you like roses?"

A river of anguish flowed from Lily as Mary patiently plucked the barbs of rose thorns from Lily's wounds.

And Lily told the gentle lady everything.

Everything.

Life as it had been before.

Mama. Papa.

Old friends and neighbors. The elders of Capernaum driving her away.

Stumbling into the Valley of Sorrow one morning half starved and terrified.

Deborah and her family taking her in during those first terrible weeks. Jekuthiel. Still half strong with his half hands. Still handsome and beloved in Deborah's eyes.

Their sons. Two little boys.

Lily, like a sister to them.

Lily learning to laugh again as they lived together in the cave just above the Valley floor.

Jekuthiel kissing Deborah farewell.

Jekuthiel setting off to find Messiah. To bring Him back. To beg Messiah to set free the 612 captives of Mak'ob.

Jekuthiel never coming back.

Rabbi Ahava who taught Torah to dying children as though they would live forever. Yes. Forever.

The children of Mak'ob singing in the choir.

Yes. So many children.

Children in the dying cave crying for their mothers.

Palm-leaf shrouds enfolding tiny remains like gentle hands.

Yes. Gentle hands.

Cantor's gentle hands.

Lily beside Cantor as they sat on the stone in the night. Naming stars. Learning names. Wondering about the One who made them. Wishing. Hoping. Searching for that glimmer of first light that might be The Light they all longed to see soaring down from heaven to set free the 612 captives of Mak'ob!

Soaring. Yes.

Cantor and the Hawk. Soaring.

Cantor with the children.

Cantor. Beloved friend.

Cantor. Lily's dress. Beautiful.

Lily. Beautiful. Beloved in Cantor's eyes.

The wedding. Their little house. The night. The one night.

The joy. Together.

Gentle hands. So gentle.

Deborah's baby born. No room for even one more life in the Valley of Sorrows. Six hundred and twelve.

Cantor. Leaving without Lily. Leaving Lily without Cantor.

The shroud of palm branches. Gentle hands holding Cantor like a bird. Cantor in the grave. Cantor.

Lily longing for death. Lily. If she could see Mama one more time. Offer Mama this baby. A living child in place of the child who lived in living death.

The baby. Deborah. Jekuthiel.

The baby. Six hundred and twelve.

The journey Outside.

The night beside the stream of rejoicing. The wedding dress. The house. Mama! Mama! The light in the windows lying to Lily's heart. Telling her that everything she ever longed for was inside.

Mama gone. Mama exiled like Lily. Driven out because of Lily.

The faces of strangers. Curious. Suspicious. Hostile.

The roses she and Mama planted by the walk.

Roses. Thorns. The tearing of her wedding dress.

A final mocking of her journey home.

All. All of this and more, spilled from Lily's broken heart in a torrent. She lay facedown on the mat as Mary's gentle hands plucked the broken thorns from broken flesh.

Gentle hands. Unafraid to touch the untouchable. Washing. Anointing. Bandaging.

Gentle heart. Listening. Listening. Listening.

Gentle fingers taking up the ruined wedding dress. A needle. Thread. Yes. What was torn could be mended. Yes. Better than before. Everything was possible.

By this kindness, this courage, touching what was untouchable, loving the soul within the ragged flesh, Mary plucked thorns from Lily's heart.

Then peace, like Mama's roses, bloomed in the twilight.

Fragrant. Gentle. Peace.

How long had it been since . . .

There, in the little cottage, Mary embroidered rosebuds while Lily slept.

The miserable blanket Simon curled up in was not adequate, even though the night was not especially cold. Why offer anything better to a *chedel?* his captors questioned. It would just go into the desert with him or have to be burned. No need to give something better to someone stricken by *tsara'at.*

Simon was unable to sleep in the comfortless pit. The stones under him were cruelly uncompromising. Facing an uncertain future, Simon had plenty of time to think.

Other people became *tsara'im,* not Pharisees. Certainly not Simon ben Zeraim, the Pharisee. The *am ha aretz*—they who were not careful about the washings—they became *tsara.* Gross sinners, unrepentant, wicked hearts, greedy, self-righteous souls—they became *tsara.* There was some cosmic mistake at work here . . . unless . . . unless . . .

Unless Simon really was being punished for allowing that woman from Magdala into his home. He had not been strong enough in denouncing her, hadn't spoken up soon enough against the wiles of that so-called Teacher from Nazareth. Simon resolved that as soon as he put this misunderstanding behind him he'd go back to Jerusalem. He'd offer his full services to the high priest. Simon now understood what damage Yeshua's heretical preaching could do. He had to be stopped. Simon would take a personal interest in seeing it done.

In all other matters Simon knew himself to be guiltless. He kept the commandments. He offered the sacrifices. He tithed of all he owned, even down to counting out the tiny grains of poppy seeds and specks of cumin so as not to deprive the Almighty of His due.

Simon turned over and shivered as air sneaked in under the thin cover. He struggled to find a comfortable place to lay his head.

There was none.

Maybe it was a curse.

That was it. That magician named Yeshua, or Miryam the harlot, the witch, had put a spell on him.

"*Simon!*" Jerusha hissed his name.

"Where are you?" he called.

"Shhh! The guard is asleep under the fig tree. I brought you some things." Over the ledge she pushed a bundle wrapped in a warmer cloak. It landed with a soft thud. "There's a skin of wine and some bread and dried fish. It's all I could get for now without raising suspicion."

"Bless you!" Simon whispered back. All Simon had been allowed by order of the synagogue council was a jug of murky water and a stale loaf of barley bread. "Thank you, Jerusha. You're the best! The best wife, the best companion, the best helper."

"They won't let me see you," Jerusha explained. "They think I might help you escape . . . or maybe they think I have it too! Oh, Simon, I'm frightened! What're we going to do?"

"Bring me the chaulmoogra," Simon instructed. "I'll use it even if I'm here. When the priest checks again I'll already be cured."

Silence.

"Jerusha," Simon whispered urgently, "did you hear? I said, bring the potion."

"Simon," Jerusha said wearily, "I've been watching you rub and swallow that oil every day. Don't you think I know the truth? It hasn't done a thing, except maybe make you worse."

"No!" Simon exploded. He stopped to listen, afraid his outburst had awakened the guard. Then when things continued quiet, he resumed, "It just needs more time." Simon would not admit that it was hopeless.

Jerusha continued timidly, "I have another idea. My father knows the Healer. We could ask my father for help. Maybe he could get us to see Yeshua of Nazareth. He's done so much good, and they say he can heal anyone."

"Never!" Simon shouted. "He's the reason I'm here! It's a curse!"

"What? Who's there?" challenged a sleepy but belligerent guard.

"I love you, Simon," Jerusha said, disappearing in the darkness.

"Not Yeshua!" Simon bellowed. "Bring me the priest! I know what to do. Bring him!"

Gideon lay perfectly still, listening.

Peniel's breathing could be heard in the gaps between Amos' snores. The dwarf's sonorous buzz was enough to wake the dead. Of course, in the case of the beggars, dead *tired* was beyond the reach of even that.

Farther away, under the overhanging boughs of an oak, lay Jekuthiel. His halting breath came first in hesitant sips, like the call of a hidden night bird. These noises gave way to the desperate gasps of a drowning man before he subsided again.

Gideon rose from the ground, wrapped his cloak around him, and set out in the dark.

On the heights above the canyon in which the travelers were camped was a village appropriately named Shion—"wall of strength." At sunset only a handful of windows glowed orange, but that glimpse was enough to give Gideon his direction.

Fifteen paces beyond the olive press at the south end of the settlement he turned sharp left. A few minutes' walk brought Gideon to a deserted farmhouse, tumbling down and surrounded by weeds.

From the acacia trees on either side of the path three shadowy figures rose from the gloom. A knifepoint at his stomach and the clout of sour wine in his nostrils halted Gideon's progress. Alek's recognizable accent confirmed the identity of his assailants.

"Take me to Captain Eglon," Gideon demanded.

"That I can and that I will," Alek concurred. "But alive or dead? Now that's the question, eh? That's the question."

"Tickle his ribs with the blade," one of the other troopers suggested. "See how well the cripple dances."

"Bring him here!"

Eglon's gruff interruption put an end to the horseplay, but not before Gideon's forehead and face ran with the sweat of fear.

Inside the wooden hut Gideon was thrust into a corner, a lone oil lamp on a shelf above his head. The cripple was confined within a cone of flickering illumination.

Parts of the roof were open to the sky. Sharp-nailed fingers of the acacia trees scraped the back wall when the wind urged them.

Bats roosted inside the shack, leaving urine-soaked piles of their droppings under the rafters where they hung. If any place could be the dwelling of demons and ghosts, this shack fit the requirements.

Eglon paced in front of Gideon, playing with a pair of daggers. The shadow on the wall displayed a demon with long claws.

"We're close," Eglon stated. "Yeshua. What'd you learn?"

"He'll be preaching near Shunem. We can get there by noon and—"

"Quiet!" Eglon barked. "I'm changing the plan. Look for me tomorrow at dawn. I'm only warning you tonight so you'll keep your yap shut."

"Dawn? What?"

A horrible stench wafted in on the night breeze. "Must be something dead. Something dead under the floor," Alek complained.

"I'm taking your place, see?" Eglon continued. "Herod Antipas and Lord Caiaphas want this job finished up. So when Peniel meets Yeshua, I'll be the one with him."

"But Peniel knows you! He'll never . . ."

A knife hissed past Gideon's right ear, impaling a heart-shaped pattern in the wood grain of the wall.

"He won't dare say no to me now, will he?" Eglon chided.

"I . . . I'm sure you know what you're doing."

"See you remember that." The guard captain's fist slid into Gideon's vision and the cripple flinched. Eglon wrenched the knife free of the wall. "Don't get any idea of backing out," Eglon warned. "You can't run far enough or hide well enough to escape me if you cross me. Now get out of here."

Gratefully, with many muttered pledges, Gideon escaped the hut.

Alek helped the cripple on his road by a well-aimed kick that sent the beggar sprawling.

When Gideon returned to the camp, Peniel and Amos were still sound asleep. They gave no sign they'd even moved.

Gideon peered into the cave of murk under the oak boughs. He could not see Jekuthiel. Gideon strained his eyes to confirm the leper's presence but made no move to get closer to where the *chadel* lurked. The cripple concentrated on separating Jekuthiel's tormented breathing from the rustle of wind in the oak, but eventually Gideon fell asleep without succeeding.

Peniel awoke before dawn and climbed a low ridge to gaze west across the fields of Issachar. The great dome of Mount Tabor sprawled in his view, anchoring the southeast corner of Galilee to keep it from flying up into the azure bowl of heaven. The mountain summoned Peniel to Shunem and the reunion with Yeshua—something he craved above all else.

It was a glorious morning. The fields stretching across the plain toward Tabor were a patchwork cloak of muted golds and browns, greens and grays. Shorn of their coats of barley, stubbled fields grazed by sheep were stitched together by stone walls. Dark green squares of vineyards alternated with the lighter greens of olive orchards.

How greatly he had changed, Peniel thought, as he reveled in the vision.

Not long ago Peniel had found his way around Jerusalem in perpetual darkness . . . and had not been afraid. Then new light dawned and for a time he had been lost, confused by the jumbled images presented to his untrained eyes. At first he had to shut out the tidal wave of vision-born impressions in order to go forward.

But since? Peniel desired light, craved light, moved toward even the lamp in the graveyard like a moth to a flame.

He'd witnessed the horrors of cripples and emaciated children and the ravages of leprosy, and yet . . . and yet he could not conceive of going back to the eternal night of being blind.

Not now that he had seen the honey and ginger stones of Jerusalem . . . the blue-and-white banners streaming above the Temple . . . the flower garden of faces.

Peniel saw the aroma of a ripe fig resting in his hand.

He had observed the wind wrestling with tree branches. Before there had only been its sigh in his ears and the tug of its invisible hand on his cloak.

He had seen the image of his own features, and now when he thought of himself, his self—his identity—irrevocably included that view.

He had seen Yeshua's eyes and smile. He longed to see them over and over again.

What an amazing gift was sight, too precious to imagine.

Peniel resisted leaving his personal watchtower. Finally the sounds of rustling in camp reminded him that Yeshua was only a half-day's hike away. Time to get the others up and moving!

The ashes of last night's fire were a soft-edged puddle on the stony ground. A handful of dry brush and scraps of oak bark would get a blaze going again.

Gideon sat on the ground, leaning back against a boulder. The cripple's eyes were wide, staring. He did not speak.

"You're awake?" Peniel asked with surprise. "Waiting for me to build the fire? Where's Amos?"

Then Peniel saw the dwarf. The small man's frame was pressed against the trunk of a tree as if he were tied there. Amos did not speak either. His hands seemed stuck behind his back and across his mouth a rag was knotted.

"What's . . . ?"

Relentless arms grabbed Peniel from behind, pinned his arms to his sides. When he struggled, a bony fist struck him behind the ear, making his head ring like a bell.

Peniel called out for Gideon to help him, but the cripple raised his hands helplessly. They were tied together, as were his ankles.

Eglon appeared in front of Peniel, smirking. "You really think you'd get away? Think you could wander halfway to Damascus without a by-your-leave from your betters? Think again!"

"Leave from a Samaritan pig?"

A backhanded cuff from Eglon's knuckles tore Peniel's lip. "Save the compliments for later. You're taking me to Yeshua, see?"

"To Yeshua!" Alek cackled from behind Peniel's left shoulder.

"Not a chance," Peniel replied. Where was Jekuthiel? Was the leper still free? Or was he already dead? How had the others been captured so easily?

"Oh, I think you will," Eglon corrected. "Bring them back to the farmhouse," he brusquely ordered the other soldiers, "where we won't be interrupted."

"What about the leper? The leper?" Alek asked. "Not here, is he?"

Peniel's hopes jumped. So Jekuthiel remained free.

Eglon sneered. "Probably crawled off somewhere to die. You want to search through the bushes for him, you go right ahead, Alek."

"Not me! Not me!"

"What's he able to do, anyway?" Eglon laughed harshly. "Ask someone for help, and him a leper? Not likely, is it? All right, bring 'em on."

Lily awoke wondering, staring up at an unfamiliar ceiling.

Not a cave in Mak'ob.

Not a starry canopy.

Not a mournful memory of her childhood. A real home—unpretentious but pleasant.

Lily recollected that she was in the gatekeeper's cottage of a rich woman's villa in Magdala.

How long had she slept?

She stretched, yawned, felt refreshed. Better physically than any time in recent memory. Rubbing the stub of her left hand with her right, she reconfirmed the reality of her leprosy. The numbness of encroaching *tsara'at* was still there. The long nightmare of being *chedel* had not vanished with the morning light.

Yet Lily had a great sense of peace. She tested the instinct the way one climbs a rickety ladder, uncertain if it will bear the weight. But the sensation held. There was no fear here. Instead there was unexpected kindness.

Sitting up, she studied the bandages wrapping her legs. Blood from her wounds had seeped through. She felt no pain. The dullness was a reminder that the warning of pain was necessary in life. Lily considered again what Cantor had told her about souls grown hard and unfeeling from the leprosy of sin and bitterness. How easy it was for those without compassion to view the open wounds of another's life as weakness.

Only one person had entered the cottage and sat unafraid at Lily's bed. Only one had dared to touch her. Feed her. Carry the burden of her story.

In the neatly overlapping layers of dressing Lily sensed again the gentleness and caring of that one fearless woman.

"Good morning, dear," said Mary. "I'm almost done here."

The cheerful woman sat in the corner of the room behind the head of the bed. Light from a narrow window streamed over her shoulder. Across Mary's lap was Lily's wedding gown, washed. Restored. Mended. A garden on the fabric. Mary put a final stitch in the hem, raised the pattern to the light to examine her work, and nodded her satisfaction. She bit the thread and tied it off.

Mary passed the dress to Lily. Rents and snags were all neatly repaired, every wound replaced by tiny, finely embroidered roses. Somehow Mary had worked the restoration into a pattern of tendrils and blossoms. The result was no patchwork of mismatched renovation but a flawless whole. It was as if the end result had been in the mind of the maker all along but hidden somehow.

"Thank you," Lily breathed. Overwhelmed by the love and compassion in every stitch, she repeated, "Yes. Yes. Thank you."

With a matter-of-fact nod Mary said, "You're rested. And that's good. You've a journey ahead of you. There's someone you've been searching for. Yeshua is his name. Yeshua of Nazareth."

Lily's heart beat faster. "The Prophet." Couldn't she just remain here in this place of solace, sheltered from the scorn and loathing of the world?

Mary seemed to read her thoughts. "You *must* go to him," she instructed. "He can mend much more than a torn garment." Retrieving the gown from Lily, Mary folded it carefully.

"How will I find him?" Lily asked, trusting Mary's word.

"Follow the road leading south from Magdala toward Shunem.

You'll find him near there. A few others will be going that same way I imagine." Mary's eyes twinkled. "I've made up a package for your journey. Food enough. A half-dozen smoked quail. You like quail? And bread too. A skin of water for you."

Lily thought of the lone quail she had lost when she ran from the traveler with fire in his hand. And now even that loss was somehow restored.

"The One. They say he's the one all Israel has been looking for."

"Yes. All of Israel. One person at a time. That's the way he likes best to meet the needs of the world. Yes. One at a time. Lily, he's the One you've been searching for."

"But even if I do locate him," Lily fussed, "how will I ever get to see him? Up close, I mean. Thousands crowd around him. And if I get close enough . . ." She paused and gestured with her blunt limb at her bandaged legs. "Even if . . . I'm still *tsara.*"

Setting the mended dress on her chair, Mary approached a shelf near the head of the bed. From it she took a small parchment scroll tied round the middle with a scrap of pale blue yarn. "I know Yeshua well." She smiled with amusement as she handed the roll to Lily. "This is a personal petition from me on your behalf. When you get near enough to see one of his talmidim, hand this over. Say it's for Yeshua from me. From Mary who tends the babies at Magdala. They'll take you to him," Mary concluded confidently.

"But what then?" Lily queried. "Even then . . ."

Mary acted as if she didn't hear the question. She busied herself wrapping the wedding dress in clean folds of linen, securing the bundle with more of the sky-colored yarn. "You'll be wanting this," she said, tucking the parcel into a leather pouch by the door. "And don't fret about the baby. He'll be here, fed and cared for. He'll be all right till you come back for him."

Come back for him? Lily could not imagine what those words could mean. Such a hope was too far out of all experience—a distant mountaintop hidden by too many intervening hills and valleys.

Once more Mary stood beside the bed, this time waiting for Lily to rise. When she did so, Mary reached out and grasped Lily's half hands . . . lifeless hands. Dying hands.

She lifted Lily's decaying fingers and brushed them with her lips. As a mother kisses the wound of her child.

Mary searched Lily's eyes and found her soul. "Give Yeshua this from me, will you?" Folding Lily in an embrace, Mary kissed her on both cheeks. "Yes. Give him a kiss from me."

The Sadducee *cohen*, Eli ben Sholom, came to Simon just after sunrise. With him was Simon's friend, Melchior, and the moneylending Pharisee, Judah of Bethsaida. The three lined up on the edge of the pit, looking down at him.

"He looks even worse this morning," the priest remarked. "Notice his ears, the loss of his eyebrows, and the beginnings of a second spot on his left hand."

The commentary began without any greeting of Simon, as if he were a caged animal in a stock pen.

"You try sleeping in a stone pit," Simon muttered. Then, recollecting that the support of these three men represented his best chance of escape, he gritted his teeth and said politely, "Good morning to you all. Thank you for coming to check on me. A little like Dani'el in the den of lions, eh? I'm still here, still alive."

There was no responding chuckle at his wit.

"Eli," Simon said to the priest, "I've always had the greatest respect for your impartiality and integrity. I know you don't want to be part of any miscarriage of justice. Surely you can see that what I have is not really *tsara'at*, not at all. I have a fine medicine that will have me cured in no time. If I could just be allowed to go home."

"We've already been to your home," Eli said scornfully. "You know the clothing and the dwelling of a suspected *tsara* must be examined for traces of the disease."

"My . . . house?"

"What we found there was worse than just *tsara*," Judah interjected. "Magical books of pagan sorcerers!"

"Medical texts only, I assure—"

"Evil, forbidden potions!" Judah corrected.

"Oil! Health-giving medicine—"

"Heathen practices!" Eli summarized. "Of course we destroyed it all. Burned scrolls, potions, and notes!"

"Burned it all?" Simon wailed, and yet he was overwhelmed with gratitude at the foresight Jerusha had shown. At his wife's insistence he had scrubbed out the chalk marks on the floor of his study. If Eli had found those, Simon would be stoned for practicing witchcraft!

"Judah!" Simon appealed, recovering a little from the multiple shocks. "Brother Pharisee. How can you let this Sadducee priest lord it over me this way?"

"Where is the money you borrowed from me?" Judah said coldly. "I want it back."

"You know I can't repay it until after the next vintage is sold!"

"Where is it?"

"I . . . I don't have it."

"And where did you spend it? Did you invest it in your business as you claimed?"

Simon's head drooped. "I needed it to buy the seeds for my medicine," he explained.

"So on top of sorcery you took my money on false pretenses? And you were leaving the country?"

"Only for a short—"

"Bah!" Judah snorted. "Do what you want with him," he said to Eli. "It doesn't matter if he's *tsara* or not. I want a judgment for the full amount I loaned him, even if it costs him his business and his house."

"Judah!" Simon appealed, but the moneylender turned his back and stalked away. "Melchior?" Simon pleaded with his best friend. "Do something! You said you'd always stand by me. Help me!"

"I think," Melchior said slowly, deliberately, "I think this is the last time I can speak with you. You are a dead man: *chedel. Tsara.* Deceit with your brothers? Lying to your friends? Claiming high status of purity while living with defilement, and then carrying that corruption into the synagogue? How wicked were you long before that? How evil must you be for El Olam to do this to you?" Scooping a handful of dust from the ground, Melchior threw it into the pit on top of Simon's head. "I will grieve for you," he said, turning his back.

"Melchior!" Simon called after him.

Bright white spots rimmed with red stood out on Simon's forehead and cheeks. Simon's right hand and right foot cramped and turned inward as if all the emotion coursing through his body made the *tsara'at* even more powerful.

"It's a curse," Simon protested to Eli. "Yeshua of Nazareth laid a curse on me! He should be in this pit, not me!"

"Even if that were so," Eli noted, "it doesn't change the fact that *you* are *tsara*, you are *chedel*, you are *baza*. No matter who you blame, you are afflicted, despised, rejected . . . and one of the walking dead. In fact, there is no doubt about the outcome of your case. If you agree to banishment to the wilderness now, you can be let out of the pit immediately."

Out of the pit. At least it was something.

"Yes," Simon agreed. "Banish me."

Though the words of the ceremony and the attention of the crowd were directed at him, Simon was barely listening. He felt dull, every sense muffled, as if his sight, his hearing, and his thoughts were all wrapped in heavy cloth. He found it difficult to breathe.

"Simon ben Zeraim," the *cohen* Eli intoned, "According to the Law of Mosheh, you've been examined."

His head bare, Simon was ringed by clumps of the curious, the openly hostile, and the wary. Former friends, old enemies, and total strangers were all grouped around him outside the limits of Capernaum in the middle of the Damascus Road. Their hands were filled with rocks, pebbles, and gravel.

"You are found to have *tsara'at*."

Simon's right hand was now so drawn as to be almost useless. The back of his left was completely inflamed, the sore covering everything from wrist to knuckles. There were seeming scorched marks on his forehead and behind both ears. One of his earlobes was twice the thickness of the other.

Chaulmoogra oil had failed.

"You must from this moment on cover your face, from your upper lip down to your beard. As a mark that you're *tsara*, you must wear torn clothing."

At a nod from Eli the two synagogue stewards stepped toward Simon. Each grasped a shoulder and lapel of his robe. Simon did not resist.

They ripped downward.

In the noise of the rending fabric Simon heard the tearing apart of his entire life.

The action left two drooping folds of cloth hanging across Simon's chest. Then each attendant clutched a sleeve and rent the seams up to the armpit.

The sign of mourning, as old as Job. Grief for loss, for affliction, for being smitten by God.

Only Simon mourned for himself; it was his own life that was forfeit.

The robe was fine linen, woven by Jerusha's own hands. Strange how Simon had never valued it before. Now it was both a worthless rag—and the only thing he was allowed to wear.

"You must call, 'Unclean! Unclean' to give a warning to any you approach or who approach you."[75]

The Pharisee, whose whole life had been structured by the demands of purity and a proper regard for keeping kosher, winced.

"You may not live in any walled city. If you're found there you'll be stoned to death. You may beg at the city gates, but you may not live where you'll contaminate others. In fact, anyone may stone you to drive you away and no guilt attaches to them."

Staring at the priest, Simon asked. "Then I'll live . . . where?"

"There're only two places where you may not be stoned out of the way of decent people," Eli said grudgingly, as if the exceptions were too merciful for a leper. "You may live in a graveyard. Since graveyards are already unclean, your kind may live there unmolested."

His kind.

Simon refused to accept the connection. His kind were scholars and leaders, righteous and upright—not outcasts, the permanently defiled, the dregs of society.

"Where else?" he cried in anguish.

"There's one place in the wilderness set aside for your kind," Eli allowed. "It's known as the Valley of Mak'ob."

Mak'ob . . . anguish.

"You're accursed. From now on, unless you're healed and present yourself to the Temple to prove it, you're *chadel*, 'rejected,' and *chedel*, the 'walking dead.' Go away, dead man! We drive you away from us!"

A shower of gravel rained down on Simon's head. Most of the crowd were no longer murderously angry. They flung the prescribed stones underhanded, symbolically casting Simon out.

But some wanted to emphasize their rejection of him. They wanted the onlookers to know the seriousness of the decree and that no exception would be made for former friendship. The stone that struck Simon on the cheek was tossed hard and straight, aimed to injure. So was the one that hit him on the crippled hand. One was thrown by Melchior; the other by Judah. Nor were theirs the only missiles hurled with brutal force.

Simon stumbled away, pelting toward the graveyard as the closest temporary refuge from the storm of hatred and cruelty.

27

The hut was uncomfortably warm from the fire blazing on the hearth. Peniel was tied to a pole supporting the roof in the center of the one-room shack.

"Yell if you want," Eglon offered as Peniel shouted for help. "Won't do any good. Way out here? Nearest village deserted. All traipsed off to see that charlatan friend of yours. 'Course, every time you irritate me, you pay me a drop of blood."

As Peniel watched in horror, Eglon yanked Peniel's hand up and nonchalantly sliced a four-inch-long cut across Peniel's palm. "Now, that's just to prove I'm serious," the guard captain said. "Next time I might cut your ear off or . . ." The tip of the dagger danced mere inches from Peniel's right eye. "He never really opened your eyes, did he?"

"Of course he—"

"Alek!"

Across the hut Alek plucked a burning brand from the fire and thrust it into Amos' face. The dwarf shrieked and writhed in his bonds. The stench of burning hair from Amos' beard filled the hovel.

Alek stepped back.

"Wouldn't that be sweet?" Eglon pondered aloud. "Two blind beggars. One big and one small. Make quite a scene I should think."

"Quite a scene!" Alek chortled.

"Maybe Herod Antipas'd keep you around for sport," Eglon said. "Dress you alike and have you perform for his guests. Now, consider your next answer carefully. 'Stead of speaking lies for a trickster who never really opened anybody's eyes, don't you think it'd be smart to oblige me, 'cause I really can make people blind! I've done it before. Makes me kind of a god, eh?"

"Kind of a god!"

Gideon was trussed up in another corner. His arms and legs, though loosely bound, were pressed tightly together. Horror was stamped on his face.

"So?" Eglon persisted. "He never opened your eyes, did he?"

"He—"

The tip of the knife touched Peniel's eyelid, pressed in slightly. "Maybe you think he can fix you up again, eh? Care to chance it? Care to chance it for your friend as well? Alek?"

The flames singed all the hair off one side of Amos' face as the dwarf screamed and pleaded for Peniel to make them stop! When Alek removed the torch, the dwarf's cheek was angry red, blistered, and swollen.

"Just say it," Eglon encouraged. "He never healed you, did he?"

Blind again! To walk again in a world without colors, without forms. What if he had to live the rest of his life on the memory of what he had lost?

Peniel whimpered. "He never . . . healed me. It was a lie."

Alek crowed. "Ho, ho! Hee!"

"There now," Eglon said in mock sympathy. "Wasn't so hard, was it? Don't expect him to do any more tricks for you now, do you? No?"

Peniel's head hung down on his chest. He stared at the gray earth of the floor of the hut. Tears welled up and dripped soundlessly into his lap. Yeshua had given the gift of sight. And to keep the gift, Peniel had denied the gift giver!

"Now here's what we do," Eglon said, wrenching Peniel's chin up. "You and me, we're going to Yeshua, see? You're going to send him word you want to talk to him alone. Just him and you . . . and me. Now we already know you're a coward, don't we?"

"Cow—ward! Cow—ward!" Alek mocked.

"But just in case you think you'll warn him somehow, Alek here is staying with your friends. Anything goes wrong—anything at all—your friends die. Maybe I let Alek play with them first, though. Roast dwarf over a slow fire. Tasty, eh?"

"Tasty!"

The road from Magdala to Shunem passed well away from Herod Antipas' capital of Tiberias, then dodged through hilly country on the east side of Mount Tabor. Without the child to carry or the goat to lead, Lily made faster time. Her only delays were when she saw approaching travelers to whom she gave the full width of the track. Lily did not want to be stoned or driven away when she was this close to the Healer.

Could it be? she mused. Was it possible El Olam interested Himself in the lives of *chadel* after all? Was restoration of humanness something Messiah could and would perform? Or would He, like all the others outside the Valley, turn and shun and reject those Inside?

I'm praying again, Tender-Mercied One. You brought the baby to a good place, to be sheltered and loved. If you have any compassion remaining, please don't let me be hurt again. The baby is safe. I can go back to the Valley and die among friends. But if this Healer can't or won't heal me, then stop me from going to him now. I don't think I can bear another disappointment. I'd just die out here instead. So please, you who can be kind, keep me from having to live with any more regret.

Lily was so deep in her thoughts and prayers that some time passed without her noticing the absence of Hawk's bell.

So he was off hunting by himself? Lily had neglected him lately she knew. She shared her meager meals with him, but his training exercises had been overlooked entirely.

Lily whistled shrilly, the way Cantor taught her, then stood perfectly still, listening.

Nothing. Not the faintest tinkling penetrated the rustle of the leaves on the olive trees lining the road.

Lily felt faint. She put out her hand to steady herself and touched the cold roughness of the stone wall.

Was this the way her petition was answered? An enormous joke, taking away her one remaining prop, her final connection to Cantor?

I'm praying again, O God of the Helpless . . .

What was the use?

Her eyesight was full of dust and blurred with self-pitying tears. Her vision was so bad that only by screwing up her face could she see into the distance. At the extreme range of her sight a tiny black dot bobbed on the horizon. Something small and dark, well away to the southeast, rose above the olive branches where they gestured to the sky, rising and falling on the wind.

"Hawk?" she breathed. Then louder, "Hawk!"

Lily ran, stumbled, jerked upright, and ran on. It was him; it had to be.

The path snaked down a hillside and into a ravine. Lily's heart pounded as her feet carried her down the slope, and she lost sight of the bird on the breeze. She held her breath until she thought her chest would explode, just as she reached the top of the opposite wall of the canyon.

It was still there! The fluttering, diving, reappearing spot in the distance. Lily signaled again and again, but Hawk did not return. Always beyond reach, yet always within sight, Hawk drew Lily on.

The road forked. The main branch continued toward Shunem, toward Messiah, toward hope and healing.

The other offshoot turned east, toward the Jordan.

The message from Mary weighed heavily on Lily's mind. What if Yeshua pushed on before Lily could get to him? What if she was too late?

She could not continue whistling and running at the same time. In the same moment she abandoned calling to Hawk, she also discarded the route to Shunem. Lily felt she had to catch up with the bird before nightfall or he'd be lost forever.

Alek yawned and stretched. He arched his back and lifted his jaw. His Adam's apple grew still more prominent, as if his throat had developed a second chin to wag in time with the one on his face.

Gideon and Amos remained tied in their respective corners of the hut.

"Wonder if that Galilean prophet's dead yet?" Alek mused aloud. "Eglon'll be on his way back here to take care of you two then."

Gideon looked startled. "What? What do you mean?"

"Tidier that way. Eglon hates loose ends, see? Loose ends are bad, he says."

Amos hunched miserably. His undamaged cheek was curled against his shoulder. The dwarf sat very still as if at the slightest movement, his scorched face would crack apart.

Gideon straightened up, shook his shoulders, cleared his throat. "Not me," he said. The cripple studied Amos, then appeared to make up his mind about something. "Untie me," he demanded. "Enough with this charade. No reason to keep pretending now."

Alek's grin widened. "You really think he'd let you go? Ho, ho! Hee! Planning on spending your share of the reward?"

"I've done everything he asked!" Gideon protested. "Gave you reports. Kept Peniel from getting suspicious when you idiots showed up in villages!"

"Good boy," Alek offered. "Good! Sure that'll be comforting to you in Sheol. In Sheol!"

"Cut me loose!" Gideon shrieked. "Cut—"

Amos opened one puffy and smoke-blackened eye. Through cracked and swollen lips he growled, "Better hope Eglon kills you quick. If I get a chance, I'll sit on your chest and gnaw your liver myself."

"Ho!" Alek gurgled. "Pay to see that, I would! Yep! Pay to see it."

"Let me go!" Gideon screamed. He lunged sideways and rolled thrashing toward the door.

Alek laughed and let Gideon flail helplessly before pursuing him. The cripple sprawled athwart the doorsill, the upper half of his body outside the hut. Alek bent over to grab Gideon by the feet to drag him back.

The stench of an open tomb filled the air. A horrible moaning voice shrieked, "Now . . . death . . . comes for . . . you!"

Alek crouched, trembling. "What? Where?"

A hooded figure stood framed in the doorway. Alek was transfixed by the claws protruding from the sleeves . . . but even more rooted by the space within the cowl.

The thing had no face. Eyes, yes, but no face.

It lunged for Alek, wrapped long, bony arms around his neck, pressed its horror of a mouth against his cheek. "Another soul . . . for the . . . living dead! By the time . . . I count three . . . you'll be . . . one of us! One! Two!"

Alek gave no thought to dagger or club, never considered defending himself from Jekuthiel. He did not know how lepers got made. He only knew he didn't want to become one.

With a scream and a backwards lunge, Alek wrenched himself free from Jekuthiel's embrace. Two strides took him across the room to the window. Alek plunged headfirst out the uncovered opening. Lighting on his back, he rolled onto his feet, ran, and kept on running.

"Get . . . up!" Jekuthiel urged Gideon. "Untie Amos. We're . . . going to . . . Shunem."

"Not with him, I'm not," Amos corrected. "He can still go to Sheol . . . lousy traitor. Untie me so I can cut his throat!"

"Let me get out of here!" Gideon pleaded with Jekuthiel. "Eglon'll kill me if he catches me. Kill all of us . . . by now he's killed the Teacher! Let me go."

Shucking his bonds, Gideon bolted from the room.

His last words seemed to have struck Jekuthiel like a blow in the midsection. The leper sank down on the dirt floor clutching his head and rocking. "Messiah . . . dead? What's . . . the point? No use. No . . . use."

"Come on, Jekuthiel," Amos urged as the dwarf in turn escaped the knotted cords. "There's still a chance."

But Jekuthiel had clearly reached an end. "You go. Leave me. No more . . . no more . . . strength. I'll be . . . dead soon . . . anyway."

Along the highway Lily encountered other travelers. Keeping her distance, she overheard scraps of repeated tales.

"Blind men could see again."

"The demon-possessed were set free."

"Yeshua, the Teacher . . ."

"Yeshua, the Healer . . ."

At the junction of two roads, Hawk's flight veered right. She called to him. Whistled, then whistled again. He did not circle back to her but lighted on a stone wall some distance away. When she followed him he lifted off, drawing her farther and farther down the secondary road. Again and again the bird played his game, allowing her to come almost near enough to touch before he lifted off again.

Yard by yard plains gave way to rolling hills. The route ascended into them, skirting the sharper peaks and steeper gorges. Glancing back, Lily saw how far she'd come. Mount Tabor blocked the sinking sun. Its shadow darkened the surrounding villages and fields. Encroaching haze further blanketed the scene, a curtain of reproach drawn across Shunem, shutting her out. Yeshua, salvation, were within just a few miles. But she would never reach the encampment before nightfall. The mountain called Purity by the sages seemed to reject her as she turned away from it.

Lily felt a renewal of the creeping numbness. The loss of sensation in her limbs moved inward to deaden her heart with hopelessness. Why had she taken this road? Why had she followed Hawk's course instead of taking the way she knew was correct?

The separation between Lily and the Hawk decreased. At last Hawk reached the thick stand of an olive grove. Lily trailed haltingly after him. Inside the canopy of tree limbs Lily couldn't see him. She whistled and called to him. Would he dart away again?

In a clearing Lily spotted a tumbled-down hovel, the ruins of a farmhouse. She heard a low moan, and on a broken stone wall she saw the figure of a little man sitting, head in hands. Was he a statue? She squinted. The thing moaned again. It was human! Or demon. Dwarfish, of half height to a man, his face was blackened and creased like a carved image.

At the snap of a twig beneath her foot, he gasped in fear and turned toward her. "What's this? What's this? Just a woman. A woman is all," he muttered to himself.

"I'm sorry I frightened you. I'm looking for my Hawk. A hunting bird. Have you seen a hawk? Heard his bell?"

The dwarf made a dismissive gesture, waving her away. He shook his head mutely, as if nothing in the world mattered but meditating on his own misery.

Then the bell tinkled from the far side of the grove. Hawk swayed on the topmost branch of an olive tree. He ruffled his wings as if to show her where he was.

Angry now, she whistled. Whistled. Whistled again!

Lily neared the tree. He launched from the olive tree, then skimmed the orchard to perch on top of an acacia.

As she approached, Hawk once more dove from his outpost. This time he did not soar away. Sideslipping, he veered between tree limbs to land atop the sagging roof of the deserted farmhouse.

"Hawk!" she demanded. Another whistle. "Hawk!" Lily lifted her fist aloft to coax him to her. The bird remained pinned like a sentinel. "You! Bird! You've cost me everything! Everything! Why have you done this?"

After these furious words she heard a weak reply, "Lily? Lily? Is it you?"

Could it be? She recognized the voice.

"Jekuthiel?" She gawked at the hut. A chill of apprehension coursed through her. She wondered if she had died somewhere on her way to see Yeshua. Or if she had fallen into a deep sleep and was dreaming the dream of walking forever on the road to nowhere.

The Hawk made no attempt to fly again. She stared at him. Had his sharp eyes seen Jekuthiel somehow? guided Lily to him?

"Is it you, Jekuthiel?" She approached the building.

"Lily." One word. Her name only.

She entered the hut. It took a moment for her eyes to adjust to the dim interior. What she saw shocked her. She did not recognize Jekuthiel. Nearly five months outside Mak'ob had changed him.

Jekuthiel's breathing was shallow. He was nearly blind. At the sound of Lily's approach his body convulsed with sobs. Weeping without sound. Without tears. He lay propped against a wall. Flies swarmed around him.

"Oh!" she cried, knowing how little time was left for him. "Oh, Jekuthiel! My dear brother! My old friend."

Lily held a cup of wine to his mouth. For the next hour she cleaned maggots from his wounds. She poured wine into the open sores and bandaged them with strips torn from her robe.

I'm praying again, God Who Knows My Path. No mistake this! No accident! You carried me to this desolate place on the wings of the Hawk. Led me here to my dear Jekuthiel!

In halting phrases Jekuthiel pestered her with queries. "What . . . are you doing . . . here? Deborah . . . how is she?"

Patiently, kindly, Lily explained about baby Isra'el—Jekuthiel's child, the boy he would never see or hold.

Jekuthiel feebly nodded his approval. "It's . . . best. You've . . . done well . . . Lily."

"I've come looking for the Healer. The Prophet from Nazareth," Lily added. She stopped and shrugged. "But, Jekuthiel! To find you here! Oh, my heart is glad to see you! Glad!"

"Yes. Yes . . . but . . . what's the use . . . of any . . . of this? All of it? Finished . . . finished . . . so long . . . we've been searching . . . for him. Now . . . the Healer's . . . dead . . . by now."

"Dead?" Lily drew back from Jekuthiel. How could this be? All hope was obliterated from her soul. It became a tree struck by a lightning bolt. "Oh no! No! We've come too late? We're too late?"

"Over. Done," Jekuthiel wheezed. "What's the . . . use?"

Drawing the scrap of parchment from her tunic, she stared at the distinct lettering of Mary's handwriting. "Poor woman. Poor dear lady. Oh, Jekuthiel! What's it all been for?" Lily cried out in anguish, crumpled the scroll, then threw it against the wall.

"Dead," Jekuthiel repeated. "And . . . so are we . . . Lily. No hope left. Nothing left . . . to stay for."

"Yes . . . then let's go home, Jekuthiel. Cantor's dead. Soon Deborah too. She needs you. Oh! What was the use! Why? Why? Oh, Jekuthiel! Let's go home."

"Yes. Yes . . . back . . . Mak'ob. The Valley of Sorrow . . . where we . . . belong."

The full weight of Simon's loss slammed down on him like a hammer. Between the blows of reality his heart continued to beat.

He was still alive. There was some consolation in that. He tried to comfort himself even as truth chipped away the stone of his resolve.

No use. No use. No use.

Every step felt as if chains of iron bound his ankles. He shuffled forward blindly, scarcely caring where we went.

Simon pictured his life like an hourglass turned upside down by his own leprous hand. Sand at the top—reputation, status, self-esteem—all these flowed away with the first grains. But the outsurging tide did not stop with those things he had once held so dear.

His business was gone, now and forever. Who would deal with the House of Zeraim, the cursed of God?

Sinking, sinking, the level in the glass dropped.

Friends abandoned him, welcomed the opportunity to distance themselves from him.

His son, driven away first by Simon's pride and self-centeredness, now lost to him forever.

Deeper and deeper.

Simon's vital parts—what he kept most concealed from everyone else in the world—approached the lip of the abyss.

"Jerusha!" Her name leapt from Simon's lips unbidden. How he loved her! Relied on her. Counted on her. Always there, never complaining, never rebuking.

Simon . . . always before too proud to acknowledge how much he cared for her. His greatest fear had always been of losing her.

Oh, God! Everything I feared has come upon me!

The last grains of life slipping, slipping toward the edge.

Only now, when the glass was completely empty of self-delusion and pride was there room for new thoughts to enter.

What if Jerusha is right? What if I had only gone to Yeshua openly, admitted my needs, my fears?

Begged for help.

Too late now. He'd never help me now. I've taunted him. Libeled him. Abused him. Born false witness against him. Hated him . . . and he saw through me all the time.

Saw me washing the outside of the cup while the inside was . . .

Too late now, though.

Simon was a leper. Lower than every publican he ever heaped abuse on. More tainted than any *am ha aretz* of unwashed hands.

Images of what he had done to others who had needed his mercy tumbled into his mind like an avalanche.

He had evicted the tenant family of a young girl with leprosy.

What was the little girl's name? Lily. Yes, Lily. No doubt dead by now. Her mother. Poor woman. Broken woman. Oh! What have I done? Where did they go after I drove them away? How could I know what they felt?

Simon had separated Jerusha from the love of her father and mother.

Zadok! The old man. Forbidden by my edict to ever see his daughter or hold his grandson! Punished by the withholding of love! Was there ever a more brutal weapon than love? Zadok! Exiled from everything he ever lived for. Now driven from his flocks. And I gave the high priest my approval for his expulsion! What have I done? What have I done?

Along with these two streams of unkindness flowed a thousand insignificant others. Rivulets of wrongdoing and neglect.

Anger! Envy! Resentment! Gossip! Coveting! Small wrongs he had committed against others! Small acts of mercy he had failed to do *for* those in need! All these together became a broad, deep river washing away the last pretense of righteousness!

Simon the Pharisee had lived a lifetime without true *chesed,* mercy! Yet how desperately Simon the Leper longed for mercy to be shown to him!

A whitewashed tomb, full of dead men's bones.

Lie down and die then.

He was dead already inside. The stink of his own corruption was rank in Simon's nostrils.

The stench of death.

One more agonizing stride and then: *My stubbornness is killing me.*

Startling thought. Simon grasped for it like a drowning man clutches at a vine. Urgently he told himself not to let that idea slip away unexamined.

It wasn't the *tsara'at* killing him.

It was Simon's stubbornness!

Everything Yeshua said was true. Every word about cleansing the inside! And I hated him for it! The blind beggar . . . healed. All the others . . . cured. What if I'm limping away right now from the only possibility of hope, of salvation, of safety?

Naaman the Leper was healed of leprosy when he dunked in the Jordan seven times.[76]

But Naaman had to overcome presumptuous pride first. He almost allowed his hard-hearted arrogance to stop him from obeying Elisha. The Syrian captain had to be instructed by his servants: "If the prophet of God told you to do a difficult thing, wouldn't you have agreed?"

Go to Yeshua and admit my need, my failures, my sin? Otherwise, hard-hearted stubbornness will kill me. Otherwise, presumptuous pride will be my death . . . not tsara'at.

Simon stopped in his tracks. Yeshua was behind him! Hope lay in the opposite direction from where he was headed!

The only hope left for me is the One I rejected, ridiculed, resisted! Turn around! Turn around! Maybe it's not too late!

With a groan, Simon turned. Set his face toward Yeshua. Took the first limping step back.

28 CHAPTER

Sun hammered on the anvil of Mount Tabor where Yeshua taught. People stretched out on the slopes like a vast field of wildflowers.

Avel, Emet, and Ha-or Tov sat in the shadow of Zadok. Emet dozed with his head on Red Dog. They were lucky, Avel thought, to be on the left outside flank of the crowd, still close enough to hear Yeshua.

"Protect your hearts and minds from false prophets. They come to you in sheep's clothing, but inwardly they are ferocious wolves." Yeshua gestured at the apple orchard halfway to the summit, where a small group of Pharisees stood talking urgently with their heads bent together. "By their fruit you'll recognize them. Do you pick grapes from thornbushes? or apples from thistles? Every good tree grows good fruit, nourishing others freely. But a bad tree produces inedible fruit. Wormy to the core. It's impossible for a bad tree to give good fruit. And every tree that doesn't bear good fruit will be cut down and thrown into the fire."[77]

Voices. Voices.

All around, the news about Simon the Pharisee was whispered.

"Aye. It's true. So falls the tree of the House of Zeraim. Simon the Pharisee, son-in-law of the old shepherd! A leper! That's who!"

"At last he's got what he deserved. After all those he's turned away! I always knew he was hiding something. Cut down to size now, that one is!"

"So, there's justice in the world after all."

"Now he's sent packing by his own kind! Driven from his own family and society. He won't be around to pester Yeshua ever again!"

Avel studied Zadok's expression as this triumph was relayed from one man to another on the knoll of the hill. The old shepherd did not seem pleased at either his own vindication or the destruction of his bitter son-in-law. Instead Zadok stared at his gnarled hands for a long time as though they too were covered in the blood of another.

At last Zadok looked up. The old shepherd's gaze, like a questing dog's, seemed to run across the space, turn, come back. Again and again he stared, almost in disbelief, at a woman and a youth in the crowd opposite. The boy and the woman, expressions desperate with longing and sorrow, raised hands in tentative greeting across the gulf.

Yeshua's warning continued. "Not everyone who says to me, 'Lord, Lord,' will enter the kingdom of heaven. Only those who from clean hearts do the will of my Father who is in heaven. And what is his will? That you love one another as I have loved you! Many who seem to be righteous in this life will say to me on that last day, 'Lord, didn't we prophesy in your name? And in your name drive out demons? And in your name perform many miracles?' And yet, they did not do the will of my Father because they didn't love others. Refused to forgive. Clung to bitterness until it became a millstone round their necks pulling them down into the depths of the sea. So I'll tell them plainly on that day, 'I never knew you. And you never knew me. Depart from me, all you who hold fast to the evil which has taken over your hearts!'"[78]

Avel sat up attentively as the woman and the youth began to inch forward through the seated throng. Her eyes seemed riveted on Zadok as she stepped over this one and that in a desperate effort to reach him.

Staff in hand, Zadok rose majestically to his feet. Rooted like an oak on the edge of the crowd, he followed her progress and that of the young man. Zadok lifted his chin as she approached. *Yes*, his expression seemed to say. *Yes! Come on, then! Don't be afraid! I've always been here. Waiting for you.*

Yeshua gazed approvingly toward the old shepherd and spoke these words to the multitude:[79] "Therefore, everyone who hears these words of mine and puts them into practice is like the wise man who built his house upon the rock."

Nearer the woman came. Nearer. "Pardon me. Pardon . . . I must . . ."

Shielded in Zadok's long shadow, Avel remained seated, watching as the old shepherd's face clouded with emotion.

Yeshua smiled enigmatically as He taught. "The rain came down. The streams rose. The winds blew and beat against that house. But it didn't fall . . . no . . . it didn't fall . . . because it had its foundation on the rock."

Halfway home.

Zadok muttered a word. A name. "Daughter. Jerusha?"

Her lips moved in an inaudible response. "Papa. Papa. Papa. Help me. Help . . . us . . ."

And Yeshua nodded once in unspoken approval as Zadok stretched out his arms in welcome, drawing her in.

So Yeshua taught the multitude about families. About love. Sorrow. Anger. Separation. About kindness . . . forgiveness and reconciliation. "But everyone who hears these words of mine and doesn't act on them is like the foolish man who built his house on sand. The rain came down, the streams rose, and the winds blew and beat against that house, and it fell . . . and it fell with a great crash."

With a groan, Zadok enfolded the woman in his arms. "Daughter! Daughter! My own Jerusha! Oh!" Then, with a laugh, Zadok playfully doubled his fist and tapped the youth in a manly greeting. "And y'! Look at y'! Jotham! What a strong buck y' are!"

Jerusha wept. "Papa! Oh, Papa! You know! You know? Oh, Papa! They've driven him away. Yeshua is the only hope left for us. Can you help Simon? Help him come near enough Yeshua to ask?"

"Gladly, daughter. Gladly. Y' have my help. Simon has my help. Always. I'll do what I can to help . . . If only he'll let me."

His hands were hidden within the length of his sleeves. The torn shred of robe was flung across his face. Simon the Leper reached the edge of the crowd around Yeshua.

He hesitated just out of reach of recognition . . . and downwind of detection.

Simon had so many enemies. Could he ever hope to approach the Teacher? Yeshua's talmidim would bar Simon's way for his previous hostility. Those Simon had abused and misused would jeer him. His own brother Pharisees would stone him away to banish the taint of his leprosy.

Yet what other choice did he have?

Over and over again, Simon proved himself to be an enemy of Yeshua. How could he ever expect help, even if he got close enough to ask?

But what other hope was there?

"Don't condemn others," Yeshua taught the crowd, "and God won't condemn you. God will be as hard on you as you are on others! He will treat you exactly as you treat them."

The breeze, heaven-sent, carried Yeshua's words to Simon.

A knife in the heart!

When had Simon ever considered the needs, the feelings, the concerns of others? Were the words a final condemnation? Could Simon hold despair at bay long enough to make the attempt? Was any path not blocked?

Simon scanned the crowd. His eyes were drawn to a trio who stood opposite him, behind Yeshua. Jerusha, Jotham . . . and his father-in-law, Zadok. Zadok's arm was draped around his grandson's shoulders.

Was this the end of all hope? Had his wife and son made common cause with the father-in-law Simon had despised and rejected?

"Treat others as you want them to treat you. This is what the Law and the Prophets are all about," Yeshua continued.[80]

The message was one of forgiveness and compassion. Simon noticed that Zadok and Jerusha listened, nodded gravely.

Was there room for hope?

"Go in through the narrow gate," Yeshua said. "The gate to destruction is easy, and the road that leads there is easy to follow. A lot of people go through that gate. But the gate to life is very narrow. The road that leads there is so hard that only a few people find it."

Zadok! Zadok was the narrow gate, the hard road.

The only choice.

Simon circled the throng, fearful of being denounced as a leper.

Then, before he was ready, Simon was face-to-face with Zadok. The old man's glaring eye lit with recognition.

Jerusha gasped as if Simon were a ghost.

His back to the crowd, Simon thrust out his hands to his father-in-law. His *hands*.

"Help me," he said. "Zadok! Please, help me to *him!*"

One hand was contorted, knobby, blackened; the other, red-spotted, angry, fevered . . . *tsara'at*.

"I have . . . I am . . . *tsara!* I have no right to claim your help. No right at all . . . except . . . I have nowhere else to go."

Simon held his breath.

Zadok grasped his hand. Embraced him. "Son. My son. Oh! My son! How I prayed for this day! Come on, then. Come! I'll take you to him."

Dragonflies cruised lazily up and down the dry creek bed. Sunlight, fragmented by overhanging willow leaves, shattered the sand underfoot into shards of bright and pale spearpoints.

Insects ticked in the brush. The hum of bees around the elderberry flowers merged with the drone of human voices from just up the hill.

Peniel squinted up into the translucent green canopy. He marveled at the interplay of sharp edges and muted forms . . . and was roughly yanked back to a different reality.

"Pay attention," Eglon demanded, squeezing Peniel's right elbow. He kept his hand there. "No slipups, see? There won't be any second chance. You get me close enough to do this right or your friends are dead. If I'm not back by nightfall, they're finished."

Peniel nodded once. He understood. Amos' life. Gideon's life. Peniel's eyes. These were forfeit if he failed his part in Eglon's quest to assassinate Yeshua.

Peniel was the betrayer, the failure, the worse-than-useless destroyer.

His mother had been right after all: Peniel should have died. He would never amount to anything. He was now poised to be remembered as the most ungrateful wretch. The most false friend in all of history.

No more time to think about it now. When Peniel and Eglon climbed the riverbank, they were among the outer fringes of the crowd, near a knot of Pharisees. Peniel heard Yeshua speaking.

"When you fast, don't try to look gloomy as those show-offs do when they fast," Yeshua instructed. "I can assure you that they already have their reward."[81]

"He's talking about us." One of the religious brotherhood sniffed. "Scandalous. Somebody should do something about him."

Eglon's laugh rumbled from deep in his chest, like the warning growl of a savage dog.

It was happening too fast. Peniel had no time to think, no chance to plot a warning and an escape.

Did even the flitting of the words through Peniel's pounding head send out an alarm? Eglon compressed Peniel's arm tighter and forced the young man forward quicker. "Here we go," Eglon said, nodding toward a pair of Yeshua's talmidim confronting them.

"Shalom," one of them said, holding up a cautionary hand. "We try to keep the space around the Teacher clear so all can see and hear."

"He . . . he sent for me," Peniel lied nervously. "I'm Peniel . . . Peniel. The blind beggar of—"

"Nicanor Gate! Of course you are! Come, brother, and welcome. And your friend is welcome too. Sorry for the delay. We've heard rumors that Herod Antipas has assassins after the Master, so we try to be extra careful. Just a moment and I'll tell him you're here."

Someone else had received a private meeting with Yeshua. A man dressed in an expensive but ragged robe stood before the Teacher. In an arc back of him were a sternly erect white-haired man, a woman, and an adolescent boy.

Peniel watched the supplicant drop to his knees at Yeshua's feet.

Simon, kneeling at Yeshua's feet.

Humbled.

Apprehensive.

Simon, head bowed, spoke to Yeshua without daring to lift his face. He wanted to fall, face downward, at those feet. Simon wanted to grasp

Yeshua's ankles and cling to them, to hold on as the patriarch Ya'acov had refused to release the Angel of Adonai.

Trembling, fearful, but no longer stubborn.

Or prideful.

"I gave you no . . . no . . . kiss of welcome," he stammered. "I offered no water for you to wash your feet. I thought the core of my life was righteousness . . . righteousness. I criticized you harshly for not knowing Miryam's sin. Didn't see that you both saw—and forgave. I didn't value mercy more than justice . . . until now."

Simon thrust his hands out of his sleeves, held them in the glaring sunlight, revealing his leprosy. "I asked for . . . I *demanded* a sign from you! While I never showed *my* true heart to anyone," he admitted. "But these are my true hands . . . washed but still unclean!" The cry of *unclean* wrung a groan from his innermost part, as if a portion of his soul tore like the fabric of his robe.

Jerusha stifled a sob.

"This is my *true* heart: I am a leper! Inside *and* out, I am unclean."

"Father!" Jotham said, agony in his voice.

Simon heard Zadok's soft remonstrance, holding back Jerusha and Jotham.

Simon's plea, not theirs.

Simon's *teshuvah*, his turning about . . . not theirs.

"There is nowhere else for me to go," Simon concluded simply. "I . . . I need to be forgiven. Oh, Lord! Clean the inside of the cup as well as the outside! You can heal me if you want to!"

A beat . . . a pulse . . . a breath . . . a lifetime!

Kneeling, Yeshua grasped both Simon's hands in His own. He looked into Simon's reddened eyes, childlike in their fearfulness.

"I want to." Yeshua pressed His lips against each of Simon's palms in turn, then lifted him to his feet.

Whispered in his ear.

Then Yeshua gave Simon more than the first touch of mercy. More than the coin a passing stranger gives a lowly beggar . . . more than a kind word . . . more than reserving instead of passing judgment. The Master enfolded Simon in His arms, embraced him, adopted him.

The second touch of kindness Simon had refused to give Yeshua, he now received from Yeshua multiplied a thousandfold.

The second touch of forgiveness.

Yeshua offered, "I take your leprosy from you." The Teacher thrust His own hand inside the folds of His robe and drew it out, whitened and shriveled.

Tsara'at!

Simon stared in wonder and horror at Yeshua's fingers. Cried out as he read the name hacked into the wound of Yeshua's bleeding palm!

Then Simon glanced at his own hands.

They were healed, clean, pure. His own hands as he remembered them. Feeling restored! Well and strong! Able to draw a bowstring and send an arrow to its mark!

Yeshua spoke gently. "Go now. Tell no man what has happened. Only take the offering to the Temple as Torah commands. Show yourself to the priests. This is sign enough."[82]

Peniel stopped. Resisted Eglon's forward movement. The knifepoint pricked his back, goading him on.

From the group closest to Yeshua, exclamations of amazement rang out.

The talmidim were distracted by the miraculous occurrence. Their attention no longer centered on holding back the crowd; they too looked toward Yeshua.

Only a few paces separated the assassin from his target.

Eglon relinquished his grasp of Peniel's arm, shoving him out of the way.

A pair of eager onlookers surged into the gap. Peniel was a pace ahead and to one side. Eglon, momentarily blocked, pushed harder to clear a path.

Peniel opened his mouth to shout a warning. But fear stifled him. Fear for Amos and Gideon.

Fear of being blinded again.

The words of alarm died, unspoken, on his tongue.

Then Peniel saw Yeshua's face clearly, saw the Teacher's eyes connect with Eglon's. Brown eyes, flecked with gold, full of compassion, met dark orbs of cold fury and merciless concentration.

Eglon lunged forward, brandishing the dagger.

Simon felt dizzy. He was grateful when Jotham rushed to provide support under one arm. Zadok put both hands on Simon's shoulders: a blessing, a welcome.

Touch! How grateful Simon was to experience it again. He had not known how cut off from all he loved and from those who loved him he had been. His life was brand-new.

A thousand unanticipated joys spread in front of him.

The air hummed with questions: What had just happened? Had a miracle occurred? Who had been healed?

Simon turned, faced a throng pressing inward, their visages full of inquiry. All of them, pushing, shouting, cheering, struggling to get close!

Yet a few feet directly in front of Simon was one face not suffused with wonder or praise. Unmistakable marks of antagonism were printed there.

Simon knew that face! Eglon, assassin of Herod Antipas' court! Eglon! Confidant of the high priest!

Eglon was within the circle nearest Yeshua! Simon glimpsed a spark of sunlight on a burnished blade!

A dagger! The knife, now upraised, gleamed in the Galilean sunshine.

"No!" Simon shouted, shaking off the vertigo and the encumbering arms.

"No!" Zadok echoed.

Simon leapt forward. No thought that his life, so recently reborn, could end, impaled on six inches of steel. Arms extended to block the blow, he rushed beneath the descending weapon, colliding full force with Eglon.

The crowd erupted in shrieks of dismay and confusion!

Simon and Eglon tumbled backward on the slope, knocking Peniel sprawling.

Eglon flailed at Simon's back, nicking his clothes with the tip of the instrument.

The point snagged a trailing length of torn lapel. Eglon struggled to pull it free, changed his grip, and lost his hold on the weapon when Simon rolled away from the blows.

The ragged cloth, symbol of the leper's impurity, snared the assassin's tool . . . and flipped it harmlessly out of reach.

It slid beneath Peniel, who snatched it up and dropped to the ground to cover it with his body.

Eglon leapt to his feet. Locked eyes with Yeshua. The predator bared his teeth with the rage of a cornered animal. He backed away, cursing Peniel and Simon. Damning Yeshua. Threatening to finish what he was sent for.

Yeshua, calm and assured, said, "Tell the foxes who sent you: 'Not today.' "

"Get him!" cried John and Ya'acov.

Eglon roared and slammed into three stunned watchers in his bid to escape. Yeshua's talmidim in pursuit, Eglon ran toward the creek bed and disappeared into the willows.

"Let him go!" Yeshua called after his talmidim. "Let him go!"

They halted their pursuit reluctantly, returning to Yeshua.

Yeshua gave Simon a hand up. The Master guided the shaken but uninjured man into the care of Jerusha, Jotham, and Zadok. "I thank you," He said. "Simon of Capernaum. Simon the Pharisee."

"No, Lord," Simon corrected. "From now on I'll be called Simon the Leper. A badge I'll wear with honor."

Yeshua nodded, approved the title. "Go home then," He instructed, signaling for a group of three small boys and a red dog to join them. "Go home, and begin your life again."

Peniel cowered where he had fallen. Huddled over the dagger, he gasped for air as if his lungs were as full of remorse as a drowning man's of seawater.

He wished the earth would open up beneath him. Swallow him up! Hide him from his shame!

He recognized the feet that appeared in his view.

Peniel sobbed. "Take back my eyes! I don't deserve them!" He gripped the dagger, revealing it to Yeshua as if offering the Teacher the opportunity to strike Peniel with it. "I betrayed you. I would've stood by and let you be killed!"

The words of Simon's miracle still reverberated in Peniel's ears: *healed and forgiven.*

Yeshua kneeled, stroked Peniel's hair, lifted his face. Wiped away the tears.

Brown eyes, flecked with gold, penetrated Peniel's soul.

"I betrayed you," Peniel sobbed. "After what you did for me. And I'm a traitor to you!"

"Yes."

"*Can* you ever forgive me?"

Yeshua answered, "Yes, Peniel. Have you forgotten? That's why the Son of Man was sent. Sent to heal . . . sent to be betrayed . . . and sent to forgive . . . again and again."

Between gasps, "Then . . . Lord . . . please! A second touch! Forgiveness! My heart will break if you can't forgive me!"

"I can. And I do. With all my heart. I will never forsake you. Peniel. You have forgiveness the moment you ask," Yeshua said.

Then stronger, bolder. "My friends," Peniel begged. "I'm afraid for them. They're tied up . . . helpless. Can you . . . would you . . . go with me to help them?"

"Yes. They'll be needing our help." Yeshua raised His chin, sniffing the danger on the wind. "Come on. You and I. We'll go together."

Jekuthiel leaned heavily against Lily. Although she was the stronger of the two, her strength drained with every mile. Hawk, dozing, rode on her shoulder as they struggled to reach the Valley of Sorrow before morning.

The moon rose late, illuminating the road before them. Lily was grateful for its glow. Thankful to be traveling through the night.

In dark houses and quiet villages ordinary people dreamed their dreams, unaware two untouchables passed so near. They were like the shadows of two birds brushing the landscape. They left no mark, made no difference to crops, or commerce, or joys, or sorrows in the world they moved through.

No one cared for them. No one would remember their names. How short their journey had been in the scope of things. Meaningless. This was suddenly surprising to Lily, who had begun her time on earth with such expectation.

I'm wondering again. Is it not said that before a soul enters this world and breathes its air, the Lord conducts it through heaven? He shows it what it's leaving behind when it comes to earth? Last of all it is shown the First Light which, at the creation of the world, illuminated all things. That Light God removed from earth when mankind became corrupt.

Once I asked Rabbi Ahava, "Why, since I was meant to live as an outcast, stricken by God's hand, why was my soul shown this Light?" He told me it was so my soul would yearn to see the Light a second time. Search for it. Seek it.

Oh, Lord! My soul has longed to see your Light. Longed for the second touch of your Light upon my face! But you, O Lord! You've kept the Light from shining on my dark life! And now I will die. I will die wondering what point my brief years ever made in your plan of eternity.

We are nothing. Our lives less than nothing.

I'm praying again, You Who Never Hear Me Pray. Look at your creatures. Those of us, multitudes who suffer, while the rest of the world turns away, afraid to look at us. Despised. Rejected. Scarcely human in our bodies. Yet wholly human in our longings! What are we? We are the faint stirring of curtains in a sleeping child's room. The echo of a voice in a dream that cannot be understood. The disturbing sense that something ominous passed near which cannot be remembered upon waking.

It was, Lily thought, as though she and Jekuthiel were already dead. She felt her own deadness fully for the first time.

The wilderness reared up before them like a wall. With difficulty they ascended the road. As they labored between the windswept mountains the sky began to lighten. Stars dimmed. The moon grew pale in the sky behind them.

A mile farther through the pass Lily stopped in amazement. The gatekeeper's cottage had burned to the ground. The evil Overseer had vanished.

And so, at last, Lily and Jekuthiel came to the end of their journey. The Valley of Mak'ob lay below them.

29

Yeshua carried the clay lamp along the dark path toward the tumbled-down house. Peniel darted ahead, came back. Tried to match his pace to Yeshua's steady footfall.

No use. Too slow. Too slow. Peniel rushed ahead again. Stopped. Looked back. Waited as the bobbing lamp approached.

Sheep stirred behind a stone wall as they passed. Insects buzzed in the brambles. Peniel heard the wind stirring in the green trees beside a creek.

"I've never been afraid of the dark before," he said, trying to explain his fear. "But what if they're there? waiting in ambush?"

Yeshua walked on, never varying His pace.

The moon glowed behind the mountain like a fire dimming the stars.

Peniel worried. "If they're there, they'll spot us in the moonlight. See us coming up the path."

Yeshua said, "Come here. Walk beside me. Let's be silent for a while and listen."

Beside Him Peniel felt safe. Like lying behind a wall when the wind blew. Yet still the night whispered terrible thoughts in Peniel's brain.

What if his friends had been murdered? What if Eglon had circled back and slit the throats of the helpless ones just for spite?

Yeshua and Peniel crossed a ridge and descended into the swale where the prisoners had been left.

"The house is just there. No light."

Yeshua held up the lamp and examined the tracks on the path. He rose with a sigh and proceeded without caution to the dwelling.

With His foot, Yeshua nudged the door open. It groaned on its hinges as it swung back to reveal . . . nothing. Rubbish. No one.

Peniel's eyes leapt from one heap of rubble to the next in the interior. He spoke softly, "Shalom? Gideon? Amos?"

Gone. Gone. An owl hooted in the tree.

Peniel, stung by their absence, shouted out the window, "Jekuthiel? Where are you? Hey! I brought him! He came with me! Hey! Amos! Eglon's . . . gone!"

By the lamplight Yeshua examined the interior of the room. He stooped to retrieve a wadded-up scrap of parchment. He opened it slowly and read silently.

"What is it?" Peniel asked.

Yeshua did not reply. He stood in the center of the broken house and listened. Listened as though He could hear voices, discern all the reasons why the house had fallen in on itself.

And then from behind a heap of trash came a whimper. A cry like that of a wounded animal.

"Who's there?" Peniel's heart pounded.

The voice of Amos replied. "Peniel?" A scruffy head poked up. "Peniel? I was hiding. Heard someone coming. Saw the light. I was hiding."

Peniel threw himself into the dwarf's arms. "Ah, Amos! I thought they'd killed you!"

"Not so far. But I believe it now. If you live long enough you see everything. Who's this with you?"

"The one we came looking for."

"Are you *himself* then?" Amos stood up slowly. "Yeshua of Nazareth?"

"Yes." Yeshua extended His hand to the dwarf.

"I thought you were dead. I'm glad you're not."

"The others are gone?" Yeshua asked.

"Gideon bolted. Off to start a new life as a thief and a liar elsewhere, I suppose. As for the leper? Jekuthiel. Back to Mak'ob. Gone back to die there with his wife and child. I wanted to remind him that life is the candle we put out when morning comes. Good one, eh? But I was too heartsick to speak when they left."

Yeshua replied, "Well spoken. A good proverb."

Amos regained some of his brass. "Good if you've got a large candle and a long way to travel till morning comes. Little comfort, I suppose, if you're going to die soon . . . like the leper. Better a single candle in the darkness than . . . oh . . ."

Yeshua reached out and grasped Amos by the shoulders. Gripped him hard. Gazed straight into his face. "A true word, Amos. Rightly spoken. One to remember."

Amos stammered in a drunken voice, "I didn't . . . didn't get a chance to . . . to . . . to . . . tell him and the girl. She was a leper as well . . . well . . . well . . . I suppose. Came looking . . . looking . . . for a bird wearing . . . a bell. The bird wore the . . . the . . . the . . . b-b-bell I mean. A very strange p-p-pair. I would have liked to . . . to . . . to send Jekuthiel off with a word of w-w-wisdom."

"I'll tell Jekuthiel when I see him." Then Yeshua asked, "Now Amos, what is the proverb about things that grow overnight? Tell me."

"Rents . . . debt . . . girls . . ." Amos finished with a sigh and sank down on the ground, exhausted.

Yeshua, towering over him, whispered, "You'll have something new to add to that list now."

A long, deep snore replied. Amos was asleep.

Peniel gaped at his friend. Long legs protruded from a too-short cloak. Arms extended from too-short sleeves. Big feet. Very big. Peniel gasped, "It is written . . . when Messiah comes, all the sick will be healed. The undertaker will be out of business and the shoemaker will have new customers! Look at his *feet!*"

"Such a tall man needs feet in proportion to his height."

Peniel said in awe, "He'll be amazed come morning."

"It'll take a few days but he'll get used to it," Yeshua replied with a smile.

"I would have liked to have been here to see him when he wakes to find his clothes are too small."

"He'll stitch a proverb to fit."

Nothing is too hard for God.

Suddenly it came to Peniel that Yeshua had much more to accomplish. *Jekuthiel!* "Lord! I want to go with you."

"Yes."

"We have a long journey ahead of us, don't we?"

"Yes. Yes. Come on then, friend. They'll be waiting. The candle is almost out."

Peniel stood at Yeshua's right hand as they surveyed the deep canyon of Mak'ob.

"They say only a leper can enter that terrible place," Peniel observed. "How will you get word to them that you've come? That you're here?"

Yeshua did not answer.

The shadows of late afternoon filled the Valley with gloom. Far below the precipice tiny antlike figures moved in the gardens. Walked slowly along paths. Drew water from the well. Tended cook fires. Lived on in the midst of dying.

The tangy scent of woodsmoke curled heavenward. So ordinary. Like any other impoverished village on the rim of this wilderness.

Peniel spoke. "From this distance, Lord? Up here? Look! They're just people. They seem no different than anyone. Could be anyone. Like everyone."

Yeshua smiled faintly, amused that Peniel still did not understand. "I tell you the truth, Peniel, they *are* everyone. Or rather, *everyone is them.* No difference. No. None at all."

"I'm not a leper."

"Don't you see? The true sickness in a man's heart is pride. Pride justifies wrongdoing and conceals the truth . . . even from a man's own self. Every person is a leper on the inside, Peniel. That is the condition of each soul trying to live outside God's sovereignty and purpose. What you see on the outside of the people of Mak'ob is an image of what's inside everyone."

At this insight, Peniel considered again what had driven him to do what he had done. "Point taken. Well spoken. I was so proud, Lord. Proud when you healed me. As if I somehow deserved it. And I wanted to prove to everyone that I was right about you! So I brought my friends and they betrayed you. And I betrayed you too! I was so proud! And yet I failed!"

What remained after Peniel's failure? Shame and disgrace! If left to fester, unconfessed and unforgiven, such emotions would have eaten away at him like a sort of leprosy, rotting his heart beat by beat.

And yet Yeshua *had* forgiven him. Fully. Loved him. Unconditionally. Even before the act of betrayal had been fully played out, Yeshua had immersed Peniel in mercy as deep and wide as the sea! Peniel's heart had felt the second touch of forgiveness from the hand of the One he had betrayed.

"Peniel, Peniel! The Son of David was sent to this world for this single purpose! *Chesed.* Mercy."

"Lord, I was too proud. I didn't know my heart needed mending."

"Yes—" Yeshua put His hand over Peniel's eyes—"even something small . . . small as a hand . . . can block the eyes from seeing an object as big as a mountain." Yeshua took away His hand. "So it is with the eyes of the inner man. Do you understand what I mean?"

"Yes. Yes. I need you to cleanse my heart even of small wrongs. Lord!"

"Gladly! With joy! Such a request is always answered! The cry for mercy is always heard and never refused! Your sins *are forgiven.*"

If this was true for Peniel, could it also be true for others? For everyone, as Yeshua said? Could it be that the inside of every person was as much in need of healing and forgiveness as the infirmity of blindness or leprosy?

Peniel asked, "The rabbis teach that in the Valley of Mak'ob there are always 612 lepers. The same number as the Hebrew word for *covenant.* Six hundred and twelve stands for the covenant: *Beriyt.* No more, no less. Add one more and that completes the number of laws in Torah."

"This is true."

"The rabbis teach also that Messiah will be a leper. According to Isaias, the rabbis call Messiah 'the Great Leper, our Redeemer.'"

"And so they are also correct in this. Six hundred and twelve is the number that stands for the Lord's covenant with Avraham. Six hundred thirteen is the number of laws in Torah. Yes. And look. Look down there, Peniel! Look deeply into the Valley of Sorrow! Here is what remains of the covenant between Avraham and the Lord. That is what results from mankind attempting to gain eternal life by keeping laws yet forgetting to love. A shambles. Decaying flesh. Defeat! Death and sorrow because no man has ever fulfilled all 613 laws of Torah! No man can earn his own salvation . . . and so the Law has brought death. Who can give mankind eternal life? Who can break the curse of death?"

"No man . . . *Lord.*"

"So, Peniel, salvation is all about God's mercy. How can broken lives be healed? You understand the words written by the prophet Isaias about the Great Leper?

> *"He was despised and rejected by men,*
> *A man of sorrows, and familiar with suffering.*
> *Like one from whom men hide their faces*
> *He was despised, and we esteemed Him not.*
> *Surely He took up our infirmities*
> *And carried our sorrows,*
> *Yet we considered Him stricken by God,*
> *Smitten by Him, and afflicted.*
> *But He was pierced for our transgressions,*
> *He was crushed for our iniquities;*
> *The punishment that brought us peace was upon Him,*
> *And by His wounds we are healed."*[83]

Peniel nodded, swallowing hard as he realized that the sign of leprosy Mosheh had shown him in the dream was the sign of the Messiah. The words Isaias used to speak of the Messiah were the same used to describe a leper. "Where is the Great Leper, Yeshua? When will he show himself? Where is the one who is the final fulfillment of everything written in the Law and the Prophets?"

At this, Yeshua placed His right hand inside His cloak, just as Mosheh had done in the dream.

And then, slowly, Yeshua drew it out again.

It was a hideous claw covered with leprosy! Rotten! Decaying! Infused with death!

Peniel did not draw back. He knew what it meant. Perhaps he had always known!

So terrible was the price God paid for men's redemption!

"You are the Great Leper, Lord! Surely you've come to take our infirmities upon yourself! I see the truth of it now, fully! You are the perfect of heart, righteous . . . who knew no sin . . . was sent to become sin for our sake! You who embody life eternal have become death so that we may live!"

Yeshua said nothing for a long time. His brown eyes brimmed with emotion. "Yes. That's it. I'm glad you understand. Someday many others will come to understand the true meaning of *Chesed*, God's Mercy for his children." Yeshua glanced at His leprous hand, then held it out for Peniel to see. Carved into the flesh of His palm was the name *Peniel*.

Peniel grasped it, laid his cheek upon it, and cried. "For me! For me you've done this, Lord! You've taken my infirmities as your own! You become what I am . . . so I can become what *you* are! You take my inner leprosy upon yourself and make my heart pure! To save me from dying you give your own life. You do this for all who call upon you!"

They stood together for a long time on the verge of the precipice.

At last, filled with gratitude and peace, Peniel let go of Yeshua's disfigured hand. "Down there in the Valley so many suffer and don't know why. They're all waiting for you, Lord. Hoping. I reckon they've been waiting for you to come to them a long time."

"Yes." Yeshua nodded and pulled out the petition written by His mother. He read it over again, pressed it against His heart, then turned His face heavenward and began to pray silently. At last He received some answer. He whispered, "Yes. Yes. Yes. Not my will, but yours, Father! Now and for all time and eternity the wait is over."

Peniel stepped back, bowed slightly, and sank down on a stone to wait. "I'm all right now. Go to them. I'll still be here when you come back."

"Thanks, my friend. Shalom, then." Yeshua sighed deeply and set off down the trail.

A lone hawk circled high above Mak'ob, as if trying to catch a final glimmer of sunset. Wind held the creature aloft, floating almost motionless. Sunlight glinted on dappled wings. Golden. For a moment the

Hawk seemed to study the lone sentinel perched on the outcropping a thousand feet above the Valley floor.

Peniel raised his hand in a kind of salute to beauty and skill at riding the updraft.

Satisfied with the compliment, the raptor cried shrilly three times. Banking, it glided down and down, vanishing into the spectral twilight of the leper colony.

Peniel strained to see the Great Leper as He descended into the Valley of Sorrow. *Yes. There. Just there.* At the switchback, midway between sky and earth. Yeshua! A slender man in a tan-and-green-striped cloak, gazing ahead, impatient to reach His destination. His footsteps swallowed the distance eagerly in giant bites, without bothering to chew. And then the darkness of Mak'ob swallowed Him whole.

Here and there, flickering campfires seemed to hang suspended in the blackness, like stars against the night sky. The universe turned upside down.

Immanuel!

Peniel clutched his knees and inhaled the aroma of woodsmoke, reminding himself that this was indeed earth. He watched and waited for some sign.

An hour passed, then two. Near the center of the Valley a new light grew, blazing up into a beacon, glowing red and yellow and white-hot, like a new galaxy.

Peniel could see Yeshua sitting on a stone beside the fire. At His feet was an old man. Waiting. Waiting for what was to come. The old one stood and raised a shofar to his lips. The first blast of the ram's horn resounded, echoing into the hills above the Valley and beyond. The second call! Strong! The third! Joyful! Certain of the message it proclaimed.

Then, oh wondrous sight! *Beautiful! Beautiful!* From each cave, crevasse, hut, and hovel, light appeared. It was as if everywhere on the Valley floor stars awakened, danced, and bobbed to some unheard melody. Those dwelling in darkness and despair, like the molten ore of first creation, flowed in thin rivulets toward the Great Light! This pit of anguish was, for the Son of God, a wondrous mine of human souls. The cauldron glowed golden, promising new life.

From his high place on the rock Peniel watched it all with his new eyes.

They drew near to Yeshua. Not stars, but broken men, women, and children. One at a time they approached. Hobbling on crutches. The strong ones helping the weakest. Carrying those who could not walk. Guiding those who could not see. Half hands. Faceless faces. Legless stumps.

Yes. And Yeshua reached out, embraced each one. Every one. One at a time. Stroked the head of a child. Caressed the face of a woman. Grasped the hands of a man.

Time? What was time to Him? The stars stood still for Him. Time obeyed Him. Time enough to hear the cry of every heart. Yes. Time enough.

The brightness of the fire grew as, one by one, crutches, no longer needed, were tossed onto it. How it blazed! On and on! As Yeshua, First Light of every soul, reached out a second time and touched each one and healed them all.

One at a time?
Yes.
Each one?
Yes.
Every one?
Yes.
Deborah? Jekuthiel? Baruch? Rabbi Ahava? All the others?
All. Read for yourself. It says . . . He healed them all.
Lily?
Yes. All.
But . . .

First Light pushed back the darkness of Mak'ob. Hawk soared high on the winds as, single file, the people of the Valley ascended the long path to freedom.

Everything foretold by the prophets of old had been accomplished.

Lily remained behind. Well and whole and beautiful, she took the hand of Yeshua and led the Great Leper to the graveside of her beloved. They stood together for a long time in silence.

"Cantor's grave," Lily said.

"Yes."

"Even Cantor?"

"Yes."

"But . . . do you mean *Cantor*?"

"Yes."

"Can it be? Is it possible?"

Yeshua smiled, nodded once, and from inside His cloak, removed the parchment written by His mother. He closed Lily's fingers around it. Then He opened His hand and held it out for her to see. Two names were inscribed together on His palm.

"Yes. *Lily. Cantor.* Yes."

And everyone who calls on the name

of the Lord will be saved.

JOEL 2:32

Digging Deeper into
<u>SECOND TOUCH</u>

Dear Reader,

It is a dark, tumultuous time in first-century Israel. Secrets and deceit abound; it seems no one can be trusted.

When the lepers in the Valley of Mak'ob hear rumors about a miracle healer, they wonder, *Could this be the One God has promised to send to those who are suffering? To bring healing to those who, day by day, have lost hope?*

Yet the journey to investigate will be fraught with danger and risks. Dare they send someone out of the Valley to see if Yeshua *is* indeed the Messiah? if He is the healer they have waited so long for?

"But what if Yeshua's claims are false?" the lepers argue. Then they might as well just wait out life—and death—in the Valley, where at least they are known and understood.

What about you? When have you experienced "valleys" in your life? Maybe you're experiencing one right now.

Perhaps you feel like Lily, who remembers even the joyous moments of her past with bittersweet sadness, knowing she will never be able to rejoin her family. Because of her leprosy and its social stigma, she has been forever cast away from them. She knows reconciliation is impossible, and yet she constantly dreams of it.

Or Peniel, who owes so much to Yeshua . . . but still agonizes because when the going got tough, he made a wrong decision. Will his betrayal separate him forever from the One he loves the most?

Or Simon, the wealthy, influential Pharisee who looks good on the outside, but is playing a dangerous game. If his secret is revealed, he will be embarassed, discredited in business, and cut off from his colleagues and friends.

Or the lepers—including Cantor, Rabbi Ahava, and Jekuthiel—who see themselves dying slowly, one piece at a time. All in the Valley appears hopeless. And yet their trust in God shines forth as bright beacons as they comfort others.

What about you? How will you choose to handle your own valleys?

Following are six short studies designed to take you deeper into the answers to your questions. You may wish to delve into them on your own or share them with a friend or a discussion group.

As we have walked through the valleys in our lives, we've discovered two humbling truths that help us keep life's happenings in perspective:

- Each of us, like Peniel, is a beggar. We can never be or have "enough" (money, material possessions, talents, etc.) to be accepted by God into heaven. Without a personal relationship with God we can never be whole and complete in body or soul.
- Each of us is also like Simon: a leper on the inside. We are unclean and unholy before God, the only One who can cleanse us and

give us a life purpose that will satisfy on this earth and for all eternity.

We all need the bright hope of Yeshua's touch. And some of us need His *second touch*—to know, once again, that God doesn't hold the past against us. That His love, mercy, and grace are unmerited.

Unconditional.

Unlimited.

And free for the asking.

1 | WHO NEEDS GOD?!

Had they all come because of a hunger in their souls? Or had they only come for bread?
—P. 294

Think of someone you know who believes in God. What reasons does that person give for believing?

_____

_____

_____

Now think of someone who says he/she does not believe in God. What reasons does that person give for *not* believing?

_____

_____

_____

There are many reasons to believe—or not believe—in God.

You may believe in God because you were taught about God and His Son in Sunday school. But that head knowledge hasn't reached your heart or your day-to-day life.

You may be convinced of Scripture's truth and that Yeshua is the Son of God. You are aware, every waking minute, that God is in control not only of the universe but of *your* life. You have experienced His breathtaking grace and limitless mercy.

You may not yet be convinced that the Bible's words are true. You're investigating . . . but cautious.

Perhaps you've seen the "misuse" of religion, and you're suspicious.

Maybe you've experienced enough of life's hardship to believe that there couldn't possibly be a God. Or if there is a God, He is certainly incompetent since He's allowing this world to spin out of control.

No matter your reasons for believing or not believing in God, it all comes down to one simple question: Do you think you *need* God?

Or is God simply a useful tool for when times get rough and you need somebody or something to lean on? Is He merely a topic for sarcastic and lively discussion? Is He someone you've decided to ignore . . . for now? Or have you chosen to acknowledge that He has played an active role in your life from the very beginning of time and continues to do so minute to minute?

READ

It was the same in my time as now. Humans seldom listen. Not really. The truth is inconvenient. The rulers have their own agenda. The common folk don't want to be bothered.
—MOSHEH (P. 92)

These people honor me with their lips,
but their hearts are far from me.
They worship me in vain;
their teachings are but rules taught by men.
—MARK 7:6-7

"If you want the people to believe in you, show us a sign. What'll you do for us?"
—A STURDY FARMER (P. 211)

"In their pride they demand a made-to-order miraculous sign. They refuse the evidence of the powerful things Yeshua has already done. . . . They plant doubts. They stir people up."
—ZADOK (P. 293)

"Some folk want him to feed them *every* day. Back to the wilderness, ha! Never work again, they mean! Paradise on earth."
—ZADOK (P. 211)

ASK

In what ways are believing in God and the truths of the Bible "inconvenient"?

_____

_____

_____

How do we try to use God for our own purposes?

_____

_____

_____

Do you agree with the following statement? Why or why not?

"The true sickness in a man's heart is pride. Pride justifies wrongdoing and conceals the truth . . . even from a man's own self. Every person is a leper on the inside. . . . That is the condition of each soul trying to live outside God's sovereignty and purpose. What you see on the outside of the people of Mak'ob is an image of what's inside everyone."

—YESHUA (P. 348)

_____

_____

_____

We all want to go our own way. It's called _human nature_, and it's a condition we are born with as a result of the Fall of Man. Adam and Eve bungled it for all of us when they chose to do what _they_ wanted to do, rather than what God had commanded them to do. As a result, pain and suffering entered the world.

Isaiah 53:6 makes it clear that _all_ of us have this condition:

We all, like sheep, have gone astray,
each of us has turned to his own way.

However, each of us must choose how we will respond to God's promises in the light of our daily circumstances. And the responses vary. Take a look at Deborah, Mosheh, the Canaanite woman, and Simon.

READ

"God has forsaken us. We are the ones who are Outside. Outside the love of God. How can we think otherwise? Rabbi Ahava? He's lying to us. We aren't loved by God!"
—DEBORAH (P. 205)

Adonai showed me the truth of what I really was! Unclean! Corrupt! Powerless! I cried out in anguish at the sight of my own mortality.
—MOSHEH (P. 94)

"Have mercy on me, O Lord . . . Son of David!" the Canaanite woman begs Yeshua. Then she asks Him to heal her little girl, who is tormented by a demon. When Yeshua tells her that her request is granted, she bows, then cries for joy—she believes! "It was obvious from the change in her demeanor and energy she had complete trust that when she arrived home, she'd find her daughter completely delivered and healed."
—PP. 271–272 (READ MATTHEW 15 FOR THE ENTIRE STORY)

"If Yeshua is anyone . . . any sort of prophet, he'll look at me and know. He'll do something without my having to ask or grovel! I'll wait and see what he does. I'll know if he's a man from God by how he treats me, a respected ruler of Israel. By what he does! . . . I'll not bend my knee to him! I'll not beg! I'll rot away before I ask Yeshua for help!"
—SIMON BEN ZERAIM (P. 207)

ASK

Deborah was angry, and understandably so. She had to birth her baby in horrible circumstances, knowing she had to give him up in order for him to live. And all this at a time when she didn't know if her husband would ever return to her side. Imagine that you are Deborah. How would you respond to such hardship?

Has there been a time when you, like Mosheh, realized your "own mortality"? In what circumstance?

_____

_____

_____

Contrast the attitudes of the Canaanite woman and Simon.

_____

_____

_____

Which of the two are you most like in attitude toward God right now? Why?

_____

_____

_____

It isn't until Simon is completely stripped of his business, friends, his reputation, status, and self-esteem that he realizes how much he needs Yeshua. Then he is hit hard with the truth: It isn't the *tsara'at* killing him. It is his own stubbornness and pride (see p. 331). He indeed does have to "rot away" for him to acknowledge his need!

READ

"Lord, I was too proud. I didn't know my heart needed mending."

"Yes—" Yeshua put His hand over Peniel's eyes—"even something small . . . small as a hand . . . can block the eyes from seeing an object as big as a mountain." Yeshua took away His hand. "So it is with the eyes of the inner man. Do you understand what I mean?"

"Yes. Yes. I need you to cleanse my heart even of small wrongs. Lord!"

"Gladly! With joy! Such a request is always answered! The cry for mercy is always heard and never refused. Your sins *are forgiven.*"
—PENIEL AND YESHUA (P. 349)

ASK

Do you long for forgiveness? In what areas?

_____

_____

_____

Have you admitted, like Simon, "This is my *true* heart: I am a leper! Inside *and* out, I am unclean"? (p 339). If so, what encouraged you to do so? If not, what hinders you?

_____

_____

_____

WONDER . . .

"What should we ask for? If we ask anything at all?

"That the will of the Lord be done in our lives. Aye. God's will for us is never wrong. Never. The Lord feeds the humble man because he loves us. If we make the Lord as much a part of our daily lives as eating, then truly he is our 'bread of life.'"
—AVEL AND ZADOK (PP. 216–217)

> *Ask and it will be given to you; seek and you will find; knock and the door will be opened to you. For everyone who asks receives; he who seeks finds; and to him who knocks, the door will be opened.*
> —LUKE 11:9-10

How deep is your need for God? What will you ask Him for today?

2 | NO LIMITS!

"The Son of David was sent to this world for this single purpose!
Chesed. Mercy."
—Yeshua (p. 349)

When you think of the word *mercy*, what person or organization comes to mind, and why? Give a specific example.

_____

_____

_____

If someone committed a crime and then begged for mercy, would you extend mercy? Why or why not? Would there be limits to your mercy? Explain.

_____

_____

_____

Simon ben Zeraim was a good Pharisee, yet he had lived a lifetime without extending true *chesed*, mercy! It wasn't until everything had been stripped away from him that he realized how "small" a life he had actually lived. Because of his pride and self-centeredness, he had never told his wife, Jerusha, how much he loved her. He had driven away his son. He had taunted Yeshua and "born false witness" against Him. He had harmed the defenseless by evicting a tenant family with a young girl with leprosy. He had even, out of "religious principle," separated Jerusha from her mother's and father's love.

Simon came to the end of himself and the beginning of an understanding of God's mercy when he realized his errors: "*Anger! Envy! Resentment! Gossip! Coveting!* Small wrongs he had committed against others! Small acts of mercy he had failed to do *for* those in need! All these together became a broad, deep river washing away the last pretense of righteousness!" (p. 331).

Simon, a respected religious official, always fulfilled the letter of the law in every way. However, in the midst of the *duty* of fulfilling the Law, he missed the *meaning* of the Law.

How easy it is for us to do so, especially when questions abound about how mercy works in the real world. Should we always keep the letter of the law to be fair in all situations—or extend mercy? If we decide to be merciful, how far should that mercy go? Should there be any limits?

Most of us would extend mercy . . . up to a point. But when a line is crossed (such as harming a person or thing we hold dear), then we crave justice. Our vision is colored by our emotions. We have difficulty thinking in terms of eternity, the perspective from which God sees. Or we may tire of doing the right thing—such as helping a suffering friend or a person in financial need.

Perhaps that is why it is so difficult for us to comprehend the infinite number of times God forgives us, not only for what we *do* wrong (see Matthew 18:22) but for *who we are*, at the very core of our soul.

READ

"[Those who are whole] don't see that they are us. On the inside they are what we are. The same. Needing mercy. No different . . . wounded. In different ways. But still wounded. All of us. They want to forget. Not think about it. Get on with their lives."

—DEBORAH (PP. 180–181)

"Can a soul be *tsara*? Can a heart have leprosy? Can the inner man be so numb he no longer feels and so increases his injury day by day? God's mercy could heal such a heart. I believe it. Forgive and heal. Restore the feeling. Bring back what is eaten away in us."

—LILY (P. 32)

ASK

In which of the following scenarios would it be the easiest for you to be merciful? Why?

- A man on the street asks you for money.
- A friend asks you to drive her to the doctor.
- A coworker asks you to lie about his being in the office.
- A relative abuses your child.
- A homeless woman asks for food.
- A desperate friend asks you to keep her child for one day because she's exhausted.

_____

_____

_____

Are there days in which you feel "numb"—as if you no longer have feeling in your heart? Describe the situation.

_____

_____

_____

Here's Rabbi Ahava's perspective for just such a day:

"This is what the Lord says to your aching heart: '_Can a mother forget a baby at her breast and have no compassion on the child she has borne? Though she may forget, I will not forget you! See! I have engraved you on the palms of my hands!_'[see Isaiah 49:14-16] . . . Adonai, the Lord, has engraved our names. No, he's done much more than that. The word used in this passage says he _hacked_ out our names, as with hammer and chisel, into the flesh of his palms! Love for his children has made the wounds we will see one day when we look at the outstretched hands of our Redeemer!"

—P. 84

Does knowing that God's wounds are *for you*, because of His great love, change your situation or perspective in any way? If so, how?

_____

_____

_____

READ

> *He was pierced for our transgressions,*
> *he was crushed for our iniquities;*
> *the punishment that brought us peace was upon him,*
> *and by his wounds we are healed.*
> —ISAIAH 53:5

> *You are not your own; you were bought at a price.*
> — 1 CORINTHIANS 6:19-20

ASK

God truly paid a high price for you—the agonizing death of His only Son. If you had to choose whether or not to allow your only child to die to save others, even those you didn't know, would you/could you do it? Why or why not?

_____

_____

It is so easy to view the wounds of another without compassion. How does knowing that God has purchased *every* person at such a price change your perspective toward those in need? toward those who have injured you in some way?

_____

_____

_____

READ

Surrounded by the thousand-foot-high cliffs that rose from the Valley of Mak'ob, she was at home among the *chadel*, the "Rejected Ones."

Outside they were known as *chadel*, the "living dead." Strange how fear, loathing, and a vowel or two could make such a different in the definition of a person's worth, Lily thought.

    —P. 60

> *In everything, do to others what you would have them do to you, for this*
> *sums up the Law and the Prophets.*
>   —MATTHEW 7:12

"So many men know the Scriptures. And still there's the viaduct. The rubbish heap. People who exist in the long, dreary waiting, like animals locked up and forgotten. . . .

"Easy not to be bothered. Easy to follow the letter of the Law. Make a great show of keeping the Law. But men forget the true intention of the Law. . . . By turning away from those who suffer, they miss great blessings from heaven. Maybe the one they refused to help was an angel in disguise. Thus ends the lesson."

    —YESHUA (P. 9)

ASK

When have you felt judged or rejected?

_____

_____

_____

In what ways has the memory of that circumstance affected how you respond to those who are suffering?

_____

_____

_____

Have you ever received "great blessings from heaven" as a result of helping someone? Describe the situation.

_____

_____

_____

READ

"What's the best day to show mercy, Peniel?"

"Every day, I think, Rabbi."

"Well spoken."

"You know what I think. I'm glad you didn't turn away from my affliction because I'm poor and it was Shabbat."

—YESHUA AND PENIEL (P. 7)

Lily began to weep. Her shoulders shaking beneath this unexpected first touch of kindness.

How long had it been? How long since anyone but another leper had dared to reach out to her, embrace her?

—P. 302

What remained after Peniel's failure? Shame and disgrace! If left to fester, unconfessed and unforgiven, such emotions would have eaten away at him like a sort of leprosy, rotting his heart beat by beat.

And yet Yeshua *had* forgiven him. Fully. Love him. Unconditionally. Even before the act of betrayal had been fully played out, Yeshua had immersed Peniel in mercy as deep and wide as the sea!

—P. 349

ASK

Mercy. *Chesed*. Both Peniel and Lily experienced the life-changing results of unmerited, unlimited mercy.

Yeshua touched Peniel in the way that would make the biggest impact on his soul—Yeshua healed his eyes. Mary reaches out to embrace Lily, the leper, who has been longing for physical touch. And then Yeshua touches

Peniel a *second time*. He extends mercy and forgiveness after Peniel betrays Him!

When have you felt the kind touch of a friend or stranger? How did that one touch impact your situation?

_____

_____

_____

We are all human. None of us has entirely fulfilled either the letter of the Law *or* the meaning of the Law. Simon harbored a secret that destroyed his life. Is there a secret for which you long to be forgiven? If so, why not ask God today? You could write out your request as a benchmark here, if you wish.

_____

_____

_____

WONDER . . .

"No one on earth would ever go hungry or live out a life of loneliness if this was the bread we broke and shared together. That is what Yeshua is. Manna from heaven. Enough love and mercy for everyone. Enough to go around. Those who gather much have just as much as those who gather little."
 —ZADOK (P. 216)

"Be merciful, just as your Father is merciful."
 —YESHUA, LUKE 6:36

In the end all we can do is ask God for His mercy. Act on that mercy. Hold to it. Claim it. . . . Then His grace pours out life to us freely, abundantly.
 —MOSHEH (P. 155)

In what areas of your life do you need to accept God's unlimited mercy? To whom do you need to extend unmerited mercy?

_____

_____

_____

3 | WHO IS MESSIAH?

Who is our Messiah? That is the question. Yahweh's speech, Yahweh's words—the Omer—contains the answer!
—MOSHEH (P. 203)

Imagine watching a man walk down the street. There seems to be nothing unusual about him. In fact, people hardly notice him because he's so ordinary. So unremarkable. Later, his face flashes across the evening news and you remember seeing him. You're surprised by the story. Evidently this man has healed people—the blind, the lame, those tortured in soul. Even more, He claims to be the fulfillment of all the Old Testament prophecies, the Messiah sent by God. Would you believe His claims? Why or why not?

_____

_____

_____

What would it take to convince you that a God-Man was walking this earth?

_____

_____

_____

Step back into the first century, when the people had lived so long with the expectation that someday the Messiah—the One who would save them—would walk the earth that it almost seems like a legend. Or a fairy tale.

They accept that there is a God in the heavens. But a God walking around on the earth? Healing the suffering? Standing in the same places as those who have earthly flesh? It seems impossible. Especially when this Messiah doesn't match their expectations—either in looks or demeanor. They expected a "kingly presence"—someone who would sweep in to end Rome's tyranny over Israel. Someone who would be their avenger, their protector. Someone who would establish a rich kingdom right here on earth.

Instead Yeshua came gently, in the form of a baby, a lowly carpenter's son. He moved among the people, "touching flesh" with them. Walking in their shoes. Sharing their meager suppers. Experiencing their emotions. Seeing the sorrows and the dreams in their eyes. But since He was not what they expected, few believed who He really was.

Only those with "new eyes" knew. Those like Peniel, the blind man who could now see. The man who had a questing heart. The man who was content merely to walk by Yeshua's side.

READ

Unnoticed. Unremarkable. Ordinary.

Yet Peniel knew the truth.

All who sought Yeshua tested Him. When they found Him, they sized Him up, trimmed Him to fit their expectations, and tried to force His image into a puzzle of their own making.

But Yeshua did not fit.

—P. 6

Like Mosheh, Messiah is the Son of a King. The King of Heaven! The Prince of Light has laid aside His royal robes and clothed Himself in the poverty of our human flesh, taking on the appearance of an ordinary man. And yet He is the Good Shepherd [see Psalm 23; John 10:11] that David sang about in one of his psalms! He will confront and defeat the Prince of Darkness and liberate His flock, not by the rod of fear and oppression, but by raising the simple staff of righteousness and love. And by the staff of our Shepherd-King, all power that the Prince of this world has over mankind will be swallowed up just as the staff of Mosheh swallowed the serpents of Pharaoh's magicians!

    —MOSHEH (P. 94)

All these things are written not simply as stories. . . . These are prophecies . . . which speak of the One yet to come. Written so this generation and those yet to be born will read and know the true identity of Messiah.

    —MOSHEH (P. 94)

ASK

What would you expect the Messiah of the world to look like?

_____

_____

_____

_____

What character qualities do you think this Messiah would have?

_____

_____

_____

_____

Does the first quote from Mosheh change your perspective about what to expect from the Messiah? If so, how?

_____

_____

_____

_____

Numerous Old Testament references are made to the coming Messiah (many in Isaiah 53). Do you believe the Messiah has come to earth yet? Why or why not?

_____

_____

_____

_____

READ

> *The heavens declare the glory of God;*
> *the skies proclaim the work of his hands.*
> *Day after day they pour forth speech;*
> *night after night they display knowledge.*
>   —PSALM 19:1-2

Peniel needed no miracles in order to believe He Was and He Is and He Will Be and He Can and He Wants To!

Nothing is impossible with God!

Peniel sensed the stars glistening on the night wind when the city was silent, and he *knew.*

Peniel heard the echo of creation in his heart and he *knew.*

The Great Timekeeper lived outside of time. Stepped into time. Just for a moment. Dwelt in *our* time! And Peniel *knew!*

Peniel needed no miracle in order to believe these things. And so, like an unbidden wind, the great miracle had caressed him, stirred him, root and branch, and *he knew!*

    —P. 6

ASK

How does seeing creation or nature affect your thoughts about God's involvement in the world?

_____

_____

What do each of the following phrases mean to you in your day-to-day life?

- He Was
- He Is
- He Will Be
- He Can
- He Wants To

_____

_____

READ

Yeshua! Joshua, the Greeks call him. Some call him Jesus. . . . Yeshua! God is
Salvation! . . . Listen to Him and be saved!
      —MOSHEH (P. 265)

I am the way and the truth and the life.
      —JOHN 14:6

He is the WHO, the Messiah! He is also the WHAT, the Bread of Life sent from
heaven! He is also the WORD, the OMER, the full measure of truth that feeds
men's souls. There is always enough to meet our needs and to satisfy the hunger of
our hearts.
      —MOSHEH (P. 202)

The Great Potter!
    He who made eyes had seen!
    He who made ears had heard!
    Wonder Worker. Origin of First Light. Knower of Secrets. He who
sang galaxies and crickets into existence with equal delight!
    Yeshua! He had stepped from eternity into time and stooped to make
Peniel's eyes out of red clay. Paused to finish the creation of an unfinished
life! To show one born blind . . . The Face!
    —P. 6

I am the good shepherd. The good shepherd lays down his life for the sheep.
    —JOHN 10:11

ASK

Consider the names of God. How has each directly impacted your life?

- Messiah, "God is Salvation!"
- The Way
- The Omer of Truth
- The Bread of Life
- The Great Potter
- The Wonder Worker
- The Origin of First Light
- Knower of Secrets

- The Face
- The Good Shepherd

_____

_____

_____

Note: There are so many names used for God throughout Scripture. If you want to grow deeper in the knowledge of who Messiah is, why not explore one of His names each day?

READ

Adonai said, "It's not who you are . . . it's who I AM! Fear not!"
    —Mosheh (p. 94)

> *For God so loved the world that he gave his one and only Son, that whoever believes in him shall not perish but have eternal life.*
> —John 3:16

"Enter through the narrow gate. For wide is the gate and broad is the road that leads to destruction, and many enter through it. But small is the gate and narrow the road that leads to life, and only a few find it."
    —Yeshua, Matthew 7:13-14

What a relief to know that it is not who we are or what we do that can "make or break" our entrance into heaven! Yeshua, the only true Messiah, has provided a way.

ASK

Why would the gate to heaven be narrow? Wouldn't a loving God want to let as many people as possible into heaven?

_____

_____

READ

If you believe it, then why doubt? Nothing . . . nothing . . . is too hard for God.

"No one else seems to believe it."

You find this discouraging.

"Yes. Honestly. Well? Who wouldn't?". . .

Why should it matter what others believe? You've met Him. You know the truth. Is creation wiser than the Creator? Why does it matter what they think?

—MOSHEH AND PENIEL (P. 93)

"Our 'bread of life.' Y' heard Yeshua apply that name to himself. Has he not proved the truth of it by the Omer, the measurement of his words and deeds? Anyone who calls himself 'the bread of heaven' must be measured, judged, by the Omer, the standard of God's Word. . . . In every way, Yeshua measures up! Yeshua is truly the bread sent down from heaven. His words spoken to us are the daily Omer, the exact measure that feeds our souls."

—ZADOK (P. 217)

ASK

In what ways do others' beliefs or doubts about God affect you?

_____

_____

_____

Today's headlines are rife with those who claim to be "the Messiah." What "measurement" can you always use when you are in doubt about whether someone's claims are true?

_____

_____

_____

WONDER . . .

The answer to our questions is found within the Omer, like gathering a container of miraculous bread. More than just a measurement of man's physical need, the Omer—the Word, the Answer—is the daily ration of Yahweh's voice, revealing eternal answers to our souls. The Omer of Yahweh's revelation never runs dry. There is always truth to nourish us!

      —Mosheh (p. 203)

One is coming—no, He's already here living among you—He is the true bread sent down from heaven! He is the WHAT! He is the WHO! Those who eat this bread will have eternal life.

      —Mosheh (p. 203)

Yeshua *is* the true bread sent down from heaven. But is He the WHAT? the WHO? your very existence? How can you bring Him into the epicenter of your life?

4 | STANDING STEADFAST

Between the Alef and the Tav of eternity, our life on earth is the Mem,
the forty years of trials and testing.
—MOSHEH (P. 264)

Whom do you know personally who is going through trials and testing right now? (Perhaps it's yourself.) What is that person's current situation?

_____

_____

_____

How has that person responded outwardly to those trials?

_____

_____

_____

Does that response make you respect and trust the person more—or break down your respect and trust for him/her? What makes the difference?

_____

_____

_____

Mosheh was right. All of us go through trials and testing. If not in the present, we have in the past or we will in the future. Trials have been part of the human condition since the Fall, when Adam and Eve chose to go their own way.

Each character in this book faced his or her own trials. And each dealt with the stress of the testing differently. Peniel caved under it . . . and lived with intense regret that plagued his every waking moment. Deborah grew bitter and questioned God's love. Simon hoped that if he acted "religious enough," God would simply make the situation go away. Lily struggled to continue believing . . . yet went on comforting others, even when she felt little comfort herself. Zadok was a rock who refused to be moved by any of his circumstances.

What made the difference for these characters? The genuineness of their beliefs . . . and their ability to act on those beliefs even when all around them seemed dark.

What does this say to us today? Trials and testing *will* come. But we need not be consumed or destroyed by them. We can stay steadfast, even when our world is shifting under our feet.

READ

Peniel huddled in the doorway of the shoemaker's shop. Even though darkness concealed him, closed around him, sleep would not come. He felt shattered, like one of Papa's clay lamps thrown against a stone wall.

Despite Peniel's new eyes, Mama and Papa could not accept him. Nor would they hear the good news he had returned to share. Fear of being separated from all that was familiar prevented them from embracing him.

Messiah had come at last . . . and there was no one he could tell!

All his life Peniel believed blindness had separated him from his family. He imagined that if he had vision everything would be different. Mama and Papa would love him. Accept him. They would be a family, whole and happy.

And now that he could see? Now that he could prove his worth? Ah, well. What difference did it make? Nothing changed. Mama was still Mama, hating him. Papa was too afraid of her to argue. So. Having sight made no difference to the one thing in the world that mattered to Peniel.

He was useless. No one listened to him when he was blind; no one would listen to him now that he had eyes. Why not lie down here and . . . wait to die? He could never, ever go home again.

In all the years Peniel had been blind he'd felt grief, yes. Sorrow, in plenty. Aching loneliness, often.

But never despair. Not like this.

The miracle had been wasted.

—P. 90

Create in me a pure heart, O God,
and renew a steadfast spirit within me.
Do not cast me from your presence
or take your Holy Spirit from me.
Restore to me the joy of your salvation
and grant me a willing spirit, to sustain me.
  —PSALM 51:10-12

ASK

What one thing matters the most to you in this world?

_____

_____

_____

How would you respond if that one thing was taken from you? Would any of your responses be similar to Peniel's ? Which ones?

_____

_____

_____

Peniel is feeling low, and it's no wonder. His biggest fear is that he will be cast forever from Yeshua's presence, just as he had been cast away from his family. Even though he has walked and talked face-to-face with The Face, Peniel still isn't immune to the troubles of life on earth. Nor are we. But will we choose to respond like Peniel . . . or a different way?

READ

"Everyone who lives anywhere dies. Everywhere. It's just that the people Outside aren't smart enough to know they're going to end up the same as us. Rabbi says we're God's reminder, so they hate us."

"They have a life before they die."

"So do we. It's what you make of it, Cantor says."

Deborah snapped. "Stop!" What do you know about it? You weren't even grown when you came here? What do you know about living? I had a real life Outside. . . . Pleasant. Other people. People with hands. People with human faces." Deborah touched her deformed face with her claw. "What can you know about it?"
—DEBORAH AND LILY (P. 35)

ASK

Deborah is living in "what if?" land. Her "what if this had never happened?" questions are destroying her. And her *I'm so miserable that I might as well make somebody else miserable too* thoughts are affecting her relationships.

Whom do you know who lives their present in the light of "what if?" questions and the *I'm so miserable* thinking? In what tangible ways can you see these questions and thoughts affecting their attitude? their relationships? their decisions?

_____

_____

_____

Do you agree with Lily's statement: Life is "what you make of it"? Why or why not?

_____

_____

_____

READ

Step into Simon ben Zeraim's world . . . and his thoughts for a minute.

"Blessed are you, O Lord, King of the world, who forms the light and creates the darkness, and in your goodness day by day and every day renews the works of creation."

He spoke the words, though he no longer believed them. No longer believed in God's goodness.

Now only the formula remained.

—P. 15

Each terrible new day he said the prayers and clung desperately to the outward image of what he was. Proud, arrogant, rich, an expert in the law and in the enactment of Pharisaic ritual, Simon ben Zeraim was among the most respected men of Israel.

No man imagined Simon's terror at what lay ahead.

—P. 15

ASK

Now that you're wearing Simon's shoes, answer these questions:

- What would your greatest fear be?
- What would you want to say to God?
- What plans (if any) would you make for the future?

Simon ben Zeraim is a self-righteous man, a man who is indignant that "a notorious sinner, a true harlot, a jezebel of scandalous reputation for her loose living" (p. 54) would dare to enter his home in order to kiss Yeshua's feet. He spends every possible moment trying to be spotless, "Hoping . . . *hoping* . . . the Eternal took note of his piety" (p. 14).

He worries about the leprous sore on his hand. "How long could he keep his secret? How long before he became an object of public humiliation and condemnation?" (p. 13). And yet his soul is far more leprous.

Do you know someone who looks good on the outside, and yet is leprous in soul? who treats others with disdain and contempt, similar to how Simon treats Yeshua? Why do you think this person responds as he/she does?

READ

For an instant, an image threatened to overwhelm Zadok. He gazed solemnly around the room where they had lived together. Where their little sons had died at the hands of Herod's soldiers. Where Zadok and Rachel, after they had wept together, had somehow rebuilt a life.

How to capture a lifetime in one last, long look?

—P. 121

> *The God of all grace, who called you to his eternal glory in Christ, after you have suffered a little while, will himself restore you and make you strong, firm and steadfast.*
> —1 PETER 5:10

"It is not for me to show the justice of my cause or complain how I am abused. The sheep are his, my life is his, and what he chooses to do with either is for him to say. My only concern is to commit my way and trust. All else is up to him."

—ZADOK (P. 123)

ASK

What was Zadok's first response when he was told he'd be turned out of his position as Chief Shepherd of the flocks of Israel? (See p. 47.)

If your job was on the line because someone had unjustly accused you, and then you'd been judged and sentenced by a partial jury, how would you respond?

Zadok is a wonderful example of one who stood steadfast in his beliefs in spite of dire circumstances. Was his life easy? Certainly not! His young sons had been murdered by Herod's soldiers, he lost an eye and gained scars, his wife died, and then he lost his job because he claimed that Yeshua was the Messiah. But when he is told that he will be turned out of his position as Chief Shepherd of the flocks, he shows no fear, only resignation.

Zadok could easily have responded with the "Woe is me" speech. Even Job, the Old Testament man known for being godly and righteous, did so after he lost his entire family (with the exception of a nagging, bitter wife) and all his possessions. (If you think you have something to complain to God about, read the entire book of Job. It will give you a soul mate for your own journey . . . and an eternal perspective.)

But instead, Zadok chose to stand steadfast, even if that meant he was jobless and homeless—with three orphan boys to take care of.

READ

Commit your way to the Lord;
Trust in him and he will do this:
He will make your righteousness shine like the dawn,
the justice of your cause like the noonday sun.
—PSALM 37:5-6

Do not be afraid; do not be discouraged. Be strong and courageous.
—JOSHUA 10:25

ASK

What makes the difference in how Peniel, Deborah, Simon, and Zadok responded to their life trials? (Hint: Look for key words in the verses above.)

After her beloved Cantor dies, Lily's faith grows dim. Rabbi Ahava tells her, "You can go on in bitterness, but why not ask Elohim for new purpose instead?" (p. 240). What new purpose could you look for in the midst of your trials?

_____

_____

_____

WONDER . . .

"El Shaddai knows our names. Knows our stories. . . . He hears us when we cry to him."

— LILY (P. 33)

"This is My promise to you! I AM speaking here! . . . My Word will feed your souls as you cross the wilderness of life! Until the end of time there is a battle raging against you, but I, Yahweh, will win the battle for your souls! I, Myself, will lead you and provide for you, if you will only trust Me!"

— MOSHEH (P. 202)

*You will keep in perfect peace
him whose mind is steadfast,
because he trusts in you.*
— ISAIAH 26:3

Like Joshua, who stood at the brink of the Promised Land, we all stand at the brink of choice. Rabbi Ahava's words to Lily are wise: "Even if you submit to the will of Elohim, if you submit without believing in his love, all your life will be is bitter" (p. 241).

Will you choose to be bitter . . . or better?

5 | BEYOND BOUNDARIES

Adonai spoke to her softly as He formed her.

I AM sending you.

Adonai loved her, created her as a reflection of His great love. He swam beside her as she emerged from the warmth of the womb into the cold, far country called Life.

She hesitated. Tried to turn back.

He compelled her to go on. *Breathe! Don't be afraid! You are sent by Me beyond what you imagine are the boundaries of your world.*

　　—PROLOGUE (P. VII)

Think of one person (from personal experience or in history) who has courageously stepped "beyond the boundaries" of his or her world. How has this person impacted history? the lives of those around him or her?

_____

_____

_____

What "boundaries" hold you back from reaching a dream or a goal?

_____

_____

_____

History books are packed with stories of men and women who went beyond the boundaries of their world. People like David Livingstone, who brought God's light to the dark continent of Africa; Mother Teresa, who compassionately gave of herself to the "lowest of the low"; Rosa Parks, who changed the course of history for African-Americans by simply taking a seat on a "whites only" bus and refusing to move.

The first-century lepers, of all people, knew what it was like to live within tight boundaries. Once they arrived in the Valley of Mak'ob, they did not leave until their death. The consequences for doing so were severe. If a *tsara* (a person with leprosy) was found outside the Valley, he or she could be driven out, stoned, or even killed. Citizens were terrified of lepers, since being a leper meant that nothing of your life would remain. You were forever cast out of your family and your community. The gulf separating you was the gulf between life and death, since you were now a walking dead person.

Lily lived within these boundaries. She'd been cast out when she was twelve, when the signs of *tsara'at* had appeared. It is no wonder she asked, *Where was the One who formed her? Why had this happened? Where was His voice of comfort in all this?* (p. x).

Aren't her questions the same ones we ask?

READ

Her father named her Shoshana, which means "Lily." She was a beautiful child, almost perfect. Everyone said so. Flaxen hair, oval face, large blue eyes that gathered in the sky. Small nose. Mouth like a rosebud. Teeth straight and white. Ears petite and perfectly formed. . . .

Papa used to say Lily was the most beautiful flower in his garden. . . . Mama had so many wonderful hopes and dreams tied up in Lily. Lily would grow up, get married, bring the grandbabies home to visit. . . . But it was not to be as Mama hoped.

Life ripened to become bitter, not sweet. So unfair. So full of suffering! Things never, ever turning out the way they ought!

—Prologue (p. viii)

ASK

Imagine you are Lily. You've grown up in a loving home, with a loving father and mother who doted on you as the only daughter in a household of boys. Then within twenty-four hours, *everything* you know literally goes "up in smoke" (p. ix). You lose your family, your home, all your belongings, and you are pronounced dead even though you are alive. How would *you* respond? What thoughts would run through your mind as you sit outside in the dust?

Now imagine you are approaching Mak'ob, the Valley of Sorrows, for the first time. You know this is the place where lepers live until they die. Once you enter, you will never be allowed to leave it. The boundaries of the Valley are permanent. What emotions are you experiencing, and why?

The leper Tobias was also twelve, as Lily had been, when he was driven away from his family. Like Lily, he faced myriad questions and emotions of rejection, fear, betrayal, abandonment, terror (reread this young boy's story in his own words on pp. 87–89).

READ

He . . . touched her face in the night and comforted her. *Don't be afraid of anything! You are a tree. . . .*

He commanded her to go forward on her journey. *I AM your ship, your sail, your captain. I AM the wind, the water, the lighthouse guiding you to your destination!*

Together we will sail a great distance, face many sorrows, overcome great trials. Do not fear the journey. Trust Me! We travel together, you and I. Together! Together we carry priceless treasure to those who wait on the desolate shore!

Go on then! Live! Fearless!

—Prologue (pp. vii–viii)

Do not be afraid, for I am with you.
—ISAIAH 43:5

ASK

If you truly believed these words about having no fear, no boundaries, and that God will always go with you, in what ways would your life change? Make a list.

_____

_____

_____

READ

You will find the lost ones, like driftwood twisted and forsaken, strewn along the path of your own suffering. Find them. Embrace them. Feed them. Carry them. I AM at your side every step of the journey! And when we return home again together? Together those who were lost before you came will travel back with us!
—PROLOGUE (P. VIII)

> *The Lord does not look at the things man looks at. Man looks at the outward appearance, but the Lord looks at the heart.*
> —1 SAMUEL 16:7

> *If anyone has material possessions and sees his brother in need but has no pity on him, how can the love of God be in him?*
> —1 JOHN 3:17

ASK

When you see people, what do you see first? Eyes, clothing, hair, facial expression? Something else?

_____

_____

Although Lily was bound by horrible life circumstances (she herself was dying), she chose to be a light of comfort to those who were also dying. Her prayer was always, *Help me see them, not with my eyes, but as you see them* (p. 44). What would you see with God's eyes?

_____

_____

_____

Do you agree with this statement by Mosheh: *Messiah makes provision for those who believe they are outside the boundaries of His love. For all the nations and peoples of the world* (p. 154)? Why or why not? Is anyone outside the boundaries of God's love? If so, who?

_____

_____

_____

Who are "the lost ones" around you? What is one way you could bring joy, love, and healing to them?

_____

_____

_____

WONDER . . .

Give is a word that never ends. Never runs dry. An eternal word. Past and present and future. . . . God's love for us is a palindrome.
　　—MOSHEH (PP. 203–204)

*Let your light shine before men, that they may see your good deeds and
praise your Father in heaven.*
— MATTHEW 5:16

Review your list of ways your life would change if you faced it with no fear,
no boundaries, and knowing that God always traveled with you. Star one of
your ideas. Then act on it this week with bold courage! Let your light shine
forth out of the darkness!

6 | SEEING HEAVENWARD

> The worries of this world blindfold our souls. Little things keep us from really seeing. You know? . . . But look up. See? That's how it is when worry doesn't block our vision. And when we die, the blindfold will be altogether gone. That's what we have to look forward to.
> —CANTOR (P. 67)

When you hear the word *heaven*, what images come to mind? (Fluffy clouds, angels playing harps, golden streets, rest and relaxation . . . ?)

_____

_____

_____

What worries or "little things" keep you focused downward on this earth, rather than heavenward, toward God and eternity with Him?

_____

_____

_____

In the Valley of Mak'ob heaven is the only hope. As the lepers die physically, piece by piece, they long for a place where their bodies can once again be whole. Where they no longer are labeled *untouchable*. Where they no longer have to stay in a community of the dying. Where they don't have to call, "Unclean!" as they pass a "whole" person.

As Shoemaker, one of the lepers, declared, "Hope's all we've got left. . . . We're condemned anyway. If this fellow can heal us and we miss him because we're all snug and content to live and die in this open tomb, think what we might miss" (p. 103).

What we might miss, indeed! All of us are lepers at heart; we *need* the limitless grace, mercy, and love that God extends to us through the person of Yeshua—God, who took on flesh for us.

We crave a "larger vision"—the hope of heaven—for that is what brings ultimate fulfillment and meaning to our lives. It gives us purpose, in spite of personal pain along the way.

But perhaps it's this "larger vision" that we struggle with the most. After all, if our image of heaven is of wimpy-looking angels with halos walking among soft clouds, heaven may seem a bit dull. *Perhaps heaven isn't such a great place after all*, we think. And then we lose perspective. The "little things" of life become blindfolds that prevent us from seeing beyond the small confines of our earthly life.

What will heaven be like? It will be far more glorious than we can ever imagine! (For a preview, read Revelation 21–22.)

READ

Do not store up for yourselves treasures on earth, where moth and rust destroy, and where thieves break in and steal. But store up for yourselves treasures in heaven, where moth and rust do not destroy, and where thieves do not break in and steal. For where your treasure is, there your heart will be also.
    —MATTHEW 6:19-21

Seek his kingdom. . . . For where your treasure is, there your heart will be also.
    —LUKE 12:31, 34

ASK

What do the verses above say about what heaven is like?

_____

_____

_____

Why is it so important to focus on God, the ultimate treasure?

_____

_____

_____

There's an old adage: "You have to lose what's really important to find out what really matters." Has this adage proven true in your life? If so, how?

_____

_____

_____

Losing someone or something often carries pain beyond measure. But it can also develop within us a heart of empathy for others if we allow God to use our pain for benefit, rather than becoming bitter and turning against Him. Lily, Rabbi Ahava, and Cantor are shining examples of those who shine as beacons of God's light, in spite of their own suffering.

READ

Lily smiled. It was good to talk of *olam haba*, the life of the world to come. "Rabbi Ahava says on that day the Knower of Secrets will reveal every secret thought. Every good deed will be rewarded and every neglected kindness will be clearly seen. Beneath the gaze of the Lord, darkness will become light."

With his gentle hand Cantor touched Lily's shoulder. "And we'll know the truth of who among mankind was merciful and whole. And also whose half-eaten hearts were beating inside trivial existence. We'll know who secretly blessed others. Helped the helpless. Touched the untouchables. No, more than that . . . who *embraced* the untouchables."
—LILY AND CANTOR (PP. 33–34)

"There is nothing concealed that will not be disclosed, or hidden that will not be made known."
—YESHUA, MATTHEW 10:26

Behold, I am coming soon! My reward is with me, and I will give to everyone according to what he has done.
—REVELATION 22:12

ASK

On the day you enter "the life of the world to come," what do you think will be said about your good deeds?

_____

_____

_____

About your neglected kindnesses?

_____

_____

_____

It's so easy to think, *No one will get hurt if I do (or don't do) that.* But Scripture states clearly that all secrets will be revealed. Would knowing that someone else will eventually know your secrets change your actions in any way? Why or why not?

_____

_____

_____

READ

Will you come tonight? Tonight? . . . We're hoping you'll come! To save us. We're watching for you to come! . . . Hoping!
—LILY (PP. 4–5)

You also must be ready, because the Son of Man will come at an hour when you do not expect him.
—LUKE 12:40

ASK

If someone asked you, "Do you think the Messiah is coming soon?" what would you say?

_____

_____

_____

Exact times have been predicted for centuries . . . and those days, months, and years have passed. The truth is simply this: Messiah will come back to earth *when He is ready.*

Not before.

Not later.

Exactly on time.

God's time.

That means we will never know the exact time because it is not for us to know. But we must always be ready.

How can you become more ready for the Son of Man's return to earth? What specific steps do you need to take?

_____

_____

_____

READ

What will heaven be like? Here are a few snapshots:

"All the light from unseen stars will arrive with him when he comes to Yerushalayim! Blast the earth at once! Light! No north, south, east, or west

anymore. Just light. Angel armies filling the sky everywhere we look! Singing! Singing."
—Cantor (p. 5)

Now the dwelling of God is with men, and he will live with them. They will be his people, and God himself will be with them and be their God. He will wipe every tear from their eyes. There will be no more death or mourning or crying or pain.
—Revelation 21:3–4

I tell you the Truth! There is coming a moment which will stand forever in the center of all eternity! The Mem of forever!
Messiah will be lifted up as the Light to the nations. He will draw all men to Him. And all those who call upon His name . . . those who acknowledge that He is the Way, the Truth, and the Life [see John 14:6] . . . will hear His voice cry out to them, "I AM the Truth! . . . AM . . . The Alpha and the Omega! The beginning and the end! . . . I AM the One who leads you and brings you home to eternity!"
—Mosheh (p. 264)

The city does not need the sun or the moon to shine on it, for the glory of God gives it light, and the Lamb is its lamp. . . . On no day will its gates ever be shut, for there will be no night there.
—Revelation 21:23, 25

Just imagine—a place of endless, dazzling light and the most beautiful songs you have ever heard. A place where you will meet Messiah face-to-face and be joined with those from all over the world who believe in Him too. A place where your talents (or lack thereof), your skin color, your past or present, your clothing size, and your financial status don't matter! A place where all boundaries stop. Where there is limitless time to spend with the One who has created you, loved you always, and now brings you home . . . for all eternity!

WONDER . . .

"Messiah waits at the end of life to welcome us! Don't be afraid of darkness. There is light at the end of the dark journey!"
—Rabbi Ahava (p. 44)

Now we see but a poor reflection as in a mirror; then we shall see face to face. Now I know in part; then I shall know fully, even as I am fully known.
—1 Corinthians 13:12

Is your heart eager for the Messiah's return to earth? Is your soul content in the "now," even while you long to be fully known? Is your spirit willing and happy to serve others "in the meanwhile"? Then you are truly "seeing heavenward"!

Dear Reader,

You are so important to us. We have prayed for you as we wrote this book and also as we receive your letters and hear your soul cries. We hope that *Second Touch* has encouraged you to go deeper. To get to know Yeshua better. To fill your soul hunger by examining Scripture's truths for yourself.

We are convinced that if you do so, you will find this promise true: *"If you seek Him, He will be found by you."* —1 CHRONICLES 28:9

Bodie & Brock Thoene

Scripture References

1. Matt 22; Luke 14:15-24
2. Matt 23:37-38;
   Luke 13:34-35
3. John 9:39
4. John 9:41
5. John 10:1-5
6. Psalm 23:1
7. John 10:11
8. John 10:16
9. John 10:17-18
10. John 10:20-21
11. Isaiah 45:23
12. Psalm 34:4
13. Psalm 34:6
14. Psalm 34:7
15. Luke 7:40-50
16. Matt 23:27
17. Isaiah 26:3
18. Isaiah 49:14-16
19. Isaiah 53:5
20. Exodus 3:11
21. Exodus 4
22. Psalm 37:5-6
23. Isaiah 53:5
24. Exodus 4:19-23
25. Genesis 17:14
26. Exodus 4:24-26
27. John 3:16; Acts 2:21
28. Exodus 20:3
29. Exodus 15:27
30. Exodus 16
31. Deuteronomy 8:3; Matt 4:4
32. Exodus 15
33. Exodus 16
34. Deuteronomy 32:2
35. Psalm 19:1-3
36. John 3:16
37. John 6:30-31
38. John 6:32
39. John 6:33
40. John 6:34
41. John 6:35
42. John 6:47-51
43. John 6:52
44. John 6:55-56
45. John 6:60
46. John 6:67-70
47. Matt 22: 37, 39; Mark
    12:30-31; Luke 10:27
48. 1 Kings 19:1-18
49. Mark 7:5-13
50. Isaiah 29:13; Mark 7:6-7
51. Mark 7:14-15
52. Matt 15:14; Luke 6:39
53. Matt 15:16-20
54. John 8:31
55. Deuteronomy 6:4;
    Mark 12:29
56. John 14:6
57. Matt 15:21-24
58. Matt 15:23-24
59. Ezekiel 34:10, 22
60. Matt 15:26-28
61. Matt 15:27
62. Matt 15:28
63. Luke 11:5-10
64. Luke 11:11-13
65. John 6:27
66. Matt 15:32
67. Matt 15:33-34
68. Matt 15:35-39
69. Isaiah 9:1-2
70. Matt 16:1
71. Matt 16:2-4
72. Matt 16:5
73. Matt 16:6-10
74. Leviticus 13:2-8
75. Leviticus 13:45-46
76. 2 Kings 5:1-14
77. Matt 7:15-19
78. Matt 7:21-23; John 13:34
79. Matt 7:24-27
80. Matt 7:12-14
81. Matt 6:16
82. Matt 8:2-4
83. Isaiah 53:3-5

Authors' Note

The following sources have been helpful in our research for this book.

- *The Complete Jewish Bible.* Translated by David H. Stern. Baltimore, MD: Jewish New Testament Publications, Inc., 1998.

- *iLumina*, a digitally animated Bible and encyclopedia suite. Carol Stream, IL.: Tyndale House Publishers, 2002.

- *The International Standard Bible Encyclopaedia.* George Bromiley, ed. 5 vols. Grand Rapids, MI.: Eerdmans, 1979.

- *The Life and Times of Jesus the Messiah.* Alfred Edersheim. Peabody, MA: Hendrickson Publishers, Inc., 1995.

About the Authors

BODIE AND BROCK THOENE (pronounced *Tay-nee*) have written over 45 works of historical fiction. That these best sellers have sold more than 10 million copies and won eight ECPA Gold Medallion Awards affirms what millions of readers have already discovered—the Thoenes are not only master stylists but experts at capturing readers' minds and hearts.

In their timeless classic series about Israel (The Zion Chronicles, The Zion Covenant, and The Zion Legacy), the Thoenes' love for both story and research shines.

With The Shiloh Legacy series and *Shiloh Autumn*—poignant portrayals of the American depression—and The Galway Chronicles, which dramatically tell of the 1840s famine in Ireland, as well as the twelve Legends of the West, the Thoenes have made their mark in modern history.

In the A.D. Chronicles, their most recent series, they step seamlessly into the world of Yerushalyim and Rome, in the days when Yeshua walked the earth and transformed lives with His touch.

Bodie began her writing career as a teen journalist for her local newspaper. Eventually her byline appeared in prestigious periodicals such as *U.S. News and World Report*, *The American West*, and *The Saturday Evening Post*. She also worked for John Wayne's Batjac Productions (she's best known as author of *The Fall Guy*) and ABC Circle Films as a writer and researcher. John Wayne described her as "a writer with talent that captures the people and the times!" She has degrees in journalism and communications.

Brock has often been described by Bodie as "an essential half of this writing team." With degrees both in history and education, Brock has, in his role as researcher and story-line consultant, added the vital dimension of historical accuracy. Due to such careful research, The Zion Covenant and The Zion Chronicles series are recognized by the American Library Association, as well as Zionist libraries around the world, as classic historical novels and are used to teach history in college classrooms.

Bodie and Brock have four grown children—Rachel, Jake, Luke, and Ellie—and five grandchildren. Their sons, Jake and Luke, are carrying on the Thoene family talent as the next generation of writers, and Luke produces the Thoene audiobooks. Bodie and Brock divide their time between London and Nevada.

For more information visit:
www.thoenebooks.com
www.TheOneAudio.com

suspense with a mission

THOENE FAMILY CLASSICS™

✪ ✪ ✪

THOENE FAMILY CLASSIC HISTORICALS
by Bodie and Brock Thoene

*Gold Medallion Winners**

THE ZION COVENANT
*Vienna Prelude**
Prague Counterpoint
Munich Signature
Jerusalem Interlude
Danzig Passage
*Warsaw Requiem**
London Refrain
Paris Encore
Dunkirk Crescendo

THE ZION CHRONICLES
*The Gates of Zion**
A Daughter of Zion
The Return to Zion
A Light in Zion
*The Key to Zion**

THE SHILOH LEGACY
*In My Father's House**
A Thousand Shall Fall
Say to This Mountain

SHILOH AUTUMN

THE GALWAY CHRONICLES
*Only the River Runs Free**
Of Men and of Angels
*Ashes of Remembrance**
All Rivers to the Sea

THE ZION LEGACY
Jerusalem Vigil
Thunder from Jerusalem
Jerusalem's Heart
Jerusalem Scrolls
Stones of Jerusalem
Jerusalem's Hope

A.D. CHRONICLES
First Light
Second Touch
Third Watch
Fourth Dawn
Fifth Seal
Sixth Covenant
Seventh Day
and more to come!

THOENE FAMILY CLASSICS™

✪ ✪ ✪

THOENE FAMILY CLASSIC AMERICAN LEGENDS

LEGENDS OF THE WEST
by Bodie and Brock Thoene

Legends of the West, Volume One
  Sequoia Scout
  The Year of the Grizzly
  Shooting Star
Legends of the West, Volume Two
  Gold Rush Prodigal
  Delta Passage
  Hangtown Lawman
Legends of the West, Volume Three
  Hope Valley War
  The Legend of Storey County
  Cumberland Crossing
Legends of the West, Volume Four
  The Man from Shadow Ridge
  Cannons of the Comstock
  Riders of the Silver Rim

LEGENDS OF VALOR
by Luke Thoene

  Sons of Valor
  Brothers of Valor
  Fathers of Valor

✪ ✪ ✪

THOENE CLASSIC NONFICTION
by Bodie and Brock Thoene

  Writer-to-Writer

THOENE FAMILY CLASSIC SUSPENSE
by Jake Thoene

CHAPTER 16 SERIES
  Shaiton's Fire
  Firefly Blue
  Fuel the Fire

✪ ✪ ✪

THOENE FAMILY CLASSICS FOR KIDS
by Jake and Luke Thoene

BAKER STREET DETECTIVES
  The Mystery of the Yellow Hands
  The Giant Rat of Sumatra
  The Jeweled Peacock of Persia
  The Thundering Underground

LAST CHANCE DETECTIVES
  Mystery Lights of Navajo Mesa
  Legend of the Desert Bigfoot

✪ ✪ ✪

THOENE FAMILY CLASSIC AUDIOBOOKS

Available from
www.thoenebooks.com or
www.familyaudiolibrary.com

CP0064